Political and Social Issues in British Women's Fiction, 1928–1968

Also by Elizabeth Maslen

DORIS LESSING

Political and Social Issues in British Women's Fiction, 1928–1968

Elizabeth Maslen
Queen Mary College
University of London

First published 2001 by
PALGRAVE
Houndmills, Basingstoke, Hampshire RG21 6XS and
175 Fifth Avenue, New York, N. Y. 10010
Companies and representatives throughout the world

PALGRAVE is the new global academic imprint of
St. Martin's Press LLC Scholarly and Reference Division and
Palgrave Publishers Ltd (formerly Macmillan Press Ltd).

ISBN 0–333–72953–6

This book is printed on paper suitable for recycling and made from fully managed and sustained forest sources.

A catalogue record for this book is available from the British Library.

Library of Congress Cataloging-in-Publication Data
Maslen, Elizabeth
    Political and social issues in British women's fiction, 1928–1968 /
    Elizabeth Maslen.
        p. cm.
    Includes bibliographical references and index.
    ISBN 0–333–72953–6 (cloth)
     1. English fiction—Women authors—History and criticism. 2. Politics
    and literature—Great Britain—History—20th century. 3. Literature
    and society—Great Britain—History—20th century. 4. Women and
    literature—Great Britain—History—20th century. 5. English fiction–
    –20th century—History and criticism. 6. Political fiction, English–
    –History and criticism. 7. Social problems in literature. 8. Politics in
    literature. I. Title.

    PR888.P6 M37 2000
    823'.9109358'082—dc21
                                                        00–049142

10   9   8   7   6   5   4   3   2   1
10   09 08 07 06 05 04 03 02 01

Printed in Great Britain by Antony Rowe Ltd, Chippenham, Wiltshire

For BLAD, RKB, JY and TS
with love

Contents

Acknowledgements

I should like to thank Queen Mary and Westfield College, University of London, for awarding me a sabbatical year in which I was able to complete a large proportion of this book. I am also enormously grateful to all those who have read parts of my work in progress, and who have offered helpful comments. I should particularly like to thank Rebecca Beasley, Vesna Goldsworthy, Jenny Hartley, Maroula Joannou, Joanna Labon, Robert Maslen, Catherine Maxwell, Janet Montefiore, Brian Place and Morag Shiach, who have all given me the benefit of their expert knowledge – and special thanks to John Chalker who has read the entire typescript with his meticulous eye for detail, saving me from the embarrassment of a number of incautious comments. I should also like to thank my postgraduate students for their stimulating ideas, especially Alexa Alfer and Nattie Golubov, and my friends Bernard Correy and Pam Hampshire for invaluable discussions about the four decades I write about here.

The jacket illustration is adapted from the original jacket illustration for Storm Jameson's *The Journal of Mary Hervey Russell* (London: Macmillan, 1945). We have tried to track down the copyright holders without success, but will be pleased to make suitable arrangements at the first opportunity.

Introduction

This is a book about continuities, about threads which run through four troubled, complex and confusing decades, linking two years which have a certain symbolic value: 1928, the year of universal franchise in Britain, and 1968, the year of the Paris students' revolt, the Prague spring and the date usually chosen to mark the emergence of new-wave feminism.[1] Tracing the changes in political and social priorities throughout this period, as they are reflected in many novels by women, has been a profoundly illuminating experience. As a result, this is a book that sets out to celebrate a wide range of women writers, most of them sadly no longer in print, many in danger of being entirely forgotten, whose works offer insights into political and social issues of their time. Inevitably, I have had to be selective: nothing useful could be said if I had attempted to include all contenders in this remarkably rewarding period, or if I had strayed beyond Britain. I have, therefore, concentrated on less well-known names rather than on those who have already received considerable critical attention. This of course does not mean I underestimate the achievements of such writers as Dorothy Richardson, Virginia Woolf or Ivy Compton-Burnett, but that I want to show how rich and varied other women's writing was throughout the period. The considerable contemporary critical acclaim which consistently greeted the publication of works by Storm Jameson, Phyllis Bottome, Pamela Frankau and Susan Ertz, to name only a few, invites investigation as to why so few, if any, of their works are still remembered. This is not a book, for reasons which will become clear in the following pages, that deals predominantly with the political and social issues affecting women, which still demanded action after franchise had been achieved,[2] nor is it a book about the writers' commitments (or failure to commit) to specific political parties. Novels, after all, often set out to show the clashes and

1

contradictions amongst a wide range of views; whatever the specific intention which lies behind the text, it is the testimony of the text itself which we hear. So what I have tried to do is to trace the shifting priorities of the novels I engage with throughout the period, to unpack the texts, and to offer possible explanations for why their priorities change.

I have concentrated on fiction rather than nonfiction for very specific reasons. On the whole, a nonfictional book, essay or article, because it makes no secret of the subject its audience is to address, attracts readers who already have an interest in whatever subject it debates; many will fail to read an article or essay dealing with a subject which does not attract them. Moreover, nonfiction very frequently simplifies issues or responses to issues in order to strengthen debating points, giving, for example, essentialist views on men and women. Fiction, in contrast, can show the diversity that exists among individual human beings, as E. L. Doctorow asserts:

> Fiction is a not entirely rational means of discourse. It gives to the reader something more than information. Complex understandings, indirect, intuitive, and nonverbal, arise from the worlds of story, and by a ritual transaction between reader and writer, instructive emotion is generated in the reader from the illusion of suffering an experience not his own.[3]

Similarly, Martha Nussbaum claims that the novel is valuable to philosophy precisely because 'the novel as genre is committed, in its very structure and in the structure of its relationship with its reader, to the pursuit of the uncertainties and vulnerabilities, the particularity and the emotional richness, of the human form of life'.[4] Or indeed, as Michel Foucault argues more provocatively, making a case for his own tendency to resort to fiction in order to strengthen an argument,

> the possibility exists for fiction to function in truth, for a fictional discourse to produce effects of truth, and for bringing it about that a true discourse engenders, or 'manufactures', something that does not yet exist, that is, 'fictions' it. One 'fictions' history on the basis of a political reality that makes it true, one 'fictions' a politics not yet in existence on the basis of a historical truth.[5]

Fiction, moreover, may well reach a wider audience than nonfiction, because it is also a vehicle for entertainment, and entertainment need not by any means only function as escapism. This could well account for why we find so many novels adopting a realist frame in which to challenge their readers with political and social issues, since the reader's familiarity with the realistic construction of a recognisable if fictional world can lull them into acceptance of a perspective on that world which is far from conservative, or supportive of the status quo. The writer can use the entertainment potential in fiction to entice readers into contemplating issues to which they have a certain amount of resistance, enabling her (and here the realist mode again proves itself a valuable tool, since 'realism' lends itself to the illusion of representing a proven 'reality') to get past psychological blocks set up in a reader by social conditioning, which may act as a kind of internal censorship. It is of this kind of censorship that Sigmund Freud speaks, drawing on his central European experience, when he likens the distortion, the dissimulation present in dreams to the strategies used by the political writer,

> who has disagreeable truths to tell to those in authority. If he presents them undisguised, the authorities will suppress his words . . . A writer must beware of the censorship, and on its account he must soften and distort the expression of his opinion. According to the strength and sensitiveness of the censorship he finds himself compelled either merely to refrain from certain forms of attack, or to speak in allusions in place of direct references, or he must conceal his objectionable pronouncement beneath some apparently innocent disguise . . . The stricter the censorship, the more far-reaching will be the disguise and the more ingenious too may be the means employed for putting the reader on the scent of the true meaning.[6]

We find such evasion developed to a highly sophisticated degree in fiction of both Tsarist Russia and the Soviet Union (where it was known as Aesopian writing), largely to evade official censorship.[7] Even in Britain, as the thirties progressed, we find writers of nonfiction faced with increasing restrictions as to what certain journals and newspapers would accept: while the *Left Review* grew less tolerant of departures from the party line than it had been earlier in the decade,[8] many conservative journals and newspapers showed an increasing tendency to adopt strategies which echoed something of the far right in Europe.[9] Moreover, while the use of fiction does help to evade what I have called (drawing on Freud) the reader's internal censorship, the novelist is not always successful in bypassing prejudice, as Naomi Mitchison's experience showed in the thirties; whereas her novel *The Corn King and the Spring*

Queen (1931) could explore sensitive political and sexual issues in conjunction as it was set in the far past, her next novel, *We Have Been Warned* ((1935), set in her own time, provoked adverse reactions in both her publishers and her readers when she included elements which had caused no such outrage in her historical novel – elements such as a condoned political murder, a rape which is forgiven, free love within an 'open' marriage, all within the context, described in a realist mode, of a Labour candidate's campaigning for a seat in Parliament.[10] Although Mitchison did not have to face a court case, as Radclyffe Hall did over her lesbian novel, *The Well of Loneliness* (1928), her readership diminished.[11] Mitchison did not attempt to approach readers of her fiction so openly again with provocative issues situated in her own time; she stuck to the disguise of history, where she could use epigraphs to invite the bolder reader to make contemporary connections. Most of her writer contemporaries did not fall foul of their readers' internal censorship precisely because they took steps to evade it, by strategies which will be explored in the next chapter; matters which could not be located in contemporary Britain could reach readers if they were situated in the past, the future, abroad, or in the realm of fable or fantasy. Paradoxically, however, in World War Two, when official censorship might have become a problem for novelists out to probe or question official propagandist lines, writers won the right for fiction to be spared, for the most part, the attentions of officialdom with which nonfiction had to contend. As a result, many novels are able to criticize aspects of wartime happenings in ways which would be impossible in nonfiction, although writers still have to use strategies to evade their readers' and their publishers' internal censorship, when writing about sensitive issues. Thus we have, for instance, Eunice Buckley's novel *Destination Unknown* (1942), a work which begins with a standard expression of patriotism, only to reveal as it progresses the cruelties suffered by refugees forcibly deported to the then Dominions by the British,[12] or we have Edith Pargeter's novel, *She Goes to War* (1942), the story of a WREN in England, her friendships and love life, ingredients which offer no affront to expectation, until she offers us in the final pages a savage attack on the mishandling of the Cyprus retreat in the letters her protagonist receives from her lover after his death in the debacle.[13]

Writers of fiction, then, have the chance to set issues they wish their readers to explore within the context of a fictional world, where political or social comment may catch their attention once they have become absorbed by the stylistic texture of the narrative or by a lively plot. Yet the writer is always a creature of her/his own age, and, in confronting complex issues of their own times, faces the problem which Gillian Beer describes:

> Our thinking is often at the mercy of our communal metaphors, and though we may develop a sharp eye for those favoured by people with a different ideology from ourselves, we need to remain alert to our own and not to allow them to bed down into our consciousness so far that they become determining.[14]

While many of the writers whose works I explore are remarkably alert to aspects of the dominant 'ideology' of their own place and time, we shall none the less find in these works certain blind spots, and inevitably also a mixture of conservative and radical points of view, since, as Alison Light has reminded us,[15] any age is made up of both tendencies, and indeed this is also true of the individual reader or writer. Indeed, modernity, we have to acknowledge, is never 'pure': alongside what we recognize as modern, there will inevitably be strands of habit, tradition, convention, by which we maintain some element of continuity with the past. Moreover, there is the further problem of expression and form, which complicates both communication and reception; for, as Rachel Blau DuPlessis warns, 'literature as a human institution is ... organized by many ideological scripts. Any literary convention – plots, narrative sequences, characters in bit parts – as an instrument that claims to depict experience, also interprets it'.[16] Furthermore, while the writer interprets issues of their time within every text, so of necessity does the reader, and this act of interpretation may differ in different eras with different priorities. Novels which have particular political or social import for the reader today may well not reflect the same political or social perception on the part of the writer, which does not make their novels any the less valuable as reflecting political or social issues of their time. Italo Calvino's comment echoes something Doris Lessing found in the reception of *The Golden Notebook*, when he says,

> We can never forget that what books communicate often remains unknown even to the author himself, that books often say something different from what they set out to say, that in any book there is a part that is the author's and a part that is a collective and anonymous work.[17]

The writers I am discussing are products of the political world in which they operate, even when they have no overt commitment to a particular cause, while we, as readers, bring to their texts our own cultural baggage, our interpretations of, say, their portrayal of gender issues inevitably affected by our current debates. But we do them a disservice if we do not recognize their insights within their own time, and fail to acknowledge that things taken for granted now were radical departures from convention when first conceived.

Social and political issues run together in the novels I am discussing. For many women writers, the issues they see as political are not included in the policies of the political parties of their day, or are only discussed on the fringes of the party. What Keith Williams and Steven Matthews say about the thirties can usefully be extended to cover the four decades explored in this book:

> Definitions of the political underwent significant metamorphoses in practice. Besides the public 'macropolitics' of the decade – the clashes between Fascism and Communism, dictatorship and social democracy – a whole new agenda of 'micropolitical' concerns was being opened up, consciously or unconsciously, and addressed by writers. Take, for example, the explicit and implicit social values of style [... and] not least, the politics of gender, unfairly regarded as neglected in thirties writing, [while] in fact objectified and scrutinised in the later work of Virginia Woolf and her acolyte/antagonist, Winifred Holtby and others ... In this way, the writing of the thirties emerges as both *less* and *more* political than hitherto assumed, in more complex and inflected senses.[18]

This is the kind of definition which informs Margaret Atwood's comments in 1981:

> We are good at measuring an author's production in terms of his craft. We are not good at analyzing it in terms of his politics, and by and large we do not do so. By 'politics' I do not mean how you voted in the last election, although that is included. I mean who is entitled to do what to whom, with impunity; who profits by it; and who therefore eats what. Such material enters a writer's work not because a writer is or is not consciously political but because a writer is an observer, a witness, and such observations are the air he breathes.[19]

So it is rather dismaying to find that a number of writers, with such an interest in what Williams and Matthews call 'micropolitical' concerns, are dismissively categorized as 'writers of domestic fiction' or indeed omitted, even in feminist companions to literature. This is frequently the fate of Susan Ertz, for instance, and yet she has in *Woman Alive* (1935) produced a shrewd dystopian novel linking pacifist and gender issues of the day, while in a work like *Anger in the Sky* (1943) she uses a family setting to explore a vast range of the pressing wartime debates of the day, including American isolationism, French support for the Vichy government, class divisions, as well as a range of issues which will appear as by no means lightweight to a later generation of feminists.[20] Moreover, even when we encounter writers who deliberately concentrate on 'domestic' or 'romantic' fiction, it is worth recalling earlier uses of the apparently 'lightweight' novel as a weapon for change, as Barbara Christian reminds us:

> the novel constructed as a romance had been one of the most effective propaganda techniques that abolitionists had used in their fight to change public opinion about slavery...the romance novel had popular appeal in a way that political treatises, detailed journalism or even erudite poetry did not, for it stirred the emotions through the vehicle of a good story.[21]

In this work, I devote the first chapter to an exploration of what kinds of fiction women write during these four decades. For there seems to be a good measure of truth in what Margaret Atwood has said about common critical evaluations of kinds of writing:

> In some countries, an author is censored not only for what he says but for how he says it, and an unconventional style is therefore a declaration of artistic freedom. Here we are eclectic; we don't mind experimental styles, in fact we devote learned journals to their analysis; but our critics sneer somewhat at anything they consider 'heavy social commentary' or – a worse word – 'message'. Stylistic heavy guns are dandy, as long as they aren't pointed anywhere in particular. We like the human condition as long as it is seen as personal and individual. Placing politics and poetics in two watertight compartments is a luxury...Most countries in the world cannot afford such luxuries.[22]

The kind of division with which Atwood takes issue is clear when we read, for instance, V. N. Volšinov, proclaiming in 1976:

> If political communication establishes corresponding institutions and, at the same time, juridical forms, aesthetic communication

organizes only a work of art. If the latter rejects this task and begins to aim at creating even the most transitory of political organizations or any other ideological form, then by that very fact, it ceases to be aesthetic communication and relinquishes its unique character.[23]

In stark contrast to Volšinov, there is Kiernan Ryan, insisting in 1987 that

> The essential function and value of fiction as such, and of a *consciously* materialist and dialectical fiction above all, reside in its relentless, uncompromising interrogation of the received in the light of an ever-changing reality, its restless explorations beyond the given horizon of experience and knowledge – including, where truth and need demand, beyond the hitherto accepted formulations and prescriptions of socialism.[24]

These are strong words. But it is true to say that, when we revisit, for their political implications, texts which are not markedly experimental, we do not always pay close attention to the ways in which they are written, as if only those novelists who experiment have taken style seriously. Yet this is very far from the case. While such writers as Dorothy Richardson and Virginia Woolf are experimentalists who look closely at the relation between who one is (gender, sex and so on), how one writes and what one writes about, there are many other women writers, like Storm Jameson and Rebecca West who, while not markedly experimental in the majority of their works, discuss in essays, articles and reviews what they clearly consider to be the responsibility of the novelist in marrying style with subject matter. And there are many others who, while they do not discuss the matter of form and content in essays, none the less demonstrate in their work a keen awareness of ways in which to draw readers into the world of their text. It is easy to forget that the writer of whatever period is facing choices about subject matter which for them are novel and complex. As Storm Jameson says in 1947 (and she is not dividing content from form here, given her distrust of the consequences of Joyce's experimentation which I shall discuss later):

> Every age asks its artists, its thinkers, a question. In the end it is always the same question: What is man? Why was I born? What does my life mean? But every age asks it in a different form, and it is quite easy for an artist to spend his whole life struggling to find out exactly what the question is that he is being asked . . . Or a writer may

spend his whole life answering a question which has not been asked yet – so that his contemporaries do not understand a word he says: he is incomprehensible and useless to them.[25]

Inevitably, in this period, the debate about what constitutes a style which adequately represents its modernity must be considered. Yet, as every critic who confronts the issue knows, this is no mean task, since there is no consensus about what we mean by the main labels which have been adopted for the novel in the twentieth century. We could, for instance, take at least three approaches to literary modernism, either separately or in combination: we could define it by period – yet opinions differ as to whether the period should extend back into the nineteenth century, acknowledging the legacy of such writers as Baudelaire, or whether the nineteenth century offers a kind of proto-modernism, giving rise to 'true' modernism, that is to say, 'high modernism', in the early twentieth century.[26] Then, again, we could define modernism as a mode of writing, with characteristic traits such as a skill in depicting consciousness, viewing time and space through the lens of interiority, a devotion to myth, a merging of popular with high culture, formal self-consciousness and so on; yet the more ingredients we add to the definition of modernism as style, the more we confine it to a very few practitioners – Richardson, Woolf, Joyce, Eliot, for instance – and the more we have to question the intrinsic modernism of others. Thirdly, we could define modernism strictly in terms of its relation to modernity – yet then there is debate as to the kinds of modernity it can express; clearly, a critic like Volšinov is not going to accept that there is any 'literary' merit in an engagement with political or 'any other ideological form' – yet macro- and micro-political issues cannot be disentangled from interiority, from consciousness, as many writers of these four decades know.[27] The problem is inevitably increased because so many references to modernism do not acknowledge the complexity which lurks beneath the label. As Michael Levenson warns:

It will prove better to be minimalist in our definitions of the conveniently flaccid term *Modernist* and maximalist in our account of the diverse *modernizing* works and movements, which are sometimes deeply congruent with one another, and just as often opposed or even contradictory.[28]

And the debate becomes all the more complicated when we introduce the label of realism, which has in the past been seen as anathema by many modernist critics. The reason is not far to seek, for just as modernist critics often refer to modernism without making clear whether they are referring to it under one of the three areas I suggest above, or under a combination of these, or indeed by some other quality, so realism has often been presented, as Elizabeth Ermarth has shown, without specific definition:

> Most discussions of 'realism' were entirely inadequate. Either 'realism' was treated as a norm of art to be accepted without discussion, or it was a straw man set up for rejection; in short, this cultural argument between realists and anti-realists used the term 'realism' variously as term of opprobrium or of praise, but rarely as something to be defined.[29]

Equally commonly, we find many blanket dismissals of realism as a nineteenth-century form of expression, with an omniscient narrator, only capable of confirming the ascendancy of the dominant culture, tidily accepting cause and effect, and largely interested in surface detail to the detriment of consciousness. Samuel Beckett, for instance, referred in 1931 to Marcel Proust's

> contempt for the literature that 'describes', for the realists and naturalists worshipping the offal of experience, prostrate before the epidermis and the swift epilepsy, and content to transcribe the surface, the facade, behind which the Idea is prisoner.[30]

Yet while, inevitably, crude practitioners of the kind Proust deplores do exist in the twentieth century, realism cannot be so easily swept aside. Chris Baldick could have been responding to Beckett on Proust, as well as to more recent theorists, when he commented ironically in 1985 that

> Among today's theoreticians of post-modern writing, some remarkable legends about the Dark Ages of nineteenth-century realist fiction have been allowed to gain currency. It can now go without saying that the objective of realist fiction was to inhibit any questioning of the world, to induce complacency and stupefying ideological amnesia.[31]

Yet Gunter Gebauer and Christoph Wulf, looking at mimesis in conjunction with realism, focus on something which many novelists would seem to have spotted in the four twentieth-century decades I am exploring, namely that 'the aesthetic principle of mimesis is generalized far beyond the sphere of art into a constitutive characteristic of class society',[32] and that 'reality is mimetically constituted' to represent the ideas of the dominant culture.[33] Gebauer and Wulf argue that nineteenth-century writers like Stendhal, Flaubert, or Dostoevski

> discover in society a fictional principle; they recognise that the formation of the social world proceeds in the same way as the formation of a novel. Society, in important aspects, is constituted in terms of the same principle as the novel. Put another way around, this claim reads as follows: the novel is constituted in terms of a principle that informs and dominates the social reality of its time.
>
> (p. 237)

Nineteenth-century writers respond to the constructions of their dominant culture in a wide variety of ways, and writers like Storm Jameson, Phyllis Bottome, Rebecca West and Doris Lessing, for instance, tell stories of later decades which show the same perception, and emphasize, true to the changing priorities of their time, how a number of perceived 'realities' can coexist.

What I shall be arguing is that realism is not intrinsically tied to any one period. The kind of realism we encounter in the four decades I am exploring has been exposed to the theories of Darwin, Nietzsche and Freud as have more obviously experimental texts, even if the realist mode also caters for what I argued earlier was that strand of continuity, of tradition, which is an inevitable ingredient of a modernity which is never purely modern. For while we accept tensions between tradition and change as playing a part in the content of the modern novel (as when Stephen Dedalus wrestles with the moral code laid down by his religious training), we have sometimes treated the modern style as one that prioritizes change over continuities, labelling realism 'middlebrow', as if it were intrinsically prioritizing tradition over innovation. However, the realism of the four decades I explore learns lessons from the more experimental works of its contemporaries: interiority and consciousness figure largely in the works of the women novelists I consider; their novels rarely end with closure; and, moreover, realism is well suited to imitate tensions between continuities and change. Furthermore, realism becomes a vehicle for exploring different constructions of reality than that of the dominant culture. In *Imaginary Homelands*, Salman Rushdie makes much the same point as Gebauer and Wulf, arguing against those who claim that too often novels that describe an alternative reality (novels emanating from the working class, for instance) simply accept the status quo. Cairns Craig, for instance, while he defends what he terms 'a critical realism', equates the 'reluctant realism' of many working -class novels with a kind of debased naturalism, arguing that:

> the major working-class novels of the fifties and sixties all end in the defeat of the hero – not a tragic defeat asserting positive values, but a miserable submission to living with the inevitable, not a critical realism that enforces the demand for change, but a reluctant realism that can see no way out.[34]

Rushdie rejects this position, insisting that

> description is itself a political act. The black American writer Richard Wright once wrote that black and white Americans were engaged in a war over the nature of reality. Their descriptions were incompatible. So it is clear that redescribing a world is the necessary first step to changing it . . . Writers and politicians are natural rivals. Both groups try to make the world in their own images; they fight for the same territory. And the novel is one way of denying the official, politicans' version of truth.[35]

The novel is also an admirable vehicle, even if incidentally, for exploring ways in which modernity is constantly changing, as part of a background or a passing topic of debate. Yet ways of writing, whether given the labels modernist or realist (and while the extremes of modernism and realism are far apart, there is a considerable blurring of territories at the centre), inevitably must practise selection, and must interpret what they select;[36] by definition, then, they are never entirely representational, and at the same time must respond to the changing priorities of the world in which they exist and of which they form a part, if they are to survive. And of course they will have their blind spots, as I have already noted. Bruce Robbins argues, for instance, that

> One specific social reason for the theoretical suspicion of representation, at least since the 1960s, has been the sensitivity of actual, vocal constituencies (racial, ethnic, sexual and so on) . . . about their misrepresentation and under-representation in the dominant cultural discourses.[37]

This is an issue which I shall be exploring in subsequent chapters, and yet what is remarkable, I think, in so many of the novels of these forty

years, is the slow but sure changes in perceptions which they demonstrate. Many of the novelists of these years show awareness that they are
confronting times when there is no one shared view of reality, but rather
a series of realities which differ according to different points of view, and
many of them strive to express this perception. As Robbins observes of a
later period, 'the issue is not between representation and nonrepresent-
ation...but between differing representations' (p. 230).

The period I am exploring is a period of rapid and often bewildering
change, where confusion rather than consensus is the most striking
quality. What Jeffrey Richards has argued for the thirties is relevant for
the period as a whole:

> people define themselves in different ways at different times. They
> define themselves as male or female, as being from a particular family
> or faith, from an individual town or specific region, from a defined
> race or class or country...Equally some people view the world from
> a class perspective, others from a moral one, and still more from a
> gender standpoint.[38]

In response to such a modernity, realism can play a part by offering
what may at first sight appear to be a familiar pattern in which to
explore its often disturbing perceptions. For as every artist knows,
there are problems in challenging tradition and its continuities, especially in times of great uncertainty. The good entertainer, however
committed to revolutionizing the audience's perceptions, must surren-
der something to expectation if the shocks are to make their mark; too
many shocks will be rejected by the bulk of readers since they make the
universe of the novel incomprehensible, and will only be acceptable to
the few, so succumbing to elitism at the very moment when a wider
audience was being sought. Yet shock, 'disequilibrium', is crucial if the
reader is to be stimulated into critical awareness of the contemporary
world, as Ernst Gombrich says of the visual arts: 'We notice only when
we look for something, and we look when our attention is aroused by
some disequilibrium, a difference between our expectation and the
incoming message'.[39] Yet, again, expectation will change as society
moves on and its priorities change. So it should not be surprising to
find from the thirties on, both in literature and in visual art, that, as
James Malpas puts it, 'in comparison with the late nineteenth century, a
new diversity of what was thought to constitute realism appears, a
mirror to the fracturing social and political structure at this time'.[40]
Yet, as I touched on earlier, there will always be a blend of conservative

and radical in society and in the individuals within that society. There is, of course, a great deal of truth in Terry Eagleton's claim that

> Until quite recently, most men and women lived their modernity as tradition: truth was a contract between yourself, your ancestors and your progeny, and radical innovation was either wicked or unthinkable... One moved backwards into the future with one's eyes fixed on the past, and in this way was less likely to come a cropper. The present was what had the most history behind it, not what was struggling to awaken from it; and if the present knew more than the past, it was the past that it knew.[41]

Yet while some, like Stephen Dedalus, are struggling to awaken from history, others are trying to situate themselves within it, struggling to understand how they have arrived in the confusing world which they now inhabit. This is not to say that the novelists who take this path accept unquestioningly versions of history which they have inherited from past analysts; often their perceptions of how the worlds of the thirties, forties, fifties or sixties have evolved will vary in their subversiveness. But the traumas of world war and cold war do not allow all writers to abandon a desire to discover and reassess their roots in the light of what has happened to their world, however painful the process is. Nor do most of these women writers make the mistake of haranguing their audience about the present; they wrap their message within the texture of story. Most would seem to agree with W. H. Auden that

> you cannot tell people what to do, you can only tell them parables and that is what art really is, particular stories of particular people and experiences, from which each according to his own immediate and peculiar needs may draw his own conclusions.[42]

What we find is that many of the women writers of these four decades do not adopt one unvarying approach to the issue of how to relate their work to the shifting perspectives of modernity. Jacqueline Rose, probing the fractures in literary theory in *Why War* (1993), observes that:

> One of the oppositions which often appears in literary theory is between a concentration on the literary or aesthetic movement of the writing and a reading of literary texts in the name of something called history or materiality, with the corresponding insistence that the latter grounds the text in a more concrete, referential domain...

Both halves of the opposition need to be troubled by what they encounter on either side of the binary. So there [may be] an appeal to the category of the aesthetic, but through history and the psyche on the one hand, and to that of history, but through linguistic and unconscious processes on the other.[43]

Such perceptions of the interlinking of the elements which Rose lists here may offer an explanation as to why so many women writers are continually changing the way in which they address their age – fantasy, fable and fairy story exist alongside or merge with political debate and acute social comment; there is less sense of a sharp division into camps than later theory might lead us to expect. True, Storm Jameson, for instance, does make passionate pleas for documentary realism at the beginning of World War Two, excoriating as she does so the work of James Joyce, but even she does not always stick to this mode of writing – she also turns to fabular fantasy (*Then We Shall Hear Singing*, 1942) and a novel structured like a Greek drama (*The Fort*, 1941) to focus her readers' attention on certain issues during the war, and her work frequently eases into the language of interiority, drawing on stream of consciousness techniques. Experiment with form and language is also a feature of work by Rebecca West in *Harriet Hume* (1929), Sylvia Townsend Warner in *After the Death of Don Juan* (1938), Naomi Mitchison in *The Bull Calves* (1947), Pamela Frankau in *The Offshore Light* (1952) and Doris Lessing in *The Golden Notebook* (1962), to name only a few novels of a few writers who engage in a variety of ways with issues of their time and whose fiction I shall be exploring in subsequent chapters; and many of these works are well worth reading, not just as social documents but as excellent novels in their own right. Yet so many of them have vanished from library shelves. Here we come to a crucial issue, and one that needs to be considered by those who establish any canon, whether it be modernist, feminist or any other kind. For it may be that the difficulty of placing such writers securely in any one category has led to their subsequent neglect – they fail to comply with the main divisions which later critics have decreed to be paramount within the period. As critics, we have too often chosen to discuss modernity as if it were 'purely' modern. The writers of these four decades knew it was not: they catered for an element of continuity, of habit if you like, within their changing world, and cast round for the best ways of expressing both the old and the new. The manner in which we have defined the modern in recent years makes it hard for us to admit the variety of ways in which its confusions and continuities are evoked in different works. Yet we do fiction no favours if we insist on consigning so many of these writers to the ranks of the 'middle-brow', implying that they are not worthy of serious critical consideration. For many of these works are important precisely because they blur the boundaries between 'modernism' and 'realism' until it appears to be meaningless, since within their diversity there is a constant: the urge to communicate with an audience, the urge not to let a readership fall into easy expectation of what they will receive from any one author, and this is a key issue which I shall be discussing in my first chapter.

When it came to selecting what areas to explore in this book, I have had again to be highly selective. The way women write throughout these decades clearly has both political and social implications, but the choice of what to highlight in their subject matter was not easy. In the end, the issue of war, attitudes to violence, and the clash between opposition to fascism and a commitment to pacifism seemed to select themselves, since the threat of war dominated the thirties, war itself giving way to the cold war in the following decades, shaping the ways in which writers conceived of their world. What is striking about the period is the way in which the issue of war and violence overshadowed so much else; when we contemplate this, it becomes easier to see why feminist issues, while never entirely lost to view, are not the first priority for many writers – the survival of the human race, the appalled dismay at the barbarity which Western civilization was capable of, inevitably loom large in much of the fiction of the time. There was a pressing need expressed in many novels of the time to identify the roots of violence; in the thirties and forties, a kind of sex war develops with some arguing for the guilt of men as the main perpetrators, while others insist on the complicity of women, or even their active instigation of or participation in acts of violence. After World War Two, the emphasis shifts, the roots of public violence being frequently sited within the family or within a dominant culture's response to what it regards as unacceptably aberrant members of its own community or of other races. Writers either have to engage with such issues, or resolutely turn their backs; both responses exist, but it is those who engage whose work I shall be exploring in my second chapter.

The crisis of confidence in the validity of many former perceptions which the revelations of World War Two provoked affects a whole range of issues. I had originally intended to devote my third chapter entirely to changing attitudes to race and empire, but the novels I read encouraged the idea that class could usefully be explored alongside these other pressing issues, the marginalities within each category having certain things in common. These concerns, above all, gain by being examined in context; what may well strike the reader at the moment of entering a new millenium as crude or patronizing are often first, tentative steps on the way to massive changes in thinking – and blindspots are also well worth exploring. Where a number of writers in the thirties, for instance, are alert to the implications of anti-Semitism both at home and abroad, far fewer are ready to address similar racist issues in the context of empire; and while some writers are alert to the iniquities of a racism which extends beyond anti-Semitism, seeing the connection between the fascism in Europe with colonial practice, few renounce all faith in what they vaguely describe as the higher ideals of imperialism. And prejudices against other races living within the home community are even more persistent. The novels which I cover reveal that such blind spots are slow to disappear.

A number of writers during the period make connections between the working class and non-white races. Yet matters of class are also subjects which produce confused responses; more recent postcolonial debates on who should write about whom have their equivalents in the thirties, but chiefly the matter at stake is who has the right to explore working-class territory. There is also the further problem, which Bridget Fowler considers, that those with the worst lives, who might gain most from the ideas put forward in works about such issues, were those with least access to them; the readership throughout the period I am exploring was predominantly middle class.[44] Gradually, throughout the decades covered by this book, more working-class writers find publishers and, increasingly, basic tenets of British imperialism are questioned – but the absence of non-white women writers in the lists of British publishers tells its own tale. None the less, the places where margins are set do shift and change throughout the period, and there are the beginnings of an awareness in many novels that silences imposed by an earlier dominant culture are on the wane.

My fourth chapter explores matters of gender; and I locate this towards the end of the book because much of what has gone before illuminates the issues I wanted to discuss, and gives grounds for some of the questions I raise. Writing of this period, Dale Spender observed in 1984 that

The quiescence of feminist issues apparently substantiates the myth, conveniently soothing to anti-feminists, that the suffragettes had 'packed up the hammers, and picked up the stones, bundled up the banners and ... returned, tired but contented, to the confines of domesticity'.[45]

Certainly domesticity does feature largely throughout the period; what
Nicola Beauman says of the early years of the century could be extended
to cover the four decades I explore:

> Very few novels by women in the period 1914–39 described a woman
> finally giving up love and marriage for her career. The moral was
> almost always that in order to be happy, to fulfil herself as a
> woman, it was important for her to sacrifice, to dote and – eventually
> – to self-abnegate. After all, the staple readership of the circulating
> libraries was largely women who had done just this, or if they were
> unmarried, they were presumed to be longing not to be.[46]

Yet while a woman of one generation may retreat into the home, her
daughter may either move out, or may at the least start to reassess
her position within the home and in relation to her value to the
society in which she is situated. As with other issues, it is impossible to
be essentialist about what was happening, as the novels of the period
show.

Of course, masculinities were also inevitably under debate after the
traumas of first one and then two world wars; the old idea of man as
warrior had proved hollow, just as the links between violence in the
world outside and its relation to domestic life within the family could
no longer be ignored. Men begin to be seen as victims of social expectations which can be quite as damaging as those which women have
experienced. But issues involving women are more frequently and
more intensively examined as the period wears on; particularly after
World War Two, we find many women writers highlighting the price
women can pay if forced into roles which do not suit them – those
suffocated by domesticity and the kitchen sink stand beside those who
feel pressured by suffragette expectations of the woman's place in the
workplace. During the fifties and sixties, women's propensity for breakdown and madness, for instance, come under scrutiny, and in many
novels is linked directly with pressures to conform to ideas which fail to
accommodate those who are temperamentally unsuited to the roles
social expectation thrusts upon them. Indeed, many women novelists
of these four decades keep the problematic issues of gender vocal and
challenging, paving the way for the feminist movements of the sixties.
We also find that the issue of same-sex relationships, while still treated
cautiously in the thirties and forties, comes to be addressed more openly
during the fifties and sixties; women novelists are very often testing the
limits of their readers' tolerance, and finding it more receptive, in fiction

at least, to explorations of the political and social margins, than some accounts of the period would suggest.

Any one of the issues I explore could be profitably extended; I have barely scratched the surface of this extraordinarily rich period. And other approaches too would be revealing; it would, for instance, be valuable to extend the work Janet Montefiore has done for the thirties, and to examine men's and women's novels side by side.[47] But at least what is here may prompt others to discover the range of highly intelligent, well-constructed novels which I have found so illuminating.

1
Women's Ways of Writing

Christine Brooke-Rose has observed that:

> to practise seeing, for a lifetime, a living 'reality' (the 'truth') in order the better to transform it (since human kind cannot bear it) has always been and always will be the painful and splitting dilemma of the artist, the truth and the lies that already so tormented Plato. And the 'reality', the 'truth', changed with each period and generation. The difference is that today we cannot believe in truth any more: the more one practises looking for it beyond appearances, the less it is there.[1]

Her comments on the writer's dilemma today can be extended back to the four decades covered in this book. For the period 1928 to 1968 is one that has put enormous pressure on writers, if only because of the drastic and rapid changes in their world, politically, materially and spiritually: 'reality' and how to capture such a shifting and complex concept pre-occupied the most perceptive of them in these four decades. So when we explore ways in which women writers communicate through their novels, it is both crucial to keep that context in mind and important not to blur the distinction between how they write and what they write about. Clearly this is not to say that the two aspects are not inevitably linked, but rather to alert us to the ways priorities may well shift in line with the writer's main concerns. What is written about and how it is written about may well be very much affected by the historical context at the time of writing – and we should try to avoid being blinded by priorities of our own period at the time of reading. For example, as regards content, while women writers may not always put feminist issues to the fore as the thirties, forties and fifties progress, such issues are rarely ignored; however, they often tend to be subsumed under pressing concerns about the human condition as a whole. Issues such as fascism, communism and the role of violence in our lives loom large; or in the post-Holocaust, post-Hiroshima era, many writers struggle to come to terms with what human nature is capable of, whether masculine or feminine; or, as old-style imperialism disintegrates, they may see as their chief concern the deconstruction of racial and cultural stereotypes.

All kinds of decisions confront writers then, and they may well come to feel, alongside or despite their critics, a need to reassess the whole question of the function of art and the responsibilities of the artist. Rebecca West shows us how seriously writers could take this when, in *Black Lamb and Grey Falcon*, she says: 'Art is not a plaything, but a necessity, and its essence, form, is not a decorative adjustment, but a cup into which life can be poured and lifted to the lips and be tasted.'[2] But later she admits:

> Art covers not even a corner of life, only a knot or two here and there, far apart and without relation to the pattern. How could we hope that it would ever bring order and beauty to the whole of that vast and intractable fabric, that sail flapping in the contrary winds of the universe?
>
> (p. 508).

As the narrator says in Storm Jameson's *Europe to Let* (1940): 'I understand at these moments how provisional and insecure is the shape, the timing of reality that we have agreed upon'.[3]

George Orwell's well-known comment on art being of necessity political in the thirties is by no means confined to that decade, and what constitutes the 'political' as well as what constitutes an aesthetic capable of responding to it are matters which tax writers throughout the period.[4] They have to decide what audience is being addressed – those already committed to the ideas being suggested by their fictions or those who must be enticed into interest: the balance in the latter case between expectation and surprise must be carefully judged and the decisions taken by the writer can be very varied. For instance, in the thirties, Naomi Mitchison sets up a historical fiction based in antiquity, *The Corn King and the Spring Queen*, which interweaves with the personal quest of the protagonist, Erif Der, political questions about democracy, autocracy and tyranny, highly relevant to Mitchison's present;[5] in the forties, Ethel Mannin writes a romantic fable, *The Dark Forest*, which

invites readers to confront the difficult contemporary issue of fraternization with an enemy;[6] in the fifties, Sylvia Townsend Warner offers a
historical fiction beginning in Victorian times, *The Flint Anchor*, subtly
revealing the pressures of patriarchy not only on its women victims but
also on the man who feels socially obliged to practise its tyrannies,
mirroring changing views of masculinity after World War Two;[7] and in
the sixties Muriel Spark, in *The Prime of Miss Jean Brodie*, uses the frame-
work of a 'rites of passage' fiction to expose, with her usual wit, the effect
of a kind of fascistic programming on the children Miss Brodie 'edu-
cates', imposing roles on them for the present and the future, and
demonstrating how the politics of the wider society have their roots in
the intimate everyday world – a growing preoccupation of novels written in the late fifties and sixties.[8]

Furthermore, what is written about must involve decisions, not only
on the forms selected but also on how to write within them: at an
obvious level, if inner consciousness is a priority, as with Woolf, it will
be expressed differently from observation and meticulous recording of
an outer reality which readers may not necessarily wish to acknowledge
as their own reality, as in Doris Lessing's early novels revealing the dark
side of colonial society.[9] And of course there is no easy either/or decision. How writers solve the problem of expression is remarkably varied
throughout the four decades; as Andrzej Gasiorek says: 'realism and
experiment mean different things to different novelists'.[10] And indeed
the ways of addressing the problem may vary widely within the output
of individual writers. Most women writers seem to be not so much
looking for a woman's style, a woman's language (on an obvious level
'he' continues to be used throughout the period to refer generally to
man or woman, even by the most notably feminist). What seems to be
their priority is the search for a voice which will engage the reader, a
voice which will express various aspects of the writer's perceptions of
modernity, and which will encourage the reader to participate in those
perceptions.

While Gasiorek asserts with some truth that 'modernism had produced often dazzling works of art but had driven fiction so deeply into
subjectivism that it had been left with few resources for dealing with
social issues' (p. 1), it is in fact often less than useful to attempt to
separate those who use modernist techniques or who are clearly experimental from those who lean towards realism. The whole question of
what art is for, the responsibility of art to the society from which it
springs, are things which deeply concern many of the writers of the
period, whether they discuss such issues in articles and essays or show

the results of their thinking within their fiction. Moreover, experimental poetics does not necessarily involve radical politics; as Gillian Hanscombe and Virginia Smyers say, 'to the political activists, artistic radicalism seems all too often traditionalist in its assumptions of the primacy of art over all the other workings of the world'.[11] And conversely, we might also see Celeste Schenk's comment as relevant for fiction: 'Might it also be true that the seemingly genteel, conservative poetics of women poets whose obscurity even feminists have overlooked, might pitch a more radical politics than we consider possible?'[12] Certainly, since all versions of events can now be perceived as story (and Christine Brooke-Rose reminds us that ' "living" history is also permanently falsified, not just by totalitarian systems that efface and reinterpret, but by liberal systems that exploit, and, in particular, that present it only as "story" '),[13] each fictional construct must be scrutinized for the politics within its writing. A traditional vessel reused, as Raphael Samuel has pointed out, does not serve, cannot serve, the same function as when it was first used.[14] Or as Naomi Mitchison says, after dicussing her reasons for decisions about the language in *The Bull Calves* (1947), her novel set in eighteenth-century Scotland: 'In a book which has the social and political implications that this book obviously has, one's motives are not purely artistic – if such a thing is ever possible'.[15]

What in fact we find, in the work of most of the writers discussed in this book, is that it is often impossible to draw a line between 'modernists', experimental writers and users of realism; and, certainly, not all those using so-called realism are formally conservative backsliders. As Gasiorek says of many writers after World War Two, they 'try to reconceptualize realism rather than to reject it outright in the wake of modernist and postmodernist critique'. He goes on to say that:

> following Brecht, I view realism not in terms of more or less fixed formal techniques but as a family of writings that share a certain cognitive attitude to the world, which manifests itself in a variety of forms in different historical periods...On this view, there is no necessary link either between particular narrative strategies and the goal of accurate representation or between realism, however it is conceived, and any given political position.[16]

Furthermore, he says, 'Realism, I suggest, is flexible, wide-ranging, unstable, historically variable, and radically open-ended' (p. 14). There is much to be said for this approach, as many writers reshape realism from within, often using techniques drawn from modernism.[17] Indeed, what emerges is that choice of form, mode of writing of whatever kind, is in itself amoral; it is what the writer does with such choices which decides whether they support or query contemporary versions of the 'real'. What is crucial is to see how aware writers are of the changes in the reality they seek to convey throughout the period, changes affected as much by the impact of, say, philosophy, psychoanalysis and scientific advances as by events. The problem for the critic is whether what is being written about and the way it is being addressed combine to change the impact of what may at first seem a traditional vehicle.

The presence of what may be presented as an objective narrator is as misleading in the writings of these women novelists as in the writings of George Orwell, especially when linked with the growing use of documentary realism during the thirties and subsequent decades. Those writers who adopt this last approach aim to give the illusion of authority to certain views of the present moment which may not be universally accepted, addressing readers who may not have confronted ways in which their world is changing. The reasons for such an aim are understandable in context, as is clear when we look at the passionate advocacy of Storm Jameson in *Civil Journey*.[18] In the wake of what was widely perceived among intellectuals of the time as the irrationalism of Nazism, she attacks the surrealists, urging us to 'distrust a movement that begins by asking the intellect to circumvent itself' (p. 298), and she argues that 'Since the century opened, we have seen pass into popular speech any number of phrases to express an almost religious belief, garbled and distorted from its true origins, in the supremacy and rightness of purely emotional activity' (p. 195); the language of metaphor has gained ground over the language of pragmatic precision. What we must recall so as to understand her apparent extremism in *Civil Journey* is the popular appeal of the non-rational in Nazi discourse of the time. It is in answer to this that she claims writers should be willing 'to sink themselves for the time, so that they become conduits for a feeling which is not personal, nor static' (p. 267), and that they should aim for a rational, objective discourse. But as Brecht warns:

> less than ever does the mere reflection of reality reveal anything about reality. A photograph of the Krupp works or the A.E.G. tells us next to nothing about these institutions. Actual reality has slipped into the functional. The reification of human relations – the factory, say – means that they are no longer explicit. So something must in fact be *built up*, something artificial, posed.[19]

Indeed, Virginia Woolf, commenting on those Edwardians who made earlier claims for the accurate representation of 'reality', asserts that 'whether we call it life or spirit, truth or reality, this, the essential thing, has moved off, or on, and refuses to be contained any longer in such ill-fitting garments as we provide';[20] and Rebecca West also addresses the problem when, in *Black Lamb and Grey Falcon*, she castigates:

> fake art, naturalist art, which copies nature without interpreting it; which believes that to copy is all we can and need do to nature; which is not conscious that we live in an uncomprehended universe, and that it is urgently necessary for sensitive men to look at each phenomenon in turn and find out what it is and what are its relations to the rest of existence.[21]

But documentary realism is only one of the modes practised throughout the four decades. Many writers of the period experiment with a range of subgenres: science fiction, murder mystery or the historical novel (in which they may look at the past so as to trace possible roots for tendencies in the present, to give a context and structure to such tendencies so as to see them more clearly), and indeed, even the kind of realist novel which explores domesticity, are in many cases far from disengaged from the public sphere, as the public is seen as rooted in the private, more and more insistently as the century progresses. Many writers move from one kind of writing to another, continually challenging the reader, not allowing expectation to dominate over surprise. Indeed Storm Jameson, despite her passionate advocacy of 1939, by no means always chose to practise documentary realism herself. At various times she writes, for instance, futuristic fiction (*In the Second Year*, 1936), a novel based on Greek tragic form (*The Fort*, 1941) and a fable (*Then We Shall Hear Singing*, 1942).[22] This varied approach is a marked feature of many writers of the period, as for example Naomi Mitchison, Sylvia Townsend Warner, Doris Lessing, Maureen Duffy and Christine Brooke-Rose. Fantasy and Utopian fiction also have their place in women's writing, either as modes for entire novels or as aspects of novels, and, in this diversity, women writers of these four decades show their links with a nineteenth-century preoccupation to which Anne Cranny Francis points:

> What Morris and others recognized was that any change in their own society required a complete change in people's perception of their

reality: they needed to scrutinize the category of the real, to see reason and reality as arbitrary, shifting constructs – only then could they be free to formulate alternatives, to challenge institutions and practices they found irresponsible and morally reprehensible.[23]

It can also be argued, as Christine Brooke-Rose does, that 'realism of a kind is necessary to all fictional modes'.[24] Ultimately, the sheer variety of form and merging of forms practised by many writers of the four decades I am exploring mirror the volatile mix of conservative and radical threads running through the period.

As always, it is all too easy to criticize, from the safe distance of the 1990s, choices which past writers have made. Apart from anything else, it is all too easy to overlook what was, at the time of writing, a subtle blend of what the reader might expect, and what constituted surprise or shock. For what offers surprise in one age becomes the norm for another, as the reception of Beckett's *Waiting for Godot* shows, and new possibilities of countering expectation have to be devised. So it is important to attempt a kind of dual perspective on the choices made in the past, remembering, for instance, that, as the European crises of the thirties loomed, the options to engage, to concentrate on aesthetic issues or to evade engagement were by no means as clear-cut as they seem to us now – while the writer in World War Two and throughout the Cold War had different but comparable choices to make, choices which for the thoughtful writer were not to be made lightly.

The form of the novel is not the only aesthetic issue which the writers of these four decades have to resolve. There is also the question of the kind of language they are to use, a question very much tied to the kind of audience the writer visualizes, and here they may well come into conflict with the prevailing aesthetic criteria of the day. As Deborah Cameron observes,

> so far as I know...there has never been a culture which did not believe that some ways of using words were functionally, aesthetically or morally preferable to others – though equally there has never been one that did not violently disagree about which ways these were.

For, as she goes on to say, 'language is not just about representing private mental states, it is also a public affirmation of values',[25] and, in a later article, she reminds us that 'Whenever some aspect of a language is codified and standardised, the standard is invariably based on the usage of an elite class. Their norms are universalised, while others are stigmatised'.[26] But what we often find is that writers who are perfectly capable of conforming to such literary norms may choose to write much more simply, even colloquially, so as to reach a wider audience and to entice them into considering issues the novel raises. It is revealing to note, for instance, that as Naomi Mitchison wrote her Scottish novel, *The Bull Calves*, during the Second World War, she read passages aloud to her fisherman friends to make sure that she was catching the nuances of their speech accurately – and they were valuable critics. Mitchison is particularly sensitive to the need to shift rhythms and verbal register so as to capture the language of different elements in society and so to make her novels accessible to a wide range of readers. Of course, the decision to reach a wider range of readers can lead to aesthetic problems, but what I am stressing is that Mitchison, for instance, is not taking her decisions on language without weighing the advantages and disadvantages of what she may do. She throws light on the issue in her Notes appended to *The Bull Calves*, saying:

> In my novels of the ancient world I have transcribed Latin, Greek, or whatever it may be, into current English, using slang or debased forms when it seemed as though this was the best way of giving the reader the feel of how people were talking. Sometimes I overdid this, using a transient slang, which has now dated that bit of the book.[27]

Then, referring specifically to *The Bull Calves*, she insists, passionately if somewhat inaccurately, 'I could never have written this book in the academic English of the literary tradition – Shakespeare to Virginia Woolf' (p. 411). Nor is this just a question of atmospherics, for she argues for the power that words have to mirror changes in society, where

> reader and author join in a conspiracy of moral fervour either to restate the old standards or to affirm a new stopping place in the process of change . . . Sometimes we forget that this moral structure of society is temporal in history, above all in economic history, and held together by words.

Importantly, she then goes on to affirm the importance of knowing what audience to target: 'My book is mainly written in the hopes of being read by the generality of Scottish folk, whether or not they have had a secondary education, but not in hopes of being read by more than a minority in southern England' (p. 457).

In the end what we find is that, just as realism is not necessarily bound to nineteenth-century conservatism, so all aesthetic criteria, when closely scrutinized, are amoral, as Leverkuhn's music proves to be in Thomas Mann's *Dr Faustus* when he uses the same sequences for angels and devils in his great Oratorio. Everything depends on the use to which they are put and the context in which they emerge; only then can we judge their moral status. A resistance movement, after all, uses many methods which are similar to those of the dominant regime. Again, what Rebecca West says at the end of *Black Lamb and Grey Falcon* is relevant here as she reflects on the question,

> What is art? It is not decoration. It is the re-living of experience. The artist says, 'I will make that event happen again, altering its shape, which was disfigured by its contacts with other events, so that its true significance is revealed'; and his audience says, 'We will let that event happen again by looking at this man's picture or house, listening to his music or reading his book.' It must not be copied, it must be remembered, it must be lived again . . . But such deliverance will not come soon, for art is a most uncertain instrument. Art cannot talk plain sense, it must sometimes speak what sounds at first like nonsense, though it is actually supersense. But there is much nonsense about, full of folly packed so tight that it has assumed the density of wisdom.[28]

And she reminds us of a mistake she made earlier in her travels through the troubled Balkan states: 'The figure standing on the balcony . . . announcing with his arms that he was about to proclaim deliverance to the plains and mountains, was a scarecrow stored from the weather' (p. 1128).

'An uproar of voices' in the thirties

As Patrick Deane says, the thirties was a decade typified by an 'uproar of voices'.[29] Throughout the period, several women writers discuss their craft in articles, while others demonstrate how they perceive it within their fiction. And certainly throughout the inter-war years there was no consensus as to how they chose to write or how they should write. Early in the decade, for instance, we hear the confident voice of the influential critic Queenie Leavis adopting the words highbrow, middlebrow and lowbrow as 'convenient' terms of distinction.[30] We might feel surprised that, despite her left-wing credentials, she seems unconcerned about the biological implications of this terminology, but, a pioneer in her field, she gives us a valuable glimpse of a shrewd critical intelligence at work in the early thirties: she identifies, for instance, a potential deterioration in literary standards, claiming that 'the critical minority to whose sole charge modern literature has now fallen is isolated, disowned by the general public and threatened with extinction' (p. 35). Certainly high modernism, as we have come to call it, did not appeal to the bulk of readers;[31] and Leavis herself acknowledges, if ironically, that one can only read Woolf if the mind is 'absolutely fresh'.[32] She seems to agree with the letter, if not entirely with the spirit, of Roger Fry who had said in 1928, 'the artist of the new movement is moving into a sphere more and more remote from the ordinary man. In proportion as art becomes purer the number of people to whom it appeals gets less'.[33]

But Leavis is not by any means esoteric in her view of the novel. She suggests that

> The best that the novel can do . . . is not to offer a refuge from actual life but to help the reader to deal less inadequately with it; the novel can deepen, extend, and refine experience by allowing the reader to live at the expense of an unusually intelligent and sensitive mind, by giving him access to a finer code than his own.[34]

She is, in fact, less concerned with promoting the priorities of writers like Woolf than in deploring the fact, as she sees it, that the ordinary reader is no longer able 'to brace himself to bear the impact of the serious novel . . . a novel, that is, in which words are used with fresh meanings and for ends with which he is unfamiliar' (p. 257); and urging that

> The peculiar property of a good novel . . . is the series of shocks it gives to the reader's preconceptions – preconceptions, usually unconscious, of how people behave and why, what is admirable and what reprehensible; it provides a configuration of special instances which serve as a test for our mental habits and show us the necessity for revising them.
>
> (p. 256)

Another critical issue of the inter-war years was the long-standing debate over what mode of writing lends itself to women's particular concerns, an issue which sometimes seemed to mirror the split between 'old' feminists (Winifred Holtby calls them Equalitarians) and the 'new' feminists who, like Eleanor Rathbone, concerned themselves chiefly with women's problems. What constitutes 'women's writing', both in subject matter and narrative mode (sometimes extending to how women 'ought' to write) has been an issue for most of this century and indeed earlier.

Marion Shaw has examined Holtby's position on whether women's fiction 'could or should be distinct from established literary practice'.[35] 'Established literary practice' refers primarily to realism, as many feminists tended to see realism as the preserve of men and the patriarchal state, reflecting a social status quo. Many feminists therefore urged the need for a new literary mode to map 'the largely uncharted territory of women's subjective lives' (pp. 177–8); yet, as Shaw observes, Holtby was not happy about this exclusiveness: 'To her, the threat from the "new" feminist novelists, as from the "new" feminists like Eleanor Rathbone, was that gender would usurp humanity as a primary condition' (p. 190). In recent years, critics have given a lot of attention to this issue. Sandra Kemp, for instance, explores how Dorothy Richardson's fiction attenuates 'human agency' and abolishes 'the distinction between "external" and "internal" worlds"'.[36] These were characteristics, as Kemp reminds us, of what Richardson calls 'feminine prose', in her 'Foreword' to *Pilgrimage*, describing how she became aware, as she wrote,

> of the gradual falling away of the preoccupations that for a while had dictated the briskly moving script, and of the substitution, for these inspiring preoccupations, of a stranger in the form of contemplated reality having for the first time in her experience its own say.
>
> (p. 102)

However, as Michèle Barrett points out, Virginia Woolf does not see this 'different' style as a 'biological imperative but rather the result of conscious choice by a woman writer whose "new" subject matter of "the psychology of sex" requires new methods'.[37] For, she says:

> Other writers of the opposite sex have used sentences of this description and stretched them to the extreme. But there is a difference. Miss Richardson has fashioned her sentence consciously, in order that it may descend to the depths and investigate the crannies of Miriam Henderson's consciousness. It is a woman's sentence, but only in the sense that it is used to describe a woman's mind by a writer who is neither proud nor afraid of anything that she may discover in the psychology of sex.
>
> (p. 191)

And indeed, if we look at the practice of other women writers during the inter-war years, the chief concern seems to be the development of a voice to cope with the realities which they perceive. It is, for instance, illuminating to see what Rebecca West focusses on in her collection of essays, *The Strange Necessity* (1928).[38] In the title essay, an analysis of her reaction to Joyce's *Ulysses* leads to a meditation on 'Why does art matter? And why does it matter so much? What is this strange necessity?' (p. 58). She argues that 'throughout the whole of his life the individual does nothing but match his fantasy with reality and try to establish, either by affirmation or alteration, an exact correspondence between them' (p. 62), and she concludes that a writer takes words that others use everyday and compels them 'into forms and patterns which are concentrated arguments concerning reality and their opinion of it' (p. 63). But, she says, it is not enough to combine a novel of character and a novel of plot into a whole, for 'the novel must have a theme. Its story must be a myth, in which bodies which are embodiments enact an event which is a type of event' (p. 86). Ultimately, she sees art as 'out to collect information about the phenomena of the universe just as science is; and its preference to do this by the study of imaginary material shows its loyalty to the scientific spirit'; and, like scientists (being of her generation, she believes in science as the ultimate in objectivity), writers must transfer 'their empathy to fields where they can reap no advantages or disadvantages', that is, no subjective advantages or disadvantages, so that, again like scientists, they can 'be trusted to make their records truthfully' (p. 118).

Arguably, Richardson has learnt from the insights of early twentieth-century psychology, and West's stress on 'objectivity' is also affected by scientific tenets of her age (she claims in her essay an affinity with Pavlov), yet, while West meets Richardson on what Kemp calls the 'attenuation of human agency', she is also paving the way for the arguments in favour of documentary realism which gain in urgency as the thirties progress. For in her essay in the same collection entitled 'Uncle Bennett', she asserts that 'life unlit by excitement is nevertheless a light shining in the darkness of the universe' (p. 212); and, furthermore, that 'like Wordsworth, [Bennett] has triumphed over the habitual; he has not let it disguise the particle of beauty from him' (p. 213). These assertions sound very much in tune with what Evelyne White recalls in her memoir of Winifred Holtby, published a decade after West's work. White writes of Holtby's social conscience and of her preference for:

> books that help us to know and understand something of the world and its people ... It might be a pity to remain in ignorance about [the

world], enclosed in the snail shell of our private interests and circumstances, never putting our heads outside to see, and never attempting the stimulating and healing adventure of extended comprehension.[39]

For while we know from Holtby's book on Virginia Woolf, published in 1932, that she could also admire Woolf's skills prior to *The Years*, even if with reservations, Holtby's concerns would prove more in accord with those of Storm Jameson who, as the thirties moved towards their increasingly troubled end, would utter an impassioned plea for documentary realism in her essay 'Documents'.[40] Over the years, Jameson would keep repeating why she could not share an admiration, like West's, for Joyce, whom Jameson unnervingly politicizes as:

a purely disintegrating force, a sacred monster, uprooting established forms to create a waste land, a great anti-humanist, the destroyer by his devilish skill and persistence of the thin walls against barbarism. Writers who give themselves up to the disintegration of language are, so far as they know, innocent of the impulse to destroy civilisation, but the roots of the impulse run underground a long way, to the point where the smoke from burning books becomes the smoke issuing from the ovens of death camps.[41]

When reading such diatribes, we have to remember that Jameson knew of the suppression of languages other than those of the conquerors under totalitarian regimes, and of how such suppressions coexisted with far more drastic persecutions, all in the name of a Nazism which she equated with non-reason.

But in 1937, in the essay 'Documents', she is more intent on pointing a positive way forward for writers and she clearly shows that she shares Holtby's preferences. However, she goes beyond Holtby (writing as she does after Holtby's death, and as the political situation of the thirties had grown ever more critical) in insisting:

We need documents...as timber for the fire some writer will light tomorrow morning...As the photographer does, so must the writer keep himself out of the picture while working ceaselessly to present *fact* from a striking (poignant, ironic, penetrating, significant) angle

and the language for such an enterprise should be 'decent, straight English – not American telegraphese'.[42] It is intriguing to see her advocating abandonment of subjectivity in such a very different way from Richardson. Indeed, Jameson is clearly aware that subjectivity does intrude on documentary when she comments on the problem for a middle-class writer who tries to identify with the workers, acknowledging that he (like others of her generation, Jameson always refers to the writer as 'he') can be seized by 'a dreadful self-consciousness':

> He does not even know what the wife of a man earning two pounds a week wears, where she buys her food, what her kitchen looks like to her when she comes into it at six or seven in the morning...he does not know as much as the woman's forefinger knows when it scrapes the black out of a crack in the table or the corner of a shelf...too much of [the writer's] energy runs away in an intense interest in and curiosity about his feelings.
>
> (p. 557)

But she does not acknowledge that photographic images are far from proof against subjective manipulation. Woolf, for instance, manipulates two sets of photographs in *Three Guineas* (published in 1938), one originally printed with the text, the other described verbally. The set Woolf describes, of dead civilians in the Spanish Civil War, she treats as objective, documentary evidence; the printed set, showing a series of professional men, she analyses as propaganda for patriarchy.[43] Documentary realism, then, is going to be a creation of the writer rather than an objective mirror of some version of reality.

Woolf herself was very much aware of how not just photographs but words develop a life of their own, as she shows in a witty radio talk given in 1937 and published in *The Listener* in the same year as 'Craftsmanship'. She has no great faith in the capacity of what Jameson describes as 'decent straight English' to offer us straightforward interpretation, giving a mischievous example (and sacrificing the constraints of context to whimsy):

> Take the simple sentence 'Passing Russell Square'. That proved useless because besides the surface meaning it contained so many sunken meanings. The word 'passing' suggested the transiency of things, the passing of time and the changes of human life. Then the word 'Russell' suggests the rustling of leaves and the skirt on the polished floor; also the ducal house of Bedford and half the history of England. Finally the word 'Square' brings in sight, the shape of an actual square combined with some visual suggestion of the stark angularity of

stucco. Thus one sentence of the simplest kind raises the imagination, the memory, the eye and the ear – all combine in reading it.[44]

More seriously, she urges the importance of this power of suggestion in
words, 'because the truth they try to catch is many-sided, and they
convey it by being themselves many-sided' (p. 255); and Woolf matches
Leavis's protest of 1932 ('The idiom that the general public of the
twentieth century possesses is not merely crude and puerile; it is made
up of phrases and cliches that imply fixed, or rather stereotyped, habits
of thinking and feeling at second-hand taken over from the journalist')[45] when she voices her sense of the danger of mediocrity if 'we pin
[words] down to one meaning, their useful meaning, the meaning
which makes us catch the train, the meaning which makes us pass the
examination'.[46] So we find Woolf apparently close to Leavis's thinking
on language, while Jameson, also close to Leavis, is more concerned to
deliver the 'shocks [the good novel] gives to the reader's preconceptions'.

As we look closely at the way novelists of the thirties express themselves, what becomes clear is that there are more connections than splits
in the way they view their writing. In 1933, the year after Leavis's book
was published, the first novel of a new writer incorporates discussion of
how to write, and clearly responds both to Woolf's attacks on Arnold
Bennett and to Woolf's own stylistic skills. In *The Mere Living* by
B. Bergson Spiro (after her marriage, Betty Miller), views on art as on
life reflect the personalities of those who hold them. So Paul, the
aesthete, thinks:

> The representation extracted the sting of the actual: gave it back,
> lovely still, but conquered. It occurred to him that this was the
> function of art. But if it were so, then art was an admission of defeat:
> art effected a prudent castration so that inoffensively and pleasurably
> beauty might enter the harem of the perceptive emotions.[47]

Paul is clearly a throw-back to the decadence of the 1890s. But Paul's
friend, Richard, engages directly with the debates on style in the thirties.
He says:

> I don't for a moment believe that the highbrows who set out to tap
> the 'stream of consciousness' get any nearer reality than the solid
> novelists who produce Old Wives' Tales...Each method merely
> approaches its own reality. It requires all the methods in the world

and several more, to get near to any central Reality. If you limit yourself to one, external or internal or whichever you choose, you merely deny all the other aspects which all the other methods portray: no single method has a monopoly on reality. Diversity is essential... If there is a 'monologue intérieur', there is also a 'dialogue extérieur' of the senses with the objective world. An equal combination of *Ulysses* and *The Old Wives' Tale* would succeed in giving a reasonably comprehensive portrait of life, I think; but it requires the two. The price of stocks and shares and the stream of consciousness. Is it reality to flay a man of his social position, antecedents, clothes, flesh and bones and entrails, and merely listen in to the non-stop psychological station? Of course not. No more than it is to mention exclusively his digestion and his bank balance and his woollen combinations.

(pp. 221–2)

However, Paul points out a snag: 'unluckily a writer can only do one thing at a time. He has to space out these activities in sequence, whereas in real life they all go on simultaneously' (p. 222). And in this novel, Spiro demonstrates the limitations of both the modes which Richard describes. For in *The Mere Living*, stream of consciousness reflects inner lives but also fails to communicate, and, when the outside world is described, it is caught in scintillating detail, yet each of the four main characters reflects rather different realities: the father is absorbed by his job, the mother by domesticity, Nancy by her body and sensation, Paul by aesthetics. Only Richard, outside their immediate circle and so the observer of them all, can attempt a synthesis and then only in theory.

But despite Richard's vision of synthesis, and despite the fact that writers with different priorities sometimes appear to agree, as we have seen, there is, as I have demonstrated, no consensus about style in the period 1928 to 1939, and this lack of consensus is not surprising, given the dramatic changes in realities at home and abroad. At home, the issue of unemployment, for instance, sits side by side with the issue of careers for women and conflicting views on relationships and marriage; abroad, there are the growing crises in Europe, and increasing unrest within the Empire. Different writers will make different decisions as to whether they address these issues or attempt to evade them, reflecting the apparently secure middle-class life found in so many popular novels of the time; but women writers of the thirties who address various social and political issues do not adopt a mode of writing which is already in existence, either realist or modernist, without 'changing the model',[48] if what they wish to say requires such changes. As I have argued above, the dividing lines between such modes are not clearly marked among those writing about their craft, and the same blurring of boundaries occurs in many novels. Realism moulded by women who wished to use their fiction as something more than a vehicle for entertainment cannot be dismissed as a vehicle for cultural conservatism or as a hostage to patriarchal modes of writing. It is reshaped and adapted, sometimes borrowing techniques from modernism, always probing for satisfactory ways of conveying commitment to causes or ideas. As Tony Davies says: 'realism, in all its multiple incarnations, is not really a literary form or genre or movement or tradition at all but a contested space, the scene of an unfinished argument'.[49]

Writers with any kind of political or social agenda also have to persuade their readers to engage with the issues of their age. Both Alison Light and Gill Plain have demonstrated how we must acknowledge the conservatism and radicalism which exist side by side in any age, and that both will be reflected in the works of writers and in their readers' responses.[50] Fiction, with its capacity for 'entertainment', and realism, with its strong story line, characterisation and settings, together make an ideal vehicle for persuading readers to engage with radical ideas, while sustained by familiar conventions. As Anne Cranny Francis says,

> the realist text may uncritically (re)present ideological forms, representations and apologetics, which require a critical reading to decode or deconstruct. Or the realist text may encode a self-referential function which continually interrogates its own meaning-making or representational practices. Or it may do both, to a greater or lesser extent.[51]

It could be argued that, for those women writers who engage with the changing realities of their times, aesthetic priorities will increasingly be seen as means to an end, but this does not mean that technique, style, no longer matters to them. If we are to appreciate what these writers achieve, we have, as Valentine Cunningham has said, to abandon 'the very traditional assumption that overt political propaganda, in fact instrumentality of any kind, let alone sentimental dispositions of materials, and simplicity of address to readers, will axiomatically mark a poet or a poem down'.[52]

What is remarkable is the variety, not just in thirties writing in general, but within the work of so many individual writers of the inter-war years. Sylvia Townsend Warner is a shining example of this, as Gillian Beer observes:

> If *After the Death of Don Juan* had been published, not in 1936 but fifty years later, it would have been greeted as a magic-realist fiction; if *Mr Fortune's Maggot* had been published, not in 1928 but, likewise, fifty years later, it would be read as a post-colonial text; while *Summer Will Show* would be seen as part of the current vogue for novels that rewrite the nineteenth century, and the medieval *The Corner That Held Them* as a follower of Umberto Eco's *The Name of the Rose*.[53]

Woolf writes *Orlando, The Waves* and *The Years* between 1928 and 1937, ranging from fantasy to her own version of 'realism';[54] West ranges from the fantasy *Harriet Hume* to another version of 'realism' in *The Thinking Reed*;[55] Susan Ertz, regularly dismissed by later critics, if mentioned at all, as a writer of 'domestic' fiction (a strange reason for dismissal, given Jane Austen), produces a tersely witty futuristic fable, *Woman Alive* (1935), showing the one woman survivor of a war waged with biological weapons, who refuses to reproduce until men have abandoned war and indeed become 'new' men.[56] And even Storm Jameson, the champion of documentary realism in 1937, has earlier in the decade written satiric fiction, historical novels and the futuristic *In the Second Year* (1936), where she sets up a fascist regime in England.[57]

As I suggested in the Introduction, some explanation for this diversity can be found in the need to get past censorship, if the writer is to deal with contentious issues; in the thirties, the cases against *The Well of Loneliness* and *Lady Chatterley's Lover* were still fresh in the mind. But there is the problem not only with the legal constraints of thirties' society, but also with personal and consensus censorship which readers may have absorbed from their specific political, cultural and moral environment. I mentioned earlier the fate of Naomi Mitchison's *We Have Been Warned* (1935), set as it was in modern times. But, while the novel frightened off publishers because of its frank sexual elements in the context of Labour Party canvassing, one of the reasons for its failure has to be Mitchison's attempt to marry too many elements from different styles of novel; there are aspects of thriller, fantasy, dystopia, romance, political realism and stream of consciousness, jostling each other in unlikely combinations.[58] Be that as it may, most women writers of the thirties avoided Mitchison's fate, by writing in ways which supplied entertainment for those who looked only for entertainment, but also offered signals (by epigraphs, for instance) that the story cover could be penetrated by readers who shared the writer's political concerns, and could then be read at another, subversive or polemical level. A number of women novelists, when they want to address some aspect of the contemporary crises, turn to historical or futuristic fictions. Sylvia Townsend Warner, Katharine Burdekin, Susan Ertz, Edith Pargeter and, frequently, Naomi Mitchison herself are obvious examples.[59] Things which could not be tolerated by publishers or readers in a contemporary setting were readily acceptable if set in the past or the future. But all the women writers I am discussing, whether opting for futurist, historic, contemporary or fantasy modes of writing, share one feature: complacent closure is definitely not an option for thinking novelists of these four decades – the endings of their works always have implicit question marks hanging over them.

Arguably, as I suggested earlier, the main reason for the rich diversity in the writing of women committed to social and political issues throughout the inter-war years is their need to come to terms with the changing world around them, and to persuade their readers to join them in this enterprise. So Ellen Wilkinson, the Labour politician, offers in her novel, *Clash* (1928), plenty of romantic interest to entice readers into contemplating the realities of the General Strike, as the protagonist, Joan, learns that selling feminist principles to wives whose husbands are on strike is fraught with unexpected difficulties.[60] Threaded through this are the personal dilemmas which Joan must face: on the one hand, as in many a contemporary film, the working-class girl is tempted by the comfort and security of a wealthy friend's lifestyle, but in Joan's case does not succumb; and on the other, the more alluring of her lovers wants her to give up her political career if she marries him, while the one she ultimately chooses will work at her side. The happy ending is rewritten, pointing away from the cosy assumptions of romantic love. Wilkinson's approach is strictly realist, but her use of accessible, colloquial language as well as the vividness of her engagement with contemporary issues reshapes parts of that realism from within. We find something similar in Winifed Holtby's *South Riding* (1936), where the schoolteacher protagonist is shown to be attracted by a man who has clear affinities with Charlotte Brontë's Mr Rochester, and who, for a time, seems likely to sweep this modern Jane Eyre off her feet.[61] But in the end, the novel celebrates the protagonist's engagement with the problems of her school and the local community, enticing us into accepting her reality over and above literary intertextuality, although that intertextuality has been one of the ways in which she has tempted the reader to confront the graver issues which rewrite the priorities of

Brontë's text. However, many writers look beyond the subversion of realism from within. For instance, in *Harriet Hume* (1929), Rebecca West offers a fantasy which shows Harriet (a 'birdwoman built by a magician expert in fine jewellers' work and ornithology' [p. 11], an ethereal forerunner of Angela Carter's Fevvers)[62] able to read the mind of her ambitious lover; the novel follows them through the years as their relationship ebbs and flows, Harriet always retaining her delicate independence, the feminine penetrating and influencing the masculine. But while this theme shows man and woman as eternally distinct, the protagonist in the novel is arguably London, a London defamiliarized with Dickensian flair, where there are:

> dining-room windows, broad and slightly protuberant, like the paunch of a moderate over-eater; and their stockade of area railings, boasting with their lance-heads that there were points, such as the purity of cooks and the sacredness of property, concerning which the neighbourhood could feel with primitive savagery.[63]

Here, as with Holtby, the literary connections are clear, as they pave the way for the fantasy level; the smugness of the house facades prepares us for the complacency of power which corrupts Harriet's lover. Or there is *The Fourth Pig* (1936), in which Naomi Mitchison goes into fairy tale mode to disarm us, rewriting the stories so as to bring out both feminist and antifascist concerns;[64] or there is *The Arrogant History of White Ben* by Clemence Dane (1939), the story of a scarecrow who is brought to life by a child's mandrake root.[65] Here the elements of folk tale are employed to draw us gradually into an analysis of the birth of a tyrant, a relatively harmless protagonist at the outset, whose mission to kill crows is gradually manipulated into metaphor by those with their own agendas for power. The analogy with Hitler is clear, but, as with Storm Jameson's earlier *In the Second Year*, the analogy is made intimate by the English setting; the countryside is lyrically beautiful, while the final massacre is set off by the darkly humorous fall of Nelson's Column.

Stevie Smith's *Over the Frontier* (1938) employs yet another stratagem, the deceptively scatty outpourings of Pompey (a kind of faux naif version of stream of consciousness, poured out as 'speech') leading to a dark fantasy/dream sequence, where woman is shown to take over man's militarist role once she is in uniform.[66] Again we are drawn into this final sequence by a literary echo; the old lady at the German castle where Pompey is staying is called Mrs Pouncer, the name of the witch in John Masefield's *The Midnight Folk* who prompted the boy-hero Kay's

excursions into a fantasy dream world. But here Mrs Pouncer signals a
far more serious project on Smith's part. Indeed, a number of critics
commented at the time on the novel's Kafkaesque quality: Marie Scott-
James, for instance, describes the 'shadowy world' in the dream fantasy
part of the book as 'part Kafka, part Carroll, lacking in the precision of
the best fantasy, yet with a sort of wild poetry of its own';[67] and we know
Smith read *The Castle* in German in the late twenties, as she wrote at the
time that it was 'a bureaucratic nightmare – brilliant'.[68] Yet, in the light
of Storm Jameson's impassioned plea for documentary realism in 1937,
it is interesting to find Smith in the following year having doubts about
modes of writing which require a reader's interpretation. She discusses,
in a letter written to Scott-James on 9 December 1938, Naomi Mitchison's forthcoming novel, *The Blood of the Martyrs* (1939), set in Nero's
Rome and using the persecution of the Christians as an analogy for Nazi
pogroms:

> I saw Naomi Mitchison the other day and she had my book and kept
> saying: It is impossible you do not take life seriously. She is writing a
> book about the early Christians all the characters get thrown to the
> lions and . . . 'mind rather'. I said: 'You are a cruel girl, Naomi' and she
> implied I was a frivolous one, so you see it is difficult not to impute
> motives I see that. But also perhaps there is something frivolous in
> this throwing of one's characters to the lions and showing that they
> 'mind'. It is a dangerous book, I shall be interested to see how it
> comes out.[69]

But then, as I mentioned earlier, even Storm Jameson did not always
conform strictly to her plea of 1937 for documentary realism. The same
year that she made it, her novel *Delicate Monster* came out, a satirical
look at the writer's world. The tone is witty, urbane and surely subjective, inviting interpretation as Mitchison does, but in a very different
vein; one suspects Jameson is enjoying herself as her narrator observes: 'I
dislike extremely your *healthy* school of novel-writing. I like a novel to
be sharp and bitter, or else so artificial that the manner is everything and
the matter nothing';[70] but Jameson has appointed a narrator who is
untrustworthy, so we are left to draw our own conclusions. This is a far
cry from her novel *Europe to Let*, published in 1940 but based on her own
journeys in Europe in the late thirties. This novel is indeed documentary
realism as she defines it, but Jameson is careful to distance her narrator,
Esk, from her own passionate commitment; Esk indeed is disturbingly
wedded to detachment:

I was still intimately aware of Europe beating in the darkness, the Danube a vein...I am resistant and responsible. What is happening to the men and women clinging to Europe as to a raft does not move me. There have been too many disasters: too many bad jokes...Nothing, nothing, nothing. The dumb weight of this city on my northern skull. I have been hundreds of years fetching to this place my awkward body, clouded blue eyes, and clumsy tongue, but to no purpose. I am still shut in my peasant's mind, avaricious, sly.[71]

However, Esk's view is deliberately presented as that of a man deadened by the effect of World War One, and does not dominate the novel's message, which won the admiration of Desmond Hawkins for the very qualities of writing which Jameson was promoting in her earlier article. In his *Time & Tide* review he wrote that it was:

not so much a novel as a documentary. Its characters have no more importance individually than the many faces of a news-reel ...this is preeminently a book of public events and private conversations, the kind of journalism that only a writer of uncommon imaginative power could produce... *Europe to Let* commands respect by the sharply phrased and stinging intensity with which it is written.[72]

The forties as 'a series of transformations'

During World War Two, the novel could take very different routes. Memorably, Woolf's enigmatic last novel *Between the Acts* (1941) sets a view of history as an 'interrupted structure' in Miss La Trobe's pageant against an audience involved with imminent world war, each with their own priorities expressed in subtly interwoven images, both linguistic and visual. Jean Radford sums up the conclusions of Judith L. Johnson and others, saying, '*Between the Acts* is a major example of the Modernist challenge to the notion of a continuous, ameliorative cultural history' where

this triumphalist history is staged as a construction, a story line whose authority is subverted by characters who forget their lines, the audience interpolate their own comments, and the natural world disrupts the human when the gramophone fails and cows add their voices to those of the script.[73]

Yet while Catherine Wiley claims that 'despite her own despair, Woolf holds out the hope that when the documents of civilisation are rewritten by those whom history has acted upon, those documents will not also be records of barbarism', that hope is at best ambiguously expressed, given the violence involved in the crushing of the serpent and toad (both, given Woolf's view of war, equally crushed), and some of the petty uglinesses of the behaviour of the guests and family among the audience.[74] Of course, fiction in the War could offer escapism, giving respite to its readers from the realities of war – and even writers who wrote about such realities could offer some respite, as Susan Ertz shows when she dedicates *One Fight More* (1940) 'To those who asked for a light book for dark times'.[75] Some women found the writing of novels incompatible with their experiences of the complexities of war; Elizabeth Bowen wrote only short stories, Lettice Cooper wrote nothing. But the novel also offered opportunities which the strict press censorship made impossible in articles and public debate; fiction was exempt from censorship for the most part (other than the voluntary censorship sometimes applied by publishers), so many women writers used fiction to address the War directly – and, on occasion, they are highly critical. During the War years, Storm Jameson presided over the PEN Club (International Association of Poets, Playwrights, Editors, Essayists, and Novelists), and her address to the opening meeting of the London Congress of PEN, held on 11 September 1941, is extraordinarily impressive. In this address, she offers a challenge to her audience: 'The writer must decide whether his work justifies him in ignoring a crisis which may lead to millions of deaths – including the deaths of colleagues he does not like'.[76] What is more, at one of the grimmest moments of the War, she dares to think of the future, saying 'writers lucky enough to be free to act as writers can – why not boldly say should? – turn their energies to the task, so complex that it alarms all but the stupid and frivolous, of preparing to renew life after the war' (p. 168); and she urges her audience to stand out against 'anything like the moral collapse after the last war', as 'the idiot rejoicings, the ignorance, the short-sighted greed, the apathy, would ruin us' (p. 169). She amplifies what she said in 1937 in her essay 'Documents', insisting that

> to put it brutally, the writer is not born to express himself. His natural egoism is worthless unless it embraces the egoisms of others; he does not know anything about reality if the only reality he knows is that of his own suffering and pleasures.[77]

Later in the same year, she was to write, revealingly, 'we cannot even take refuge in a severe realism . . . What we are looking at is never still, a series of transformations, not an event.'[78] Not very surprisingly, writerly anxiety about the nature of reality continued. Dorothy Sayers, for instance, objects in 1942 to what she terms the 'ill-directed argument' about the word 'reality'. She argues that 'creation proceeds by the discovery of new conceptual relations between things, so as to form them into systems having a consistent wholeness corresponding to an image in the mind, and, consequently, possessing real existence'.[79] Like West, she turns to science to illustrate a sense of a structured reality:

> Boiled down to the last proton and neutron, everything in the universe is the same thing . . . Indeed, there is, in a sense, nothing very much to show where you and I leave off and the rest of the universe begins. When we ponder this too closely, we may begin to wonder whether we possess any reality at all. But (escaping from the hypnotic power of words) we may console ourselves with the thought that the reality of the atom, or of ourselves, consists precisely in the relation that binds us into a recognisable unity. Our behaviour corresponds to a mental concept which sees us as a whole.
>
> (p. 49)

Such a setting of humanity within an apparently stable universe must have seemed ironic a few years later, given the disasters made possible by the splitting of the atom.

When we read the novels of women writing during the War and engaging with all that the War implied, especially in the early years when the outlook was by no means certain, what is particularly impressive is the discipline and creative energy evident in the structuring of their works. The quality of writing is often remarkably high. For instance, Storm Jameson's *The Fort*, written between October 1940 and February 1941, is based on a play she had already written on issues leading to the fall of France in June 1940.[80] The structure of her novel follows the rules of neo-Greek tragedy: place, time and action are unified; only once are there more than three characters appearing together, and that is in the central moment of the work, a sort of choric moment of crisis. No violence occurs, as it were, on stage, and the final scene, we gradually realize, is a kind of Hades for dead characters, since the dialogue reveals that one of the speakers was killed in World War One. It is a spare, controlled piece of writing, an extraordinary and moving response to very recent events. Jameson's characters debate the legacy of the Great War, older men and the young confront each other, French and English state their positions, and different French opinions (for capitulation and resistance) clash. But the writing is classically unjudgemental: the young German prisoner, a committed Nazi, is seen as a tragic figure, a boy of promise in the grip of fate, coming from a past when present opponents were friends, sharing common ground. There is no propagandist zeal in this impressive little work, but a finely conveyed sense of the pity of war.

Very different in content, but also impressively structured is Inez Holden's *Night Shift* (1941), dealing with factory work on the home front.[81] This novel covers six days, the first five situated entirely in the factory, with a workforce of strongly drawn characters, and the book ends with the bombing of the factory seen from outside. The dialogue is racily written, catching the spirit of gossip and tiffs between the characters, but the grey monotony of their work is enlivened by strands of images. One such strand sees the workers as animals; at one moment they are, for instance, 'like cats from a damp garden' (p. 58); or one who does not fit in is 'like a lonely colt' (p. 68). Casts of mind are revealed as the week progresses, like that of the girl who is always reading at break: she 'did not look very interested in these stories, but she did not want anything more from the printed word than the usual formula, the same story with the names changed and slightly different pictures' (p. 30). There is nothing of Leavis's judgemental disapproval in this comment; we are simply shown reading as a ritual of relaxation rather than an exploration, a rest rather than a stimulus for the mind.[82] As the narrator observes on the Saturday of the bombing: 'The extremes of fatigue brought about by long hours in the workshop and air bombardment could make an individual into another person, a half-conscious creature removed a little way from the things which were happening' (p. 120). In a later work, *There's No Story There* (1944), another finely crafted tale of factory life, Holden develops the use of stream of consciousness to present Julian, a young man incapable of speaking after the trauma of being torpedoed; he 'talked in silence', 'he thought in words'. He even creates, like a novelist, putting 'thoughts into words, then going through them in his mind'.[83] Both Holden's works cut through class boundaries unpretentiously but incisively, capturing the idiom of chatter with appropriate wit and a sense of pathos which never becomes maudlin. Storm Jameson offers yet another way of presenting current concerns in her futurist fable, *Then We Shall Hear Singing* (1942). While clearly the work refers to the fate of Czechoslovakia (the work is dedicated to 'Liba Ambrosova and her country'), it is set far in the future; it is also set in a province (a so-called 'Protectorate') 'with the longest memory in the world for freedom, among a people most resilient under poverty and richest in inner resources, sceptical, enduring'.[84] This novel by its tone establishes a strongly partisan support for the beleaguered peasant community, as the scientist sent by the regime sets about removing their memories so as to make them into a docile workforce, but, by using many of the features of folktale, Jameson is able to tap into the tradition whereby the lowly born triumph over all hazards to suggest that the future will bring release. This is a satisfying fable to read today but, like so many folktales of the past, reads very differently when set in the writer's context, as a cry of pain and solidarity controlled by the contrivances of art.

In a different vein, Ethel Mannin, in *The Dark Forest* (written early in 1945, although published a year later), addresses the sensitive question of fraternization by offering a love story, complicated by war and ideological conflict, where the lovers Paul and Anna try to force a happy ending against the public concerns of their time, and inevitably fail.[85]

In her first war novel, *She Goes to War* (1942), Edith Pargeter takes yet another approach.[86] This work is written in a lively epistolary style, from a former journalist to a crippled World War One pilot, now permanently flat on his back. Many of the details are autobiographical; Pargeter's protagonist's involvement with the sinking of the *Bismark* (although not at close quarters) mirrors her own, as *The Bookseller* for 1 January 1942 tells us.[87] But the structuring stops the work becoming no more than a confessional diary, and there are some hard-hitting comments on bungled military operations. We get vivid glimpses of a Wren's way of life, her private concerns about day-to-day living, together with her meditations as an individual caught up in war; we also catch glimpses of the war overseas from the letters of her lover, Tom, ending with the inevitability of his death as a result of a series of tactical blunders. What is striking about this novel is the polished liveliness of the structuring, the well-judged combination of poignancy and wit, especially given the speed at which it was responding to the events of war. Different realities confront each other: the Wren's, the ageing, crippled pilot's, and Tom's; and the epistolary method means that we seem to have access to three very different perspectives on the War, without the interference of an overall narrator. In her later War trilogy, Pargeter abandons the epistolary style, and turns to documentary realism to give a vivid account of a man's war on various fronts.[88] These novels, in their psychological insights, anticipate Pat Barker's trilogy of the First World War, and are all the more impressive for having been written so close to the event. Realism is a favoured medium throughout the war years, but those writers who engage with the issues of the moment can hardly be accused of conservatism. Susan Ertz, for instance, opens her novel *Anger in the Sky* (1943) as if offering the 'country-house' convention of the pre-war years, only to undercut any expectation of an old familiar friend by having all its inmates gradually choose to abandon it, given the new priorities which war reveals to them; the 'reality' constructed by earlier fictions centred on the country house is shown as quite inadequate for the current situation. And here, too, we find what happens on the personal front inextricably tied to public events: one French refugee is a Vichy supporter while her daughter favours resistance; one daughter falls in love with an American who, at the outset, supports isolationism; the other daughter is killed in an air raid because she wants to experience conditions in the East End, having felt challenged by a socialist friend's scorn for her 'safe' environment. The realism of the 'country house' novel has been moulded to fit very different realities, no one of them dominant, no one of them judged. Naomi Mitchison would also make the link between public and personal in a very different vein, when, in *The Bull Calves*, the historical novel she was writing throughout the War years, she opens with a poem blending her grief at the loss of a baby with her reaction to the War, personal suffering intensifying her sense of public disaster.

'The dangers of insufficient symbolism' after the War

While there are, of course, writers who try to avoid themes with obvious political or social resonance (however we may read them now), a real sense of anxiety about the role of the writer affects many novelists as the War ends. The implications of Hiroshima and the Holocaust made the entire concept of Western civilization questionable, and furthermore underlined the helplessness of the individual. In Stevie Smith's *The Holiday*, for instance (updated, and published in 1949, but originally written during the War years), while the style is that of her earlier novels, the thinking as shrewd as ever, Celia, her heroine cries, 'One wishes...to write something that is truly noble, but the times are wrong, they are certainly wrong, at least in the West they are wrong';[89] and later she reflects, more seriously:

> if the writers like to think they are persons of general influence and
> leadership, we need not grudge them the pleasure they derive from

this notion, for there is in fact no substance in it; they are neither influencers nor leaders, they are indeed wholly unattended to. Nor can it be found, in the history of the whole world, that any writer has influenced the course of history, though by their written propaganda they may have advanced the causes already in existence which gained their approval and the use of their ready pens.

(pp. 157–8)

Naomi Mitchison, in her Notes to *The Bull Calves* (published in 1947, but written throughout the War years), expresses another concern, commenting on the danger of degenerating symbols, as, she says, is 'only too plain in modern Germany';[90] we need new ones, she insists,

as social glue...many modern writers are aware of the dangers of insufficient symbolism and are hunting around for something. But, besides satisfying them, it must be reasonably universal. Auden and Eliot both use symbols and redescribe some of the major archetypes. They do not do so, however, for the general reader.

(p. 516)

As one of Bryher's characters says in her novel *Beowulf* (1956), 'These extraordinary events needed...a new and quite other vocabulary'.[91] And at the end of the forties, Storm Jameson addresses the form of the novel once again. She claims that the contemporary novelist is 'threatened, perhaps crushed...by the sheer ugliness of the world he lives in', while in the nineteenth century 'language itself did not, as it does now, break in their hands. Words had not been emptied of their meaning'.[92] Of course, she says there are still important matters like birth, death, conflicts of love and loyalty, but 'it needs an almost inhuman detachment to forget that we are living in the darkness of the atomic age' (p. 71). As always, she looks beyond the immediate situation in Britain and addresses the dilemma of those living under oppressive regimes: 'unless he is free to speculate, completely free, absolved from the fear of being punished if he puts searching questions about morals or motives or religion or politics, the novelist is ruined' (p. 73); and 'we are free only when we engage ourselves to fight for the freedom of all oppressed and enslaved men' (p. 76). Ultimately, she concludes that new novelists 'will need...to discover some new method':

What we need now may be just that insolent irresponsibility, the contempt for safety and comfort and riches, the passionate delight in freedom, the curiosity, the blind hunger for experience and new knowledge, of the medieval wandering scholar: even – perhaps more than all – his disreputable carelessness. We have really become too respectable.

(pp. 81–2)

Certainly Elizabeth Bowen is not 'too respectable' in her novel published in 1948, *The Heat of the Day*.[93] In this work she draws on the thriller mystery, using a number of modernist techniques to demonstrate, among other things, the ultimate unknowability of a fellow-creature's identity; by the end of the novel, we are no longer sure where treachery begins or ends, or how to evaluate human loyalty. As Bowen's narrator observes of Stella and her visitor, Harrison (the good or the bad guy?):

That, of course, was the core of their absolute inhumanity together. His concentration on her was made more oppressive by his failure to have or let her give him any possible place in the human scene. By the rules of fiction, with which life to be credible must comply, he was as a character 'impossible' – each time they met, for instance, he showed no shred or trace of having been continuous since they first met.

(p. 140)

This uncertainty about identity is a persistent theme in the work of many women writers of the late forties and fifties, and they shape their novels to accommodate this theme in many different ways. Elizabeth Taylor, for instance, in her novel *Palladian* (1946) follows a popular model, using, as Paul Bailey says, the 'formulae of romantic tosh', but the formulae are there to be exposed; the heroine is called Cassandra Dashwood, and her capacity for self-knowledge is grounded entirely in literature.[94] She sets out to be a Jane Eyre, and casts her employer (ironically named Marion Vanbrugh) in the role of Mr Rochester. Others fall prey to this fantasy of romance, which mischievously incorporates disastrous reminiscences of both the Brontës and Jane Austen (an uneasy combination at best, since their styles and senses of decorum differ so much); the redundancy of the formulae if transposed to the post-war years is wittily exposed. As Marion's cousin, Margaret says, this is 'not a fairy tale in which I should want to be the heroine...One begins to see what is meant by "they lived happily ever after"' (p. 190). Others pay a heavy price for Marion and Cassandra to achieve this traditional ending.

The same exposure of lives built on what is read (and, given the advent of film, what is viewed) is there in Doris Lessing's first novel *The Grass Is Singing* (1950), where Mary, who is quite happily unmarried, is driven to conform to the priorities of her time and place by the magazines she reads as much as by the opinions of her friends.[95] And Taylor's novel *Angel* (1957) returns to the dangers of relying on literature more than life;[96] here the protagonist is a writer of the sort of bad fiction which influenced Lessing's Mary. Taylor never mocks her character, Angel, but shows her to be the victim of her own fantasies even as she victimizes others. Angel, the writer, is 'solitary without knowing' (p. 14), creating a world where 'experience was a makeshift for imagination' (p. 51), so that her husband can say 'you communicate with yourself, not with your readers' (p. 133) even as he recognizes the appeal that this kind of writing would have for the unsophisticated reader. Significantly, when war is declared, Angel will not engage with it, as it has not affected her personally; and she eventually dies, destitute and forgotten. Taylor's exploration of a certain kind of popular writing in this novel recalls many of Leavis's concerns, but without the acerbic tone; Taylor is always compassionate, even comic, as she demonstrates in her own work the very antithesis of the writing she is exposing as fraudulent; and, by implication, both she and Lessing show the inadequacy of all such formulaic writing for their postwar world.

In a different vein, Barbara Comyns, whose *Sisters by a River* was published in 1947, explores the theme of how the young build their identities in a world made uncertain by the failures of family life, mirroring the failures of the larger society.[97] This is a work that conforms to no previous convention. The style mingles naïvety with subversiveness, and there is an element of magic realism too, as when the child narrator sees a door where 'the Big Bacon Cock was standing... welcoming hens from the other side, he shook hands or rather claws with each hen as she entered, then he looked at me in such a haughty manner that I felt ashamed and went away, I never saw the door again' (p. 89); or when her father, drunk, 'broke the key to pieces and threw the bits out of the window, and where they fell a small tree shaped like an umbrella grew' (p. 94). As with Angela Carter's novel, *The Magic Toyshop* (1967), this is no reminiscence about a happy childhood; we are shown instead a violently dysfunctional family, the private world mirroring the war that had just passed.[98]

Some writers choose to offer potential explanations for the present by extending the range of realist fiction imaginatively from within, as does Storm Jameson in *The Green Man* (1952), to explore the gradual disintegration of a family against a background of the growing crises in Europe;[99] or Sylvia Townsend Warner in *The Flint Anchor* (1954), exposing how a man could be trapped into his patriarchal role by the moral code of his day.[100] Dysfunctional families abound in such novels, and act as microcosms of the wider social disasters. Others extend the realist range beyond European points of view: Attia Hosain and Doris Lessing, for instance, write fictions based on and shaped by lives in India and Southern Rhodesia.[101] Then again, Iris Murdoch, responding to Sartre's existentialism, also remodels the medium. In an article of 1962, she says: 'We are not isolated free choosers, monarchs of all we survey, but benighted creatures sunk in a reality whose nature we are constantly and overwhelmingly tempted to deform by fantasy'.[102] She is very alive to the problem of how to write, saying, for instance in her essay 'Against Dryness' (1961):

> Our sense of form, which is an aspect of our desire for consolation, can be a danger to our sense of reality as a rich receding background. Against the consolation of form, the clear crystalline work, the simplified fantasy-myth, we must pit the destructive power of the now so unfashionable naturalistic idea of character.
>
> Real people are destructive of myth, contingency is destructive of fantasy, and opens the way for imagination . . . Too much contingency of course may turn into journalism. But since reality is incomplete, art must not be too afraid of incompleteness. Literature must always represent a battle between real people and images; and what is required now is a much stronger and more complex conception of the former.[103]

But we have to beware of taking what Murdoch says about writing as the blueprint for what she writes. In her early works, such as *Under the Net* (1954) and *Flight from the Enchanter* (1956), elements of magic realism, of myth and fantasy insistently appear, enhancing the mystery of the realities she perceives, as her characters weave in and out of one another's lives.

What is clear, in both these and other more experimental fictions, is that, after World War Two, writers no longer felt at ease using older modes for the novel without major modifications, either in content or style. A striking example is Christine Brooke-Rose who, in the fifties, was still writing a kind of realism, but it is as if realism is the chrysalis for her later experimental writing: at her best, her images continually threaten to break out of her novels' structures. In *The Languages of Love* (1957), for instance, she describes Hussein: 'like a shade spattered and then extinguished by strong white light, he filtered through them and slipped quietly away';[104] and later, cats: 'Their screeches clawed at the night, striping its silence to a tiger-skin, streaking across the jungle of twisted chimney-pots to mate in the sultry air with other screams, hisses and wails from beyond the sleeping ocelot eyes of the stretched yellow houses' (p. 166). Her next novel, *The Sycamore Tree* (1958), even more emphatically acknowledges language as an imperfect vehicle for meaning; yet when Antrobus, a critic, subscribing to what he calls 'New Subjectivism', explains: 'In the last analysis, a poem is the sum of all the meanings read into it by everyone. All these meanings are there, whatever the poet may have consciously intended', a publisher ironically replies, 'That would certainly explain why there is such an abundance of critics these days'.[105] Brooke-Rose clearly teases the extremes of interpretation, even while she wrestles in these early works with the curiously uncertain relation of words to meaning.[106]

Mary Borden also experiments during the fifties, with form rather than language, in *The Hungry Leopard* (1956), a novel which centres on the disappearance of a writer and the attempt of various characters to lay hands on his letters.[107] This is a strikingly postmodern work, structured as a collage of fragments, flashbacks and anticipations, centred on different consciousnesses, with each character interpreting according to their own temperament. There are echoes of Ivy Compton-Burnett in the use of dialogue, yet the two central characters, Amanda and Jaques, cannot speak for themselves as the verdicts are reached; the core of the novel again centres on the problem of identity, exploring the impossibility of creating a complete picture of another person. The experimentation here has something in common with that of a younger writer, Muriel Spark, whose first novel, *The Comforters*, was published in 1957.[108] In this novel, we find the same collage of fragments, the same swings between times past, present and future. There is also a similar use of a popular genre as a basis, the thriller mystery, but there the similarity ends. For Spark shares Brooke-Rose's keen ear for language, and has at the same time her own voice in the witty, tersely epigrammatic style of her novels. *The Comforters* also explores the nature of writing; Caroline hears a voice (at first, seemingly, voices) through the wall which record not her thoughts but the narrative of Spark's novel and which Caroline does not of course hear as repetition since she is living the events in the novel rather than experiencing Spark's way of recording these. As Caroline observes,

> Her sense of being written into the novel was painful. Of her constant influence on its course she remained unaware and now she was impatient for the story to come to an end, knowing that the narrative could never become coherent to her until she was at last outside it, and at the same time consummately inside it.
>
> (p. 181)

The author plays god then, with predestination and foreknowledge (also reflecting Spark's Catholic preoccupations), and Spark revels in playing games with her self-reflexive text: the first few pages signal something of her method by a continual switching of tense. Caroline as character will on occasion alter and shape this story which is created by someone else but in which she is prime mover, but sometimes the narrative will state what she will do in the future, or what other characters are doing; the character Mrs Hogg literally disappears when she falls asleep. At the end of the novel, when Caroline has gone away to write a novel (Spark's novel?) herself, Lawrence, her fiancé, tears up a letter he has written to her, and

> he saw the bits of paper come to rest, some on the scrubby ground, some among the deep marsh weeds, and one piece on a thorn-bush; and he did not then foresee his later wonder, with a curious rejoicing, how the letter had got into the book.
>
> (p. 204)

Not surprisingly, since Caroline earlier in the work was writing a book about fiction, we hear that she had trouble with the chapter on 'realism'.

The 'socially determined fiction' of private life in the sixties

Yet realism continued to be a valuable vehicle for women writers throughout the fifties and sixties. Lynne Reid Banks, for instance, in *The L-shaped Room* (1960), moulded it as a vehicle to explore the life of a single woman, pregnant, in a house with other marginalized characters; here flashbacks avoid linear narrative, while cause and effect, past invading the present, are dominant themes of the novel.[109] Yet content rather than form is what makes this novel something of an innovation; it is one of many novels by women of this period which insistently show the effects on women of the kind of social code which promotes rigid definitions of virtue (meaning chastity for women), marital duty (as applied to women only), and the pressures which can lead to breakdown.[110] Then again, some women who are exploring the realities of working-class life offer their own versions of socialist realism. Menna Gallie, for instance, in *Strike for a Kingdom* (1959) and *The Small Mine* (1962), explores the effects of a strike or of a miner's death on a vividly drawn Welsh village community, where the language of the narrative gains greatly from the injection of Welsh humour and the Welsh love of dramatic images; *The Small Mine* opens with: 'The wind howled over the mountain and swept down on Cwmardy as though chased by a million nightmares'.[111] Similarly, Attia Hosain, in *Sunlight on a Broken Column* (1961), may use realism as a vehicle, but enriches it memorably by drawing on the rhetoric of Urdu.[112] In all these cases, it would be problematic to suggest that the writers are being conservative because of their choice of form, for what is achieved within this protean mould is a striking diversity of views of widely differing realities.

The most striking of those who reconfigure their realist vehicle is surely Christina Stead, as Angela Carter maintains. Carter says that:

> for Stead, pity is otiose, a self-indulgent luxury that obscures the real nature of our relations with our kind. And to disclose that real nature is her purpose. She does this through the interplay of individuals with one another and with the institutions we have created that now seem to dominate us: marriage, the family, money.[113]

Carter argues that 'for her, language is not an end-in-itself in the post-modernist, or "mannerist" mode, but a mere tool, and a tool she increasingly uses to hew her material more and more roughly' (p. xii); and urges that:

> The way she finally writes is almost as if she were showing you by demonstration that style itself is a lie in action, that language is an elaborate confidence trick designed to lull us into acceptance of the intolerable . . . And that truth is not a quality inherent in any kind of discourse, but is a way of looking at things, not any aspect of reality but a *test* of reality . . . she has latterly gained a reputation as a writer of naturalism, which she certainly is not. If her fiction is read as fiction about our lives rather than about the circumstances that shape our lives, it is bound to disappoint . . . For Stead, however, private life is itself socially determined fiction, the 'self' a foetus of autonomy that may or may not prove viable and 'inner freedom', far from being an innate quality, is a precariously held intellectual or emotional position that may be achieved only at the cost of an

enormous struggle, often against the grain of what we take to be human feeling.

(p. xiv)

I have quoted Carter at length as her enthusiasm for a writer so different, on one level, from herself should give us pause about pigeon-holing modes of writing too readily. There is much in common, for instance, between Stead's novel *Cotters' England* (1966) and Carter's *The Magic Toyshop* (1967).[114] Both explore the dysfunctional family in a style which frequently borrows from surrealism; the fantasies which characters create to sustain their own existences permeate the world of those around them, often with disastrous results. Stead's Nellie drives her friend Caroline into 'the deep river of a lucid delirium' (p. 290); Eliza thinks Nellie and her brother Tom each have 'a floating soul' (p. 342). Melanie, in Carter's novel, is caught in Uncle Philip's puppeteering trap. Both novelists show how disastrously manipulation can break down the barriers we think we have between fantasy and the real world, both drawing on animal imagery and folk tale. But whereas Carter tends to give a feminist slant on society, Stead, in this novel, takes us into the heart of a woman who tyrannizes others as a means of confirming her own identity – the domestic world of power politics finally celebrates itself in a literal witches' Sabbath that drives Caroline to her death.

The means by which women manipulate their realist vehicle to their own ends and also explore other forms of fiction show remarkable adaptability in responding to a rapidly changing world. Naomi Mitchison, for instance, makes her first experiment in science fiction in *Memoirs of a Spacewoman* (1962), with a subtle and witty view of a distant future from the point of view of a female communications expert.[115] Here she explores genetic engineering, intervention in other civilizations, sexual practices; her skill is in treating her reader as partially in the know so that some things but not all are explained. So the narrator, the protagonist, can make comments which suggest new possibilities for the reader, but the comments are not necessarily developed; the result is an open-ended fiction, where by no means all the answers have been found by the end of the novel and there is no neat ending; we are left to review our own present and its potential for progress and catastrophe without tiresome moralizing.

Then there is Brigid Brophy, whose *The Finishing Touch* (1963) may recall *Olivia* in its evocation of the sexual preoccupations of a Finishing School in France, but whose prose looks towards Angela Carter's magic realism. Miss Braid, for instance, opens the novel with a voice 'deeper than the average man's voice; deeper, even, than the average frog's voice';[116] and these French frogs haunt the text, creaking 'as though at a mad dinner party every guest had simultaneously seized his pepper mill' (p. 8). Brophy, like Spark, plays deftly with time sequence, and she also shares with Spark a fine capacity for satirizing the mores of her time. Her *Hackenfeller's Ape* (1964) is a further development of comic satire, where Brophy again looks towards magic realism.[117] Here, the plight of an ape in a zoo merges with Mozart's *Marriage of Figaro* in the mind of the zoologist who espouses the ape's cause; fable is the vehicle in this novel for some shrewd cracks at the state of Western civilization. Meanwhile, Spark continues to develop her own experimentation; in *The Bachelors* (1960), for instance, she offers a glimpse of society where, by non-sequential dialogue, we are shown people chattering self-absorbedly, failing to hear others, while the repetition of phrases within apparently unlinked scenes set against one another, cast light on each other. The barrister prosecuting the medium, Patrick, for fraud, is himself exploiting his lover, and we hear the echoes; the medium is convicted for fraud on dubious evidence, but is prevented, as only the reader knows, from murdering his lover, Alice. 'Law' and 'justice' ironize each other, and Alice's cry after the verdict, 'I don't believe in God', only adds to the irony, given that her life will be saved by Patrick's conviction.[118] Memorably, *The Prime of Miss Jean Brodie* (1961) uses similar techniques to expose the fascist tyranny a teacher imposes on her charges. By Spark's weaving of the present and future together, we see the effects of Miss Brodie's assigning of roles to her girls: Mary, for instance, always labelled as stupid, 'later, in that hotel fire, ran hither and thither till she died' (p. 43). Yet, ultimately, Miss Brodie is something of an innocent, if a charismatic one; even Sandy, who sees through her while still at school, will come to recognize that Jean Brodie has merely reflected aspects of a wider society. Later, the title of Sandy's 'strange book of psychology, "The Transfiguration of the Commonplace"' (p. 186) surely suggests, as Mann had done in *Dr Faustus*, that what is inspirational can be used for good or ill. Spark is always witty, but never less than serious, never simplistic. As Duffy and Lessing do, she uses stylistic tricks to forestall complacently easy answers to the complex problems she exposes within society. For Doris Lessing also moves into a new mode of expression with *The Golden Notebook* (1962).[119] This self-reflexive novel explores the nature of fiction among other things, since the sentence Saul gives Anna in 'The Golden Notebook' section towards the end of Lessing's novel is/will be the first sentence of Anna's novella 'Free Women' which begins Lessing's *The Golden Notebook*. Saul says:

'"I'm going to give you the first sentence…There are the two women you are, Anna. Write down: The two women were alone in the London flat' (p. 615). So, while Lessing's novel, divided as it is into a series of notebooks, offers different perspectives on Anna's material, Anna has to accept her own divided nature, and indeed 'write' herself, since she does not exist outside the pages of her own short fiction 'Free Women'. The construction of identity becomes, then, in Lessing's novel a matter for self-knowledge, self-construction; yet, since Lessing tells us in her preface, added ten years later to the novel 'we…must not compartmentalise' (p. 10), her characters can be read as individuals or, as Saul suggests, as aspects of the self. So Saul himself may stand for the partner in a heterosexual relationship or for a necessary acknowledgement of masculinity's contribution to Anna's creative process; Anna, after all, supplies an aggressively masculine first sentence for Saul's own novel, a novel he knows only he can write, yet which is set in motion by a woman's contribution. Lessing's extraordinary novel has been read many ways, as she acknowledges in her later preface, and its complexity is achieved by the vivid construction of the notebooks, the novella, and the demands which such a complex construction makes on readers.

Maureen Duffy also departs from 'realism' in her novel *The Microcosm* (1966).[120] This is a novel which begins in midstream of consciousness with a gradual revelation that someone is dead, 'one of us' (p. 6); mystery generates the text, including the gender of one of the narrators, Matt; past, present and future tenses jostle each other on the page; and there are long stretches of dialogue which act on us as if we are outsiders, straining to understand what is going on. There is a parodic passage telling of the doings of 'the adventurer', a female disguised as a male, from the period of *The Beaux Stratagem*, and a Beckettian monologue on illness. Gradually it becomes clear that the world Duffy lets us glimpse is a lesbian world of alienation, a working-class world for the most part, a 'House of Shades' haunted by 'The lonely ones' (p. 35). And the novel, by not offering easy access to its world, mirrors the situation of its characters who feel themselves driven through evasion, disguise and rejection into a tragic underworld; this is a bleakly disturbing novel where the language of internalization challenges the kind of communication still demanded by dominant elements in the society of the sixties.

Christine Brooke-Rose makes an even more dramatic break from her previous 'realist' novels, when she starts to experiment with aspects of the French *nouveau roman*. However, as Patricia Waugh maintains, to 'foreground the aesthetic' need not be 'a withdrawal from political commitment or ethical concern';[121] and, as Heather Reyes argues, the novel *Out* shows inward experiences as utterly bound up with global events and power structures, by no means offering an 'aesthetic cul de sac'.[122] As Reyes says, Brooke-Rose uses parody, exaggeration or other 'shaped' discourses or clash of discourses (e.g. *nouveau roman*, colonial oppression, film clichés, media interview, language of advertising) to explore big moral themes. In *Out* (1964), for instance, the way in which perceptions of reality depend on where we are coming from is revealed by minute descriptions of the same scene as seen from the big house and the shack/bungalow; while on another level, we find the 'Colourless' Uessayans and UKayans as the inferior race, driven to dependency on the charity of their black employers by some nuclear disaster (obsessive descriptions of disease and medicaments mark the Colourless, who are dying of the 'malady'), while wittily exact descriptions of flies copulating bind the work together with a kind of Blakean subtext (repeatedly, we hear how, from the shacks, the drive leading to the Big House can be seen as a 'network of bare branches [which] functions in depth, a corridor of cobwebs full of flies').[123] Brooke-Rose's next novel, *Such* (1966) demonstrates, among other things, how shifts of linguistic register alter what we perceive as reality. Everyday experiences expressed, for instance, in the language of physics, are defamiliarized, as when the narrator tells how the death of the professor now 'moves through me with its vibrant atoms that whirl round mine, create resistance' (p. 326); later, love is described in language combining astro-physics and biology:

> Some argue nevertheless that parts of a divided nucleus recede from one another at great speed, the shock process involving ejection of high energy particles that must ultimately form a human element, a star where the taste of love will increase its luminosity until it cools in quiet rage at all that tenderness that went to waste, accumulating only the degenerate matter of decay. Well, what did you expect, a Blue Giant? We love like ancient innocents with a million years of indifference and despair within us that revolve like galaxies on a narrow shaft of light where hangs the terror in her eyes as the life drains away from blood-vessels, nerve cells, muscle spindles, bones, flesh and such.
>
> (p. 390)

Brooke-Rose is constantly showing how language shapes experience, either wilfully or unintentionally, but her experimentation is never purely for its own sake, and she speaks out unequivocally on occasion, as when we are told, the 'great failure of our century [is that] we don't heal, merely create new dependencies' (p. 341).

A novelist who experiments in a quite different way is Ann Quin who responded to the paintings of Francis Bacon and to *nouvelle vague* film. Her novel *Berg* (1964) treats the dysfunctional family comically, beginning: 'A man called Berg, who changed his name to Greb, came to a seaside town intending to kill his father...', and exploring, like Stead and Carter, the blurred boundaries between fantasies and reality with echoes of Joyce and Beckett.[124] Quotations from Shakespeare appear frequently, and there are clear links with *Hamlet*: Berg's closeness to his mother, for instance, and his contemplation of suicide. But he is also very much an alienated child of his own time, reacting to a bleak, indifferent society:

> a sticky, sickly child, who longed to be accepted with the others, by those who were healthy, tough, swaggered in well cut suits, brilliantined hair. Your stained, rat-bitten cuffs, and collar, patched behind, the mud squelching through your shoes. But once on your own when you lorded it with beast and flower, striding the hills, welcomed by a natural order, a slow sensuality that circled the sun, rode the wind through the grass-forests, then nothing mattered, because everything comprehended your significance.
>
> (p. 11)

Comedy of a kind dominates this novel, as Berg only succeeds in 'murdering' a ventriloquist's dummy belonging to his father. But Quin's next novel, *Three* (1966) is much darker.[125] In this work, scenes are presented like stage or film directions, reflecting the way in which even characters who 'know' each other intimately, play roles; and dialogue between the two characters, Ruth and Leon, is set up like stream of consciousness, in paragraphs, where we cannot always tell who is speaking which phrase. The reader is, as in Duffy's *Microcosm*, listening to a conversation between intimates, straining to interpret the implications, as when Leon apparently refers to some problem in the War, saying: 'Never forget those weeks we should have really been shot Mother and myself no doubt would have been if it hadn't been for our connections' (p. 7). Later the text offers a poem, and a series of notes where some link, others do not, as if the thread binding them has been forgotten. We hear about a girl who has apparently died, a fact we discover in what is a stream of dialogue (not consciousness) and routine, everyday actions. But, gradually, the violence which exists beneath the banal surfaces.

One entry in the dead girl's notebook, for instance, puts her in the role of tormentor: 'My hands instruments of torture. Hers butterflies, when excited, flustered. His feed the goldfish. Fingers snap like crickets in long grass, as he enters, leaves a room' (p. 58); the girl was, we find, 'pursued by a compulsion to jeopardise such a bourgeois stronghold' (p. 71). Quin links the public and the private, as have earlier novelists, but her way of keeping the reader at bay mirrors the secrets practised by this apparently close couple, as Leon furtively watches pornographic movies, and Ruth, when alone, plays back his personal tapes where she hears him saying,

> The little soldier playing with real lives to create a bigger and better world where all things everybody would be equal. You believed in that. He did at least...Only the whole a love affair yes not unlike ...Yes a game you – he watched played out against a background of subterfuge. Violence. Torture. Never witnessed. Only whispered about behind locked doors. Down with the Capitalists. But not the family the girl who cried when they took her parents away. Then was it then awareness shook the sleep-walker? The idealist. Tin soldiers grew life-size. Screamed. Shuddered. Between their legs a bridge that had beginning no end. Contradict that if you can. I can. But this now brings no such certainty.'
>
> (p. 120)

Leon finally rapes his wife, and there is a hint that he or they have murdered the girl with her consent. Dysfunctional relationships, the hauntings of past guilt, the linking of pornography and violence both in that past and in the novel's present make this a powerful and disturbing work which refuses to accept suburbia at face value.

Quin and Brooke-Rose take the novel further into experimentation than any British woman writer since Woolf. Both make a claim for a powerful new voice, dealing with such concerns of their time as the inner workings of the mind, and the alienating effect of linguistic registers which do not speak to one another and interpret (create?) realities very differently. But that does not mean that women's issues are seen by either as ultimately dominant; both are more interested in the workings of society as a whole, while certainly exploring roles which women have within that society. But Brooke-Rose, writing in 1991, is wary of what she sees as an extreme feminist stance.[126] While, she says, women writers have undoubtedly been ignored or imitated silently, it is unwise to claim such things as 'circular structures, open endings, nonlinearity' as primarily women's territory since they can be found in men's writing as well; and she points out that 'early feminist arguments' claimed rationality for women. 'The present and constant emphasis on certain structures as "masculine" and others as "feminine" is a gross over-simplification',[127] Brooke-Rose argues; and she further claims that too insistent a claim for 'feminist aesthetics' can be counter-productive:

> Feminists, then, should perhaps beware, when they use the term 'aesthetics' or 'feminist aesthetics', of its history and of all its manifold implications, not only of 'inferior sisterhood', 'enervated', 'frail', ... and so on (as opposed to the 'dignified' rational, which they prefer to call 'master-structures' and such), but also of the insidious power and coercion contained in the concept...It is not only 'not concerned with art' but it implies a de-moralizing of ethics into the agreeable and the disagreeable...Is that what feminists want when they use the word?
>
> (p. 283)

It is hard not to respect what Brooke-Rose says, when, as a woman writer, she manipulates language so powerfully and effectively to her own ends. Difficult she may be, but never prioritizing her experimentation above the contemporary issues she addresses. Curiously, she is not as far as she might at first appear from Storm Jameson's concerns in an article of 1965. Jameson argues:

> When too much is said too quickly, by men or machines, or by men using machines, the danger of slipping into jargon is hideously easy; your perpetual task, today, tomorrow, forever, is the sharpening of language into a more precise and flexible instrument, as far removed as possible from the automatic response, the empty abstraction, the flabby half-exact phrase.[128]

What Jameson deplores is what Brooke-Rose often explores, to expose the effects of jargon (or indeed specialist registers) on the shaping of realities, and she certainly sharpens language.

Although Jameson could never come to terms with an experimentation which she saw in terms of 'disordered language',[129] she does admit in *Parthian Words* (1970) that the camera, which she once saw as the ultimate exponent of documentary realism, cheats, as language does if it only documents; and she goes on: 'What I want is not the face of that old woman stooping over the bombed-out ruin of her house, but what is passing through her mind in the moment when she runs a caressing hand over a cracked cup' (p. 44). This too is the concern of a writer like Brooke-Rose, just as it was Brecht's. What we find, at the end of the period I am exploring, is that women writers echo the concerns of what were known in Holtby's day as Old and New Feminists: some are what Holtby would have called 'Equalitarians', others concern themselves primarily with women's issues. Often, the old antagonisms between the two camps reassert themselves as well. But both camps offer extraordinarily inventive exponents of language and form whom we ignore at our very great loss.

2
Wars and Rumours of Wars

Throughout the period from World War One to the present, war or the threat of war has never been far away. Already in 1915, Sigmund Freud was warning that the Great War 'threatens to leave a legacy of embitterment that will make any renewal of those bonds impossible for a long time to come';[1] and women writers were quick to be among those assessing the legacy which Freud foresaw. As early as 1922, in her novel *The Clash*, Storm Jameson writes:

> The Peace conference sat in Paris. Liberty, with a bloody pate, stalked famished on the ice-bound Neva. Grand Dukes and generals ran about two hemispheres crying Murder, Revenge, and moved by the thought of so much suffering, the victors of the war blockaded Russia, so that Murder had to tighten his belt across his hollow stomach... Lord Weaverbridge groaned in travail and the new world was born, by the fecund will of one terrible old Frenchman and passionate lover of his country. He had faith only in the negation of faith and saw that an eyeless malice broods over the destiny of man. Lusts meaner than his, and greeds poorer, served him. Youth, that was to have swept the world, rotted unseen to manure it, or living, became absorbed in a search for excitement or bread. The old men did as they pleased.[2]

As the thirties progressed, the threat of fascism became ever clearer to those who turned their eyes to Europe. Literature was being put at the service of fascism in some quarters, echoing the thinking behind Marinetti's Futurist Manifesto (1909), which had championed the 'aggressive' heritage of great literature, insisting that:

except in struggle there is no more beauty. No work without an aggressive character can be a masterpiece...We will glorify war – the world's only hygiene – militarism, patriotism, the destructive gesture of freedom-bringers, beautiful ideas worth dying for, and scorn for woman.[3]

Walter Benjamin responds to the fascist renewal of this claim in the inter-war years, warning that:

Fascism...expects war to supply the artistic gratification of a sense perception that has been changed by technology. This is evidently the consummation of '*l'art pour l'art'*. Mankind, which in Homer's time was an object of contemplation for the Olympian gods, now is one for itself. Its self-alienation has reached such a degree that it can experience its own destruction as an aesthetic pleasure of the first order. This is the situation of politics which Fascism is rendering aesthetic. Communism responds by politicizing art.[4]

It is not surprising, therefore, that, as Maroula Joannou observes, questions of gender were a secondary concern for many women, their first priority being to defend democracy. Joannou quotes Hilary New-itt's assertion that 'only under western democracy is it still possible for a feminist movement to exist';[5] and this idea is reflected in such novels as Naomi Mitchison's *We Have Been Warned* (1935) and Storm Jameson's *In the Second Year* (1936), warning of fascism at home, and preeminently in Katharine Burdekin's *Swastika Night* (1937), transposing the legacy of fascism into a future where women are caged breeders.

This opposition to fascism confuses another key issue of the inter-war years, pacifism, a cause which was espoused by many women writers in response to the carnage of World War One.[6] Virginia Woolf, in *Three Guineas* (1938), is of course the best-known advocate for opposition to war; some, like Vera Brittain, continued to support pacifism throughout World War Two.[7] But the issue became more complex as the thirties advanced, for the Spanish Civil War complicated the issue; opposition to fascism was not always easy to accommodate with pacifism, and many found their principles hard to maintain consistently. Rebecca West, for instance, pours scorn on Naomi Mitchison in 1939 for supporting the Spanish Civil War while opposing the coming conflict;[8] and Storm Jameson lost Brittain's friendship when she finally confessed that she had ceased to support pacifism after the invasion of Czecho-slovakia.

Furthermore, while Joannou argues that in opposing fascism 'the pendulum had swung a long way from questions of gender',[9] the issue of who was responsible for the eruption of war and violence was reviewed constantly throughout the thirties and forties, and continued to haunt the post-war decades. Many women writers succumbed to the essentialist mythologizing of Marinetti by tying the responsibility for violence to masculinity, a responsibility which some men had indeed claimed as their prerogative after World War One, as Joanna Bourke demonstrates, showing how, after World War One, women teachers were frequently accused by their male counterparts of 'feminising the male body'.[10] Bourke quotes from a 1923 issue of *New Schoolmaster* which brags:

> When men wavered, the sports-masters came to the fore, the real men, those who had done the big things in the war... Where sports-masters lead, the victory is assured. Sports-masters are the real live men, men who know boy-nature, men who mix with men of other walks of life. They are the men who count.[11]

So it is not surprising to find, in the collection of essays *Man, Proud Man* (1932), some of the women contributors attacking men's inclination for war, albeit wittily.[12] Susan Ertz in particular makes the same connection between sport and war as the *New Schoolmaster*, when she observes that the 'Englishman's feeling for cricket is close to reverence' and that 'when a man can forget himself he is usually happy. Hence the fact that wars are not yet outlawed';[13] while Storm Jameson, more seriously, quotes Sir Arthur Keith's reference to the 'pruning-hook of war', commenting in her footnote:

> The learned gentleman was clearly under some misapprehension of the uses to which sane gardeners put their pruning-hooks. Did he, perhaps, imagine that they pruned away only the best and lustiest shoots? Now, if in the next War, recruits were strictly chosen from men between the ages of fifty-five and eighty-five, Sir Arthur would be able in person to justify his metaphor. Would that not be a profound satisfaction to him?[14]

Yet there are also those who take the broader view of human nature, perceiving women as either capable of war and violence or condoning it. There is, for instance, Stevie Smith in *Over the Frontier* (1938) or there is Amabel Williams-Ellis in *Learn to Love First* (1939), novels

I shall be discussing in due course.[15] Later, too, women writers show how war can arouse a violence in women which can certainly match the male's, as, for instance, in Storm Jameson's novel *The Hidden River* (1955) or, more poignantly, in Rose Macaulay's *The World My Wilderness* (1950).[16]

The War itself gave writers the chance to express in fiction what could not be said in articles or essays, for, as Jenny Hartley records, censorship of fiction remained voluntary, although kept under observation by the Scrutiny Division of the Ministry of Information; 'the only fixed prohibition on fiction was against passing information to the enemy'.[17] As a result, we find some novels which are openly critical about the running of the War, as is, for instance, Edith Pargeter's *She Goes to War* (1942). Writers like Pargeter, Storm Jameson, Ethel Mannin and Phyllis Bottome do not hesitate to address issues connected with the War in Europe, although the bulk of writers concentrate on the home front, giving graphic impressions of the blitz, the fate of evacuees and refugees, work in factories, hospitals and on the land. Here again, writers do not necessarily follow the propagandist line: instances of panic and disaffection are confronted; lack of organization is exposed. What is extraordinary about these novels is the way in which they grapple with events almost immediately after they have happened, without, in most cases, resorting to a purely journalistic approach.

Immediately after the War, most of the women writers I am examining were either revisiting the past, trying to set the conflict in some sort of context, or were concerned to ensure a lasting peace, for even those who had abandoned pacifism for the duration of the War never lost sight of the barbarisms which war exposes. As early as 1941, in her opening address to the London Congress of PEN, Storm Jameson had urged writers to 'turn their energies to the task, so complex that it alarms all but the stupid and frivolous, of preparing to renew life after the war'.[18] And she for one did indeed turn her mind to the task. She faced considerable difficulties. There was, for instance, a strong body of popular opinion which resented any attempt to put Germany back on its feet, so it took courage to look squarely at the confusion, violence and suffering in post-war Berlin as she did in *The Black Laurel* (1947).[19]

But by the mid-fifties, as the full horror of Hiroshima and the Holocaust had sunk in, and there had been renewed conflict in Korea, there was more questioning of the concept of Western civilization, since the horror of mass destruction seemed to have outstripped that civilization's power to contain it. Most works of the fifties and early sixties have characters who live their lives in the shadow of the bomb, and most see humankind as innately responsible for its own tragic conflicts. While many writers actively supported the Campaign for Nuclear Disarmament (CND), many, in their writing, were looking within the family and the community to explore the potential for violence. In this category, there is Sylvia Townsend Warner's *Flint Anchor* (1954) and Christine Brooke Rose's *The Sycamore Tree* (1958); and within a few years, there are many examples of violence practised on the marginalized within society. Works like Veronica Hull's *The Monkey Puzzle* (1958), Jennifer Dawson's *The Ha-Ha* (1961), Penelope Mortimer's *The Pumpkin Eater* (1962), Paddy Kitchen's *Lying-in* (1965) and Maureen Duffy's *The Microcosm* (1966) all, in different ways, explore what is inflicted on those who are seen as legitimate targets for physical or psychological violence.[20] Freud's conclusion in 1915, that we should not find the violence which human beings perpetrate as shocking, since 'in reality our fellow-citizens have not sunk so low as we feared, because they had never risen so high as we believed', is very much the underlying theme of these novels, written as they are in parallel with Michel Foucault's *Madness and Civilisation* (1961).[21]

Alongside these novels, the larger view is not absent from women's fiction, particularly in those coming from former parts of empire. Doris Lessing, for instance, names her sequence of five Martha Quest books 'The Children of Violence', showing the shadow of world war hanging over Southern Rhodesia, where the sequence starts, together with the barely contained violence of the young men of the white community. And Attia Hossain, in her novel *Sunlight on a Broken Column* (1961), movingly evokes the tragic violence that erupts in India with approaching independence and partition.[22] Some writers also begin to look to the future, suggesting where nuclear war and the collapse of society may lead, as do Naomi Mitchison in *Memoirs of a Spacewoman* (1962) and Doris Lessing in her complex novel, *The Four-Gated City* (1969).[23]

In the end, it would be unsafe to ascribe fixed attitudes to war and violence in the novels of women writers during these years of rapid change. While freedom from tyranny is the main priority of most, and while most show opposition to the use of violence, they vary dramatically in the perceptions of how this may be achieved. What must always be remembered is that the view from the end of the millenium must be different from that of writers confronting war and violence at the time, and that we miss a great deal if we assume our view justifies a sense of superiority or dismissal.

Hauntings and forebodings of war in the thirties

While front-line experience of World War One is often seen as exclusively male, women's works being written from the perspective of home (as, for instance, Rebecca West's *The Return of the Soldier* [1917]), this is by no means always true, as Yvonne Klein and Claire Tylee have shown.[24] Mary Borden's *The Forbidden Zone* (1929) is made up of poems and sketches which were written, for the most part, during her four years with the hospital unit she provided for the French Army (her help having been refused by the British).[25] This work is graphic in its descriptions of the *poilus* she encounters. The glamorizing of warfare is thrust aside for the real thing: 'You see those men, lolling in the doorways – uncouth, dishevelled, dirty? They are soldiers. You can read on their heavy jowls, in their stupified, patient, hopeless eyes, how boring it is to be a hero' (p. 2), she comments in 'Belgium'. In other sketches, she describes the horrors she encounters among the wounded. There is the huge man in a coma, who, if he lives, will 'be court-martialled and shot . . . for attempting suicide' (p. 98); for, she writes in 'Conspiracy', 'it is arranged that men should be broken and that they should be mended' (p. 117). She exposes her own reaction to what she sees, part detachment, part a strange, halucinatory happiness which seems to her inexplicable afterwards. Yet as the war drags on, there is only longing for an end, as her final poem shows in its plea to 'The One who drowned mercifully the children of men;/Let the waters cover the earth again, Let there be an end to it – an end' (p. 186).

Helen Zenna Smith's *Not So Quiet: Stepdaughters of War* (1930) comes to the same conclusion, but by a rather different route. The novel was commissioned to be a parody of Erich Remarque's *All Quiet on the Western Front* (1929), but was initially misread, as Barbara Hardy shows: 'the novel's first readers assumed it was a memoir, though no attentive reader of Remarque could have thought so, since aspects of his structure, language, and action are remodelled, freshly but faithfully'.[26] Smith refused the publisher's original idea of a more superficial parody, basing her work on the diary given to her by Winifred Constance Young, who had been an ambulance driver in France. This is not a case of plagiarism, as some have claimed, but a skilful fictionalizing of another's fact, with Young's consent. The novel is written in the present tense, conveying the immediacy of involvement; here, the emphasis is on the women's experience at the front rather than on the patients as Borden's was, and the narrator's world is evoked in graphic, staccato sentences, with vivid images. The roots of pacifism are planted firmly in this experience: one driver says, 'I would rather see a child of mine dead than see him a soldier' (p. 55); and the women at home are savaged for their mindless support of the war effort. Confronting her mother, in imagination, with the image of a gassed man, the narrator says:

> He's about the age of Bertie, Mother. Not unlike Bertie, either, with his gentle brown eyes and fair curly hair. Bertie would look up pleadingly like that in between coughing up his lungs... The son you have so generously given to the War. The son you are so eager to send out to the trenches before Roy Evans-Mawnington, in case Mrs. Evans-Mawnington scores over you at the next recruiting meeting... 'I have given my only son'.
>
> (p. 93)

Raw emotion is expressed throughout, loss of faith in things human and divine. One colleague is nearing breakdown, another is no longer committed to the chastity she once regarded as paramount; and there is a growing anxiety as to what will become of the young after the War. When finally the narrator gets leave, she cannot at first bear to go home because of her family's blinkered support of the War; finally, she re-enlists as a domestic worker, in revolt against her mother's snobbery, and back in Europe becomes the 'ideal' worker, because she has ceased to care.

These two novels give some insight into the kinds of experiences which bred inter-war pacifism. But very early in the thirties, as I have indicated, the rising tide of fascism complicates the picture. Nor is the threat necessarily seen solely on mainland Europe. Naomi Mitchison, for instance, in *We Have Been Warned* (1935), ends the novel with a graphic vision of a not-so-distant fascist counter-revolution in Britain, after a Labour victory, a clear reference to the dangers of Mosley's movement; and in her short story *The Fourth Pig* (1936), she gives a grim reworking of the folk tale of the little pigs, as Four tells how his brothers now live in fear in the brick house, for 'might not the Wolf have so practised his huffing and puffing that even this may not be strong enough to stand against him?'[27] Meanwhile he himself is 'without shelter and without hope' (p. 6); and he concludes, 'Three was afraid, but yet he thought the time would come when no pig need fear the Wolf. But I – I know I am afraid, and afraid almost all the time' (p. 7). The story gives a vivid picture of the enemy without, powerful and menacing, all the more effective for the message being cloaked in what had been an optimistic fable where good sense triumphed over brutality.

Equally powerful is Storm Jameson's *In the Second Year* (1936), which is set in an imminent future and in a vividly drawn England. Here, Hillier's National State Party is brought to power by Richard's National Volunteers. The 'liberal-cum-bolshevik scum' are to be exterminated, while Richard and Hillier preach pure nationalism and xenophobia. Jameson, drawing on the rise of Hitler, gives a compelling picture of how a tyrant is made, while her language and setting convincingly warn that it could happen in Britain, as business interests so strengthen the Prime Minister as to turn him into a dictator. As Hillier's tyranny becomes more bloody, Richard decides to rebel, but is betrayed, arrested and finally shot, while Hillier now plays the role of a mystic messiah, ready to die for the greatness of his country. Jameson gives a bleak view of the innate conservatism of the British, and her observer figure (clearly based on E. M. Forster, with his eloquently expressed liberal views) finally leaves the country, without hope.

In 1939, Clemence Dane adds her voice to the warnings against fascism in Britain, this time in the form of a fable, *The Arrogant History of White Ben*.[28] In this novel, a scarecrow becomes a populist leader in a Britain of the fifties, towards the end of a devastating war. White Ben, the scarecrow, used by others for their own ends, but soon charismatic enough to spellbind them for his own, is a fine blend of entertainment and a grim mirroring of Hitler's rise to power. Ben, brought to life by a little girl's mandrake root hidden in his chest, sets off to kill the crows he hates, only to have his mission interpreted as parable by the people he meets so that, gradually, he is encouraged to see crows as metaphors for enemies at home and abroad. He discovers the power he has for haranguing the poor, and the narrator warns of a future possibility: 'In those days women were the inflammable element in any crowd. The women had lost their patriotism when they lost their men and their homes: and when the first war-prosperity ended in penury they became dangerous' (p. 246). War, Dane warns, clearly breeds violence, and women will not be immune; an ugly alternative to women as the champions of pacifism is suggested here. Meanwhile, Ben himself, we are told, is 'a lunatic who had dived into the deeps of unreason to bring us hope' (p. 250), a linking of fascism with unreason which is widely repeated in the writings of the thirties and forties, as writers strove to cling to the idea that reason, rationality, the bedrock of humanism, could still be an article of faith.[29] The climax of the novel comes as Ben addresses the mob in London and Nelson's Column falls, sparking the outbreak of revolution; parliament is dissolved, Ben's government takes over, and concentration cages are set up in Richmond Park for 'crows', who die there quickly.

Fortunately, Ben eventually loses his mandrake root to the little girl who gave him life, but Dane ends her novel on a note of warning: 'Time travellers report indeed that the savants of a thousand years hence have proved . . . that White Ben Campion was no more than the wish fulfilment of a backward people, and that he personifies in their folk-lore the natural human instinct to maltreat the harmless and destroy the happy' (p. 420), both an echo of Freud's conclusion of 1915, that humankind's instinct for violence is very basic, and an endorsement of Jameson's view of the innate conservatism of the British. Furthermore, Freud, it is tempting to think, provides a link between Dane's novel and Rebecca West's experience of a scarecrow during her travels through Yugoslavia in the late thirties and recorded in *Black Lamb and Grey Falcon*. West sees, as she thinks, someone making a speech, and

> the proud stance of his body showed that he had dug the truth out of the earth where it lay under the roots of the rock. The force of his right arm showed that he had drawn fire from heaven, so that he might weld this truth into our life, which thus shall not perish with our bodies.

But he was merely

> a scarecrow dressed in rags which had been plastered in mud to give them solidity against the winter, and he had been stored on the balcony till it was time to put him out among the fruiting vines. His authority was an exhalation from a bundle of straw.[30]

The perception of the populist orator in both works as no more than an apparently charismatic scarecrow recalls Freud's comment towards the end of his reply to Einstein in 1932, when he acknowledges that 'our mythological theory of instincts makes it easy for us to find a formula for *indirect* methods of combating war'; West and Dane also offer a means of combatting the idea of the unspeakable, reducing Hitler, the charismatic orator personified, to a headpiece 'filled with straw'.[31]

Dane's warning of how dangerous women may prove gives the lie to the equating of women with a passive as opposed to a pacifist stance. Katharine Burdekin, in *Swastika Night* (1937) had shown women reduced to passive victims of fascist oppression; but in a novel written, although not published, in the thirties, *The End of This Day's Business*, she creates a world four thousand years in the future, where women have subjugated men after a series of disastrous wars and have created a world without nationalism, violence, or war.[32] Susan Ertz also creates a future woman who is far from passive in her championing of pacifism in *Woman Alive* (1935), set in the 1980s.[33] In this novel, after years of conflict, all the women are dying as a result of biological warfare. When one woman, Stella, is found alive, initially she refuses any part in keeping the race going because of man's obsession with violence. She sees her world as evidence of 'men's mess' (p. 81), sees man as merely 'a fighting animal' (p. 97), and grieves for her lonely status: 'a world without women is no world at all' (p. 128). Yet she also blames women as accessories to men's crimes: 'We always wanted to please men. That was our undoing. If men went to war, we played up to them' (p. 129), and she goes on to claim that 'if you're romantic, you like the idea of war and killing. Why heaven knows...But it's true that romance and killing have always gone hand in hand' (p. 130). It is not until Ertz introduces Alan, an embodiment of the recent conception of the New Man, that Stella agrees to procreation. But while Ertz pins her hopes on an altered male consciousness, the underlying fear is that mankind as a whole will always be the same.

Other writers treat the theme of women's relationship with violence more harshly in the years leading up to World War Two. Amabel Williams-Ellis, in *Learn to Love First* (1939), adopts the idea of women colluding in men's violence. Her story begins like a typical magazine romance, with a beautiful bride marrying an air hero. But we soon learn that, while Nikolas thinks his new wife is simply shy, a 'snow maiden', she is in fact the mistress of the dictator, Stekker, and Nikolas is simply being used as 'someone utterly loyal';[34] Renata, we are told, still enjoys 'rhinoceros-taming' and its perks (p. 138). She accepts everything that the dictator tells her, failing to see what would distress her; and only when she begins to imagine herself as a possibly discarded mistress, and is asked to learn brothel tricks, does she consider revenge and finally kill him – we are left doubtful as to whether she acts either out of repugnance for his slaughter of his opponents or out of personal outrage – as often in women's fiction, gender-based abuse is presented as having inextricable links with wholesale violence. Ertz's Renata has much in common with the women whom Richard Baxter, the political journalist, will condemn far more viciously in his immensely popular tirade, *Guilty Women* (1941), targeting those women he accuses of backing fascist partners or breaking those opposed to fascism during the thirties, in a tabloid blend of fact, sensationalism and supposedly first-hand assertions. Yet Williams-Ellis is also making the point that if a woman is conditioned only to see herself through a man's eyes her judgement of both public and personal issues may be catastrophically distorted.

However, women are also portrayed as actively engaging in violence by some writers. In Sylvia Townsend Warner's *Summer Will Show* (1936), Minna is seen fighting at the barricades in the Paris of 1848, and when she is shot by Caspar, her lover Sophia's kinsman, it is Sophia who shoots him in the face, a grimly dark moment which has little to do with the revolution. Sophia, the text suggests, kills for personal revenge rather than commitment to a cause, just as Williams-Ellis's Renata does, although Sophia does not die as a result. This is an ambivalent moment in Warner's presentation of commitment to the left, as Caspar is the black pawn in the struggle between Sophia and her husband, the victim of racial prejudice in those who ostensibly protect him.[35] Stevie Smith shows women's capacity for violence less ambivalently in *Over the Frontier* (1938), when Pompey, her protagonist, in a dream sequence, dons a uniform and kills the 'Rat-face' she abhors, because:

> I have seen it before, this rat face; in London, Berlin, Paris, New York; in the villages of Hertfordshire. And now here, in this Ultima Thule of beyond the frontier, and now here? *We are so many.* You shall be so many, less one. And to my liberalistic world-conscience, that is still persisting in Opposition, I might say: He must not live to tell the tale, to put something in jeopardy that must be secure.[36]

As I commented earlier, the dilemma of defending democracy against tyranny while temperamentally subscribing to the cause of peace is far from being easily resolved in many of the novels written at this time.

This dilemma is immediately apparent when we turn to works written about the growing conflicts in Europe. Sylvia Townsend Warner, for instance, was a passionate supporter of the republican cause in Spain; in her short story, 'The Drought Breaks' (1937), she tells of a woman in a Spanish town, whose husband has been shot because he was a member of a Trades Union. She has no food, as it is being eaten by the Italian and German soldiers in the Nationalist army, her children have been taken by the church, and so, when the bombers come, she greets them because they are 'ours'; and she turns up

> her face, her heart, to the death falling from the air, as though to a greeting from the dead, as though to a greeting from life . . . It was like the noise of earth, thirsty with long drought, clucking with parched lips as it drinks the rain.[37]

Again, in her novel *After the Death of Don Juan* (1938), set in the eighteenth century, Warner shows how the local peasants gradually realize that, whether the oppressive aristocrat Don Juan lives or not, their traditional oppression by the Church and the landowners will not be eased without their own efforts. As Warner herself explains in a letter to a friend in 1945, the novel is: 'a parable if you like the word, or an allegory... of the political chemistry of the Spanish war, with the Don Juan – more of Moliere than of Mozart – developing as the Fascist of the piece'.[38] And, as Warner shows in her novel, he has to be confronted, either with a passive acceptance that violence is necessary, as the peasant woman does in 'The Drought Breaks', or with arms, as the peasants attempt to do in the novel. Phyllis Bottome also confronted the conflicts in Europe, but in her case as an adherent of the medical psychologist Alfred Adler, whom she worked with in Vienna. Adler was a passionate advocate of 'social interest' (an idea associated with 'Love thy neighbour as thyself') in the face of European totalitarianism in the thirties. Where Freud saw humankind's animal instincts only contained through repression, Adler saw inborn trends (for social interest and the striving for superiority), whose development could perfect the personality. Interestingly, although he and Freud had gone their separate ways in 1912, in the thirties Freud was coming to accept a number of Adler's views in the face of the increasing violence in Europe. In 'Why War?', Freud admits that love or at least identification may be the only means of avoiding war.[39] And this is Bottome's starting point in her extremely successful novel *The Mortal Storm* (1937), which was reprinted several times throughout the War years.[40] The novel tells the story of Freya Toller and her family; her half-brothers are both Nazis, the mother being Aryan, while Freya and her younger brother are classified as Jews, Catholic Jews, like their father. The anguish of a loving family remorselessly driven in different directions and into conflict with each other is told with keen intelligence and a fine perception of the psychological complexities. Freya, studying medicine to follow her father who, like Adler, preaches the importance of love rather than violence, falls in love with a communist peasant, and, while gradually becoming aware of the gravity of the political situation, conceives his child. Her half-brothers refuse to meet her lover, Hans, and eventually kill him; the Brown Shirts visit her father, who opposes their nationalism, saying 'a country is a mere lump of earth – without qualities or desires' (p. 130). When the father is awarded a Nobel Prize for his achievements in medicine, he is not allowed to receive it, his fortune is sequestered and his wife told to leave him; as he says, 'It is a war to exterminate the brotherhood of man' (p. 183). Inevitably, he is taken to a concentration camp, where two months later he dies. Published as the novel was, in 1937, it is a stark reminder of the problem facing those, like Bottome, who wanted to defend democracy while continuing to espouse pacifism; Freya's father's philosophy, admirable though it is, does not penetrate the minds of his stepsons, and the killing goes on.

Storm Jameson's rough, bleakly honest novel *Europe to Let* (1940) also exposes the dilemmas for pacifists which are endemic in the European situation.[41] In this work she looks back at its cumulative horrors and traces the gradual, inexorable process by which events on the continent have led to World War Two. Jameson offers a passionate authenticity as her narrative is a fiction based on fact, an example of documentary realism. Her strength lies in weaving together into a dismayingly cohesive whole a host of personal tragedies which will create in the fulness of time the tragedy of world war. As the novel opens in 1923, in a 'starving, bankrupt' Germany, we hear how the French have marched into the Ruhr where they behave 'like people living in a house of which the windows look over a slaughter-yard; ignoring the fear, pain, rage that touched them, they kept up a civilized life behind blinds' (p. 6); and the German Hesse tells the narrator how, sooner or later, 'we shall set fire to the house...How you will hate us. And how in our hearts we shall blame you, for leaving us to play with matches in an icily cold room' (p. 36). Later, Emil, a Jewish surgeon in the Vienna of 1938 who has just had his fingers broken by his Nazi tormentors, so that he can never operate again, speaks bitterly of how truth is denied:

> It's not true that thousands of people in Austria have been robbed of everything. That thousands are slowly dying of hunger. That the prisons are crowded with people charged with having been born. That others have been existing for weeks on a rotten boat in mid-Danube. It is not true that the postman is authorised to demand a hundred marks for a package containing the ashes of your son, he who was taken away last week by enemies who were amused by your tears. It is not true that when they have forbidden a Jew to work, and knowing that no country will admit him have ordered him to leave at once, officials answer the impudent question, 'What am I to do?' by the retort, 'There is always the Danube'.
>
> (p. 280)

As I showed above, Jameson saw clearly where Europe was heading as early as 1922 in her novel *The Clash*; *Europe to Let* reads like a devastating, planned sequel in its charting of a seemingly inevitable process, given the follies of the intervening years, and demonstrates clearly how painfully Jameson comes to acknowledge that pacifism cannot be justified in the face of such atrocities.

Home and abroad in the War years

The advent of World War Two caused most politically-minded women writers to put the defence of democracy ahead of pacifism on their agenda, but this did not necessarily mean that they followed the propagandist line in what they wrote; pacifism might be out, but most subscribed to what both Adler and Freud had come to agree on, an attempt at understanding and compassion for those not directly involved in atrocities. Storm Jameson is outstanding in her efforts throughout the War to make her readers think about what it felt like to be in Europe as Nazism and its allies gained the upper hand. As Joanna Labon says, Jameson defined her life by war, and her wartime fiction may well have been written to give 'accounts that could not be published elsewhere' given the strict press censorship of non-fiction.[42] For Jameson pulls no punches in what she writes. In an article of 1941, she claims that we are now 'insensitive' to what has been going on in Europe over the past twenty-five years, and as a result, 'famine, broken children, distressed areas, concentration camps, torture cells, are the crimes we shall be known by in history, not by our heroism, our endurance under air-raids'.[43] Her anger here springs from her experience in PEN, working desperately to ease the plight of refugees, and often facing the hostility and indifference of her compatriots in the process. In 1941, in her closing address to the London PEN congress, she is already pleading for understanding of those French who supported capitulation in France: 'Is he to be blamed, by an Englishman who has drunk his wine, has laid a caressing hand on the stones of his walls, for being too civilised to like the idea of total war?'[44] It is illuminating to see how this former pacifist continues to empathize with the longing for peaceful solutions, even as she has come, intellectually, to accept the necessity for the violent confrontation of fascism.

Already, between October 1940 and February 1941, she had written her tightly constructed novel *The Fort* (1941), structured, as I showed in Chapter 1, like a neo-classical tragedy, in three chapters. Her setting is the cellar of a farmhouse in North-East France, where English and French infantry officers are trapped in the face of the German advance.[45] As they wait, the older English and French officers discuss the origins of this war, while of the two young French soldiers in the cellar one is for fighting the other for capitulation. These two are also divided by class, the one who supports war, Masson, being poor, the other well-to-do; moreover, Masson is a socialist, and claims with some truth: 'I fear and hate the Nazis, you fear me [as a socialist] and you admire them because they've found ways of killing me, in Dachau, in Madrid. Thousands of deaths' (p. 31); the other, Vidal, is openly anti-Semitic: 'you haven't the wit to see the rottenness, and the Jew squatting everywhere' (p. 33). So Jameson threads into her tale many of the issues debated in the early stages of the War, but she never loses the tension of the moment. In the middle of the novel, another young Englishman is brought in, and then a young German, full of Nazi mysticism; yet these two young men find they have much in common, both being mathematicians. Eventually, the allied officers decide the German has to be shot, and the full pity of war is brought out. Inevitably, the German forces reach the farmhouse, find the cellar, and there is a fight. Then Jameson plays a neat trick, showing how the novel is grounded in drama; when the Germans leave the cellar, it is plunged in total darkness. After a moment, a light from the cellar shaft shows a young man, a stranger, standing there, while the others appear to be asleep; the young Englishman wakes and they talk, and gradually we realize they are talking about different wars. When the older Englishman wakes, he greets the stranger as 'Jamie', the young man he had earlier mourned losing in 1916. So economically, as the dead of two wars greet each other, does Jameson show the tragic irony of the same ground fought over for the second time in less than twenty-five years.

What is so impressive about this work, as with so many written at this time, is the speed with which it responds to events, and the value Jameson puts on art to structure and discipline what is, after all, highly emotive material. In 1940, the same year in which she had blamed the French, in *Europe to Let*, for being oblivious to German suffering after World War One, she brought out *Cousin Honoré*, a 'realist' novel on one level, but on another, fabular, with each character typifying some crucial stance in the debates concerning resistance or capitulation.[46] Here, as in *The Fort*, Jameson looks with understanding at the difficult choices facing the French and their allies, linking the public with the private. Strikingly, she shows where she differs from Bottome in this novel, as she stresses the importance of roots in the land to her central character, old man Burckheim. Again, Jameson's experience with PEN is clear: her close association with those dispossessed and uprooted compels her to emphasize the value of home, not nation; frequently, in subsequent novels, she returns to this theme, consistently discussing it in terms of native soil and the growing of crops – a useful reminder that the emphasis on the homeland is a common theme for both the Nazis and their victims, to very different effect.

In Jameson's moving fable *Then We Shall Hear Singing* (1942) the theme recurs, linking a village's roots in its native soil almost mystically with its memories, its identity, an idea dear to the hearts of the dispossessed of eastern Europe.[47] Here, in an imaginary country (clearly based on Czechoslovakia) which has been conquered by a Germanic enemy, a Dr Hesse arrives who can destroy 'the highest functions of the brain without affecting the body in any way' (p. 17), defending his right to experiment on his victims 'for the race' (his), since moreover the victims 'aren't my countrymen' (p. 18), and will become useful servants, 'amiable, docile, obedient. The mind is, you may say, gone...' (p. 19). He announces that he will begin by treating everyone in one village, excepting only two old women as their memories are unimportant. Arriving in the village of his choice, Hesse first takes all the men over 18, returning them changed to their women (one girl is savagely raped by her formerly gentle lover), and then he starts on the women. Eventually, only old Anna is left unaffected, the sole repository of the people's memories;[48] Jameson reiterates the theme she was developing in *Cousin Honoré*, for the afflicted people start to sense links with the earth which they cannot explain, and gradually Anna helps them to remember, the climax coming as she brings out an old bottle of wine and reminds them of their vines. As a result, the men are determined to fight their oppressors although they know the odds are against them; and the women are left alone, some uncertain, some serene, with Anna continually offering encouragement, saying, 'Our past is always here'. This, given its date, is inevitably an open-ended novel (Anna after all stands for confirmation of the past, she cannot guarantee a future), but it is unashamedly a paean of faith in survival, and demonstrates how fully Jameson empathizes, while not embracing patriotism as such, with the implications of native soil for many of her friends from occupied countries.

In 1943, Jameson returns to the dilemmas facing the French before capitulation in her novel *Cloudless May*.[49] This work offers a much subtler portrayal of a woman involved in self-centred political manipulation than Williams-Ellis's novel did. Jameson's Marie is clearly based on Reynaud's mistress, Hélène, one of the targets for Baxter's contempt in *Guilty Women* (1941). But Jameson does not take the easy option of condemning her Marie; she explores the insecurity that drives her, the childhood poverty which makes her avaricious, the fear of reprisals which haunts her – she lives a life of 'hunger and stratagems'.[50] Even her lover, Emil, the mayor of a small town, who at first fights off the determined efforts of would-be Nazi collaborators, finally succumbs to her pleas (the ugliest moment is when he agrees not to free an interned German Jew, because, Marie says, as such people are revolutionaries, they are simply 'enemies in an enemy country invaded by their enemies' [p. 233]). The many reasons for capitulation are analysed with shrewd insight; there are those who are ruthless in their self-interest ('Hitler understands how to govern', says one such character [p. 67]), as well as those who believe passionately in peace, or are simply sickened by their experiences in the previous war. Jameson never makes the mistake of painting all characters in primary colours, and it is interesting, too, to see how the term 'realist' is bandied about to describe each man's version of the situation.[51] The confusions of intentions, good, bad and undecided, are interwoven into a very human tapestry, while issues like the destruction of much of the French fleet at Oran by the British (to prevent its seizure by the Germans, but with great loss of life), or the fact that Dunkirk was seen by many French as betrayal, remind the British reader how differently 'reality' may appear when seen from another point of view.

In late 1944, Jameson took on another sensitive issue as the War drew to a close, in *The Other Side* (eventually published in 1946).[52] This novel deals with the impossible situation faced by the young French widow of a German soldier, living with his aristocratic family in Germany. She has to cope with both the hostility of her husband's family and with the initial contempt of the French officer, Aubrac, who, as a member of the army of occupation, is billetted in the family's chateau. Marie's love for her dead husband is unequivocal, but she is soon trapped by divided loyalties, realizing that the head of the German family is involved in a plot to kill a visiting English MP. After a struggle with herself, she reports the plot, and the MP is saved. The family treat her as a traitor, but finally, after coping with many insults and with her own lack of self-esteem, she allows herself to be saved, Aubrac offering her the chance to rehabilitate herself in France by helping to care for war orphans. Jameson's plea for reconciliation is clear, as the savagely anti-German Aubrac learns a degree of tolerance despite finding no answer to his initial question: 'How is it possible that everything, in a country which has pushed to its furthest point the line of technical science, corresponds to a myth?' (p. 4).[53] But Jameson does not make the mistake of either understating German resistance to the invaders or underestimating the enormity of the task of reconciliation.

In early 1945, Ethel Mannin also tackled the theme of those who fall in love with an enemy in *The Dark Forest* (published in 1946), but from an aggressively pacifist point of view.[54] In her preface she says:

> 'Ling' could be any little town in any neutral country over-run by any nation at war. The invaders could be any country that considered it expedient to occupy such a country...I have been interested in the war of emotion and intellect between people of irreconcileable ideas drawn together by a common human need.

And she adds that, while she will not quarrel with the reader who wants to label characters fascist and anti-fascist, that is not her main concern (p. 6). We are given the story of Anna, whose much-loved husband is killed by the invading force, and of Paul, the enemy soldier utterly convinced of his country's New World Order; Anna's passion for Paul overcomes her hostility, despite the fact that they continually argue about their beliefs. Anna, from being well liked in her small community, is branded as a fraternizer and indeed finds 'collaborationist' chalked on her farm walls (p. 123); but for all that, her communal loyalties are unaffected as she battles to save life in the local hospital. When the enemy force is driven out, Mannin emphasizes that Anna sees no difference between the liberators and the original army of occupation. What is interesting in this novel is the way in which the love of the young people does not affect the rational debate, or clear-sightedness about the atrocities committed – Mannin, somewhat improbably, finds no problem in drawing a clear line between passion and reason. In due course, after Paul leaves with his retreating army, Anna is sent to the former enemy country on relief work, where she and Paul meet again, and finally decide to flee to a neutral country. Anna gets away, but Paul is shot. As Anna's doctor friend remarked, thinking of the moment when Paul left Ling with the retreating army, 'A novelist writing it all as a story would have ended it there – the artistic ending, the logical ending' (p. 192); but Mannin, a committed pacifist, shows Paul and Anna trying to force a happy ending, and being thwarted by the realities of war. This is a powerful little folk tale, and, like Jameson, Mannin shows boldness in addressing one of the most highly charged contemporary issues.

However, most of the novels written by British writers during the War are situated at home, which is not to say that they are necessarily insular. By the end of 1939, Jan Struther is already confronting one of the dangers on the home front. She warns in *Mrs Miniver* that women should guard against indiscriminate anti-German feeling: 'there are no tangible gas masks to defend us in war-time against its slow, yellow, drifting corruption of the mind';[55] as Jameson and Mannin will do, she is already appealing against an essentialist definition of 'the enemy'. But not all writers hit a compassionate note as the War began. Rachel Ferguson, for instance, a writer who had an established reputation for wit before the War, damaged that reputation with her 'curiously insensitive' novel, *A Footman for the Peacock* (1940).[56] Set in the traditional country house, the story of the long-dead 'running footman' who haunts the estate is overshadowed by the self-satisfied snobbery of the family. Lady Roundelay worries about the democratizing effect of education for the masses, and, although claiming to sympathize with the German Jews, refuses to house a Jewish refugee. The Roundelays also refuse to have evacuees, perceiving them as 'deriving much stomach upset from the change of air and biliousness from unaccustomed food' (p. 224). The story of the footman may be central to the work, but the snobbery of the Roundelays is what sticks in the mind, and the uncomfortable suspicion that Ferguson may not be wholeheartedly satirizing it.

For clearly such attitudes did exist. Clemence Dane's historical novel *He Brings Great News* (1944) makes a sly dig at long-standing British prejudices against all intrusions on their insular existence, as her Frenchman says with relief as he leaves for home:

> never again shall I be stared at as you stare at a dancing-bear or a lady's marmoset . . . Think what it will be not to hear ever again the phrase 'you French', nor to be asked if you eat frogs, and why, and if many of your family have perished on the guillotine, and why you are not fighting, although they know that in the British navy and army they will not admit an emigré.[57]

More immediately, Ruth Adam's *Murder in the Home Guard* (1942) is dedicated:

> with next to no affection to those who sat tight in safe areas and billeted not the homeless, clothed not the bombed-out, shared not their rations with the evacuated, visited not the interned, but said, as they listened to the news, 'we bombed Berlin last night', trusting that they will provide themselves with a water-tight alibi before the last trump.[58]

While the novel gives a very funny picture of an incompetent German bomber pilot with his hated Gestapo minder, and also involves us in a murder mystery and a romance, the most powerful passages are those dealing with evacuees, and these are not light-hearted. The child Betty is offered comforting promises which 'bore no more relation to her silent fears and questionings than the reassuring cliches of a politician to a nation under censorship' (p. 53), and certainly bear no relation to her experiences, as she is shunted from household to household because she has nits: 'she wondered, as a man who has already been in a concentration camp may wonder, with helpless, formless fear where they would send her next and what new miseries would be waiting for her' (p. 236). Eventually, trying to escape back to London, she is found by a kindly police sergeant who takes her home to an environment which she at least recognizes and understands. Meanwhile, an old colonel is the only one to offer shelter to expectant mothers and service wives, and his intended punishment of the community for its inhumanity provides the climax of the novel.

The plight of children of the East End of London during the Blitz, children like Adam's Betty, is also the theme of Phyllis Bottome's immensely successful novel *London Pride* (1941) (it was reprinted ten times during the War years).[59] While this work in many ways shows the danger Queenie Leavis and Storm Jameson perceived, of a middle-class writer venturing into working-class territory, it was a work which confronted middle-class readers with a part of society which would be unknown to most of them. The child hero, Ben, is six in 1939, living with his family in the slums of the East End at the beginning of the Blitz. The novel tends to dwell on brave Londoners who have the right standards at heart, and gives a somewhat unlikely view of the gratitude Ben's mother feels to the 'lady' who calls to offer help and possible evacuation for the children and herself; but the children are vividly drawn, their language more realistic than that of the adults, their exploits credible, whether it is their small ventures into looting in the West End, or their terrified endurance when trapped under rubble after a raid. This work may be dated, but, in its concentration on the East End slums, it was a highly successful pioneering work at the time, aimed at the same middle-class audience which Adam would challenge in her novel of the following year.

Indeed, the way the War forced people of different classes to confront each other is a striking feature of many works written at this time. Inez Holden, for instance, in *Night Shift* (1941) takes us into a factory where people from a whole range of backgrounds work together, with the inevitable moments of tension and assertion of difference. Yet these people somehow develop into a community, against the background of 'the air-raid orchestra of airplane hum, anti-aircraft shell bursts,

ambulance and fire bells. Sometimes bomb concussions caused the floor
to give a sudden shiver' (p. 10). The same mixture of people are found in
Holden's other factory novel, *There's No Story There* (1944), where Julian
struggles with his trauma after Dunkirk, 'alone in his silence, feeling as
isolated as a man walking by himself on a heath' (p. 26). Here too there
are people from remote country districts meeting city crowds for the
first time; as the narrator observes, 'national upheaval, with all its
implications for the individual, was . . . an unknown thing, unexpected
and uneasy for many of the workers here' (p. 53). And some people
never come to terms with the mixing of backgrounds that war imposes
on them. Victoria Sackville-West, for instance, in her account of the
Women's Land Army (1944), records how two girls, tired and dirty after
a demanding day of back-breaking forestry work, go to a restaurant
where 'the guests were all in evening dress, and let us know how disgusting it was to let the Land Army in their hotel, and two left their
dinner and went out, we could have eaten it, we were so hungry'.[60]

Other novels, while paying the respect due to the courage shown by
civilians, do not hesitate to criticize where they feel criticism is due.
Phyllis Bottome's *Within the Cup* (1943) is written as the diary of a
'ghost', a Jewish Austrian doctor disowned by his Aryan wife, and now
a refugee in England.[61] This novel launches a series of attacks, ranging
from criticism of British resistance to the concept of euthanasia (an issue
particularly relevant to the horrific injuries of some victims of air raids),
to an exposure of the way in which the General Medical Council initially tried to block the employment of refugee doctors. Yet the picture
Bottome draws is well balanced. Rudi, the refugee, is welcomed and
helped by one family; and he is sustained by Adler's philosophy in his
work as a doctor. As in many novels, the intensive bombing of Plymouth
is graphically described, and Bottome shows, not only heroism in the
first wave of strikes, but those who were utterly demoralized by the
second wave, when her protagonist, Rudi, is dismayed by 'a loud-
speaker promising equal destruction to German homes' (p. 242).[62]
This novel is an intelligent, complex and finely structured tale, addressing immediate issues, as does Susan Ertz's *Anger in the Sky*, published in
the same year.[63] Ertz's novel, based initially in the traditional country
house, almost literally deconstructs the conventions attached to it. Ertz
does allow a warm family life at the centre of her work, and does end on
a hopeful note, but she aims to give a cross-section of society and
opinion. There is, for instance, the French woman, an unwilling refugee,
who supports the Vichy Government and cannot forgive the British
attack on the French fleet at Oran. There is also the young American

who is, initially, an isolationist; and the young English socialist, who cannot accept that the family are truly democratic because they are not living in the East End. The household discuss how little is heard of sexual morality in this war, unlike the last, 'was it that the subject of sex had been pushed aside by the titanic struggle between opposing ideologies?' (p. 42), while Viola, the daughter nursing in London, is having to come to terms with her lover being reduced to a vegetable existence because of his injuries. Viola also experiences the Plymouth bombing, and encounters the same 'real racial hatred' of the Germans that Bottome's Rudi heard over the loud-speaker. This is another extraordinarily rich novel which is very far from adopting the propagandist line of a united and uncritical Britain.

Betty Miller's novel *On the Side of the Angels* (1945) by no means toes the line either.[64] This work offers a scathing account of male bonding in the military, as a doctor's wife and sister suffer from his love affair with military life. As Claudia, the sister says, 'I sometimes think . . . in a sense – we're all prisoners of war' (p. 68), while Colin, her doctor brother-in-law, has no fear of danger but, seduced by his uniform, does fear that the 'war could not last for ever' (p. 127). Miller's characters are very clear on the factors in society which lead to war. Claudia's fiancé, for instance, sees the rigidity of society as its chief weakness, with everyone 'pretending to conform, pretending to be what they aren't' (p. 69), so that war, when it comes, is a form of escapism; he sees the formula 'we can take it' as a kind of morphia to counter the power of death (p. 156). But ultimately, while Miller does suggest that it is the stultifying conventions of society which make militarism so attractive, what imbues this novel is a distaste for masculine posturings in uniform, and an exposure of the price it exacts from the women who either unwillingly endure it or are seduced by it.

Edith Pargeter offers a quite different perspective in *She Goes to War* (1942). Her first-person narrator who joins the WRENS is no longer pacifist; indeed, a major theme in this novel is an attack on Britain's half-hearted measures early in the War and the appalling cost of this. The narrator cannot cope with what she now sees as the 'indiscriminate forgiveness' of pacifists.[65] She catalogues the atrocities of the War so far, the torpedoing of evacuees, events in Spain, China, Prague, convoys mined, homes blasted, Guernica, Coventry, Warsaw in ruins, and asks: 'Do we talk of forgiving the virus of a contagious disease?' (p. 93). She estimates that no more than 60 per cent of the people in England are involved in warwork of some kind and is as contemptuous as Adam about the rest, who, she supposes, 'are engaged in dodging the war,

protecting their personal fortunes from the war, or founding new and
very dirty fortunes on the chances thrown up by the war' (p. 119). When
her lover confronts death in the rearguard action in Crete, his last letters
speak of the lack of air support, saying, 'If I die here, as I believe, I die an
angry man', because of the 'muddle and half-measures' (p. 232); Britain
has let them down. His one hope is that the war will be a revolution as
well, since he believes that:

> our prized democracy is a half-hearted and inefficient business, our
> equality of sacrifice a euphemism for the most blatant exploitation of
> the great underdog, and our concern for life much less than our
> concern for property, since one may be commandeered wholesale
> and the other may not be so much as breathed upon.
>
> (pp. 238–9)

This novel in its entirety confirms that, while Pargeter picks up on issues
touched on by other writers, she is much more wholeheartedly in support of war than many of her contemporaries, her pacifism leaving little
aftertaste.

Certainly Pargeter's view of war is far removed from Rosamond Lehmann's. Lehmann's story 'When the Waters Came' (1941) makes us fully
aware of her distance from the conflict, set as it is in her country
village.[66] The narrator thinks of 'sailors freezing in unimaginable wastes
of water' and 'of soldiers numb in the black-and-white nights on sentry
duty'; but her setting stresses her apartness from such experiences: 'In
her soft bed, she thought of them with pity – masses of young men,
betrayed, helpless, and so much colder, more uncomfortable than
human beings should be. But they remained unreal, as objects of pity
must remain' (p. 108). Later, in the first of Lehmann's series of stories
entitled 'Wonderful Holidays' (1944), the narrator

> heard the rhythmical throat of night begin to throb and croon again.
> Bomb, bomb, bomb, bomb. Burn, burn, burn, burn. Down, down,
> down, down. Fuller, fuller, fainter, fainter. A strong force of our air-
> craft passing overhead. Impersonally exulting and lamenting, deadly
> mild, soothing in its husky reiterated burden as a familiar lullaby.[67]

Lehmann's aestheticizing of the sounds of the blitz is, if we recall Walter
Benjamin's comment on fascist aestheticizing, somewhat disturbing.
Her stories are far removed from the confrontation with the war over-
seas which Pargeter's narrator experiences, albeit at one remove.

Brittain is even farther from Pargeter, since Brittain never abandoned her passionate advocacy of pacifism, as is clear in her novel, *Account Rendered* (1945). In this work, all German air raids on the cities are seen as retaliation for British raids on German cities; Brittain shows no awareness of the Holocaust or of other atrocities committed by the Nazis in Europe. Her sole concern is the iniquity of the battlefield and the bombing, together with the effect these have on their victims. Within this context, her handling of the psychology of her characters is sensitive and astute, echoing the points which united Freud and Adler in the early thirties, and indeed she is responding to the same war as they were, for her main character is the victim of a form of shell-shock suffered in World War One. But she is not out of step with some of the underlying concerns of many other novelists of the thirties and forties; echoing Freud, she makes the point that: 'We all know that the darkness is in each one of us; the Nazis may be a gang of criminals, but they haven't got a monopoly of evil' (p. 124). In the end, the conclusions Pargeter and Brittain draw about the concept of warfare simply go to show that one person's conviction as to what the 'facts' demonstrate is not necessarily another's.

'The post-war': neither war nor peace in the late forties

As the War drew to an end, we find the novel being reassessed. Philip Toynbee, for instance, sees the novel as having been in decline during the War, saying: 'One may diagnose the two principal causes of temporary decline as the overweening influence of contemporary events and the vastly enlarged scope of the novelist's territory. The combination is powerful and destructive'; and urging that, while writers cannot ignore political issues, 'the novelist must concentrate on the trees and divert his attention from the wood'.[68] But the works I have discussed above do not seem to me to merit such easy dismissal. At the end of the War, moreover, some impressive books emerge, not by any means directed towards celebrating peace in the way Storm Jameson had warned against in 1941, when she urged that 'anything like the moral collapse after the last war, the idiot rejoicings, the ignorance, the short-sighted greed, the apathy, would ruin us'.[69] Phyllis Bottome's *The Lifeline* was published in 1946, an absorbing tale of an Englishman who becomes a courier for the resistance in Austria during the recent conflict;[70] this is another work promoting reconciliation, as Bottome reminds her readers of the heroism of those Germans and Austrians who opposed Nazism. Both Bottome and Jameson are tireless in making the distinction in their works between those who held out against Nazism and those who succumbed; clearly a major contribution to their war effort, as they saw it, was to use their eloquence to combat easy blanket definitions of friend and foe. Not that either of them offer a naïve view of Europe. Jameson's *The Black Laurel* (1947), for instance, begins in a POW camp in Scotland, with the impending execution of German prisoners for hanging two men who betrayed their plans to escape; for, the commandant insists,

> Any bloody thing can be justified, gas chambers, cutting a school-roomful of Bolshie children's poor little throats, injecting poison into the veins of old girls of sixty and seventy – anything. Once you decide to call a private murder justice you're done for – you and your country are going straight to hell.[71]

Jameson then takes us to post-war Berlin, into a macabre world where her protagonist, Arnold, sees: 'The hangmen had done their work thoroughly, the body of Europe, flayed while still living, was stretched below him' (p. 35). While there, he meets an embittered Rudolf Gerlach, who asks him, 'When the war starts with Russia will your people recruit us Germans as mercenaries?' (p. 71), a surreal suggestion amidst the devastation, one might think, if it were not that Churchill has been shown to have contemplated precisely such a possibility as the War ended.[72] Be that as it may, conspiracies and vendettas abound in the Berlin of 1946 which Jameson explores. The innocent Jew, Kalb, in Berlin to identify stolen pictures, is framed ('a Jew, of course, every refugee is a traitor and the Jews doubly so')[73] and executed as a looter. But Jameson, as always, is never one-sided; she rouses our sympathy for the ravages and destitution of Berlin before she gives, in vivid detail, the obscenities of the crushed Warsaw rising; she deliberately complicates the picture for her readers. On one issue, however, she is very clear: the horror of the atom bomb, which will cast its shadow across the fifties and sixties.

Jameson is not alone in assessing where war has led. In 1945, Edith Pargeter brought out the first volume of what was billed as a trilogy, the story of a soldier's war.[74] This first volume takes us through the early years of the War, from the soldier Benson's experiences in France and Belgium through to Dunkirk. As in her earlier novel, Pargeter makes clear her disapproval of what she sees as the British Government's amateurish approach early in the War; the soldiers say of the Jerries, 'Trouble is they're taking it seriously, and we're not' (p. 79). But Pargeter's own approach is far from amateur, as she traces Jim's experiences of battle and the personal tragedies of the civilians he encounters. This is a gripping novel, and Pargeter sustains the quality in the second, *Reluctant Odyssey* (1946), and in the final volume, *Warfare Accomplished* (1947), which begins in 1944.[75] The tone changes in the third volume, since Jim now feels, as D-Day approaches, 'whatever happens – this time it won't be half done' (*Warfare Accomplished*, p. 12). In Germany the soldiers are greeted by women factory workers from a medley of occupied countries, 'freed slaves of the last tyranny of history' (p. 283), but Pargeter is realistic about their excitement: 'Freedom, which in her first ecstasy had put colour back into the world and youth and hope back into the heart, might turn out in a month or two to be just another ageing drab limping along beside them' (p. 285). But the most devastating moment of this passionately delivered novel is when the soldiers are led to a women's concentration camp, 'an island outside humanity' (p. 295).[76] Jim is not only appalled at what he sees, but at the reaction of neighbouring villagers: 'No one could go near the farm, no one could walk over the hill without seeing the living skeletons ranging along the wire; but they swear with tears their ignorance and consternation, and in some quarters, beyond doubt, they would be believed' (pp. 312–13). We are so used now to exposures of this kind that it needs an effort of will to realize how quickly and effectively Pargeter is responding to the events of her own time, and how shrewdly she shapes a protagonist who is tough and cynical, so that the impact of the horrors he sees is all the greater. In the end, Jim has no sense of victory: 'He was empty, drained, and cold' (p. 340); and his return to England is a carefully muted affair.

The end of the War does bring a moment of pause, writers tending to assess where they are at and how they have reached this point, rather than putting the War behind them. The revelations of the Holocaust and Hiroshima leave a sense of horror, rather than triumphalism. Elizabeth Bowen's novel *The Heat of the Day* (1948) certainly eschews triumphalism in its superbly complex explorations of what constitutes love, betrayal and identity. Bowen cuts across class just as Holden did; Louie, the factory worker, faces confusions which are similar to those of Stella, the upper-class woman engaged in intelligence. But Bowen shows that their problems are not peculiar to war, as Harrison, the mysterious Mephisthophelean character who forms the link between the two women says:

> War, if you come to think of it, hasn't started anything that wasn't there already – what it does is, put the other lot of us in the right. You, I mean to say, have got along on the assumption that things don't happen; I, on the other hand, have taken it that things happen rather

than not. Therefore, what you see now is what I've seen all along. I wouldn't say that puts me at an advantage, but I can't help feeling 'This is where I come in'.

(pp. 33–4)

Mystery and uncertainty, as Harrison's riddling words demonstrate, deconstruct all Stella's securities. Harrison hints that her lover is a traitor, even as he himself 'looked about him like a German in Paris' (p. 44). The Blitz itself is 'the demolition of an entire moment' (p. 96), and Stella sees her own individuality as no more than the reflection of the angst of the time as war and what goes on in her tangled relationships coalesce:

> the mischief was in her own [world] and in other rooms. The grind and scream of battles, mechanized advances excoriating flesh and country, tearing through nerves and tearing up trees, were indoor-plotted; this was a war of dry cerebrations inside windowless walls. No act was not part of some calculation; spontaneity was in tatters; from the point of view of nothing more than the heart any action was enemy action now.

(p. 142)

The bitterness of this knowledge stems from the same source as Pargeter's; like Jim Benson, Stella's lover, Robert, has suffered a sea change after experiencing the evacuation of Dunkirk, as he says: 'The extremity – can they not conceive that's a thing you never do come back from? How many of us do they imagine ever have come back? We're to be avoided – Dunkirk wounded men' (p. 272).

The repeated conviction that war has its roots in each individual, which may be read as the absorption of Freud's ideas, is clear in many of the novels published as the forties drew to a close. One of these is Stevie Smith's *The Holiday* (1949), originally written and set in the War but which Smith altered to cover the post-war years. This turned out to be fortunate, since throughout the book the 'post-war' can be differentiated from peace. As the protagonist, Celia, says, 'it is a year or so after the war. It cannot be said that it is war, it cannot be said that it is peace, it can be said that it is post-war; this will probably go on for ten years' (p. 13). Smith's novel catches the antitriumphalist spirit of the immediate post-war years, as Celia is consumed by present griefs and fears for the future. She dreads the rise of nationalism as it could be 'the death of Peace' (p. 16), and asks, 'shall we win the post-war?' (p. 90). Smith's Celia

does indeed mirror the spirit of existential crisis which preoccupies
Pargeter's protagonist as the War ended; Celia's nervous chatter is darker
in tone than that of the earlier Pompey, her weeping an image of the
helplessness felt by many before the revelations which called in question all that Western civilization was supposed to stand for.

At first sight, Naomi Mitchison's novel *The Bull Calves* (1947) is out of
tune with this malaise, as it is a historical novel set in eighteenth-century
Scotland, tracing the story of Mitchison's own family. But one strand
running through this novel is an imaginatively graphic reconstruction
of Scotland as an occupied country, a reminder that this island has been
no stranger to atrocities. Moreover, Mitchison meditates on many issues
related to the aftermath of war, including fraternization and collaboration, and Mitchison's very full notes at the end of the novel make clear
the connection between her tale and World War Two. A similar link is
there in Daphne du Maurier's *The King's General* (1946), another historical
novel, this time set in the English Civil War, which tells of cruelties at
home which once were and might have come again.[77] Du Maurier's West-
country heroine recalls how the people were broken by the war: 'Long
faces and worsted garments, bad harvests and sinking trade, everywhere
men poorer than they were before and the people miserable. The happy
aftermath of war' (p. 9). As the aristocrats, the ones in power, fight over
the land, it is the ordinary people who pay the price, and the seemingly
casual reference to the main Cavalier character, Richard, being off
'slaughtering the savages of Ireland' (p. 55), also implicates colonialist
attitudes; although this is a lively tale of mystery and adventure, du
Maurier keeps the thread of comparison with modern times going.
There is a vivid account of the occupation of the protagonist's home,
and du Maurier shows clearly how war can bring out the brute in those
caught up in it, 'like those half savages of the fourteen hundreds who . . .
slit each others' throats without compunction' (p. 158). The old charge
that men 'are really bred to war and thrive on it' (p. 158) is again made, a
theme that is never entirely lost sight of throughout the forties. What this
novel achieves, as well as or because of its success as entertainment, is a
convincing case against the complacency of an England which has convinced itself that it has never been vulnerable in modern history, never
committed atrocities against its own.

This is a case to which Nancy Mitford bears witness, although perhaps
unintentionally, in her novel, *The Pursuit of Love* (1945).[78] Before the
War, in *The Vanguard*, Mitford had defended fascism and supported
Mosley who, she said, had 'the character, the brains, the courage and
the determination to lift this country from the slough of despond in

which it has for too long weltered'.[79] Unsurprisingly therefore, while *The Pursuit of Love* is an engagingly witty work, it sometimes suggests, like Ferguson's, that far-right sympathies are alive and well. Its first page, which describes the entrenching tool with its blood and hair adornment still bearing witness to Uncle Matthew's attack on eight German soldiers in World War One, reads oddly after the compassionate writings of Jameson and Bottome; even Pargeter, who treats battle violence so graphically, never makes light of the slaughter. But Mitford uses this frivolously savage and pitiless reference as a leitmotif running throughout the novel, with no hint of criticism such as we find in Barbara Comyns' disturbing novel *The Skin Chairs* (1962), where the chairs upholstered with the skins of black and white victims of the Boer War provoke a need to atone in the child protagonist.[80] Instead, a Mitford character sees a man's experience of Dunkirk as 'something out of *Boys' Own* – he seems to have had a most fascinating time',[81] a far cry from Bowen's view in *The Heat of the Day*. Indeed, Mitford offers a grim reminder that some of the less attractive political opinions of the thirties still continue to flourish at the end of the forties, despite the bomb and the Holocaust.

Under the shadow of the bomb in the fifties and sixties

In the fifties and sixties, the effects of the bomb and the atrocities of the War strengthened their hold on the imagination. There was a widespread physical fear of nuclear warfare, a sense of helplessness and unwillingness to subject children to a world where such things were possible; and there was also a growing need to make sense of the world in existential terms, as traditional faiths in higher authority had, for many, proved themselves inadequate. Accordingly we find women writers taking different paths. Some look back, often offering routes from the past which may inform and make sense of the present, or showing how awesomely the times have changed, as Rebecca West, in *The Fountain Overflows* (1957), has her protagonist observe, looking back to the end of the last century: 'It is strange how it was in the air in those days, the belief that war crime and all cruelty were about to vanish from the face of the earth, even little girls knew it to be a promise that was going to be kept'.[82] Other novelists deal with the present, analysing the sense of powerlessness in the context of the politics of the time, and exploring the microcosmic world of personal relationships to make sense of perceived dysfunctions in society; and still others looked to the future in an attempt to assess where current trends might lead.

Of those looking back, there is, for instance, Rose Macaulay in her haunting novel *The World My Wilderness* (1950), where the child, Barbary, is shown as unable to cope in a post-war world, so imbued is she with the philosophy of the French resistance movement, the Maquis. Macaulay sees the emergence of a new barbarism very much in line with destroyers of civilization throughout human history. Barbary's brother sees how:

> Barbarism prowled and padded, lurking in the hot sunshine, in the warm scents of the maquis, in the deep shadows of the forest. Visigoths, Franks, Catalans, Spanish, French, Germans, Anglo-American armies, savageries without number, the Gestapo torturing captured French patriots, rounding up fleeing Jews, the Resistance murdering, derailing trains full of people, lurking in the shadows to kill, collaborators betraying Jews and escaped prisoners, working together with the victors, being in their turn killed and mauled, hunted down by mobs hot with rage; everywhere cruelty, everywhere vengeance, everywhere the barbarian on the march.[83]

Again we find pacifism at the core of a woman writer's work, even though Macaulay was one of those who had reluctantly abandoned her former pacifist stance as fascist forces overran Europe – the Korean war, for many, reawakened a pacifist response, as a war too many. Macaulay, in this novel, no longer offers comic satire; she anticipates Lessing's *Memoirs of a Survivor* (1974), as Barbary 'translates' the Maquis ethos she has grown up with in France to the bombed sites of London.[84] The legacy which the past has bequeathed to this child offers no great hope for her future. Lettice Cooper's novel *Fenny* (1953) also explores the impact of war on a child, and on an apolitical protagonist, a governess working in Italy.[85] The public and private worlds of Ellen, the governess, are brought together by violence as the Rome–Berlin Axis is visibly strengthened; and her longing for non-involvement leads to an argument with her lover, Arturo, a member of the Italian resistance, as he protests:

> Of course you think that we should all stand aside and do nothing! It is what your own country has done! You betrayed us in Spain, in Czechoslovakia! You yourself have been living happily for years in the household of a woman whose brother is a notorious Fascist!

When she retaliates with what Italy has done, ending with '*We* haven't used mustard gas! We haven't got a dictator!', he cries, 'No! You have an ignorant and foolish old commercial traveller!' (p. 209). Inevitably, Fenny is interned by the Germans, taking on a child whose mother dies in the camp, and, when released, she suffers all the deprivation of 'war-dented Florence' (p. 226). Cooper writes a good story, but on the whole she offers little more than recapitulation of the ideas found in many of the War novels, not making much of Fenny's internment. Only towards the end of the work does she engage with present fears, when a young girl observes that '"Brief life is here our portion" was all right when people were religious and could count on eternity. Now we don't feel that we can count on three years'; and Fenny says, 'Sometimes I think perhaps [the world] has to be fully conscious of despair before it can go on to the next stage' (p. 236). The effort to remain positive under the shadow of the bomb is palpable, and in the end Fenny's life revolves about the child she has saved, Dino, who, like Macaulay's Barbary, is an 'unregenerate creature' (p. 295), inevitably damaged by his experiences during the War.

Someone who looks even further back is E. M. Butler in her striking little novel *Daylight in a Dream* (1951), which sets its tale retrospectively against the background of Butler's own experiences with a Scottish nursing unit, sent to support the Russian imperial army in World War One, only to be caught up in the Revolution of 1917.[86] Butler explores the effects that the confrontations with East Europeans and the mixing of classes within the unit has on her protagonist, Miss Rawlinson. Her later life is ruled by fantasies about the superiority of the upper-class girls in her unit, and her bitterness at failing to find the standards she ascribes to them affects her treatment of the students she later teaches – she has become 'an unwitting slave to a tyrannical ideal she had learnt to worship in the past' (p. 31). Dysfunctional aggression here stems from wartime experiences which distort a professional woman's view of her world until her fantasies are dispelled by one of the very women she has tried so hard to emulate. This representative of the upper class calls herself and all those who served in the unit 'war-victims' (p. 78), who could never fully recapture the lives they had lived before the War. Here experiences of one war and the effect they have on a post-war state of mind keep their resonance in the aftermath of World War Two.

Attitudes to the past vary enormously in these works of the fifties. Ethel Mannin, for instance, in *Lover under Another Name* (1953), takes something of the same line as Vera Brittain, but far more truculently.[87] Basing her work in London, Mannin sees 'no point' in writing about the Blitz since, she says, it would have been worse in Berlin or Warsaw or Stalingrad; and when she refers to Hiroshima, she speaks, bitingly, of 'exhilaration' as the reaction in the suburbs (p. 217). Bryher (Annie Winifred Ellerman), on the other hand, sets her novel *Beowulf* (1956) in London's West End during the Blitz, and explores the effect on a range of characters who have the Warming Pan tea-shop as their meeting place. This is very much a work centred on private lives, although there are a number of attacks on thirties' complacency as responsible for the present conflict. But on the whole the characters are concerned with more immediate issues. Selina, for instance, 'hated ration cards, less because she wanted more food for herself than because they were a symbol of some poverty of spirit' (p. 30). Yet the reassessment which asserts itself so often in the novels of the fifties is there, as when the retired Colonel thinks, 'Perhaps civilization was really unbearable, and in some rage of protest man had duplicated the conditions of the beginning of the world?' (p. 179); or when the young girl, Eve, looks at the ruins of the tea-shop, destroyed in an air-raid, and thinks:

> It was true that the dark shapes grouped themselves into the forms of some old canvas and the colours were less black and purple than a patina of oil, age, and dust. Yet there was a new element of violence that was beyond apprehension and rational emotion. It had scooped out, somehow, a part of her own being.
>
> (pp. 188–9)

Turning to Europe once again, Storm Jameson shows the same sense of a world which needs to look beyond pre-war moral structures in her haunting novel *The Hidden River* in 1955. This work again explores the difficult issues of fraternization and collaboration; as in *The World My Wilderness*, people living in occupied territory are seen as inevitably contaminated by the violence, both of the invaders and of the resistance, so Jameson turns to Greek culture to give some sense of the morality of the time. Old Marie in her black dress resembles Nemesis, the spirit of Greek tragedy; when her nephew dies, having acknowledged his guilt for betraying her son to the Gestapo and so causing his death, her implacable attitude is seen as something quite outside the accepted cannon of Western civilization – but she is not condemned for that. Jameson in her own way, therefore, acknowledges the failure of pre-war standards of morality to cope with the situations confronting Europe, and Adam, the English protagonist, as the French family's tense drama is played out, has his own sense of what constitutes tragedy revised and refocussed.

But Europe is not the only scene of conflict to be addressed by novelists at this time where a grim revision of previously held certainties has to be confronted. As I mentioned earlier, Attia Hosain looks back, in a poignant and superbly structured novel, on the effects on a Moslem family of the gradual growth of the forces in India which produced Partition. In *Sunlight on a Broken Column* (1961), Hosain shows how poor relatives of the central family are drawn to the independence movement, Asad, to non-violence, and Zahid (who will later be among those massacred on a train taking him to Pakistan) to the Moslem League. The novel tells of the gradual intrusion of violent conflict into the normal round of family affairs and celebrations of festivals; the pacifist Asad is injured in one such confrontation between Moslems and Hindus. At college, Hosain's protagonist, Laila, acquires friends representing a wide range of sympathies from passionate Hindu, or pro-British, to those of the revolutionary Nita Chatterji, who helps to organize opposition to the British, and dies from her injuries after a student demonstration. In the final section of the novel, Hosain shows the remnants of Laila's family as refugees in India, while some of its members have gone to Pakistan. Laila recalls the war, and the eruption of extreme nationalism, with the Congress leaders imprisoned in 1942; and she remembers the climactic events of 1946, the partition of 1947, and the 'putrescent culmination' after this (p. 290). Tragically, her own husband, who had suffered under the aristocratic disapproval of her family, had joined the PR branch of the Army, was sent to the Middle East, and was killed in 1942. Laila's large and lively family has been utterly fragmented by conflicting ideologies and the ensuing violence.

As all the above novels show, the urge to revisit the past to explore routes to the present, is very strong in the fifties and sixties. As I observed earlier, many of those women writers who attempt to come to terms with the present, writing under the shadow of the bomb and Hiroshima, tend to turn their attention to the roots of violence within the community or the family, demonstrating Freud's assertion that violence is an integral part of human nature. Sylvia Townsend Warner, for instance, traces the development of a Victorian patriarch in *The Flint Anchor* (1954), subtly hinting that he is as much a victim of his society's expectations as his family are victims of his destructively conscientious tyrannies. Violence simmers just below the surface in this fine novel, residing as it does in the progressive destruction of love, its place usurped by hypocrisy and deception. Storm Jameson explores comparable developments within a twentieth-century family's divisions in her novel *The Green Man* (1952), tying their conflicts very clearly with the world of war which they inhabit. As one character says: 'this time we've gone too far. We've killed ourselves with our cruelties' (p. 352), and this

becomes a leitmotif as the novel progresses. Jameson again demonstrates how acceptance of the need for World War Two does not oblit-
erate strong leanings towards pacifism as the truly civilized position. We
hear, for instance, Andrew's father debating with himself responsibility
for the atom bomb. First he blames the scientists, but then:

> his belief, his passionate belief in human freedom, answered him
> that, since we are free, each of us is always responsible for his inten-
> tions: the intentions of the brilliant minds who planned a new form
> of death – I mean, of dying – are all theirs: but not only theirs: men
> created the instrument of a fiendish cruelty, men gave the order to
> use it, and used it. Therefore all men are responsible: it is – the others
> can be dodged – the only unbreakable natural law. All of us lie under
> the judgement reserved for hubris. The idea of obliterating human
> life over a vast area, once put into practice, has no limits. In the
> agony of another war, the gesture will be repeated. The sooner it's
> over the sooner to bed, as they say. Until the moment, all regrets and
> sanctities purged, when murderer and victim lie together quietly,
> while the cuckoo sings.
>
> (p. 675)

This bleak awareness of a responsibility which is too often abused lies
at the heart of many novels of the period dealing, not only with world
war, but with those violated by their families or by the community. At
the beginning of this chapter, I noted a range of such novels, all of
which set the capacity for violence at the very core of so-called civilization, impinging on individual lives. Christine Brooke-Rose's *The Sycamore Tree* (1958), for instance, links the personal and the public use of
violence very clearly, as uneasy relationships reflect the ugliness of the
crushing of the Hungarian uprising in 1956. Ruthless invasions of privacy are tied, in the wake of Freud, to the Russian invasion; Zoltan, the
Hungarian refugee, has attempted to cloak his identity as a famous poet
to escape to England, only to be hounded by those who want his manuscript, while Nina, set on a pedestal by her adoring husband, also takes
on the identity of a prostitute to escape this suffocating role, only to find
herself at the mercy of an obsessed lover who is also after Zoltan's
manuscript. In the end, she is caught in the cross-fire, quite literally, as
Zoltan shoots at his persecutors; she dies and Zoltan destroys himself.
Brooke-Rose so entwines the fates of her characters with the world in
which they live that she does not need to spell out the extent of the
responsibility for their destruction.

The same sense that responsibility for the larger issues in the world cannot be conveniently assigned solely to the authorities is at the core of a number of novels which can be read as continuing the debates of the thirties on pacifism and on violence in the very different context of the fifties and sixties. Pamela Frankau, for instance, in *The Offshore Light* (1952), produces a novel quite unlike anything else she wrote.[88] This novel has affinities with Doris Lessing's later work, *Briefing for a Descent into Hell* (1971),[89] since Frankau's protagonist, Brooke Alder, the American President's European Adviser in the atomic age, breaking down under the stresses of his job, enters an alternative world where he inhabits an apparently idyllic island, a place that was saved 'when the world destroyed itself' (p. 61), and which is inhabited by a 'moneyless community', the majority of whom 'do not admit progress as the answer to mankind's salvation' (p. 62). But there are some who long for change. Gradually, it becomes clear that the people Alder knows in the 'real' world have been transformed into inhabitants of his island, their conflicts being played out there; and as his island life gradually encroaches on this 'real' world, Alder finally kills a neurologist, identifying him with the island's German scientist who is, he fears, developing a weapon from the island's raw material, 'a force that, unleashed, can send the whole world and the island up into nothingness' (p. 242). Clearly Alder's breakdown is directly linked with his fears in and for the 'real' world, and Frankau leaves us in no doubt that, while he may have broken down, his fears are by no means irrational. Alder says at one point that Hitler and Stalin, while maladjusted, are in fact scapegoats: 'We are as responsible as they'; since all men are potentially evil, all are to blame – 'from the philosopher to the advertizer. From the psychiatrist to the soap-manufacturer. From the delicate agnostic to the high-powered salesman' (p. 250) – all are meretricious sellers of happiness. Frankau centres the disintegration of Alder's mind upon the fear of the bomb and the general sense of a world that has lost its way, a world, as Alder says, whose aim is 'unidentifiable'.

Doris Lessing's *The Four-Gated City* (1969) also explores breakdown, but more positively than Frankau's novel. Lessing suggests it may be a way to expand consciousness and establish alternative values in a world of violence where, among other things, she shows some of the more terrifying possibilities of scientific research which could be put to military use: Jimmy's machine, 'that could stimulate or destroy areas of the brain' (p. 392), for instance, recalling the fascist doctor's programme in Jameson's *Then We Shall Hear Singing*. But Lessing is ultimately more sanguine than either Jameson or Frankau; she extends her novel into a

future, beyond a catastrophic nuclear war, where the survivors are seen
to be acquiring greater mental powers; the human race is evolving
impressively.

It is particularly striking to see so many of the novels of the fifties and
sixties exploring breakdown and madness as responses to the violence,
physical or psychological, inflicted on individuals by the family or the
wider community; it is as if the War has set all the vaunted values of
Western civilization in the dock, to be tried by those who have been
marginalized. Veronica Hull's woman protagonist in *Monkey Puzzle*
(1958), Jennifer Dawson's in *The Ha-Ha* (1961), Penelope Mortimer's in
The Pumpkin Eater (1962) and Lessing's in *The Golden Notebook* (1962) all
show how they have to fight, often literally, to retrieve a sense of their
own identity in a hostile world.[90] Arguably, this takes us back to Freud's
reply to Einstein in 'Why War?' (1932–3), when he explores the meaning
of the German word *Gewalt* which can mean both 'violence' and
'power', showing how the power of the law originally came out of
violence and can still use violence if it feels itself threatened. The threat
from within is what these novelists deal with, the little people who are
the victims of the law's power and who are being crushed for failure to
conform to its edicts, the people who would interest Foucault in his
Madness and Civilisation. This loss of faith in the structures of Western
civilization is surely a long-term legacy of two world wars.

Yet *The Four-Gated City* does suggest that there is some shred of hope
for the future; and this, up to a point, is also true of Brigid Brophy's
comic satire, *Hackenfeller's Ape* (1964), even if the future Brophy offers is,
by implication, several degrees less exalted than Lessing's. Brophy's
mischievous fable links contemporary society closely with the fate it
inflicts on a captive ape (genetically, we are told, almost identical with
its human captors), since the zoologist who champions the ape's cause
tells the animal, ' "When my species has destroyed itself, we may need
yours to start it all again." '[91] All too predictably, however, the ape is
eventually shot, for, as the zoologist comes to accept (borrowing from
Freud the concept of the inevitability of humankind's propensity for
violence), he is living in a twentieth century which is 'the Age of Cain'
(p. 65). Yet despite all this, despite man's inhumanity to man and
monkey, a baby ape is born to take his father's place. Brophy may not
have much faith in humanity, but she does allow something genetically
close to humanity to survive, even if its first response to the world is a
'roar of wrath' (p. 160). Yeats's rough beast seems to stand for the future
humanity can hope for in this novel. Naomi Mitchison's futuristic
science fiction novel *Memoirs of a Spacewoman* (1962) is rather more

optimistic, although again Mitchison is acutely aware of potential
threats to the achievement of better understanding of human responsibility. Ten years earlier, in *Travel Light* (1952), she had offered a fable
which explores personal responsibility for violence, the heroine having
to learn how to control and contain the dragonish part of her nature.[92]
In the later *Memoirs*, in tune with growing awareness about the effects of
colonialism, Mitchison extends her concern about violence and the
possibility of violation to interaction with other communities; at one
point she says of one race she meets:

> The Epsies had colonised very vigorously, and at a period of moral
> crudity, which luckily humans had lived through and put behind
> them by the time they reached the technical excellence in space
> travel that the Epsies had achieved earlier.[93]

Yet while her human space explorers have strict rules against interference with other cultures, which on the whole they observe, Mitchison
hints that humankind is still very much interested in economic interference if the explorers find something which is materially valuable to
them. Her acute awareness of economic imperialism haunts the novel,
as the sixties became aware of voices from former colonies revisioning
the past, in yet other ways than those looking to Britain and Europe. As
Freud had seen, violence is deeply ingrained in human nature; and one
of the valuable offerings made by writers of these four decades to their
readers has been a frank appraisal of what violence is capable of, both in
the public and the private world. The love or, at least, identification
which Freud advocated in 'Why War?' as the only way of avoiding such
violence is shown to be desperately fragile; the urge to marginalize those
who do not conform to the standards by which any group or society
defines itself is, by contrast, very strong. And the capacity of the very
structures which uphold 'civilization' to use their powers against those
they perceive as threats is, as Freud saw, ever present, as I shall explore in
the chapter on marginalization.

3
Marginalities of Race and Class

Marginalities shift and change, especially over a period of forty years. Beryl Gilroy notes that the struggle to define them exists 'not only between Black and white but between all those who find grounds on which differences could be pin-pointed and measured (for example, tribe, class, religion, politics, shades of colour, class and economics) – any ingredient that could produce dissension';[1] that is to say, those who stand secure in what they regard as a dominant group, whether within a country or a football crowd, will marginalize those whom they perceive as not belonging there. Zygmunt Bauman argues that:

> Modern culture is a garden culture. It defines itself as the design for an ideal life and a perfect arrangement of human conditions. It constructs its identity out of distrust of nature ... It classifies all elements of the universe by their relation to itself. This relation is the only meaning it grants them and tolerates.[2]

And he comments, ironically, that in this garden culture, 'weeding out is a creative, not a destructive activity' (p. 92).

Marginalization, exclusion, has of course always been with us; Beryl Gilroy points out its 'undying nature',[3] and we are still a long way from answering Maud Ellman's plea that we 'look beyond the pieties of identity politics to rediscover the radical singularity of human experience'.[4] Raphael Samuel, looking specifically at Britain, observes that 'Minorities have not normally had an easy time of it', as 'tolerance, though it enjoys an honoured place in the pantheon of national virtues ... hardly survives historical scrutiny as a distinctive national strength'.[5] He asserts that 'the ideas of national character have typically been formed by processes of exclusion, where what it is to be British is defined in its relations of opposition to enemies both without and within' (p. xviii); and he concludes:

> Politically, Britain may be a pluralist society, as it has been, notion-
> ally, through three centuries of representative government. Behav-
> iourally, though, it is fearful of departures from the norm ... In public
> discourse 'British characteristics' (as the Prime Minister [Thatcher]
> calls them) are still spoken of as though they were generic, the
> 'British' as though they were a single people, 'the British way of life'
> as though it were organic – a natural harmony which only the
> malevolent would disturb, a shared condition which newcomers
> must adapt to.
>
> (p. xxii)

Bryan Cheyette agrees, arguing specifically that racial minorities in this country are vulnerable to 'particularist definitions of Englishness predi-cated on the fixity of the past'.[6] What is more, as Paul Gilroy observes, race itself is a complex, 'cultural-biological' concept that: 'can change, assuming different shapes and articulating different political relations'.[7]

The most obvious marginalities in England throughout the period I am exploring are racial, but there are others. Those who are pregnant outside marriage, those seeking abortion, those whose sexual orienta-tion is perceived as deviant, are some examples of those who in their time have been thrust to the margins, as have those who cannot cope with the lifestyle of their perceived group and break down. Then too there are those who are marginalized because of class, or the region of the country they come from. And there are the particular cases that result from war, such as refugees, evacuees, internees. Most of those who exclude insist on essentialist definitions of what is to be excluded: there tends to be a refusal to see this problem in terms of the individual, as putting a face on the enemy complicates the issue, and, of course, what is perceived as marginal will differ from group to group, and the emphases will shift over time. I shall in this chapter confine myself to issues concerning race and class which women writers have addressed. Writing about such issues is inevitably full of pitfalls, since exploring prejudices can be read as a form of endorsement, as Gillian Rose warns: 'it is possible to mean well ... yet to be complicit in the corruption and violence of social institutions';[8] and it is certainly true, as Cheyette observes, that 'while literary texts might well help to change perceptions over a long period of time, they rarely have a transformative impact that is not in itself intimately related to wider social issues'.[9] Yet to address prejudices, to expose them by giving them recognizable faces, may be worth the risk, as it may at least begin to persuade readers to see the enormity of the problem, and fiction, by drawing its readers in, may even encourage them to implicate themselves. At the very least, as Suresh Renjen Bald says, 'Fiction, by creating a compact, accessible world which reflects the writer's view of reality – what is, what is not, and what ought to be – provides the reader with glimpses of the writer's world view'.[10]

Race, empire and wage-slaves in the thirties

With the growth of fascism in the thirties, the main racial issue to which writers address themselves is anti-Semitism, and there was good reason for them to do so. As early as 1933, reports about concentration camps were blocked; and, despite the activities of the British Union of Fascists, foreign correspondents reporting from Europe were treated with caution by the BBC and the press as the decade wore on, particularly if they were Jewish, as it was felt that their assessments of the situation might be biased.[11] Hopes for appeasement overrode the admission of what was happening, and Chamberlain's placing of East European suffering in 'a far away country of which we know nothing' meant that the British public did not have its attention drawn to the Nazi genocide campaign. The need for writers to address the issue was urgent, especially given the latent anti-Semitism in Britain. As Arthur Koestler and others have demonstrated, *The Brown Book of Hitler Terror* (1933) was an early attempt to publicize the atrocities committed by the Nazis, and other works followed.[12] Stevie Smith's *Novel on Yellow Paper* (1936) and *Over the Frontier* (1938), for instance, use the strategy of implicating the narrator in anti-Semitic feeling. In *Over the Frontier*, Pompey says:

> I am in despair for the racial hatred that is running in me in a sudden swift current, in a swift tide of hatred, and Out out damned tooth, damned aching tooth, rotten to the root.
> Do we not always hate the persecuted?
> ... But I have had some very dear Jewish friends.
> Oh final treachery of the smug goy. Do not all our persecutions of Israel follow upon this smiling sentence?[13]

This is a perilous tactic, but one that at least avoids any appearance of superiority. As Phyllis Lassner observes, 'Through her relentless questioning, Pompey Casimilus represents the possibility for historical change and for freeing the representation of the Jew from the historical dangers of ambivalence'.[14] Sylvia Townsend Warner, in *Summer Will Show* (1936), also implicates her protagonist, Sophia, in anti-Semitism, showing her contempt for Minna's Jewishness before she actually meets Minna and hears Minna's compelling story of her family's direct experience of persecution. Warner's novel may be set in 1848, but the racial issues revealed in it simply underline that little had changed in the last ninety years.

Phyllis Bottome and Storm Jameson deal much more directly with what was happening in Europe during the thirties. While Bottome tells a fine tale in her novel *The Mortal Storm* (1937), her main concern is to persuade her readers to confront the injustice of the persecution being meted out to European Jews, and, like Jameson in *Europe to Let* (1940), she delivers clear messages. Asked 'What is being a Jew?' a father tells his son, among other things, that, 'it is to belong to a race that has given Europe its religion; its moral law; and much of its science – perhaps even more of its genius – in art, literature and music';[15] and later he says,

> Italians also have dark skins and black hair – the Japanese yellow skins and shining hair – they will be, if they are not yet, the respected friends and allies of Germany – this difference of skins and features will be easily overlooked when the interests are the same.
>
> (p. 133)

Bottome does take risks. But as with her depiction of the East End slums in *London Pride*, she is addressing an area rarely portrayed in the literature of the time other than through the traditional stereotypes. It is possible, for instance, to criticize the fact that many of the Jews in her novels are presented as Christian, or, at least, non-practising Jews[16] – but is this to make them more acceptable to their readers, a kind of concession to innate prejudice, implicitly ghettoizing practising Jews, or is it to implicate the readers who cannot therefore entirely define her Jews as 'other', having to accept them as assimilated members of their community? As Bryan Cheyette says, writers 'actively construct [Jews] in relation to their own literary and political concerns',[17] and all of Bottome's career as a novelist shows her as a passionate defender of those she perceives as marginalized. But in the end, readers too construct the texts they read in relation to their own literary and political concerns; in reading any novel about the marginalized, a great deal will depend on the reader's point of view.

While the situation of Jews in Europe is increasingly a matter for concern in fiction as the decade progresses, attitudes to the British

Empire are much more complicated. In 1929, for instance, the Communist Party of Great Britain unequivocally links the fates of the colonies with that of the working class at home, asserting that:

> The present crisis of Great Britain...consists in the struggle of a decadent empire, torn with economic and social contradictions, against the forces of social revolution developing within its frontiers, as evidenced by the vast unrest amongst the propertyless masses of Britain and the colonies.[18]

Others join in this condemnation. In 1933, for instance, Winifred Holtby makes a powerful attack on colonial propaganda, in her discussion of the film *Round the Empire*. She says:

> The masterpiece comes with Africa. 'Africa is, even now,' continues that cultured voice regretfully, 'predominantly native'. How sad! Just think of that, after all these years of British rule. In Australia and Canada our virile race succeeded admirably in reducing Red Indians or aborigines to quite insignificant proportions, but the tiresome Africans continue to increase and multiply.[19]

And in her novel of the same year, *Mandoa, Mandoa!*, Holtby attempts to give an African view of Western civilization.[20] Her fictional country, Mandoa, attracts the attention of a British tourist company, but, as Mandoa has a slave economy, the directors decide it must be cleaned up so that its 'primitive world' conforms to British standards of decency. Holtby interweaves satirical attacks on the hypocrisies practised by the British both at home and abroad, in public and in the privacy of the family, with a view of how these may appear to an outsider, her protagonist, Talal. However, while Mandoa is an African country, its citizens are not black Africans but descendants of European Jesuits, which is an important if unemphatic distinction in Holtby's plot; the British in the novel call both Mandoans and their black African slaves wogs and niggers, establishing a complacent Otherness which quite fails to detect similarities in cultural exploitation. But Holtby makes the similarities clear. For instance, the Englishman, Bill Durrant, tries to explain to Talal how British society works, but:

> when Bill described the queue at the Labour Exchange, Talal countered with the slave train to Abyssinia and the Red Sea. When Bill urged the mercy of unemployment allowance, Talal remarked that in

Mandoa, if a noble allowed his slaves to starve, he lost the worth of them. When Bill conceded that Socialists spoke of the British system of wage-slavery, Talal shrugged his shoulders and observed that the attitude of the League of Nations towards his [fellow slave traders] in Abyssinia was all the more incomprehensible.

(p. 140)

Talal is no fool when it comes to interpreting what he hears; he compares the British exploitation of the Kikuyu in Kenya where 'No Briton *owns* a Kikuyu', but where the British system reduces the Kikuyu to penury and the hopelessness of indentured labour, with his own practice: 'Now *I* have slaves. I have bought them. I must feed and clothe and house them. I must make women fine and strong mothers, must buy strong breeding men, must feed children till they can work' (p. 140). Holtby's method is Swiftian here, offering a shocking reasonableness that throws into sharp relief the dystopias at home and abroad, while elsewhere the would-be 'developers' of Mandoa mouth their self-justifying fictions about the civilization the West can offer. Holtby takes the risk of ventriloquizing African voices but, by giving them a share in a European genealogy, limits the risk of the common imperialist habit of asserting, as her character Bill says, ' "I know what you want better than you do!" ' (p. 334). Inevitably, however, this strategy means that the novel concentrates on the shortcomings of British attitudes and behaviour; Holtby does not pretend to give a genuinely African point of view, hence the fact that her Mandoan characters are at least partially European by descent. Her awareness of the flaws in British imperialism is clear – yet while she is far more liberal in her views than many of her compatriots, she remains, as Barbara Bush notes, curiously 'committed to the "higher ideals" of empire'.[21] This is, indeed, another of the confusions which becomes evident in the thirties: anti-racism did not necessarily mean a total rejection of imperialism.

Jean Rhys is in a far stronger position to speak for the colonized in her novel *Voyage in the Dark* (1934), and as a result she complicates the issue of race where Holtby arguably simplifies.[22] Rhys's protagonist, Anna, is a white Creole, trying to establish a life for herself in an unfriendly England, where, to add to her problems, she has to contend with racism, since, white or not, Creoles in the England of the time were treated as inevitably racially mixed. Torn between vivid, colourful memories of the Caribbean island which she thinks of as home and the grey, rootless existence she comes to in England, Anna is, as Susheila Nasta says, an early representative in Rhys's works 'of a kind of cultural schizophrenia'.[23] And Nasta, comparing this work with novels by later black writers, continues:

> The experience of Britain does not create a simple antithesis between tropical exoticism and darkness in a cold clime, nor is the meeting of the two worlds in the imagination easily reduced to a nostalgic vision of a lost paradisaical childhood and an alien world which replaced it. The problem is, more centrally, one...of different modes of apprehending reality which have to be accommodated within a new context.
>
> (p. 50)

Rhys's Anna has to abandon an illusory idea of London based on colonial myth; and the psychological and physical abuse Anna sustains as she attempts to come to terms with the demythologized reality mirrors the kinds of violation which Rhys's heroine in *Wide Sargasso Sea* undergoes. Yet Rhys's Anna, while at times she longs to be black, knows that she cannot entirely accept or be accepted by black culture. As Elaine Savory says, 'What Rhys offers us is a chance to look at race in all of its complexity: she earns our respect by not fudging her own contradictions, her ability to be both racist and anti-racist, both resentful and sentimental about race'.[24] And Rhys stands out, in the thirties, as an authentic voice with the first-hand experience of an incomer from a colony. It is no more than appropriate that her protagonist, Anna, should stand tragically alone. A useful novel to compare is one by an established English white writer, Elizabeth Cambridge's *Portrait of Angela* (1939), which gives a liberal view of relations between white and black inhabitants of the fictional French island of Saintes Maries; for instance, white Angela says of black Marie, who is training to be a teacher, that she is 'the prototype of the girls of my own class who were battering their way into professions'.[25] Yet Cambridge is perceptive enough not to take the analogy too far; Marie does not have the career she hopes for and her frustration and disappointment are clearly shown. Cambridge does not satirize imperialism, but she is not wholly accepting; her novel is simply an indication of how subtly British attitudes were changing among those with political and social sensitivies.

Rebecca West is particularly interesting, as we can trace her gradual move to disapproval of imperialism, and we can also see how rejection of racism precedes this. In *The Strange Necessity* (1928), despite her current socialist leanings, she still speaks of empire as 'a political necessity, and a glorious one',[26] although she does not accept a nationalism that involves racism, for in her novel *Harriet Hume* (1929) she can write bitingly of the attitude of the India Office (they cannot trace the where-abouts of her fictional creation, Mondh, although it is of central impor-tance in a Treaty):

> For the sake of the British Raj no white man must ever admit to a Mango that he does not know everything. Once the secret were to leak out, the insolence of the Mangoes at present studying law and mathematics in this country would become unbridled, and there would not be a rupee or a virgin left between Middle Temple Hall and Cambridge.[27]

By the end of the thirties, however, driven to contemplate empire in view of what had happened in the Balkans under the Ottomans and what was happening in Europe under Hitler, she writes in *Black Lamb and Grey Falcon* that her attitude to empire is changing. She says: 'There is not the smallest reason for confounding nationalism, which is the desire of a people to be itself, with imperialism, which is the desire of a people to prevent other peoples from being themselves';[28] and she admits, 'I became newly doubtful of empires', since 'the theory of the British Empire that it existed to bring order into the disordered parts of the world was more than half humbug' (p. 1089). What is more, 'a conquered people is a helpless people; and if they are of different physi-cal type and another culture from their conquerors they cannot avail themselves of anything like the protection which would otherwise be given them by the current concepts of justice and humanity' (p. 1091).[29] Yet although West disapproves of the conduct of empire, although she does show some understanding of the plight of the conquered, she does not give voices to 'the natives'; they suffer, but they are silent. None-theless, we can see how the racism and imperialism manifest in fascist dealings with Jews and with the countries in Europe and North Africa which were overrun in these years opened eyes to the similarities to be found in the empires of Western Europe.

In Virginia Woolf's *The Waves* (1931) and *The Years* (1937), the ques-tion of empire and colonialism is treated subtly, and, with its elegaic undertones, is resolved ambivalently, not wholly in line with West's comments in *Black Lamb and Grey Falcon*.[30] Linden Peach, for instance, points out that Woolf is fully aware of how the British define themselves by their Empire; but it is the British angle, the 'frightfulness', the loss of identity involved in the inevitable change of such definition when the Empire finally falls, that she contemplates. Peach shows how, in *The*

Waves, the imagery of the italicized interludes gives the 'shadow' side of Englishness and empire;[31] while, in *The Years*, Woolf goes further, making criticisms of the arrogance and complacency of British attitudes by letting characters condemn themselves out of their own mouths, or by evocative images. Inevitably, Woolf treads dangerously, as, all too often, what characters say in novels is suspected of being the author's voice, depending on our view of the author and especially when, as in Woolf's case, the voice of the narrator makes scarcely any comment on what the characters say. What is significant, I think, in both West's and Woolf's cases, is that while neither looks closely at the colonized, they do in their different ways distance themselves from the self-justifying domineering of the colonizer, as when Woolf in *Three Guineas* (1938) urges those who care about peace to stay away from 'patriotic demonstrations … military displays, tournaments, tattoos, prize givings and all such ceremonies as encourage the desire to impose "our" civilisation or "our" domination upon other people'.[32] And Woolf's plea suggests the same link between fascism and imperialism which Naomi Mitchison makes in *The Moral Basis of Politics* (1938). Mitchison pours scorn on the 'moral disapproval' expressed by the imperialist West over Italy's conquest of Abyssinia:

> It seems possible that this moral disapproval might have worked had those who made the moral attack *really* believed that the Fascist vision was incorrect (but their own immediate imperialist predecessors had seen the same kind of moral vision and they had been brought up to honour it).[33]

Outright statements of support for those within the confines of empire were not always successful, as Eleanor Rathbone's wrong-headed but passionately sincere championing of Indian women in the twenties and thirties makes clear, and which Mary Stocks chronicles in detail.[34] Indeed, we regularly find in the nonfiction and novels dealing directly with non-whites that the stereotypes are still firmly in place, although whether this is the author's view or a character's is often hard to determine. In Sylvia Townsend Warner's novel *Mr Fortune's Maggot* (1927), for instance, Lueli's innocence is perceived by Mr Fortune as stereotypically childlike; yet Mr Fortune is the one who, in the end, questions his own assumptions of superiority, handing the boy back the god of his birthright while losing faith in his own.[35] Warner returns to the theme of wrong-headedness about the colonized, but far more subtly, in *Summer Will Show* (1936); and here it is much clearer that she is exposing a lack in her white characters. For Sophia's uncle, who manages the family's Caribbean estate, sends his son to be educated in England – and the son is black. As with the Jesuit ancestry of Holtby's Mandoans, it is important to recognize that Warner's Caspar is related to Sophia; both Holtby and Warner quietly insist on the brotherhood of man, or rather, of humankind. Warner depicts Caspar sympathetically, as she did Lueli, and makes no bones about the racist attitudes he has to confront while, at the same time, her Caspar becomes for Sophia a living embodiment of freedom, a kind of mascot, from all the restrictions which plague her:

> With Caspar's coming something came into her life which supplanted all her disciplined and voluntary efficiency, a kind of unbinding spell which worked upon her lullingly as the scent of some opiate flower...It was not possible, while Caspar was in the house, to do anything but enjoy.[36]

Yet Sophia decides on a grey, prison-like boarding school for him in Cornwall, and Warner makes the school's confining role all the more telling as Cornwall is the setting for Sophia's own fantasies of freedom; the price of her sense of liberation is, by context, seen as Caspar's confinement, all the more so as what sustains her country house is the income from the estate managed by her uncle in the Caribbean. Yet Caspar has set something in motion, some freeing from convention which makes possible Sophia's relationship with the racial 'other' of Europe, the Jewess, Minna. Caspar, however, does not benefit from this. When he runs away from school to find her in Paris, Sophia feels no empathy for him, despite the fact that she has run away from her own constricting marriage; indeed, he has lost what she calls his 'Sambo charm' for her, is no more worthy of being her plaything and pet, 'all his wits had been bruised out of him, his one idea was to please and he had no idea as to how it was done' (p. 298). She shows no sign of feeling any responsibility for this, and guards her new-found freedom with Minna by thrusting Caspar away; is Warner suggesting that women, however denied public power, cannot deny their responsibility for empire? Whatever the truth of this, Caspar's adulation of Sophia, his desire to prove his equal status with her, causes him to treat Minna with the contempt which he has been shown (and in a sense, he is right to see Minna, however innocently, reaping the benefit for what he has donated). In the end, he is trapped into service of the very society which Sophia herself has renounced, showing the corrupting influence of colonialism which Frantz Fanon so deplores.[37] Certainly, Warner exposes in this novel the oversimplification which is inherent in Woolf's advocacy of a 'Society of Outsiders' in *Three Guineas*; standing aside is not enough. What we find in novels like Warner's is the beginning of a movement towards recognition of the Other as an entity urgently in need of consideration, not just as the negation of what is normal and right in so-called Western civilization. Without such beginnings, the great, if gradual, changes in attitude that occurred during and after World War Two would not have come into being.

A number of women writers, as we have seen, make the link between racial marginalization and the fate of the working class. Yet the ability to show the way the working class lived was something of a problem, as most writers of the period were themselves middle class despite the fact that the working class, according to Ross McKibbin made up over 70 per cent of the population during the thirties and forties.[38] The left-wing sympathies of many of the women writers of the period inevitably meant that the cause of the underprivileged was a keenly felt commitment, yet some influential critics felt that the working class could not be represented adequately by middle-class writers. Storm Jameson, for instance, asserts that the middle-class writer:

> does not even know what the wife of a man earning two pounds a week wears, where she buys her food, what her kitchen looks like to her when she comes into it at six or seven in the morning...he does not know as much as the woman's forefinger knows when it scrapes the black out of a crack in the table or the corner of a shelf...too much of [the writer's] energy runs away in an intense interest in and curiosity about his feelings.[39]

Queenie Leavis is more personal and more cutting, and in her case we can sense a justification of McKibbin's assertion that hers was an intensely class-conscious and class-antagonistic society. In a 1935 review, Leavis showers contempt on Naomi Mitchison's attempts to represent a cross-section of society, accusing her of snobbishness, complacency and intellectual pretentiousness in her novel *We Have Been Warned*.[40] Leavis compares Mitchison's work unfavourably with Storm Jameson's novel *Love in Winter*, saying:

> Miss Jameson too has set out to give a cross-section of contemporary society, and the comparison...is entirely in her favour. She shows how much can be done by observing and composing with nothing

more showy than stubborn honesty, humility and the sensitiveness that goes with solidity of character.[41]

Mitchison suffers the same fate as Woolf, some years later when, in a review of *Three Guineas*, Leavis deplores the fact that Woolf was quite insulated by class. Yet Leavis's response was not invariably shared by those of working-class background, as Anna Snaith has shown: the letters which Woolf received in response to *Three Guineas* come from readers, most of them women, from a wide variety of backgrounds, including the working class, most of them affirming ways in which Woolf's text has touched their lives.[42] Furthermore, while Jameson earns Leavis's respect for her depiction of working-class people and issues, she did not in fact come of a working-class background, although she did hale from the north, having grown up in Yorkshire. Her background is similar to Winifred Holtby's, who also offers excellent comparisons of different aspects of society in her novel *South Riding* (1936), showing, for instance, the inequities in medical treatment available to the poor as against the well-to-do. Certainly both novelists move easily between the classes, without the sense of entering alien territory which Mitchison's Dione experiences in *We Have Been Warned*. Jameson, in her thirties trilogy, The Mirror in Darkness, gives vivid accounts of the sufferings of the unemployed, a rare subject in the thirties, particularly among women writers. In the last volume of this sequence, *None Turn Back* (1936), she sets the desperate workers involved in the General Strike of 1926 against those who were equally determined to break it, and the novel acts as a powerful continuation, not only of her own trilogy but of Ellen Wilkinson's fine novel of 1929, *Clash*.[43] Wilkinson, herself of working-class background and another northerner, shows in this novel the effect of the Strike on the miners in the north, and on their wives. Importantly, she has her protagonist, the trade union organizer Joan, face a dilemma when she realizes that her endeavours to help the wives is undermining the purpose of the men, who see themselves as acting for their families; this is a sharp reminder that middle-class feminism could not be translated into working-class situations without much careful thought. Wilkinson was a powerful advocate for the sufferings of the unemployed and as MP for Middlesborough was directly involved in the events she describes. Later, while MP for Jarrow, she wrote her non-fictional *The Town That Was Murdered* (1939), reassessing the manipulation of the fates of the northern dockers by those in power during the long years of little employment.[44] Her approach is uncompromising: 'The poverty of the poor is . . . the permanent state in which the vast majority of the citizens of any capitalist country have to live' (p. 7); and there is an echo of Holtby's *Mandoa, Mandoa!* when Wilkinson comments, looking back at the long-term exploitation of the working class: 'Some of the proprietors of [1831] were shedding crocodile tears about slavery in America, while oblivious to, or even defending, the industrial atrocities in their own country... a habit the English still maintain to the annoyance of other nations' (pp. 34–5).

Ethel Mannin also produced a series of working-class novels during the thirties, drawing on her own background. In *Venetian Blinds* (1933), for instance, she shows the stresses on a family where the wife and mother has aspirations to climb the social ladder.[45] For Mrs Pendrick thinks her husband's relations 'common', while her own are terrifyingly 'set on respectability' (p. 31). Gradually she moves her family from house to house, always upwards through the fine gradations of working class to the lower ranks of the middle class; and on the way Mannin explores attitudes to sex, gender roles and the ostracizing of German neighbours at the outset of World War I. We are shown Mrs Pendrick's illusions about the middle class (she thinks, for instance, that they are never intolerant), and her ambitions for her son Stephen; he is not allowed to be a gardener, but must go to commercial school. Ironically, Stephen's girl friend now sees the Pendricks as 'common'; and when Stephen eventually marries another girl, her mother will not go to the wedding as she works as a charwoman and might, she thinks, let her daughter down. The younger generation's obsession with material things brings them little happiness, according to Mannin; Stephen's sister Elsie, forced by her pregnancy into a loveless, 'good' marriage is in despair, while her mother insists that 'It's money that makes class' (p. 390). In the end, Stephen, trapped in a dreary money-driven existence, can only dream about the 'properly organised' society he would like, where:

> there would only be men and women, and it would be all one whether your father was a duke or a dustman – only of course there wouldn't be any dukes, or business-magnates, or parasite women such as Elsie had become, 'kept women' made 'respectable' by law; there'd be no such thing as 'respectability', either, only self-respect, and the respect of one self-supporting human being for another... There'd be no pretentious little semi-detached villas, no fetish of keeping up appearances, no tyranny of shams, the great god Money would be pulled down from its pedestal...
>
> (p. 391)

The obsession with class that Ross McKibbin identifies as paramount during the inter-war years is alive and well in this novel (Mannin herself was a revolutionary in these years), and the snobbery affecting dealings between finely separated gradations of working and lower middle class is starkly, if compassionately, exposed.

More usually, however, women writers' novels (like most novels at this date) confine themselves to the middle class, and the poor and unemployed are virtually invisible. But occasionally we find a work satirizing the inadequacies of those in power. Rebecca West does this, for instance, in *The Thinking Reed* (1936), in which she mercilessly dissects the leisured classes.[46] She sees as their main difficulty that 'They had refused all succour offered to them by the mind, and there is simply not enough for the body to do unassisted during the whole twenty-four hours' (p. 94). West shows Isabelle's husband, Marc, quite failing to see his workers' unrest, ingenuously explaining away a strike:

> A master must take more than his men, otherwise there wouldn't be any masters, and the industries would never get anywhere. But it was so cleverly cooked up by the agitators that my poor children took it seriously, and we had a lot of trouble getting them to see reason... Why, do you know they talked as if it were not my money but theirs that I had spent?
>
> (pp. 116–18)

The links with imperialist thinking are very clear.

Inevitably, there are going to be blind spots in the confrontation of some kinds of marginalizations during the inter-war years; disability, for instance, is treated warily if at all at this time, especially in relation to masculinity (an issue I shall return to in the next chapter). But on the whole, we find that the women I have been examining have a good record in their protests against injustices. Most deplore racism, whether practised against Jews or the colonized, and we also find some of them making the link between fascism and imperialism, even if this link is resisted, as in the case of Rebecca West, until the late thirties. Some writers were also making the link between fascism and the exploitation of the working class, as well as with tyrannical attitudes to women; the implications of Nazi attitudes to women, for instance, are dramatically presented in Katharine Burdekin's futuristic *Swastika Night* (1937). In attitudes to the marginalized groups they espouse, what we find in these writers is a passionate commitment to the same point of view that Freud presents in 'Why War?', when he sees love or at least identification as the only way to avoid the grossness of conflict. But just as the championing of democracy against fascism complicated for some their commitment to peace, we also find a number of women writers showing unease as they see the links between fascism, with its avowedly racist agenda, and imperialist practice. In the end, the inter-war years presented vast and troubling confusions as new readings of established thought processes insisted on their validity; at such a time, when the fascism of the enemy was gradually being perceived as having its parallels within British practice, breaking down the benevolent image of a parental, caring empire, Woolf's stress on the 'frightfulness' of the process of rethinking personal and national versions of identity is at least understandable.

Xenophobia, merging and mixing in the forties

The issue of race, the marginalization of anything other than the Aryan, inevitably continues to be important during the war years, given the role it holds in Nazi doctrine. Interestingly, several women novelists concentrate on the racism they find at home rather than in Europe; the intention is clearly to encourage British readers to confront this on their own home ground. Dorothy Sayers is subtle in her approach, treating the subject of racial purity lightly in a speech delivered in 1940, arguing that the English have always been a mongrel race, and including 'Red Indian' and 'a dash of the tarbrush' in an imaginary family tree.[47] She claims, disingenuously, that

> A direct result of the mongrel nature of the English, and a thing very noticeable about them, is that they have never in their lives been what the Germans still are, that is, a *Volk*. From the first beginning of their Englishry, they have been, not a race, but a nation.
>
> (p. 69)

Clemence Dane in her historical novel *He Brings Great News* (1944) also has one of her characters claim that the 'English' are a mixed race:

> What were the English people but valiant, foolish, quarrelsome, independent men of all nations, fighters, wanderers, merchants, looters, runaways and saints who, during the last five thousand years, had drifted in from the four quarters of the world and beached upon the shores of Britain in search of security and a home. The motherly

island had gathered them in, settled them down, and by and by so fused them that no-one could say for certain: 'I know my stock', but only: 'I know my land'.

(p. 179)

But others do not let the British off so lightly. Storm Jameson, reviewing the work of a distinguished Polish refugee novelist, refers to the current aversion to the influx of refugees, as she declares the novel's theme to be:

that Eastern Europe of whose existence we English complain, without understanding, without for a moment understanding what a country loses with its loss of certainty, of permanent addresses, of unbroken family traditions. Or what it gains – in hatreds erected as a defence against memories of defeat and weakness.[48]

Eunice Buckley is initially more circumspect. Her novel *Destination Unknown* (1942) opens with the Jew, Ebermann, grateful for 'his own privileged position as a naturalized British subject'.[49] But having lulled the reader into conventional pride in Britain as the haven of the oppressed, Buckley then shows how Jews of European descent were distrusted in the early years of the war, refugees receiving much the same treatment as enemy aliens; after Dunkirk, we hear, 'feelings have become so much more bitter against foreigners' (p. 141). But just as Ebermann's family are consoling themselves with the thought that those of them condemned to internment will not suffer the same fate as in Nazi concentration camps, a cousin is sent overseas by the Camp Authorities, and we hear that he has been shipped to Australia:

under conditions which, when they became known, had aroused general indignation and provided the occasion for an inquiry in Parliament. In charge of exceptionally tough guards, these 'enemy aliens', among whom were artists, doctors, experts along many different lines, had been subjected to treatment worse than that accorded to the average criminal; men who in several instances had endured torture in Nazi prison camps had found themselves once again in the hands of bullying tormentors, who had robbed them of their few personal belongings and forced them, for the whole of that ghastly voyage, to live in conditions so appalling that more than one had been driven to take his own life.

(p. 190)

Buckley's protagonist does maintain that England is on the whole good to its Jewish population, but this concession can hardly compensate for the appalling lapse of those deportations, or the simmering distrust of those perceived as 'foreign' at this time.[50]

Ruth Adam, in *Murder in the Home Guard* (1942), while exposing inhumanity to evacuees in a complacent village, expresses a more ambivalent dislike of refugees like Greta Schwarz, who, employed as household helps, are seen as comparing 'each house unfavourably with the concentration camps they had avoided';[51] it is not entirely clear whether the novel is suggesting that this criticism of the foreigner (likely to be a Jewish foreigner, given her name) is unjustified. Certainly Monica Dickens, in *One Pair of Feet* (1942), seems not to connect blithely anti-Semitic comments on Jewish patients (one geriatric is nicknamed 'Judas Iscariot') with sympathetic awareness of what is going on in Europe;[52] one minute she can speak flippantly of a Jewish refugee from Warsaw, irritatingly keening 'like the lost tribes of Israel', and, a page later, comment that:

> The Warsaw from which she had fled must have been a city of spying and treachery and suspicion, of whispers in cafes and menacing glances and abusive notices mysteriously appearing on walls. How could you trust anybody when the people you knew, even your friends, appeared from one day to the next in Nazi uniform, and even your old servant turned informer?
>
> (pp. 27–8)

And such treatment was certainly not unknown in Britain. Inez Holden, in her novel *There's No Story There* (1944), shows the security chief of the munitions factory calling the foreman, Gluckstein, a foreigner, although he is English; and Gluckstein also finds daubed on his house the same mark which used to appear on East End homes in the days of the Mosley marches: 'P. J.' – Perish Judah.[53]

In 1935, Betty Miller submitted her fourth novel, *Farewell Leicester Square*, to Gollancz, only to have it refused (it was eventually published by Robert Hale in 1941). It is intriguing to speculate as to why Gollancz refused Miller publication; certainly the novel gives a hard-hitting account of what it felt like to be a Jew in England during the first few decades of this century. Miller's protagonist, Alec Berman, tries to shed his Jewish heritage yet is obsessed with his sense of difference, and Miller shows how destructive racial paranoia can be. Alec's future (Aryan) wife can say carelessly that their old house has been bought by 'some awful dago, I believe'; and Alec's immediate response is to think that 'Me, she means. Dago: Jew: Outsider...'[54] Ironically, what draws Catherine to Alec is precisely what she perceives as exotic: 'his dark, screened eyes: the matt, foreign skin' (p. 113); she cannot understand Alec's explanation of 'what it means to be born a Jew', with what he terms 'the terrifying lack of security: the sense that all one has yearned and striven for (the every-day happiness which any human being is entitled to) is entirely at the mercy of politicians, is challenged by every hostile word, look, gesture' (p. 132). He tells her, 'You've never had the experience of hearing your own race casually vilified' (p. 134), and shockingly, when Catherine protests, 'this is England', Alec counters with 'Yes. The concentration camp is only *spiritual* here' (p. 135). At first, the marriage between these two seems to negotiate the minefields successfully, but this changes as their son is growing up and, when the child is involved in a fight at school because he is a Jew, Catherine leaves, taking their son (blond and blue-eyed like herself) with her, writing that '*I'm not willing to accept the same scheme of disadvantages for my son*' (p. 247).

Yet Miller ends her novel with the hope that assimilation can be achieved, a hope which Buckley's protagonist also voices at the end of *Destination Unknown*. Both novels set out the dangers of Jews continuing to hold themselves apart from other races, both advocate the idea of a future merging with others. Yet neither novelist makes this claim in her own voice. Buckley shows the anti-Semitism which still exists in the war, and Miller offers an ugly moment as Alec is confronted by a newsvendor crying, 'Buy the only newspaper not run by Jewish finance!... Clear out the Jews! England for the English!' (p. 162). Buying a copy, Alec reads of how Jews are the 'International Mischief-makers' and of how they drink the blood of Christian children. Sylvia Townsend Warner, in the historical novel which she wrote during the War years, *The Corner That Held Them* (1948), reminds her readers of just how old this calumny is, as one of her nuns demonstrates: '"No Jews now", she chirruped, "to waylay poor little lads and hang them up in cellars. It was a good day for England when they were packed off".'[55]

During the War years, attitudes to empire remain much as they were in the inter-war years. Storm Jameson, for instance, continues to be clear-minded about the War in Europe; as one character says in *Then We Shall Hear Singing* (1942), 'You can't keep a country by hating and despising it', yet Jameson does not at this date apply her thinking to empire.[56] Dorothy Sayers, however, much further to the right than Jameson in her political stance, is readier to question imperialist attitudes. In an essay 'They Tried to Be Good' (1943), she points out that while enlightened thinkers treated as Divine Law the idea that 'people in Europe who spoke the same language and shared the same ideas should be made independent of rulers with other language and ideas', these same thinkers could not see that 'the British Empire was, of course, a horrid example of disobedience to this Law. Nobody was quite ready to coerce Britain into giving away her colonies, dependencies and scattered strong-points'.[57] And in another piece, 'The Gulf Stream and the Channel' (1943), she mockingly refers to a matter which was puzzling for foreigners; they wonder 'how it is that in the British mind the word "Empire" is understood to be a synonym for "liberty"'.[58]

Novels exploring relationships between black and white continue to be popular, yet their contents reveal that the basis for this popularity is more often a fascination with the exotic, rather than a genuine concern for the Other. It is instructive, for instance, to set E. M. Delafield's *No One Will Know* (1941) beside Jean Rhys's earlier *Voyage in the Dark*.[59] Delafield has some young English characters discussing forebears who were 'Creole' and speculating that they may have been 'black' (p. 10). As the novel looks back at this Creole ancestry, it is clear that the hint of mixed race is justified and adds, stereotypically, to illicit romance. The family, we are told, are 'a feckless lot', a typical Creole family, while the fatal attraction of uncle Fred is linked to 'his Creole ancestry unmistakably shown in his dark colouring, the whites of his heavy-lidded black eyes already faintly tinged with yellow and the indolence displayed in every movement when he was not actually exerting himself at sport' (p. 198); the family is suspected of being 'some kind of niggers in disguise', and there is the stereotypical threat: 'you wouldn't like a pitch-black grandchild, I suppose' (p. 220). The tale does not suggest any progress beyond exoticism and stock prejudice; Fred destroys his brother's marriage, passion triumphing over moral integrity. Martha Gellhorn offers a more sophisticated tale in her novel *Liana* (1944), based in the Caribbean and intriguingly sharing some of the features of Rhys's *Wide Sargasso Sea*.[60] Liana is a mulatto girl whom the European, Marc, marries and then tries to groom into whiteness; the girl is indeed well drilled, but may never meet the white wives, as Marc is ostracized because of his marriage. Bored, frustrated, and now alienated from her own family, Liana falls passionately in love with the French tutor Marc has engaged for her, yet in the end the young man has more in common with Marc through their shared European background. Liana, ever more alienated and humiliated, starts to drink heavily and, when her lover leaves to fight in France, she cuts her wrist and dies. Gellhorn cannot speak for Liana, but she makes clear the insidious corruption of a young girl who will never be accepted by the very 'civilization' that has robbed her of her roots.

The works of British writers which contain black characters are few and on the whole not successfully realized. Annabel Farjeon, for instance, in her short story 'The Rose' (1943), attempts to show a black working-class character, but he is woefully stereotyped.[61] When sad, 'his childlike, pensive expression darkened and he stared around puzzled and hurt' (p. 98); when he smiles his 'lips pressed back on the ivory teeth and gums, like those of a friendly dog' (p. 100). So although he is treated as a popular member of the pub 'regulars', it is always implicitly as a member of a less than adult culture. Yet the climate is changing, if almost imperceptibly. Edith Pargeter, referring to the Emperor of Ethiopia in *She Goes to War* (1942) may describe him as a 'savage' confronting his 'civilised conquerors', but the comparison is ironic, for she adds, 'Heaven preserve us from civilisation'.[62] The loss of faith in the European civilizations which for so long had claimed superiority over other races was beginning to take effect.

And of course British imperialist illusions of superiority have not only been meted out to non-whites, non-Europeans. Daphne du Maurier, in her historical novel *Hungry Hill* (1943), shows how four generations of landowners in Ireland exploited the local Irish miners in their copper mines as thoroughly as any in Africa.[63] Brodrick sets out in the early nineteenth century with well-intentioned paternalism, meaning to give 'employment to all the poor devils who find living next to impossible in this country' (p. 10); but his son is not interested in the mines except as a source of income and cannot understand why the locals 'have no desire to see their country either great or fine' (p. 117), even as he fails to ensure the safety of his workers. Finally we meet John-Henry, who has fought in World War One, and who can see 'both sides of the question' when he returns to The Troubles in 1920. He differs from the contemptuous British officer who says of the Irish, 'they're not human' (p. 402), being only too aware of how the present has deep roots in the past, and his summing up places the Irish situation firmly alongside experiences of imperialism elsewhere:

> It was strange...that his family had striven now for generations to bring progress to the country, and the country did not want it, and his family would not learn...The first John Brodrick might have lived longer and died in blessed old age had he the sense to understand the people could not be driven, and the land was theirs.
>
> (pp. 413–14)

Du Maurier is another writer who is often labelled conservative, yet, like Sayers, she is by no means reactionary in her attitude to the oppressed.

Naomi Mitchison, in *The Bull Calves* (1947), the historical novel she was writing throughout the War years, also looked at oppression, but this time the oppression of one group by another within eighteenth-century Scotland, mirroring as it does the racist suppressions of slavery abroad. Her protagonist Kirstie recalls a Highlander, condemned to the gallows for sheep-stealing, and how her uncle

> bought him off and held him as his slave ... In those days I had no great principles about such things, for I had seen little of them, but now I am certain that it is a terrible, unchristian thing for one Scot to be slave or serf to another, as I have seen in the Ayrshire coalmines and as my William saw in America on the plantations done to his own men ... and I am against it altogether.[64]

The Highlander, we are told, condemned to wear an iron collar as the token of his slavery, eventually drowned himself; and it is the High-lander, Black William, who, having been deported to the colonies, makes the link of oppressed race with oppressed class: 'I did see the Indians in America. And they are not unlike the rest of us Highlanders' (p. 138); while Kirstie recalls the cynical injustices of slave labour at home, where the Forth salt-pans were run by slaves, 'and the Whigs thought it none of their business to interfere since the owners of the salt-pan serfs would be supporters of the Government and that with money' (p. 392). The link with the inter-war dock owners, whom Wilk-inson had savaged in *The Town That Was Murdered*, is clear in Mitchi-son's novel and confirmed in her appended notes. The injustices of the inter-war years are still being debated throughout World War Two, and for many there was the hope that war would breed some kind of social revolution. Certainly the effects of war in placing people of different classes in close conjunction, whether in the services or in war work at home, began to erode the silences about social divisions. I have already mentioned the popularity of Phyllis Bottome's *London Pride* (1941), exploring the world of the East End slums during the Blitz. This work is not in Bottome's usual style, but unashamedly propagandist, its dedi-cation being 'To The Children of Bermondsey and Bethnal Green', with Blake's 'Jerusalem' printed underneath. The cast of characters is almost entirely working class, and there is a serious attempt to show the prior-ities of slum dwellers. Bottome clearly felt this was no time to heed

Jameson's advice about the dangers of a middle-class writer venturing into working-class terrain; her aim is to open the eyes of her middle-class audience. The attempt at Cockney pronunciation, syntax and idiom is, for the most part, more literary than exact, a problem that will continue for many years, as the Ealing Comedies bear witness; on the whole, what the characters do is caught well, but how they think and speak is less successful. We are given, for instance, a graphically unromantic view of birth among the poorest part of the community, but the language used is aimed at the middle class, as when the mother's response to the doctor is described: 'Mrs Barton felt rather as a knight must have felt receiving the accolade from his overlord';[65] or again, when Mr Barton, a Communist and admirer of Stalin, thinks of his hero, we are told, 'Mr Baron's stream of consciousness, out of which expletives reared themselves like submerged rocks, flowed back into comparative serenity over Old Joe [Stalin]' (p. 34). But Bottome, although she gives a somewhat anodyne picture of relations between the classes, did succeed in directing her readers' attention into unfamiliar territory, across a major class division – and Ruth Adam had shown by the treatment of the evacuee in *Murder in the Home Guard* how much lack of understanding and compassion there was to combat.

Inez Holden's *Night Shift* is more realistic. This work has fine vignettes of a range of characters from different classes, and a keen eye for the clashes which fine gradations of class difference inspire, as when 'the shadow of the class within the class' falls between two workers.[66] She also shows the middle class as out of place in the factory; marginalization is set on its head as the narrator speculates, for instance, on

> why this girl was in the factory. She was not of the working class, and I thought she was the sort of girl who would have been 'ladying it' at a First Aid Post attached to some auxiliary service. Perhaps something had happened to shake up her journey in the slow coach of security.
>
> (p. 13)

Then there is Peggy, who acts superior

> because she had been a clerk. In the canteen I had heard her saying, 'I always thought factory girls were a low class of girl'...she ignored that we were all working in a factory and that she herself was soon to give birth to a bastard...
>
> (p. 36)

Here, while bigoted notions of class are deplored, we find the same old prejudice against bearing a child outside marriage. Yet equally, Holden's narrator has a quick scorn for middle-class views on how the working class should be bettering their lot. Her middle-class 'Feather' declares that:

> the working classes were sabotaging themselves. Why couldn't they call out together for what they wanted... When Feather talked to me I could almost hear the prompting voices of several luxurious leftists – armchair sitters, Swan-pen writers, backs-to-the-fire shouters...
>
> (p. 55)

While Ross McKibbin rightly argues that during the 1940s the working class registered the biggest gains in their standard of living and their political influence, novels like Holden's show how the middle class was also being 'educated' in other points of view by wartime experiences.[67] Clearly this conjunction of classes was not easy, as Edith Pargeter also demonstrates in *She Goes to War*. Her narrator has friends of different classes, Myra and Gwyn, who 'look at each other with alien eyes';[68] the apparent breaking down of class boundaries may create a new world, or it may be a passing illusion, as the song Pargeter uses for an epigraph suggests:

> Democracy's our watchword,
> Lifting up our hearts,
> Democracy's the ticket –
> Wake me when it starts.

Pargeter's narrator both sees war as a maturing political process (she asks, did it take this to 'make socialists out of people like me?' [p. 186]) and is appalled by the minority with 'prefeudal ideas of class distinction' who argue that 'we don't want to recruit Lancashire girls' or are crudely racist, protesting (of American soldiers) that it is 'disgusting to think these niggers walk about actually on the same pavement as you' (p. 186). Democracy, she concludes, is at best 'half-hearted', 'a bit of a mirage' (p. 187).

Sylvia Townsend Warner's historical novel *The Corner That Held Them* (1948) again shows the usefulness of the sub-genre for exposing long-continuing attitudes of mind which are still relevant during World War Two. Warner reveals an easily recognizable complacency when her medieval bishop claims that 'Whoever else is ruined and undone, the poor will always scramble out with something they have managed to snatch from the wreck'.[69] Later, another character comments more perceptively:

> the wretchedness of the poor lies below hunger and nakedness. It consists in their incessant incertitude and fear, the drudging succession of shift and scheme and subterfuge, the labouring in the quicksand where every step that takes hold of the firm ground is also a step into the danger of condemnation. Not cold and hunger but Law and Justice are the bitterest affliction of the poor.
>
> (p. 257)

And later still, the nuns' priest thinks, hearing of the peasants' revolt: 'starve a dog and it will grow wolf's teeth, was an old saying and a true one' (p. 272). Warner is one of those who hoped that the war would also bring social revolution, as does Phyllis Bottome.

In Bottome's *The Lifeline* (1946), Mark's experiences of Nazi atrocities in Austria and Germany open his eyes to oppressions at home. He

> could not forget the ugliness and evil in his own country...the mindless penal system grinding criminals down into their loveless crimes, punishing children who were the victims of a society that was itself criminal towards its uncared-for young; the base selfishness of a rich country towards those who could find no work because no one made it for them to find.[70]

As we have seen, many women writers are frank in their exposure of such marginalizations, and inevitably also reveal where blind spots continue to exist. Victoria Sackville-West, for instance, in *The Women's Land Army* (1944), comments on the northern girls coming down south to help with the harvest:

> 'Ba Goom!' one heard, as one drove them through the lanes towards their billets. It was like having three Gracie Fields in the back of the car. I don't know what they expected to find, but at least one girl had been told by her mother to leave her false teeth behind, as she might get bombed down South...[71]

Sackville-West's well-meant pleasantry serves to reveal her bland consignment of northerners into the realm of the 'foreign' (for these girls the south is, she says, a foreign country), an unthinking consignment to the margins, embracing both class and race, which survived the war years.

The shifting and changing margins of the fifties

As the War ended, the full implications of where racism could lead became clear with the revelations of the concentration camps. The implications of the Holocaust for Western civilization were hauntingly debated, but almost exclusively in nonfiction. Novels like Pargeter's *Warfare Accomplished* (1947) convey something of the horror of a con-centration camp, but do not address wholesale massacre; while other works, such as Muriel Spark's *The Comforters* (1957) tend to stick to oblique references, as when Spark's Caroline, who is half-Jewish, thinks of how she cannot stand her family's 'debauch of unreal suffering...the fireside congregation of mock martyrs, their incongruity beside the real ones...it was an insult'.[72] Spark is so oblique here that it is up to the reader as to whether 'the real ones' are seen as the martyrs of Caroline's newly espoused Catholicism, or as those consumed in the Holocaust. What shows more frequently in women's fiction is growing anxiety about British attitudes to race. Storm Jameson, in her novel *The Green Man* (1952), looks back at the kind of reception some refugees received in Britain; when one of her characters, a great Czech scholar, is told bluntly that he is not welcome, he thinks of how he has been betrayed by his reading of Shakespeare:

> It was Shakespeare who, when he was poor and in danger, had told him that the English are exasperating but loyal, stupid but brave and long-sighted. He had been told – by this same Shakespeare – that England is only another word for freedom, a different word meaning generosity. Now he knew that England is a tired elderly man, without imagination, disloyal, timid, ungenerous and short-sighted, without meaning to be, without even knowing it.[73]

Bryher also shows, in her retrospective novel *Beowulf* (1956), a bureau-crat's rejection of a friend's offer to liaise with foreign troops, as such people must be kept from mixing with the British population. This disillusionment with British liberalism towards others is still actively experienced later in the fifties, after the Hungarian uprising, in Chris-tine Brooke-Rose's novel *The Sycamore Tree* (1958), when the Hungarian refugee, Zoltan, thinks:

Of course [the English] wanted the Poles, the Czechs, the Hungarians, the Yugoslavs, the Chinese, the Indians, the Cypriots, the Negroes to be free, but it was all so difficult, they were not ready, there was one kind of freedom for the English, and one kind for the Negroes and another for the Cypriots and yet another for the Poles, the Hungarians, the Chinese . . . for if the multain complications of life, and love, and brotherhood and freedom met and clashed, then it was all so very inconvenient.[74]

Strikingly, we find throughout the fifties that liberalism and anti-racism are most commonly expressed in terms of what has happened in Europe; further afield, the old conventional references to 'savages' and the exotic remain largely in place. A particularly repellent example of racist and class stereotypes is Ann Mary Fielding's *Ashanti Blood* (1952), where we meet a small group of white gold miners in an African forest. Early on, Fielding introduces a houseboy with 'coarse negro lips',[75] while one miner has a mistress with a 'wooly skull' who, we are told, was typical of her kind as she 'lived only for the moment, found waiting no hardship' (p. 16). Moreover, there is strict class hierarchy among the white miners: the working-class Jubb and Perkins are 'undersized', and the manager's wife, kindhearted Philippa, says of them, 'You know, even in all the squalor of slums and smells, they have a sort of romance' (p. 24), while the Welsh miner's 'short sturdy legs gave away his peasant origin' (p. 62). Philippa's manager husband has no love for going underground, suggesting it is the lowly miners' natural habitat, as they cope better with an air which 'stank of mould and negro sweat' (p. 25). The tone is indeed set early on. The Hausa men's tongue has 'a sort of bleating cadence' (p. 40); the noise from the native village is an 'almost human uproar' (p. 77); the cook has an 'over-intelligent face – a type of native Robert loathed' (p. 44) – Robert dislikes 'educated natives' (p. 73). When the mine is flooded, a cry is heard from the workings: 'It wasn't a white man's cry. No white man wails in distress' (p. 118). And Fielding was a popular writer in the fifties. Her work unconsciously demonstrates Hannah Arendt's contention that:

imperialist rule, which provides an outlet for superfluous capital but without the forms of bourgeois constitutionalism and bourgeois rights, is conducted in the interests of the bourgeoisie by 'the mob', class residues from all classes, 'the human debris that every crisis, following invariably upon each period of industrial growth, eliminated permanently from producing society'.[76]

While Fielding represents the extreme of inbuilt prejudice, we do find echoes even among the most enlightened. Storm Jameson's eyes are, on the whole, resolutely turned towards Europe, and her references to other cultures may be well-meaning, but do not break through stereotyping. And the younger generation show the same tendency. Iris Murdoch, for instance, in *The Flight from the Enchanter* (1956), describes two Polish immigrants as being 'like poor savages confronted with a beautiful white girl';[77] although Murdoch also shows how limited the British acceptance of foreigners is, as one character tells another that immigrants should, for preference, be born west of a line (p. 98), while the European refugee, Nina, permanently in fear of pursuit and persecution, and hounded by immigration officialdom, finally commits suicide, her cry for help ignored by her English friend.

Yet writings about other races abroad were a continual source of interest, and the doubts about empire were steadily increasing. Phyllis Bottome, for instance, in her novel *Under the Skin* (1950), has her protagonist, the young white woman, Lucy, going out to the Caribbean with her ideas of a benevolent, imperialist patronage intact, only to have her preconceptions shattered as she comes to terms with the islanders she meets.[78] She learns, for instance, something which Caribbeans have frequently accused the British of ignoring, the fact that the islanders cannot be viewed as part of an essentialist whole; they have their own racial divisions and prejudices, which Lucy ignores at her peril.[79] Bottome shows Lucy growing to deplore the attitudes of the white settlers, and finally not only casting in her lot with the islanders, but marrying the black doctor who has shown her where the real needs of the island lie. Such a mixed marriage is rare indeed in writings of the fifties, but Bottome, in her quietly shrewd way, is often ahead of her time.

In her very different style, Stevie Smith in *The Holiday* (1949) makes an equally bold attempt to show colour prejudice from a non-white perspective, having her Indian characters say, 'we do not mind white people, of course, but . . . now we are beginning to have to combat this disgusting and so un-free colour sense . . . for the fastidious Indian there is for instance the smell of the white person'.[80] Smith is another exception at this date in that she does not treat Indians as exotic, and her narrator insists, 'we are right to quit India' (p. 94); yet ultimately she gives an anodyne account of the granting of independence, leaving the benevolent image of British imperialism intact: 'it is the first time a great colonizing Power, not driven by weakness but in strength choosing to go, has walked out for conscience sake and for the feeling that the time has come' (p. 129).

Writers who could give an Indian point of view on independence and partition are rarely published in Britain during the forties and fifties, and those that are published are mostly men, like R. K. Narayan. An exception is Attia Hosain whose collection of short stories, *Phoenix Fled*, was published in 1953.[81] Hosain came to Britain in 1947, and in this collection she writes of India both before and at the time of Partition. In the title story, for instance, she poignantly evokes the end of the former way of life by describing an old woman, her skin 'loose around the impatient skeleton' (p. 9), who finds 'her changeless, circumscribed world' is unnervingly 'quickening its step in noisy haste' as the cars and trains of Western civilization engulf the life she knew (p. 11). In this story, Hosain does not refer directly to partition; all we hear is that the villagers now 'feared the departure of the [British] soldiers as once she had feared their arrival'; and when the villagers flee, the old woman 'who had survived the threats of too many years refused to believe in its finality' (p. 14). Fatally, she refuses to go with them, staying on her string bed until 'the creaking of the door woke her. She could not see who came, how many. She smelt the flaming thatch, and as shadows came nearer across the courtyard she tried to sit up' (p. 15). We are closer to the holocaust here than to Stevie Smith's comforting view of the civilized retreat of imperialism. Other of Hosain's stories tell of the strains Westernization has imposed on traditionally raised women; in 'Time Is Unredeemable', for instance, the wife of an arranged marriage tries to adapt to what she imagines her husband will expect after his nine years in Europe, only to realize, when he returns, that he does not want her. Yet Hosain is always fair in her dealings with her characters; she never suggests that the traditional ways are flawless, and she deals compassionately and clear-sightedly with both rich and poor. Kamala Markandaya, who also managed to achieve publication in the fifties, shares this compassion. Her first published novel, *Nectar in a Sieve* (1954), is a poignant tale of a poor family of tenant farmers in India, battling poverty and dispossession as their village is gradually swamped by a modern tannery.[82] Markandaya came to England in 1948, and she writes, on the whole, for a Western audience, her characters' speech anglicized, but, again, what her early work offers is a rare chance for the Western reader to see the effects of 'modernization' on a traditional way of life. Like Hosain, too, she does not limit herself to one aspect of Indian society; rich and poor, urban and rural, tradition and innovation interact in finely crafted and thought-provoking prose.

Ruth Prawer Jhabvala was also being published in Britain during the fifties, but she is the outsider viewing India from the inside, being a

Jewish refugee from Europe who came to Britain and then married an Indian. She is poised, as a result, between cultures. Her novel *Esmond in India* (1958), for instance, is particularly biting in its assessment of the legacy which the British have bequeathed to India.[83] The Indian family she constructs at the core of the work is tragically divided between those who have fought for independence and those who have become westernized, despising their own culture. Esmond is the superficially attractive Briton, a degenerate lover of Indian culture, who has married into this family, primarily, it transpires, to have a wife as part of his 'collection' of Indian treasures. But as in Betty Miller's *Farewell Leicester Square*, the marriage becomes troubled when this couple have a son; Esmond resents Indian ways of raising a child, and finally leaves, intending to return to England; but not, we are led to believe, before he has seduced the young girl who has been brought up to prefer all things English to her own people and their needs. Certainly, when we read works written in former parts of empire or by those who have lived in colonies, the mystique of imperialism is wearing very thin. Helen Tiffin has remarked that:

> The dis/mantling, de/mystification and unmasking of European authority that has been an essential political and cultural strategy towards decolonisation and the retrieval or creation of an independent identity from the beginning persists as a prime impulse in all post-colonial literatures.[84]

This is true of both Jhabvala's and Hosain's work, and is also central to Doris Lessing's novels written throughout the fifties. *The Grass Is Singing* (1950), for instance, exposes ways in which a Southern Rhodesian settler community suppress the evidence about white Mary's murder by black Moses, forcing the new arrival, Tony, into unwilling but complicit silence. As Tony quickly learns, 'When old settlers say "One has to understand the country", what they mean is, "You have to get used to our ideas about the native". They are saying, in effect, "Learn our ideas, or otherwise get out: we don't want you".'[85] Lessing concentrates in this and in her other novels based in Africa on the behaviour of white settlers rather than on the thinking of the exploited blacks. In *Martha Quest* (1952) and *A Proper Marriage* (1954), for instance, the first two books in her Children of Violence sequence, Lessing deconstructs the romantic novel, as we see Martha both rebelling against and succumbing to the conventions of colonialism.[86] As a young girl, Martha is first alerted to racism when she sees her Jewish friends enduring the insults of anti-Semitic settlers; later she witnesses the harrying of a black waiter by the young white men of the sports club, and, later still, we see these same 'wolves' knock down a black man as they chase after Martha's wedding car. Mr Maynard, who has just officiated at Martha's marriage, sees the accident and is relieved when

> the native was getting to his feet and shaking himself. And now it looked as if silver rain were falling from heaven around the man, for the wolves were flinging handfuls of money at him, slapping him on the shoulder, and assuring him he was all right, no bones broken. They were already climbing back into the undamaged cars, to resume the chase...Mr Maynard walked on, very shaken, very unhappy. No sense of responsibility, completely callous, thought they could do anything if they could buy themselves out of it afterwards...[87]

Martha will gradually come to reject the world of these young men, pursuing her dream of a city where 'the blue-eyed, fair-skinned children of the North [play] hand in hand with the bronze-skinned, dark-eyed children of the South' (p. 21), but that vision has been pushed farther and farther into the future as Lessing has continued to write in this country.

While novels about the colonies were increasingly popular in Britain, the mental block about increasing numbers of incomers from erstwhile colonies is marked throughout the late forties and the fifties; it would seem that what Orwell concluded in his essay 'Marrakech' remains true: 'People with brown skins are next door to invisible'.[88] Muriel Spark's protagonist in 'The Portobello Road' (murdered because she knows that her murderer married a black woman in Africa) tells, for instance, of how

> I was brought up in a university town to which came Indian, African and Asiatic students in various tints and hues. I was brought up to avoid them for reasons connected with local reputation and God's ordinances. You cannot easily go against what you were brought up to do unless you are a rebel by nature.[89]

When migrants are acknowledged, whether Jewish or from the former colonies, what we find, as V. J. Mishra observes, is 'the nation-state's barely concealed preference for the narrative of assimilation', regardless of how long migrant communities have actually existed in this country.[90]

Certainly, what is marked is how few published novelists write about the non-white community in Britain, and those that do (Sam Selvon or V. S. Naipaul, for instance) tend to be men. As Susheila Nasta observes, when discussing post-war Caribbean writers:

> Few women writers, apart from Jean Rhys whose work spanned the pre-war period, were published at this time [1950s and 1960s], largely due to the fact that the first wave of immigration to Britain was predominantly male. Other women writing during this period, such as the poets Una Marston or Louise Bennett, gained little recognition in the publishing world.[91]

The Moslem Indian writer Attia Hosain does get published, but she looks back to the India she has left and which has vanished, rather than addressing the Britain where she now lives. Beryl Gilroy, writing about life for incomers in this country, found publication much more difficult, and indeed had to contend not only with the resistance of the white community but with prejudice among Caribbean men as well:

> When my work was sent to the male writers from the West Indies to be read, these men, in order to be as erudite as they were expected to be ... said my work was too psychological, strange, way-out, difficult to categorise ... My stories are being published now.[92]

Suresh Renjen Bald, discussing South Asian migrants (but his observations could be applied to migrants in general), remarks that

> because challenges to well established myths are disturbing to one's world view, they are often ignored or not given the attention they deserve. It is not surprising, therefore, that the Anglo novelists ... writing about post-war Britain tend to focus on changes of class structure, but often ignore completely the diversity introduced into British society by the racially and culturally different immigrants. Indeed, if included in the novels, the South Asian immigrants are generally presented as inconsequential figures who have absolutely no impact on the lives of the characters in the novels.[93]

Bald does cite Barbara Pym as someone who attempts something more than glimpses of South Asians in late-night restaurants or shops that never close, but Bald also claims that 'there seems to exist an irrational fear and suspicion of the South Asians among some of the main characters' (p. 416). Certainly this is a fair criticism of Pym's *Excellent Women* (1952), where there are stereotypical comments on both Indians and Africans which the narrator shares, and where it is hard to tell whether the narrator is being presented to us critically or not.[94] The tone is clearer in Pym's later novel *Less than Angels* (1955), where an anthropologist, Tom Mallow, noting the hunting trophies in a house, 'felt as if he were observing some aspect of a culture as alien to him as any he had seen in Africa'.[95] This turning the tables on English customs is a continuing theme in the novel; earlier, African carnival is linked with a flower show in Shropshire, and Tom sees 'how this or that old custom of which he had read had died out and been replaced by some new and "significant" feature' (p. 172). When it comes to attitudes to Africans themselves, we are given a satirical account of the attitude of a young man's parents when he chooses to study 'primitive peoples' rather than enter the Foreign Office; and the fatuity of Catherine, Tom's ex-girlfriend, is clear when she declares,

> How soothing it will be to get away from all this complexity of personal relationships to the simplicity of a primitive tribe, whose only complication are in their kinship structure and rules of land tenure, which you can observe with the anthropologist's calm detachment.
>
> (p. 181)

Later, it is Catherine who romanticizes Tom's accidental shooting in a political riot, presenting him as the white hero: 'It seems a noble way to die, doesn't it, fighting for an oppressed people's freedom against the tyranny of British rule?' to which another friend protests that Tom was 'in this crowd purely by accident' (p. 227). Gradually, versions of Tom's death move further into the realm of the stereotype of contemporary film, as when Rhoda thinks Tom was killed 'by natives...the shouting mob of black bodies brandishing spears, or the sly arrow, tipped with poison for which there was no known antidote, fired from an overhanging tree' (p. 229); and Rhoda is rather shocked to think Tom may have been wearing a native robe, as she sees this as 'lowering' (p. 230) – he clearly should have been in tropical whites and a topee. Such attitudes die hard, as we see in Christine Brooke-Rose's *The Languages of Love* (1957) which derides the treatment of the North African Hussein in London: he is seen as naïve, and racism is casually brutal, as when Bernard, jealous of Hussein's friendship with a woman he himself likes, 'felt irrelevantly pro-Apartheid'.[96] Yet Brooke-Rose's tone, like

Pym's, can be ambivalent; the British treatment of Hussein may be viewed unsympathetically, but he trembles on the brink of being the naïve, comic character of stereotype, as when he brings a camel through the London streets to woo Georgina. Or again, he is associated with the African as exotic when we hear that 'but for his European clothes he might have stepped out of King Solomon's Mines, he was so very tall' (p. 16), and that his 'tropical laughter, like tick-fever, is infectious' (p. 17).

Muriel Spark's 'The Black Madonna' (1958) is much more successful in mocking British racism. Her Raymond and Lou, a childless couple, whose local church boasts a black madonna carved from Irish bog-oak which is said to have miraculous powers, pride themselves on being 'progressive' and make friends with two Jamaicans. All goes well until one of these black friends sympathizes with Lou over her sluttish sister, comparing her with those islanders who have a 'slum mentality'. Lou is furious, 'thinking wildly, what a cheek *him* talking like a snob. At least Elizabeth's white'.[97] Gradually, the superficiality of Lou's liberalism becomes clear, and finally vanishes when, after praying to the black Madonna, she has a black baby. Raymond's mother quarrels with him 'through his inquiries whether there had been coloured blood in his family' (p. 55) before Elizabeth reveals that there was black blood on Lou's side. This is too much for Lou; she cannot take to the child, so they have it adopted and move to London. Spark's economy of style rules comment out, and the story works well in its stark simplicity. Lou and Raymond's abrupt loss of racial tolerance when it threatens to invade their own lives is more typical of the fifties than Barbara Comyns's wonderfully eccentric father in her novel *Who Was Changed and Who Was Dead* (1954), who speculates casually on why his favourite daughter Hattie is black, but without any suggestion of repudiation.[98]

However, although Suresh Renjen Bald observes that race in this country is much less readily addressed during the fifties and sixties than matters of class, this is not entirely true of women's fiction. There are, certainly, some novels of working-class life, as, for instance, the industrial fiction of Menna Gallie, centring on the mining community in a Welsh village, with vignettes of their working and family lives. *Strike for a Kingdom* (1959) looks back to the strike of 1926, with the people picking coal off the sidings.[99] As Stephen Knight points out, the setting and title link Gallie's work to the English-language novels of Gwyn Thomas and Lewis Jones, but Gallie uses humour to bring the social life of the village alive, the children are given a point of view, and the community of women is evoked in the theme of a still-born child. Gallie's strikers too are shown as family men, and she steers them away from the left-wing heroism depicted in Lewis Jones's novels; Knight points out that she is closer in her sympathies to Welsh Nationalism.[100] But on the whole her miners are apolitical:

> They were not trouble makers for the fun of it, they were not Marxists out to destroy Capitalism, they did not think of themselves as 'one of the Factors of Production', but they felt they were poor devils having a raw deal and they had had enough.[101]

The village Carnival evokes their desperate poverty, if with a light touch, as Joe Everynight's 12 children walk in the procession: 'the smallest child's sack trailed to the ground and the sack of the eldest scarcely covered her bottom. This one wore a card on her back, "The Bread Line"' (p. 22). Gallie weaves a murder mystery into her tale, but while this adds drama to the action, it is not allowed to detract from the keenly observed depiction of the miners' predicaments. When their peaceful protest march reaches the Owner's house, it is attacked by the police, and a few of the men are taken off to jail, the sister of one dying of consumption while they are in the cells. However, stereotyping re-emerges in this lively little novel as the link between race and class is voiced yet again; D. J., the magistrate and a miner himself, says in exasperation:

> Some think we are all desperate, violent men in the pits, like black savages from Africa, queer people who vanish under the ground like devils or goblins ... When I was at Ruskin College I sometimes felt people treated me with interested kindness and looking at me like a specimen from strange lands, brought over for their scientific curiosity.
>
> (p. 145)

On one level, he shows some sense of affinity with those brushed aside in Ann Mary Fielding's *Ashanti Blood*. But what we also see here is one form of Otherness being used to challenge another; yet again, the stereotypical view of Africans is used to denote a debasing view of British miners. As we have found elsewhere, clear-sightedness about one cause is not necessarily applied to another. D. J. is sensitive to the way in which miners will be demonized if coal goes short in homes and factories, yet Gallie has him locating demons for himself in another part of the Empire.

While gradually during the fifties working-class novels begin to find publishers, there are also novels attacking the hollowness of aspects of middle-class respectability. Pamela Frankau, for instance, in

A Wreath for the Enemy (1954), centres on a family whose father, scarred by the War, turns his back on what he sees as English smugness to enjoy a Bohemian existence in France.[102] Inevitably, his daughter Penelope longs for a 'shape' to her life which the middle-class Bradleys appear to stand for, while the Bradley children long for the freedom which she appears to have, and it is some time before Penelope realizes just how claustrophobic the Bradley parents' ideas of respectability actually are. The Bradley parents dislike Jews, cannot bear eccentrics or those who show 'character', and their daughter analyses their fear:

> 'What People Will Say' is one bit of it. Sometimes I feel as though they were waiting for an inspector to call . . . to make sure that we're all doing the things that 'Nice People' are supposed to do . . . And another bit is the fear of *seeing* that anything's wrong. Putting a bright face on it all – you know. 'Let's change the subject, shall we?' Refusal to face facts. Particularly *queer* facts. Anything that isn't 'normal' is a terror. If you ask me, I think their trouble is that they just have no imagination at all. They can't see further than their poor noses. So they've never really grown-up, and they're out of date.
>
> (p. 113)

Stevie Smith also debates the middle classes in *The Holiday* (1949), but she is much more forgiving than Frankau. Her protagonist Celia sees some of her friends 'still in this violent revolt from the virtues of the middle-classes', and confesses that these classes can be unbearable. But she adds that while revolutionaries and 'classless artists' are the salt of the earth, inspired as they are by their vision,

> you cannot make a diet of salt, and it is through the use and practice of the middle-classes that the vision is made actual. I have not found the middle-classes against the new ideas, so much as anxious how they may be applied; but of course I am speaking of the less wealthy sort of middle-class person, such as we have at home.[103]

Her cousin Caz, however, is less well disposed. When Celia cries, 'at least the English law cannot be bought', he replies,

> 'That is true . . . at least not by the poor.'   (p. 130).

As a reviewer of E. M. Butler's *Daylight in a Dream* (1951) remarks: 'Among the Victorians sex was a subject not to be mentioned except among men. We have replaced this taboo by another. We are prudish about class'.[104] Certainly Butler exposes the dangerous effect which fantasies about class have on her obsessively snobbish protagonist, based on the illusion of the superior moral code of the upper middle-class girls she served with in World War One. As her reviewer noted:

> [Butler] uses class to illuminate her real subject, the contrast between persons as they appear to us and persons as they really are. We bolster our self-esteem by indulging in censoriousness, a vice more common – in both senses of the word – than any of the seven deadly sins. By liking to impute bad motives, we lose touch with reality, and make ourselves miserable.

Yet class, like race, despite the social changes which World War Two undoubtedly made, remains a controversial issue throughout the fifties. The working class may find a voice, but all too often the standards of the 'British way of life' remain stubbornly defined by southern middle-class practice.

New voices of the sixties

The relations between the races become ever more dramatic in the sixties; the granting of independence to a whole range of former colonies must be balanced against Enoch Powell's 'rivers of blood' speech (1968) at home. On one level, the memory of the Holocaust has become an event which shapes thinking on global responsibility for race relations, on another, nothing has changed; and while old-style imperialism may be losing ground, economic imperialism is flourishing. Naomi Mitchison, in *Memoirs of a Spacewoman* (1962), stresses the importance for explorers of not interfering with cultures on other planets, but also hints that the ethos of explorers is inevitably different from that of mineralogists; clearly economic imperialism is still alive and well far into her imagined future. *Memoirs of a Spacewoman* is a powerful little novel, using the medium of science fiction dexterously to expose a number of contemporary concerns. On one expedition, it is worth recalling, the explorers meet a centipedal race that 'had colonised very vigorously, and at a period of moral crudity, which luckily humans had lived through and put behind them' (p. 27). This race shows all the symptoms of imperialist superiority to their playful, humanoid fauna; they cannot tell one individual from another, regarding the humanoids as a 'species towards which one can have no emotional feelings' (p. 31);

and there are echoes of the Holocaust in Mitchison's vivid descriptions of the coralling of the humanoids and their indiscriminate, ponderously rationalized slaughter. Interestingly, Mitchison has moved into what is for her a new genre to expose the inhumanity of imperialist exploitation, and to attack the reader's sensibilities in this episode by having the subservient race humanoid; and this has some similarities to Christine Brooke-Rose's strategy in her first experimental novel *Out* (1964), where Africans are in power after the white races have destroyed their societies and their physical health by an apocalyptic catastrophe. But there is a difference between the visions of the two writers: while Mitchison's dominant race destroys its underlings callously, Brooke-Rose shows her Africans as humanitarian on the whole, while her treatment of the whites is reductive. These people are known as the 'Colourless', who have to be given unemployment pills to ease their neuroses; as an African says, 'We have no prejudice that's an article of faith. But there is an irrational fear of the Colourless that lingers on, it's understandable, in some cases, even justifiable, with the malady still about, well, it makes them unreliable' (p. 51). We hear that the kindly Mrs Mgulu 'does not choose to be touched by sickly Colourless hands' (p. 25) (although she offers her own blood – illegally – when the Colourless Lilly is seriously ill), and we are also told that 'the Ukayans have long had a bad reputation as workers' (p. 38). All the Colourless deny having had professional status, to avoid being charged with responsibility for the effects of the radiation sickness, the mutations, the corruption. Ultimately what Brooke-Rose does is to offer a tapestry woven with bright images and wittily inventive language through which we catch blindingly clear glimpses of her contemporary world, with its fears of nuclear disaster and loss of faith in European civilization; and we are also offered the alternative world of a caring, responsible African community, exasperated by the helpless burden of the Colourless, but not vindictive. The white reader is given the illusion of seeing white civilization and its legacies from the outside.

Barbara Comyns chooses to confront racial issues through her own idiosyncratic magic realist medium in her novel *The Skin Chairs* (1962), looking through the eyes of Frances, a child narrator. Frances is taken to the General's house to see his skin chairs, and the General's wife tells her, almost casually, ' "He brought them back with him after the Boer War, isn't it horrible? Five of them are black men's skins and one white. I believe if you look carefully you can see the difference" ' (p. 19). After the Holocaust, the sense that imperialism could be as callous as the various brands of fascism repeatedly finds expression, and Comyns is particularly effective with the casual tone of this Swiftian extension of horrors revealed after the Holocaust, as with the hint that the skin colours are barely distinguishable. The child is intrigued by the novelty of what she is seeing, but also thinks of 'the poor skinless bodies buried somewhere in Africa. Did their souls ever come to see what had happened to their skins or had they forgotten all about them?' (p. 19). The chairs haunt her as the novel progresses, becoming 'fearful', and in the end she decides she must say a burial service over them, after first giving them names (and so, in the simplest sense, restoring their humanity). The horror at the heart of this novel is all the more effective for being seen from a child's point of view.

Muriel Spark uses a child very differently to inspire horror at the casualness of racial cruelties in her story 'The Curtain Blown by the Breeze' (1961).[105] We hear that a 'Piccanin of twelve' was caught and shot by Mrs Van der Merwe's husband for watching her suckling her child. The woman tells her story:

> I look up at the window and so help me God it was a blerry nig standing outside with his face at the window. You should of heard me scream. So Jannie got the gun and caught the pic and I hear a bang. So he went too far in his blerry temper so what can you expect? Now I won't have no more trouble from them boys.
>
> (p. 29)

No hint of regret there, and the husband is given a light jail sentence. However, when he comes out of jail, he shoots his wife and the white man he takes to be her lover; this, we hear, 'was a serious crime and Jannie was hanged' (p. 37). The monstrousness of the discrepancy between the sentences for the two shootings needs no further comment; the economy of Spark's style says it all.

The works I have been exploring are all written by women based in Britain, none of them from ethnic minorities, and this continued to be the norm for publication in this country. A few works by women writers from the former Empire and colonies do find a publisher in the sixties, but, when they deal with racial issues, the setting is usually outside Britain itself. This is true of Lessing's African stories, such as 'The Black Madonna' (1964), where an Italian painter, a former prisoner of war in 'Zambesia', causes trouble for the British captain by painting a black Madonna.[106] Although the Madonna reminds the captain of his own African mistress, he insists that 'You can't have a black Madonna', to which the Italian, himself of peasant stock, replies, 'She was a peasant. This is a peasant. Black peasant Madonna for black country' (p. 16). Lessing shows the empathy between the former prisoner and the Africans as Spark does, without superfluous comment.

Attia Hosain, although she had been in England since 1947, also pitches her novel *Sunlight on a Broken Column* (1961) abroad and in the past.[107] Her setting is India, before and at the time of partition. Anita Desai, who wrote the introduction for the Penguin edition, quotes Hosain as saying,

> Events during and after Partition are to this day very painful to me. And now, in my old age, the strength of my roots is strong; it also causes pain, because it makes one a 'stranger' everywhere in the deeper area of one's mind and spirit *except where one was born and brought up.*
>
> (p. ix)

The sense of unbelonging in the Britain where she lives is poignantly stressed here, but Hosain chose not to write on that theme. Instead, she explores the growth of distrust beween Muslim and Muslim, Muslim and Hindu, in the years leading up to independence and partition; she analyses, as it were, the construction of racism in areas where it had not previously existed. There had of course been awareness of difference; whites are uncomfortable at a tea party with Indians, a Muslim lady has no patience with the 'destructive non-violent nonsense' of the Hindus (p. 51), the Anglo-Indian Sylvia expresses her contempt for 'wogs' (although she later marries an impoverished Raja before running off with an American sergeant). But the descent into open enmity and violence is a gradual process within the community itself; opposition to British imperialism gives way to conflict between old friends and neighbours, where Otherness comes to override tolerance of difference. As one character says ruefully, 'God was a safer subject for discussion than His religions' (p. 127). Racism in Britain is only briefly touched on, by cousins returning from England, who say that they were left in no doubt as to where they belonged, 'we coloured people' (p. 178). Saleem mocks the old school tie tradition and recalls

> 'This key to English hearts worked like magic on what's-his-name over there. In the Forest Service, I believe. May be that is why he has that anthropoid look. Quite a zoological couple, don't you think?

His wife looks like a honey-bear. He slapped me on the back, talked of the good old school, and made me feel as if I had some special, select quality...'

'A native but one of us, what?' laughed Sita...

(p. 188)

'Down from the trees' is neatly reassigned here, but what is more central to Hosain's story are the splits within the Indian community itself.

Ruth Prawer Jhabvala's novels, written from within India, continue to be published in the sixties, giving her own view of an Indian community after partition. Her view is both that of a wife within an Indian family and that of an outsider, a member of the Jewish Diaspora; she is no advocate of old imperialism. In *Get Ready for Battle* (1962), for instance, she centres on the heartache within a traditional society as it slowly adapts to a changing world.[108] At Gulzari Lal's party we see Indian wives resigned to this westernized form of entertainment; they 'accept their boredom without resentment, for they understood it comprized the social life which, as modern women, it was their duty to take part in' (p. 8). Materialism wrestles with idealism within this society, and Jhabvala, like Hosain, is remarkably even-handed; both writers can see the strengths and weaknesses of the traditional societies they explore, and the painful process of adapting to the new ways which the British left behind them. British readers, it seems, are now ready to view the legacies of imperialism abroad in the fictions they read.

Jean Rhys's *Wide Sargasso Sea* also appealed to this taste for deconstruction of old imperial mythologizing of colonial life, since, while her novel revisits the world of *Jane Eyre*, it is largely set in the Caribbean.[109] While Brontë saw the role of woman as more important than that of colour, Rhys insists that the reader sees the implication of colour for womanhood. Rhys's Antoinette may not have mixed ancestry, but her own mother can call her a white nigger because of her cultural bonding, while those who are truly black consider her inferior, a situation which can only be resolved by a white marriage. We see Antoinette, as it were, turned into a commodity; her husband even renames her, redefining her by the image he imposes on her. Yet, like Hosain and Jhabvala, Rhys is even-handed: her Rochester is also trapped by the demands of his role, the imperialist point of view he has been conditioned to perceive as superior. He is never at ease in the Caribbean, does what he does because he sincerely believes his wife to be degenerate, and is as much a victim of his culture as she is. As we are told, 'there is always the other side. Always' (p. 106).

As I have observed, little fiction by members of ethnic minorities about their situation in Britain itself finds a publisher, and what is published is largely by men. Rhys comes close to speaking for the Caribbeans but Beryl Gilroy, for instance, sees even Rhys as wearing 'the God-given cloak of privilege...Poverty is, and was even then, relative. And she, lovely woman, wrote from within the culture, but outside of the self – the true Black self'.[110] Nonfictional accounts do occasionally give women a voice, as when Donald Hinds quotes Myrtle from British Guyana, describing her gradual disillusionment with the expatriate English parson's view of the British Commonwealth as like the Kingdom of Heaven; the parson had maintained that both 'are made up of black, white, Indians, Chinese and those whose colour defies definition. Heaven and the British Empire never think of anyone as unimportant'.[111] And Beryl Gilroy does have her stories for children published, but her adult fiction will not be published for some years. In the end, we only have glimpses of other races in the fiction of white women writers like Barbara Pym, whose *No Fond Return of Love* (1961), for instance, mentions the mixture of races in a student house, and shows a Miss Lord who is still somewhat shocked by the difference of orthodox Jews who eat with their hats on: 'A little skull cap doesn't look so bad, quite distinguished, really, but a black trilby's another thing'.[112] Later, however, we get the less inhibited (though still stereotypical) view of Dulcie who, 'now that she was alone...might well consider letting rooms to students – perhaps Africans, who would fill the house with gay laughter and cook yams on their gas-rings' (p. 285). But such liberalism remains relatively rare, in fiction as in life, during the sixties.

In Lynne Reid Banks's *The L-shaped Room* (1960), a whole houseful of the marginalized are central to the novel.[113] The first-person narrator, Jane, is an unmarried mother who is befriended by her homosexual black neighbour and falls in love with the young Jewish writer downstairs; later she is befriended by the prostitutes in the basement, one of whom is a Hungarian refugee from the 1956 uprising. This is a novel that is honest about the prejudices which can lurk behind apparent acceptance of difference; Jane's prejudices disappear very slowly. She is at first terrified of black John, only to find he is kind and gentle, while at first she despises Jewish Toby because, forgetting the horrors of World War Two, she thinks he has changed his name to hide his race. In the course of the novel, odd myths emerge, like the claim that 'West Indians' are less black than John (p. 92), or that the black smell as a matter of course; and prejudices emerge whenever tensions are roused, as when Jane's former lover, her child's father, taunts Toby, calling him

'Jew-boy' (p. 256), or when John's involvement in a fight is half-suggested by the text as having been his own fault, or when Jane is shocked to realize John is gay, but feels she has made progress as she feels no 'revulsion' (p. 263). In the end, we see how far Jane has come when she meets the girl who has taken her old room, and who is full of the old prejudices which Jane once held. Yet here again, it is important to heed Beryl Gilroy's comment in *Leaves in the Wind*, that while 'books such as *The L-shaped Room* set in Notting Hill...were filmed[,] they didn't show Black men being treated uncivilly or offered urine disguised as beer by racists' (p. 213). Nevertheless, such novels do mark a certain amount of progress, as does the fact that they were filmed; their success is a small something to set against the hostility which Powell's speech sought to fuel.

The L-shaped Room, with its boarding-house of those on the social margins sets race alongside the working class; yet the narrator is a member of the middle class who, we discover, has chosen to renounce her middle-class home after a row with her father, and ultimately she does return to him with her baby. However, a number of novels were published which gave first-hand insights into working-class life, as, for instance, Maureen Duffy's *That's How It Was* (1962).[114] This is a semi-autobiographical novel, based centrally on a vivid, multifaceted portrait of Duffy's mother, a lifelong sufferer from tuberculosis, who, in the novel, is 'held together by a steel-wire will' (p. 16). Paddy (the child drawn from Duffy herself) and her mother live a difficult life in the slums of the East End; during the Blitz, Paddy is evacuated (she thinks most people took such children 'in a thwarted missionary spirit' [p. 71]). Later, the mother marries in an attempt to give Paddy a better chance of getting on, and the struggle to give Paddy an education is graphically described, amidst the hostility of the step-father's undisciplined, illiterate family. The mother's increasing frailty, her courage and determination to keep up some sort of standard in a thankless environment where violence simmers, the haunting fear that death could strike at each coughing attack (bathing, she looks like 'something out of Belsen' [p. 194]) form the background to Paddy's childhood and adolescence. Duffy's language, colloquial, spiked with vivid imagery, constructs the world of the novel from within, a very different effect from previous attempts at a working-class world observed from outside.

The sixties also saw the publication of Margot Heinemann's *The Adventurers* (1960), a powerful evocation of a mining community in Wales.[115] Heinemann herself was neither working class nor Welsh, but the authenticity of her writing (she had worked closely with working-class representatives on political and trade union issues) won Alan Sinfield's admiration (he called her novel 'the most positive and astute representation of working people that I have seen in the period').[116] Heinemann, unlike many of her contemporaries, remained a committed Marxist after the Hungarian uprising, and the novel explores, among other things, how Marxist intellectuals had to realign their thinking to cope with their contemporary world, without self-delusion, through the character Richard, who is not working class but a dedicated Communist, betrayed by Russia's invasion of Hungary yet (like Heinemann herself) still fighting for an ideal. This is a novel of socialist realism, plotting Dan's gradual betrayal of his mining roots as he moves up and away in the world of journalism, as against Tom's integrity in staying closely in touch with such roots. As Stephen Knight observes, Heinemann 'stands outside the heroics of industrial male fiction and sees clearly the competition and the compromise of male careerism'.[117] In the larger world, we see how power corrupts, reshaping and ultimately falsifying what working men are supposed to be about, diluting and in the end betraying democracy. This is a novel of powerful, impassioned political writing, leavened with Welsh humour, earthy, far from politically correct. Tom, for instance, tells Richard that he is 'too bloody sensitive' when he objects to what the miners call him: ' "Intellectual, middle-class – that's only like saying to a chap who's pinched your shovel, you goddam thieving Irish Papist, get back to your bogs and leave decent people to make a living in peace. Doesn't mean a thing" '.[118]

Intention counts for quite a lot in the language of this novel and in its attitude to language. Lena, for instance, despite being one of the corrupting influences on Dan, catches something of the dilemma facing a writer of a novel of ideas (how far can you entice the reader in by entertainment and still keep faith with the core and rationale of your argument?), when she explains that 'the Boss says...that when you've taken all a speaker's best propaganda points out with a blue pencil, there's a chance he might begin to persuade somebody. You can't orate to a microphone' (p. 154). Yet there is real (and continuing) poignancy when Dan is told reminiscently by a Labour MP that during the War,

> I think I was a bit idealistic about the working class, I suppose we all had big ideas in those days. I used to think, if we come through this packet and the boys feel they've got their own Government, won't they just work and give and sacrifice for the country!
>
> (p. 161)

and Dan himself 'never changed his views so that he could remember. It was rather that, after a couple of years of this kind of thing [London-based journalism], one got a sense of proportion' (p.182), later adding to his credo that 'to put one's group and class above the nation was natural in those who hadn't been educated. One learned a wider view with difficulty' (p. 285). This fine novel explores the issue of loyalty (to what? to whom?), both personal and communal, and acts as an apologia for Communism, searching out the complexities of intellectual commitment to an ideal.

Menna Gallie's *The Small Mine* (1962) is lighter in tone, bringing the Welsh mining community of her earlier novel up to the present.[119] The conditions in the nationalized pit are greatly improved, as against the primitive facilities in the small, privately owned pit nearby, although the latter offers good money 'while it lasts' (p. 13). The world outside affects the miners too. They have difficulty coming to terms with an influx of German engineers, war memories and identification with the repressed complicating their thinking; as one says, 'we can't forgive on behalf of the Jews and the gypsies, those poor buggers are beyond forgiving' (p. 19), although, as one man points out, the engineers they distrust were mere children in the War. They argue about Russia and America and the bomb: 'This bloody bomb has changed everything, mun. It's put us back right back in the middle ages. It's the medieval world all over again, when one or two chaps was tin gods and all the rest didn't matter a damn' (p. 28), or, as another says, 'My father said we'll all be blown to hell in five years, so it's no good saving' (p. 47). They are alienated from their own bosses (a problem Heinemann deals with): 'Class distinction had reared out its fat belly among the higher officials of the Coal Board' (pp. 26–7). Manslaughter lies at the heart of Gallie's plotting, just as murder shaped the earlier novel, but again it is the vivid life of the community which dominates the book, and, reflecting contemporary anxieties in a rapidly changing world, the threats to that community's cohesion.

And the threat of the contemporary world of the sixties to older models of working-class life are clear; a bleak but utterly haunting evocation of a dysfunctional working-class family lies at the heart of Christina Stead's *Cotters' England* (1966).[120] This novel catches the bleakness of the post-war period, while it centres on the violence and affection in the protagonist, Nellie, her equally balanced sadism and concern for others. In a changing society, Nellie's left-wing politics are exposed as largely rhetoric (anticipating Lessing's *The Good Terrorist* [1985]),[121] and her do-gooder activities are basically exercises in self-promotion, although couched in humanitarian terms. Nellie's language is always spellbinding, her life 'nothing but a dancing in a hall of mirrors' (p. 20), a phrase which resonates throughout the novel. Yet while Nellie's activities horrify, Stead never judges her; we see the bleakness of the family which has formed her, her mother's senility, her father's wildness, her sister's crushed existence in the family home. Nellie herself takes refuge in fantasy, fantasies for which her friends and family pay dearly (she is, like Spark's Miss Jean Brodie, a manipulator). Yet the key to Nellie's dangerousness is her disillusionment with contemporary life; at one point she asks if all political action is not fascist, and yet she continues to dominate others, trying to force them to live out her fantasies. Stead gives us, at a subliminal level, a view of the demise of traditional working-class socialism, as Nellie, throwing a party, substitutes for it her tough, licentious crew of women ('In her brave bohemian democracy she allowed no question of morality' [p. 277]), which ultimately drives her protegee, Caroline, to her death. For Nellie has insisted to Caroline her true belief: 'I don't care about society. Society is a villain. It keeps on living and social arts and social sciences are charitable dames. Marxism is cruel, because it doesn't care about the individual'. In the end, Marxists are, she says, 'self-satisfied black-coated bureaucrats, a petty-bourgeois sect with canting deacons' (p. 295). The nihilism of this crisis of belief in society and political systems leads inevitably to a kind of death; it is no surprise when Nellie's window-cleaner friend succeeds in interesting her in a rather crude form of mysticism after her loss of faith and friends – Nellie must have something to believe in, however mistily.

What we find, in the 40 years which I am exploring, is that what is on the margins shifts continually. Just as there are enormous differences in how the working class is viewed from within as we move from Ellen Wilkinson to Christina Stead, Bottome's pioneering novel of the slums, *London Pride*, is inevitably dated by its patronage (or rather, maternalism) when set beside Maureen Duffy's *That's How It Was*. Attitudes to race change too; anti-Semitism is a continuing target in novels of the thirties and forties, but, after the Holocaust, the vestiges of racial prejudice against Jews tend to merge with other forms of racism in the fictions of the time; the problem of constructing responses to the Holocaust seems to defeat most women novelists, who on the whole leave the articulation of such responses to nonfiction. Attitudes to imperialism also change dramatically; from the confused mixture of disapproval and vague loyalty to the imperialist 'idea' which we find pre-war, we move to a situation where imperialism is no longer acceptable in responsible fiction of the sixties, although there is still a very mixed response to the ethnic minorities at home as opposed to the postcolonial world abroad. I have barely scratched the surface of this absorbing area, but I hope I have at least shown some of the complexities which urge us to read on.

4
Men, Women, Sex and Gender

In 1997, Suzanne Raitt and Trudi Tate raised the question as to 'why gender has become a critical orthodoxy; why critics rarely feel the need to justify an analysis of gender, especially in writing by women, to the exclusion of many other issues'; and they go on to warn that focussing exclusively on gender can 'produce a curiously depoliticised reading of our culture, its history, and its writing'. Janet Montefiore had also urged in 1996 that analysis based primarily on gender tended to ignore other areas of oppression and subordination, as, for instance, social class, race, age, religion.[1] I am in complete agreement with these necessary reminders yet, as Luce Irigaray has said, sexual difference is 'situated at the junction of nature and culture', both conditioning language and conditioned by it;[2] furthermore, it is also crucial to acknowledge that, as Catherine Hall has pointed out, 'masculinities and femininities are ... historically specific and we can trace the changes over time in the definitions which have been in play and in power'.[3] Moreover, it is worth bearing in mind Marianne van der Wijngaard's point, that traits labelled as masculine or feminine are also culturally and historically specific, even when so assigned by scientists; the laboratory is also a product of its era.[4]

While many of the women novelists of the four decades under consideration have not exclusively centred on sex and gender, sex and gender inevitably surface continually in their writing, if in subtle and complex ways. Certainly, two world wars pose urgent questions about what had been assigned to masculinity and femininity since Victorian times. While Elizabeth Badinter (who agrees that masculinity varies according to historical period, 'but also to a man's social class, race, and age') has suggested that the seventies was the decade when women (and, as a result, men) redefined themselves and their roles, the women novelists of the four previous decades, at the very least, are already preparing the ground.[5] Badinter points out that English-speaking countries may well have been prompted to redefine roles 'because these societies have always been obsessed with virility, as is evident in their history, art, and culture' (p. 5); and she warns against biological determinism, since 'essentialism necessarily ends in separation and worse: oppression' (p. 25). Essentialism of the cultural kind is explored by Kenneth Clatterbaugh in his work on masculinities, suggesting that 'when the experiences of men of a certain class and set of choices are generalized, a false universality is created that undermines or ignores the realities of men differently situated'; and furthermore, 'there will never be a final perspective on masculinity that is free of political bias and thus completely objective'.[6]

Badinter also highlights an associated problem which writers confront, the 'obsession with the norm',[7] something which is central to Nazism with its fixed images of the ideal for men and women, and its intolerance of those who do not conform; this is a theme which many writers of the thirties and forties pursue. Later, too, in the fifties and sixties, a number of writers will turn their attention to the problem of the norm in Western society, running parallel with Foucault, for instance, in their investigation of what is regarded as 'mad' in their contemporary society. Many women novelists of these decades demonstrate Irigaray's contention that literature is well suited to challenge 'the regulations of logical truth or the social order, in which the artificial scission between private life and public life maintains a collusive silence on the disasters of living relationships',[8] both in the public and private sphere.

Claire M. Tylee has commented that, from the Great War on, 'what men and women did share were the cultural myths and the behavioural inhibitions of their society. They suffered equally from the repression of their memories of traumatic experiences and from a common vulnerability to the myths of imperialism'.[9] This is to say that women, as did men, shared the confusions which the traumas of war evoked; the effects of shell shock and gassing challenged old views of masculinity and heroism, requiring adjustments from both men and women. Then there were issues of sexual morality; both wars put older codes of conduct on trial as surely as the growing independence of women (abortion, affairs and pregnancy outside marriage persistently resonate throughout the fictions of these four decades, and the price paid comes under close scrutiny). Yet for every challenge to the conventions, there was a corresponding withdrawal into conservatism; Tylee points out, for instance, that early feminists had to wrestle with the notion that 'women who took over the "masculine" privileges of education and politics lost their "femininity"': "unsexed", they lowered themselves' (p. 166), and during World War Two we find the denizens of the Women's Land Army concerned that their workers should keep their femininity. It has been frequently said that, after each war, women retreated into the home:

> The implications of war for women and men are … linked in symbolic as well as social and economic systems. During total war, the discourse of militarism, with its stress on 'masculine' qualities, permeates the whole fabric of society, touching both men and women. In doing so, it draws upon preexisting definitions of gender at the same time that it structures gender relations. When peace comes, messages of reintegration are expressed within a rhetoric of gender that establishes postwar social assignments of men and women.[10]

Yet what is often overlooked is that the next generation takes a step forward into increasing independence; we see such movements after each war. And there are further complexities. The women novelists of these years, while they continually address the paternalism of their society and the subordination of women, do not make the mistake of which Gillian Rose accuses some manifestations of feminism; they do not fail 'to address the power of women as well as their powerlessness, and the response of both women and men to that power'.[11] Woman's power, for both good and ill, balances explorations of women as victims. At the same time, novelists show the pressures suffered by the daughters of the suffragettes; not all, by any means, were temperamentally or intellectually prepared to take on careers and abandon domesticity.

Uncertainties about the roles of men and women in society parallel concerns about sexuality; throughout the thirties and forties, homosexuality and lesbianism tend to be treated circumspectly, implied rather than explored, and, when they are spelt out, often meeting a hostile reception. By the fifties and sixties, however, same-sex relationships begin to be openly addressed, despite continuing resistance from the law and areas of society. What these four decades do reveal is a steady opening up of the debate about gender and sexual roles, about 'normality' of behaviour and sexual orientation. Inevitably, as we have seen with other issues, at the heart of social and personal identity, conservatism and radicalism remain in tension, but the revelations of two world wars, with the ensuing anxieties about a civilization which has revealed itself as betraying the very precepts on which it is supposedly based, help the push for change.

Advances and exclusions in the thirties

In the inter-war years, issues concerning sex and gender are continually evident in the work of women writers. While Woolf is the most eminent of those attracted to the idea of androgyny, Winifred Holtby says,

> We still are greatly ignorant of our own natures. We do not know how much of what we usually describe as 'feminine characteristics' are really 'masculine', and how much 'masculine' is common to both sexes ... We do not even know – though we theorise and penalise with ferocious confidence – whether the 'normal' sexual relationship is homo- or bi- or heterosexual.[12]

The pronouncements of contemporary psychology on the fundamental importance of sexual difference also complicated the issue for the generation of women who had just achieved suffrage, as Marion Shaw has pointed out;[13] and Joanna Bourke has admirably reviewed the crisis of identity which World War One imposed on men and, as a result, on women. As she says, 'anatomy may not be destiny, but the belief that it is moulds most lives',[14] arguing that the term 'patriarchy', while 'drawing attention to male oppression of women ... ignores the way in which power structures oppress men' (p. 14). Holtby, keenly aware of the pressures of history and custom, cannot accept the conventional labelling of qualities as either 'male' or 'female', preferring the notion of shared humanity, and pouring scorn on

> the Ibsen thesis that women are captives, the Strindberg thesis that women are devils, the Barrie thesis that women are wistful little mothers, the Ethel M. Dell thesis that they are neurotic masochists yearning for the strong hand of a master – all these in different forms transfuse contemporary fiction.[15]

For, added to the disquiet about what can be ascribed to biological sex, there is the further complication of the roles ascribed to the sexes by their society (Holtby is an early advocate of the term 'gender' to describe such roles).[16] Victims of the Great War suffering from the effects of shell shock had already raised anxieties about the ways in which women perceived masculinity's role in, for instance, Rebecca West's *The Return of the Soldier* (1918); and novels like G. B. Stern's *A Deputy Was King* (1926) explored the frustrations for both a man and a woman as both have to come to terms with how the effects of gassing redefine a man's role both at work and in the home.[17] Alongside such traumatic readjustments are the experiences of women during that war, either in the war zone (as, for instance, Mary Borden, passionately protesting in *The Forbidden Zone* [1929], as she tends her mutilated patients, 'There are no men here, so why should I be a woman?... How could I be a woman here and not die of it?')[18] or in jobs on the home front. The subsequent disagreements about women's role in society are repeatedly rehearsed as they either willingly or unwillingly return to the home;[19] the struggle for suffrage may have been won by the end of the twenties, but women's position in society was by no means clear, and current theories of psychology eagerly espoused by those resistant to change did not help, as Holtby protests, saying that when the woman writer 'might have climbed out of the traditional limitations of domestic obligation by claiming to be a human being, she was thrust back into them by the authority of the psychologist... common humanity shrank to a small and unreliable generalization'.[20] The split in the priorities of women after suffrage widened as well; while Holtby was one of those who sided with the 'old' feminists, arguing that equality between the sexes was paramount, the 'new' feminists, which Eleanor Rathbone supported, saw issues which primarily concerned women, such as the inadequate provision for abortion and birth control, as of central importance.[21]

Added to these divisions there is the mixture of conservatism and radicalism on many gender issues which can be found in several works by women writers of the thirties. Mary Borden, for instance, in *The Technique of Marriage* (1933), gives advice on achieving equality in marriage, by no means championing the institution but examining it simply as a 'socal fact'; yet she can also admit that 'the life of the harem still has its charms',[22] and reveals strange prejudices, such as disapproval of 'sexual drive in the old' which she sees as 'a pitiful fact' (p. 155). Ellen Wilkinson, in her novel *Clash* (1929), shows vividly the dilemma of a woman torn between her career and the prospect of either a marriage which would end it or an equal relationship with a man back from the war whose 'inside is in bits – all silver tubes – and he is strapped together outside';[23] so there is the issue of marriage as against job, and a further issue, treated more obliquely, about disability in a man. Rachel Bowlby sums up the writer's dilemma admirably:

In thinking about women's writing there is a tension which comes back again and again between, on the one hand, narratives of straightforward advance, whereby modern women are taken to be slowly putting past restrictions behind them, getting to stand on their own two feet and write what they want; and, on the other, the description of formal structures of exclusion, whereby what does not go along with a norm defined as masculine is taken as disruptive of established spaces and in a certain sense feminine.

And Bowlby gives a perceptive analysis of how Woolf explores this tension in women's writing:

Sometimes she talks of 'impediments' – literally what stands in the way of the feet – obstacles without which women would be able to move on. And sometimes she talks of the outsider's place, the position of exclusion, as the origin of a difference of view which is valuable precisely in that it does not fit in with and thereby challenges the standard.[24]

For her part, Rebecca West is very clear about relationships which become 'impediments' in the four novellas which make up *The Harsh Voice* (1935).[25] In 'Life Sentence', problems arise as the woman, at first 'tender and virginal' (p. 20), finds herself a better business woman than her husband; their mutual hatred grows until they have to part, since, although desire is not dead, communication completely breaks down. The second novella, 'There Is No Conversation', also centres on a Beckettian failure of communication: 'There is no such thing as conversation. It is an illusion. There are intersecting monologues, that is all' (p. 63); and later, we are told,

no-one listens to what the other one says. But it appears that the inter-silence of the universe is more profound even than this. It appears that even the different parts of the same person do not converse among themselves, do not succeed in learning from each other what are their desires and their intentions.

(p. 127)

In the third story, 'The Salt of the Earth', West shows a woman as an obsessive medler, whose husband finally kills her to stop her destroying others. Only the final novella, 'The Abiding Vision', escapes the judgemental approach of the first three, as West tells the tale of a man who genuinely loves both wife and mistress. Otherwise, bitterness about ways in which relationships can become forms of entrapment is the prevailing tone. Again, in West's *The Thinking Reed* (1936), we find the sophisticated Isabelle (West's rewriting of Isabel Archer in Henry James's *The Portrait of a Lady*) twice having to resort to violence to have her point of view taken seriously, a humiliating experience which makes her realize how hard it is to break out of a stereotyped role:

> why should there be this feeling of oddness, of incongruity? It was perhaps because every inch of a woman's life as she lived it struck her as astonishing, either because nothing like what she was experiencing had ever been recorded, or because it had been recorded only falsely and superficially, with a lacuna where the real poignancy lay.[26]

Women, West suggests, have colluded with men in conforming to the stereotype which society has constructed for them; even Isabelle, in the end cries to her husband, 'Marc, I cannot understand it, I feel we ought to be equals, and yet I know you to be my superior and I like it' (p. 413), and again, later, she can say, 'I detest being a woman' (p. 418), coming to feel that men 'do not belong to the same race as women' (p. 429), a far cry from Holtby's faith in the ultimate unity of human nature.

West's women, while they may suffer, are from the upper echelons of society. Jean Rhys's women of the thirties, in contrast, are hovering on the edge of destitution. In *After Leaving Mr Mackenzie* (1930), the protagonist, Julia, is helpless; we hear that 'her careers of ups and downs had rubbed most of the hall-marks off her, so that it was not easy to guess at her age, her nationality, or the social background to which she properly belonged'.[27] Reduced to passive drifting from day to day, 'like a ghost' (p. 41), Julia is lost, suffering breakdown, with little chance of making a life for herself; her role is that of the archetypal victim, drawn to and degraded by the men she meets. Anna, in *Voyage in the Dark* (1934), seems set to follow Julia's route, and the protagonist in *Good Morning, Midnight* (1939) is also a woman at the end of her tether, with nowhere to go:

> In the middle of the night you wake up. You start to cry. What's happening to me? Oh, my life, oh, my youth...
> There's some wine left in the bottle. You drink it. The clock ticks. Sleep...[28]

Rhys is adept at portraying such women, sharp reminders that eman-cipation has by no means opened up opportunity for all.

Most women writers of the thirties, however, portray victims on the edges of their fictions; Ellen Wilkinson gives us vignettes of working-class poverty in *Clash* (1929), as do Naomi Mitchison in *We Have Been Warned* (1935) and Holtby in *South Riding* (1936), but usually the main characters reap some of the benefits of emancipation. They may strike out on their own, as Holtby's protagonist eventually does in *South Riding*, or they may actively work to uphold patriarchal society, as the Duchess Sophia does in Helen Simpson's historical novel, *Saraband for Dead Lovers* (1935).[29] This novel shows the strength women may have in using power, intellectually equal if not surpassing their menfolk in their capacity for intrigue, scorning men's predilection for warfare (an apt subject, given the debates about pacifism in the thirties), yet capable of their own brand of psychological violence, and quite failing to be humi-liated by the men's infidelity. But the cost is high. The Duchess is utterly ruthless in sacrificing the young Sophia Dorothea, sold at 16 into mar-riage with a man she loathes (the future Hanoverian king of England). This child is no match for her subtle mother-in-law or for her father-in-law's highly intelligent mistress, and her inevitable love affair with a dashing suitor leads to a tragic conclusion which is imposed by woman on woman, with no sign of pity or 'sisterhood'. Katharine Burdekin also looked at how women may use power in a novel of 1935 (unpublished at the time), *The End of This Day's Business*, but this work is pitched in the future rather than the past.[30] The world it constructs is one of universal peace, without violence or nationalism, ruled by women; men have been reduced to total subjection. Yet Burdekin does not in the end suggest that this is an ideal solution; her protagonist is put to death because she has attempted to educate her son, to lift him above the slavery to which he is otherwise doomed. Clearly, Burdekin implies that equality between the sexes, men's masculinity being completely re-educated, would be the best solution; yet the fact that such a drastic course as the subjugation of men must happen before this equality can be attempted does not suggest that she is optimistic about this happen-ing readily in her contemporary world. Indeed, in another novel pitched in the future, *Woman Alive* (1935), Susan Ertz kills off all women save one so as to give her protagonist sufficient bargaining power to stop men's propensity for war; essentialism is frequent in such novels, but then essentialism adds weight to any debated argument.

This essentialism is wittily exploited in the essays by a number of women writers in Mabel Ulrich's *Man, Proud Man* (1932). As I have suggested elsewhere, it is revealing to set these essays alongside the fictions which their authors write, since the essentialism which strengthens a case in debate is questioned when the writer concentrates on the fates of individuals and the complexities and contradictions within the human mind.[31] The tone of Ulrich's collection is on the whole witty. G. B. Stern, for instance, in her essay 'Man – without Prejudice (Rough Notes)', caricatures the absurdities of essentialist hostilities:

> No such thing as generic Man. No such thing as generic Woman. Therefore, no such thing as difference between them . . . But Man on the subject of Woman, and Woman on the subject of Man, are equally an expression of fundamental antagonism.[32]

Stern acknowledges her susceptibility to '"that Cranford feeling" – . . . nothing could go wrong as long as he was in the house' (p. 189), while next moment asserting that

> in a patriarchy, the women who marry into the family are assimilated into it from outside, and bring very little change into the moral blood-stream. Obviously, then, the patriarchal man subconsciously seeks a type that will not offer resistance to matter-of-fact assimilation.
>
> (p. 190)

Yet these witty, inconclusive observations acquire ballast when we turn to one of Stern's novels, *A Deputy Was King* (1926). Set in 1921, 'when the world seemed strangely empty and drained of all men' (p. 1), Toni, the Jewish protagonist, is tired of her role of business-woman and matriarch of a cosmopolitan family. Besides, 'she has learnt that directly she succeeded in noosing a man's interest in the work she did, she promptly loosened and lost it for the girl she was' (p. 4). So Toni, despite her philosophy that 'men are no good', takes a Gentile husband just back from the War, and throws herself into the role of 'little woman'. But her image of Giles's masculinity is as illusory as his of her dependent femininity. Furthermore, 'Giles has the Great War in his system' (p. 311): gassed then, he succumbs eight years later to tuberculosis and, as a result, to a redefinition of his role as a man, both for himself and for Toni. In this novel, too, traditional Jewishness problematizes generalized definitions: we learn of the old Matriarch's 'virile, autocratic epistles' (p. 126), for instance. Stern's novels demonstrate what Badinter reminds us of, and which the collection *Man, Proud Man* disguises with its witty unanimity: 'there is no universal masculine model ... Masculinity varies according to the historical period, but also according to a man's social class, race and age'.[33] And, that being so, women may well need to revise their concept of masculinity, as Toni must, so as to accommodate such variations; while men have to come to terms with women's changing priorities, as Robert Graves somewhat wryly acknowledges when discussing his first wife in *Goodbye to All That* (1929):

> Socialism with Nancy was a means to a single end: namely, judicial equality between the sexes. She ascribed all the wrong in the world to male domination and narrowness, and would not see any of my experiences in the war as anything comparable with the sufferings that millions of working class married women went through without complaint.[34]

More bitterly, in his novel *Death of a Hero* (1930), Aldington observes of George's wife and mistress,

> Unfortunately, they did not quite realise the strain under which he was living, and did not perceive the widening gulf which was separating the men of that generation from the women. How could they? The friends of a person with cancer haven't got cancer. They sympathise, but they aren't in the horrid category of the doomed.[35]

This failure to comprehend had been the theme of Rebecca West's *The Return of the Soldier* in 1918, and certainly, as Bourke says, by the late twenties, 'the sympathy allocated to the ill or diseased ex-serviceman was often negligible';[36] economic depression led to resentment against the war-damaged when others were perceived as more needy, and 'crippled soldiers had to be "made" into men again ... shrugging off what was regarded as the feminizing tendencies of disability' (p. 74). The confusions inherent in rethinking the roles of the sexes, not to mention the resistance to such rethinking, surface in many novels of the period. In Helen Simpson's novel *Boomerang* (1932), for instance, we hear that a girl with what are termed 'trousered' accomplishments loses her trousered attitude as her sexuality develops;[37] yet while this may be so, attitudes to men who try to live out the patriarchal role are ambivalent. Simpson's protagonist appreciates being treated as an equal, taken by her doctor friend through a war zone of the Great War: 'He showed me the way through a man's eyes, and better than that, let me look with my own eyes on the actual blasted places where men so casually walked and slept and accepted a three-to-one chance of death' (p. 438). Yet this equality is earned at a price; the narrator talks of 'the conscientious maleness of the woman in uniform' (p. 455), and the loss of femininity is implicitly mourned. The same complex reactions to a changing world emerge in Stevie Smith's *Over the Frontier* (1938), where Pompey recalls that before the Great War women only thought of 'love and the trials that make up the temperate hairbrushing confidences' (p. 22), while today 'we have in us the pulse of history and our times have been upon the rack of war' (p. 94). Pompey mourns the effects of war on masculinity, recalling 'the old men of 1922, the old broken shamefully broken body of the shattered soldier drawn up lifted up crucified upon his crutches' (p. 16), while later she mocks women who wear trousers: 'they would wish to approximate so closely to the masculine physique' (p. 151). Yet her whole novel questions the 'frontiers' between men and women, as Pompey demonstrates:

> Never again in England I think shall we breed exclusively masculine and exclusively feminine types at any high level of intelligence, but always there will be much of the one in the other and often it is making me laugh to see how not only the men sometimes ... but often the women too are saying Oh how much they long for the time to come again when there was nothing of this subtle overlapping at all but everything was as plain as a pikestaff.
>
> (p. 149)

This dilemma emerges in Victoria Cross's futuristic novel, *Martha Brown M.P., a Girl of Tomorrow* (1935).[38] The protagonist lives as a man-woman in thirtieth-century England, where women, as in Burdekin's novel of a feminist utopia, are the dominant sex. Sexuality is ambivalent in this work; in all Cross's early fiction, women find the adoption of 'masculinity' attractive, and Martha is no exception, as her first appearance shows:

> standing there in the doorway the lithe active figure framed in it, hands thrust deep down in the pockets of the leather coat, short pipe held firmly between the straight white teeth... Martha Brown looked, as she stood there, a magnificent specimen of bronzed womanhood.
>
> (pp. 7–8)

Yet the ending of the novel withdraws into convention; at the height of her political career, Martha leaves for America where men are still dominant, apparently abandoning her former strength even as she 'perceives her departure as a kind of death'.[39] Such novels support Catherine Hall's contention that 'feminine subjectivity presents serious problems for feminists, [as our] wants and desires might be more contradictory than we realized ... our psyches might be more resistant to change than our social selves'.[40]

The problem of how women perceived their roles was exacerbated by the fact that women outnumbered men throughout the inter-war years. Muriel Spark, in *The Prime of Miss Jean Brodie* (1961), looks back to this period and observes of Miss Brodie's contemporaries,

> There were legions of her kind during the 1930s ... women from the age of thirty and upward, who crowded their war-bereaved spinsterhood with voyages of discovery into new ideas and energetic practices in art or social welfare, education and religion.
>
> (p. 42)

Some of these found it hard to break out of the traditional role of the unmarried woman as servant to her family, as Sylvia Townsend Warner shows in *Lolly Willowes* (1926);[41] Lolly is one of those who continues to serve until she suddenly rebels, finding independence in a small village as a member of a witches' coven. Spinsterhood here is shown as a deprivation, but Lolly's conscious assertion of independence wins out in the end. Lettice Cooper's Rhoda, too, in *The New House* (1936), almost succumbs to spending her life looking after her charming but demanding mother, until finally agreeing to take up her sister's job in London on the sister's marriage (since the sister will, typically for the time, resign); but we are left in no doubt as to the family pressure she is under to do what is considered her spinsterly duty, not least from the spinster aunt of her mother's generation.[42] The protagonist of Radclyffe Hall's story, 'Miss Ogilvy Finds Herself' (1934) is less fortunate. She had flourished as an ambulance driver in the War, but the return to domestic spinsterhood brings on neurasthenia:

> during those [war] years Miss Ogilvy forgot the bad joke that Nature seemed to have played her. She was given the rank of a French lieutenant and she lived in a kind of blissful illusion; appalling reality lay on all sides and yet she managed to live an illusion. She was competent, fearless, devoted and untiring. What then? Could any

man hope to do better?...Poor all the Miss Ogilvies back from the war with their tunics, their trench boots, and their childish illusions! Wars come and wars go but the world does not change; it will always forget an indebtedness which it thinks it expedient not to remember.[43]

Under the pressures to conform to her traditional spinster's role, she begins to doubt that she ever had a worthwhile position in society; and this sense of exclusion lies at the core of Winifred Holtby's argument in *Women* (1934), concerning a high proportion of women, married or not, during the thirties.

Holtby looks at the ways various sections of a community exclude all those outside 'an arbitrary set of qualifications',[44] in the process signalling the marginalization of the Kikuyu in Kenya and the Jew in Germany. She then suggests that women's case is not so very different, and is also very ancient, arguing that, 'We call it Puritanism, but we forget that before it was Protestant it was Catholic, before it was Christian it was Hebrew; before it was Hebrew it was pagan' (p. 33). This is the sort of shock challenge which Katharine Burdekin uses in her futuristic novel *Swastika Night* (1937), when she shows women confined to cages as breeding stock; it is the sort of shock challenge which, as I have argued, is legitimate in debate to draw attention to an issue. But Holtby would certainly have a strong case if she referred to the exclusion of those whose sexual orientation was perceived at the time as deviant; very few novels appear which deal with homosexuality or lesbianism after the Radclyffe Hall case. Ethel Mannin does publish *Men Are Unwise* in 1934, but the title alone suggests a somewhat ambivalent presentation of homosexuality, whatever Mannin's own sympathies;[45] and for the most part, any reference to the subject is either implied or lurks on the margins of women's novels, open engagement with the issue being on the whole confined to debate rather than entertainment. This is also true of lesbianism; Helen Zenna Smith does write of a lesbian relationship in *Not so Quiet* (1930); but the couple who are caught are punished, and while there is some sympathy expressed, the issue, it is implied, is a consequence of the artificial grouping together of women of different backgrounds which war imposes – in other words, it is not 'normal'. Sylvia Townsend Warner offers a lesbian relationship in her historical novel, *Summer Will Show* (1936), but, while Sophia and Minna come very close to making love, Warner holds back from being explicit.

We do find more direct engagement with other sexual matters which suffer marginalization at the time. In Zenna Smith's *Not so Quiet*, the protagonist's sister, five months pregnant, begs her for the money to procure an abortion, as she dare not ask their parents; but again this is presented as one of the sad consequences of war. Rosamond Lehmann faces the issue more squarely in *The Weather in the Streets* (1936), showing the high price of an abortion; Olivia has to sell her emerald ring and cigarette case to raise the money and, again, family cannot be appealed to. Naomi Mitchison, having found that explicit issues of sex and sexuality were acceptable in her historical novel, the very popular *The Corn King and the Spring Queen* (1931), attempted to discuss modern abortion in *We Have Been Warned* (1935) but found that this was one of the issues which frightened off her publisher, Jonathan Cape, in 1933 (although it may well have been the conjunction of condoned rape, an open marriage and the discussion of the benefits of abortion in the Soviet Union, all part of the experience of a Labour candidate's wife which really frightened them off). Yet her novel was eventually accepted by Collins, who had published Jean Rhys's *Voyage in the Dark* the previous year (1934). While Mitchison's novel gives a vivid picture of the squalour of Soviet abortion clinics, Rhys's novel shows the better sort of back-street abortion which the fairly poor in this country could expect (not, that is to say, the worst version of such things) – and indeed, Rhys initially had her protagonist die as a result, although her publishers persuaded her to alter the ending, presumably for the sake of a largely middle-class readership. Rhys's novel had raised no outcry when it was published, so presumably Collins felt Mitchison's could be risked, although Mitchison would in fact lose a large part of her readership as a result of this book. Again, Phyllis Bottome, who in other novels complains of British conservatism about sex, exposes, in *The Mortal Storm* (1937), attitudes to unmarried pregnancies among the middle classes in Austria, an obvious parallel to pre-war Britain. Freya finds that high in the mountains, the poor family of her lover, Hans, 'gave her fresh dignity and strength, while down below – in her own social world – the same fact would make her feel ashamed and despised'.[46] As we can see, then, women's fictions of the thirties give a complex picture of the roles which women and men play in their contemporary society; there is no tidy thesis to be made out of the effects which universal suffrage had on attitudes to sexuality and gender roles, or out of the changes brought about by the Great War.

The gender paradoxes of the forties

The effects of warfare on men's and women's views of themselves are nonetheless considerable, if often tied to the context of war. Betty

Miller, for instance, in *On the Side of the Angels* (a novel delivered in 1944 but, because of the paper shortage, not published until 1945) explores the effect on both men and women of war service; the war service is specifically masculine, the women presented as adjuncts to this service. We see the effect on Claudia as her fiancé, Andrew, feels his masculinity challenged when he has to leave the army because of a 'groggy heart'; he repeatedly confronts her with his disability, and, for a time, she is dazzled by her encounter with the supposed commando, Herriot, only to find that his uniform is a pretence, a fantasy escape from his life as a bank manager. Herriot boosts his view of the masculine by donning a uniform to which we eventually find he has no right, Andrew feels his masculinity threatened by his disability, while Claudia confusedly half-subscribes to their assessment of themselves, before finally returning to Andrew. Meanwhile her sister, Edith, with her mask of 'self-effacing, self-concealing apathy' (p. 32), has to watch her husband's love affair with the army, that 'male world, without loyalties outside the rigid artifact of military life' (p. 39). Elizabeth Taylor's *At Mrs Lippincote's* (1945) explores very much the same area; again the novel is centred on camp life in this country, the husband, Roddy, 'that leader of men, who did not know how the world lived', living in digs with his wife and sister.[47] The sister, Eleanor, is trying to build herself up as a woman of social conscience but, being basically small-minded, is comically inept; she dreams of having lunch with Paul Robeson 'to show the world the quality of her moral courage and her indifference to its colour bars' (p. 16), and later dabbles with Communism while really pursuing a man. Roddy's wife, Julia, is very different:

> Could she have taken for granted a few of those generalisations invented by men and largely acquiesced in by women (that women live by their hearts, men by their heads, that love is woman's whole existence, and especially that sons should respect their fathers), she would have eased her own life and other people's.
>
> (p. 26)

Roddy, like Miller's Colin, is totally absorbed by military life, resenting the responsibilities of married life, while Julia thinks, as the novel draws to a close, 'Roddy wanted love only where there was homage as well as admiration. He did not want merely to be reckoned at his own worth. "How can you love what you do not respect?" he asked bitterly. "Women have to," she replied' (p. 214). Both Miller and Taylor present these marriages as casualities of a masculine bonding with military life and, more importantly, masculine acceptance of militaristic values.

Women involved in war work are, on the whole, portrayed more positively. Barbara Whitton's largely autobiographical tale of work as a land girl, *Green Hands* (1943), shows how much resilience was required to cope with the demands of the farm.[48] Often the girls came from a different class from their employers, resulting in a period of tense negotiation, especially as there was a residual prejudice against land girls left over, we are told, from World War One. Yet Whitton's narrator reports with pride that she and her friends are eventually accepted by the seasoned, working-class women, who tell them, 'We never thought you would stick it' (p. 49). Description veers from talk about 'clothes, food ... and our probable future husbands' (p. 73) to triumph at driving the very heavy tractor of the war years. Yet there are moments when middle-class ignorance of essentials is clear, together with what is considered 'polite' to discuss; we hear that the girls are embarrassed by talk of cows having abortions, or of a man's sister having a breast removed, while one of them has no idea of what is meant by castration. Marriage is still taken for granted as their goal, and ideas of a peace-time career are often modest – 'commercial designing and a bit of shorthand and typing', for instance (p. 183). The veering between conservative ambitions and radical achievement is striking.

Victoria Sackville-West's history of the Women's Land Army is a celebration of this achievement, even if 'it is a plodding story, of endurance rather than heroics'.[49] Some things she cannot applaud; attempts to assert femininity in dress do not always measure up to her standards, although she does (coyly) approve of tying the head up in a coloured scarf, as it 'puts me in mind of women turning the hay in Alpine meadows, and of women harvesting the huge orange pumpkins on farm lands in France' (p. 26). (As Antonia Lant records, the war office was concerned for women to retain their femininity during the war years so as to emphasize the masculinity of men; there was 'a male fear that the adoption of uniforms or overalls by women might actually diminish sexual difference.'[50]) However, on a more practical level, Sackville-West is proud of the girls who take on rat extermination, precisely because it defies an old stereotype, being undertaken 'by the very people who were traditionally supposed to mount a chair and scream whenever they saw so much as a mouse washing its whiskers' (p. 53).

In other areas, too, girls are defying conventions. As in World War One, sexual relations are not confined to marriage; Edith Pargeter's narrator in *She Goes to War*, for instance, accepts the feeling rather than the reality of formal marriage, claiming that if Tom 'takes me into a sort of twentieth-century sturdy-beggary, the new vagabondage, well, I always had leanings that way'.[51] Yet in professional areas, women's contributions to the war effort have their limitations. Dorothy Sayers tells, for instance, of a paper she was asked to give on the BBC's *Postcript* which was suppressed because it 'appeared to have political tendencies, and... "our public do not want to be admonished by a woman"'.[52] It is amusing to set this smug pronouncement alongside Storm Jameson's comment at the end of *Then We Shall Hear Singing* (1942), where she asserts,

> At whatever moment you choose to come into Europe, you are able to hear a woman talking under her breath about invasion or some sort of everyday violence... History, accurate history, is an affair of poor women, in spring, in summer, in autumn, in winter, in a country which has been invaded and conquered, talking... It's not of much account, what they say.[53]

The reviewing of women's lot takes many forms during the War years. E. M. Delafield, for instance, in *No One Will Know* (1941), looks back over a span of fifty years to show one woman in a family being slowly fixed in the role of spinster carer, while another, Rosalie, who never wanted marriage, and in a later era would have happily indulged in a series of relationships, is forced into a marriage which dooms both her and the two men she loves. A similar fate confronts Linda in Nancy Mitford's *The Pursuit of Love* (1945); although lively and intelligent, she is propelled by lack of education and general unhappiness into 'frippery and silliness' (p. 24). She swings from marriage to a right-wing banker to Communism when she falls in love with Christian, and finally ends up with a French lover, an aristocrat who works for the Resistance. Indifferent to the war which kills him, she dies, having his child.

Kate O'Brien is also concerned for the weight of conservatism on her women characters, exploring a whole range of issues relating to sex and gender in her novels. In *The Land of Spices* (1941) we learn that the English Mother Superior of an Irish convent took the veil because she could not come to terms with finding her adored widowed father in bed with another man;[54] yet she confronts the effects of unhappy, oppressive marriages ('No cross, no crown. He sees your sacrifice' [p. 40]) on her pupils without being judgemental, but with passionate commitment to her girls' right to fulfil their promise. Interestingly, O'Brien has the suffragette, Miss Robertson, point a parallel between her own cause and the nun's 'devotion to an idea, or an ideal. If your Reverend Mother had been in the world she might quite easily have gone to jail for the vote!' (p. 207). Then, in *The Last of Summer* (1943), O'Brien shows the devastating power of the mother of an Irish family over her children;[55] when the visit of their French cousin Angèle threatens her stranglehold, she destroys her eldest son's happiness rather than let him marry the girl, just as she has nursed her hatred of Angèle's father over the years because he saw her basic ruthlessness and refused to marry her. The narrowness of her vision corresponds to the narrowness of the opportunities which life in this intensely conservative society has given her; and her eldest son pays the price, accepting a kind of emasculation rather than break free.

Rosamond Lehmann's *The Ballad and the Source* (1944), set in the early years of the century, also explores a woman's capacity for cruelty.[56] The novel explores how women may teeter on the brink of a madness which might be brilliance (Mrs Jardine's daughter does in the end tip over), when intelligence is not allowed to fulfil its potential and as a result is twisted. Yet Mrs Jardine is not alone responsible for her cruelties; they are also constructed by the society in which she lives, something of which she is very much aware, as when she says:

> Do you know what goes to make a tragedy? The pitting of one individual of stature against the forces of society. Society is cruel and powerful. The *one* stands no chance against its combined hostilities. But sometimes a kind of spiritual victory is snatched from that defeat. Then the tragedy is completed.
>
> (pp. 107–8)

And she dreams of a better world for women where 'one day...women will be able to speak to men – speak out the truth, as equals, not as antagonists, or as creatures without independent moral rights – pieces of men's property, owned, used and despised' (p. 101). But that world is slow to come in the fiction of women writers of the time. Elizabeth Bowen's *The Heat of the Day* (1948) may show a woman with a sophisticated job during the War, but she is no nearer speaking out 'the truth', or hearing it from the men whom she cares for than the Mrs Jardines of World War One. Bowen's Stella is manipulated by one man through her love for another; she has sacrificed her reputation first for her husband and then for her lover, and she loses the admiration of Louie, the girl who has set her up as an icon, when Louie no longer thinks her 'virtuous'. Conservatism about woman's lot is a potent force in this novel, just as it is in the novels by Miller and Taylor.

But there is another side to this lament over conservatism; a number of women writers take up the effects of the suffragettes on their children. Ruth Adam's *Murder in the Home Guard* (1942) shows the nurse Sally as full of fantasy and a sense of vocation, educated by women who had fought for the vote; but Sally does not pass the matric, which would have given her access to university. There is an unvoiced gibe at the limitations of those feminists who see femininity as an enemy and attempt to destroy or suppress it; we hear that 'Sally's headmistress and mother between them had managed to eliminate the message "Just watch me" which had been imprinted by Nature when she turned her out of the womb for the sole purpose of carrying on the human race'.[57] The portrayal of the forces shaping Sally's life echoes something of the unease Dorothy Sayers expresses about feminism in her essay 'Are Women Human?' (1938).[58] Sayers comments:

> In reaction against the age-old slogan, 'woman is the weaker vessel', or the still more offensive, 'woman is a divine creature', we have, I think, allowed ourselves to drift into asserting that 'a woman is as good as a man', without always pausing to think what exactly we mean by that. What, I feel, we ought to mean is something so obvious that it is apt to escape attention altogether, viz: not that every woman is, in virtue of her sex, as strong, clever, artistic, level-headed, industrious and so forth as any man that can be mentioned; but, that a woman is just as much an ordinary human being as a man, with the same individual preferences, and with just as much right to the tastes and preferences of an individual.
>
> (p. 107)

Here Sayers eschews, not only the tendency of men to refer to essentialist woman, but of women to dream of a specific future for just such a non-existent model; and this is what we find the daughters of suffragettes having to contend with in several novels of the period. In the end, Adam has Sally escape back into femininity through her love for the dashing pilot, Tom; yet here Adam also spares a thought for the rushed love affairs which war all too often imposes, seeing something precious as having been lost to this war generation:

> All through their troubled love-affair, they had no time to search each other out, and debate and advance and retreat and play at love as though all springtime was at their disposal before they need settle

down to the serious business of mating. They must crush springtime into a few brief hours.[59]

As I have suggested, in matters of sexual orientation most novels of the War years deal with the fluctuating fortunes of heterosexual relationships. In this sphere, the things which are specifically condemned tend to centre on the effects of war. Jim's fiancé, Delia, for instance, in Edith Pargeter's *Lame Crusade* (The Eighth Champion of Christendom, 1945), abandons him for another man early in the War, and we are left with the impression that she has accepted 'missing' as 'dead' far too easily. And there are horrific instances of letters sent to servicemen, suggesting that their wives are having affairs; Pierre, in Storm Jameson's *Cloudless May* (1943), comes home and kills his innocent wife after receiving just such a letter. Yet the pressure on wives, left for years without a husband, can be treated sympathetically too; Louie, in Elizabeth Bowen's *The Heat of the Day* (1948) gets pregnant while her husband is away at the front, but she is not condemned for it, and Bowen allows her to escape her husband's anger, as he is killed before his next leave. Bowen's solution contrasts with the disturbing moment in Phyllis Bentley's fine novel *The Rise of Henry Morcar* (1946), when Henry's wife announces, on his return from the Great War, that her son is not his;[60] this, it turns out, is a lie she has fabricated to punish him because he survived while her brother did not, and the effect of the lie shapes all their lives for many years.

Hasty, passionate love affairs, pregnancies, abortions are inevitably part of the instabilities of war as portrayed in the novels of the time. And so is disability. A number of works touch on the effects disability has on sexual relations. I have already mentioned Andrew's groggy heart, which drives him out of the army in Betty Miller's *On the Side of the Angels* (1945), affecting his view of his masculinity; and inevitably the War presents wounding as causing a crisis in many relationships. Susan Ertz, for instance, in *Anger in the Sky* (1943), portrays the anguish Viola faces when her lover is reduced to a vegetable existence in an air raid; while Phyllis Bottome, in *Within the Cup* (1943), shows the beautiful Virginia, the vicar's wife who has been the lover of both the local landowner and his son, reduced to a severely mutilated invalid in one of the Plymouth raids. The doctor who has befriended her gives her the choice between life and death; she chooses life, but the struggle she undergoes to make this decision is vividly portrayed, since, for such a passionate creature, the loss of her physical beauty, her own view of her femininity, challenges the mainspring of her existence – she must, if she lives, accept a life of sexual sublimation. Disability outside the parameters of the effects of war is not, however, often visited on central characters; a rare exception is the heroine of Daphne du Maurier's historical novel *The King's General* (1946), who is confined to a wheelchair after a hunting accident, yet still retains her lover's passionate commitment, although their marriage does not take place, since she cannot have children. The radicalism of placing disability centre stage exists side by side in this novel with the conservatism of its preclusion of marriage.

While the many faces of heterosexual relationships are those most usual in these novels, homosexuality and lesbianism, when they are represented at all, are still treated, for the most part, circumspectly. We see this, for instance, in Rachel Ferguson's *A Stroll before Sunset* (1946), a novel looking back at the Edwardian stage.[61] Here, we are shown the passionate rivalry between two stars of the stage, Georgina Dempster and Grania Summet, wittily treated – but entwined with their lives is that of the ultimately tragic Lionel. While Grania's love affairs are treated robustly, in contrast to Georgina's awesome virtue ('Georgina would make a brothel into a Cranford parlour' [p. 93]), Lionel's life is filled with shadows. Homosexuality at school is implied, not stated; when he is older, he longs to be a dress designer, and designs Grania's frocks – yet whether he is gay or bisexual is never clear. He fantasizes about life with young Mary, but the relationship comes to nothing amidst hints and nudges about his past; he seems 'to combine all the worst faults of both sexes', says the malicious (and equally ambivalent, sexually) Reggie, who, for his own part, puts 'into a nutshell the male immunity from consequence which is eternally confused with morality' (pp. 228–9). In the end, Lionel overhears one of Grania's vicious comments, describing him as 'a dear thing, really: one of those nice, cosy tame cats who adore one and whose shoulder one can weep on with absolute impunity – when he isn't weeping on yours' (p. 261); already in a distraught state, he goes out and drowns himself, whereupon one character remarks that he was not gay but had a woman's mind in a man's body – a description which quite fails to satisfy.

Much more outspoken is the novel *Olivia* (1949), which is set in a French finishing school. This autobiographical novel, written by Dorothy Strachey using the pen name 'Olivia' in the early thirties, is a vivid account of passionate lesbian attractions and rivalries; publication may well have been delayed because of the Radclyffe Hall case.[62] At the core of the novel is the conflict between Mlle Cara and Mlle Julie, who own the school; the implication of a lesbian relationship which has foundered is very clear. The girls are inevitably drawn into one or other of the rival camps; Olivia's feelings for Mlle Julie are frankly erotic, and she finds her judgement entirely governed by Mlle Julie's tastes and views (Mlle Julie is a forerunner of Muriel Spark's Miss Brodie in her manipulation of the young). Gradually the rivalry between the two camps darkens; Mlle Cara now has as supporter Frau Riesener while Mlle Julie has the Signorina. Olivia declares her love, and it becomes clear that Mlle Julie's love for her girls is far from platonic. At last, the battle reaches its climax, Mlle Cara accusing Olivia of 'being led astray, demoralized, depraved[.] How idle you have become, and for all I know, vicious! Fallen into the hand of a low-born Italian Jewess – and into others, worse, worse!' (p. 73). In the end, Mlle Julie plans to go to Canada, leaving Cara and Reisener in Paris, whereupon Cara dies of an overdose of chloral, whether intentionally or not is unclear. This is a finely controlled tale, conveying the dangerously unstable aftermath of a passionate relationship which is never spelt out but haunts the work throughout, and which inevitably involves the girls who are of an age to experience rites of passage. But the attitude to lesbianism is by no means clearly defined.

Domesticity, rebels and victims in the fifties

As Gill Plain observes, after the War many women did return to the home.[63] Furthermore, for those who might be reluctant to do so, there were passionate advocates of domesticity, a cause which drew adherents throughout the late forties and the fifties. Sheila Rowbotham points to Monica Dickens, for instance, as one of those urging domesticity as the true sphere of femininity:

> There were emotive pressures within popular culture which set ful-
> filled femininity against external intellectual interests and demand-
> ing employment. Monica Dickens...warned career women in
> *Woman's Own* in 1956 that they could be endangering the love of
> their children. She portrayed shallow ambition on one side and the
> deeper virtues of homely intimacy on the other.[64]

And those of the younger generation who had no wish to pursue careers continued to be a subject for women writers. Elizabeth Taylor, for instance, in *A Game of Hide and Seek* (1951) charts the career of Harriet, a suffragette's child, who is 'heedless of former sacrifice, as history makes all of us'.[65] It is not that she is really against her mother's feminism, but that she is neither bright nor academic, so the benefits of a satisfying career are closed to her; and, aware that she is disappointing her mother's hopes for her, she comes to hate any mention of the time her mother spent in prison for the cause, as all she really craves is to be married and enclosed by domesticity. In due course, we find her daughter Betsy implying that she would have felt proud of her mother if she had been imprisoned, like the grandmother; 'How things can swing right across the heads of one generation, Harriet thought' (p. 181). This, in a nutshell, shows how the return to the home of one generation does not mean that the next may not reap the benefits for which their grandmothers fought; Betsy, by the end of the novel, is bidding fair to achieve all that her grandmother hoped for her daughter. And this difference between generations is an illuminating feature of the fifties, as Deborah Philips and Ian Haywood have pointed out.[66] They argue persuasively that feminism did not die after the War, as, despite the need to give jobs to the men returning from the War, Labour was still recruiting women actively in 1947, and many women were contemplating a wider range of careers than formerly. By this, they do not deny that there was considerable tension between marriage and a career, both in the market place and in the mind of the individual; but a social revolution was being 'unobtrusivey enacted' in the fifties, as is shown by the conference in 1956 of the Six Point Group and the Married Women's Association on 'Married Women out of Work'. Yet progress, they admit, was slow; marriage was still a priority, an alternative to a career for the majority, abortion was still illegal, bastardy frowned on, and the export of orphans continued. However, they also point to a surprisingly large number of career novels, aimed at the popular market; many were in the Mills and Boon series, but several were published by mainstream publishers. They range from novels on becoming a doctor, a librarian, a physiotherapist, a teacher, to life behind the counter and driving a car.[67] What we find in the post-war decade are the struggles which women have to reconcile the aims and aspirations of pre-war 'old' (equalitarian) and 'new' feminist priorities; careers tend to be set against the urge to enjoy marriage and family, at a time when the pill was as yet out of reach. Yet life in the fifties is complicated by a great deal more than this; after World War Two, with the horror of the Holocaust and Hiroshima, came the Korean War and the unease of the cold war. As a result, the doubts raised about the values of Western civilization, the fear of the H bomb which made many wary of having families, the end of empire, the debacle of Suez, the Russian invasion of Hungary, were just some of the issues which made the late forties and the fifties as complex and complicated as any previous decade in which to attempt to formulate definitions of masculinity and femininity.

As we have seen in previous chapters, the fifties decade was, for some women novelists, a time to reappraise ways in which the past had led to the present. Rebecca West, for instance, in *The Fountain Overflows* (1957) reviews a childhood very close to her own, looking, among other things, at the utter power an inadequate father wielded over his entire family: 'Papa was brave, he was cruel, he was dishonest, he was kind...I might have added to the list of his paradoxical qualities that he was penniless and discredited and enormously powerful.'[68] This was the father who could take on public causes quite altruistically, yet who was completely irresponsible towards his family and towards money which he treated like 'a gipsy mistress, he loved it and hated it, he wanted to possess it and then drove it away, so that he nearly perished of his need for it' (p. 56). Yet despite or because of this, 'feminism too was in the air, even in the nursery' (p. 11), while marriage still offered the only viable prospect, however unsatisfactory, for a woman's future; we see the complication for the child Rose who, although very independent-minded, adores her father and confesses 'temperamentally I was born to acquiesce to patriarchy' (p. 307). In the end, despite the love and loyalty of his wife and family, this volatile father abandons them, taking the bonds and selling the furniture which could have brought them some income. The mother remains generous ('You must be thankful, dears. Your father will have something' [p. 329]), and contrives to bring up her children with a continuing respect for their father. In this, he is more fortunate than the father in Sylvia Townsend Warner's *The Flint Anchor* (1954), another male viewed retrospectively, who is temperamentally unsuited to exercizing the absolute power of the patriarch, and who loses the love and respect of his womenfolk as he successively destroys their lives; yet Warner does not allow us to lose sympathy for him entirely since she makes clear the burden which the expectations of contemporary society placed on the Victorian male.

Such novels, looking back at past tyrannies, coincide with others which scrutinize women's lot in marriage. Christine Brooke-Rose, for instance, in *The Sycamore Tree* (1958), shows an adored wife, Nina, who has 'pride in her femininity mingled with a deep uncertainty which men were quick to sense' (p. 24); she is seen as one of those sweet, devoted wives, who nonetheless attract 'some crude reference to her physical attractions' from men (pp. 24–5). One of these dubious admirers becomes obsessed with her and, fatally, discovers her secret: occasionally, unable to cope with her image as the 'perfect' wife, she goes soliciting. He uses this knowledge to compel an affair, and the situation develops rather as in Middleton's *The Changeling*, with Nina, wretched but helpless, becoming as obsessed as her unattractive lover. The husband is not ultimately blamed for her predicament, but we are aware of the intolerable burden she carries, playing the angel in the house when the role is inappropriate for her temperament. Mary Borden handles a related theme in *The Hungry Leopard* (1956), where Amanda, who has commited suicide, has left three years of her life unaccounted for. We hear the impressions of her husband, his mistress and Amanda's closest friend, all with clear views on who she was. Most of these characters see Amanda as a side issue to their pursuit of letters she had received from the charismatic Jacques, while their accounts of her are more confusing than revealing; she was reckless, she was pampered, she was not the sort of woman 'who needed a man in her life' (p. 199). We learn from one character that she did war work as she 'wanted to win the war with her own two hands and be killed doing it, or at least mutilated because she was ashamed of her husband who didn't join up' (p. 201); when, as a result, she suffered a damaged hand, her husband could not bear this 'mutilation'. In the end, we learn that, in those lost three years, she and Jacques were lovers, and had a child which died; everyone has typecast Amanda to suit their own requirements, and with no regard for her own perception of herself.

Hers is the burden which some women take on willingly; Storm Jameson's Emmy, for instance, in *The Green Man* (1952), a woman who has given up everything for her intolerably selfish husband, even to comforting him when his love affairs founder, tells a horrified young visitor, 'We're not put into the world to amuse ourselves. That's not life – or at least it's not a woman's life. Our happiness is in giving' (p. 239). More extremely, Jameson shows a woman colluding in the patriarchal ruling of the Catholic Church of the day, when old Marie, in *The Hidden River* (1955) tells young Elizabeth, to her fury, that a wife is always expendable when giving birth to a child (p. 199). The lot, too, of spinsters can still be seen as traditionally lacking in value in works of the fifties. Barbara Pym sets about giving a subversive account of this, for instance, in *Excellent Women* (1952), where her protagonist plays the role of a Chaucerian narrator, deceptively naïve while in fact very shrewd, as she observes the politely patronizing people around her.

Yet values are changing, if painfully. In Christine Brooke-Rose's *The Languages of Love* (1957), Julia discusses the problems these changes bring with a friend, Marion, who argues:

> Of course values change. I saw a play a while ago in which the word 'mummy' was pregnant with class hatred. Recently I read a novel in which the word 'mother' became more and more ominous and freudly monstrous. Sometimes it seems there's nothing left that means anything. But the reality behind the shifting values of words and feelings remains.[69]

But this last (debatable) reassurance does not help Julia's relations with such men as Bernard, who responds to her with the 'reality' of a traditional male reaction to the female: 'When he felt serious she had to respond, but when she felt serious he accused her of being solemn, he played with words, saying, if she protested, that humour should penetrate life at all levels, and not form a separate compartment' (p.147).

Barbara Pym's novel *Less than Angels* (1955) turns to a similar theme, exploring the stirrings of rebellion against convention, even as the surface tension of conservatism is retained. An older woman, observing her niece, thinks that 'in her day [the mid-twenties] it was the men who formed the women's tastes. Now, perhaps, it was the other way round' (p. 57); yet later one of the young women says that men still 'like to form [women's] tastes for them' (p. 124). In this novel, Pym shows the young living together, and the gradual realization that there should not be 'different codes of behaviour for men and women, though of course that view *was* held, and in the highest circles' (p. 130). Pamela Frankau also shows, in *A Wreath for the Enemy* (1954), her protagonist, Penelope, caught in the toils of a changing world, part of her obstinately longing for old-fashioned romance ('my love was a haunting; an enchanted slavery, a chosen bond' [p. 142]), part of her acknowledging that she belongs to an age where such fantasies no longer satisfy for long. Indeed, in 1946 Elizabeth Taylor had demonstrated how destructive such fantasies can be in her impressive novel *Palladian*, where her heroine Cassandra (another of those children in rebellion against the suffragette generation) is ruled by the 'proper emotions' she encounters in novels (p. 5). She assigns her androgynous employer, Marion, the unlikely role of Mr Rochester, and remains obdurately insensitive to the reality of the world around her, as she has determined to fall in love with Marion 'like a governess in a book' (p. 182); yet his house is on the point of ruin, his estate neglected, the other members of the family suffering the realities of life (pregnancy, despairing alcoholism, the death of a child) which Cassandra fails to acknowledge. Her name is ironic; she rejects any glimpse of a predictable future, preferring to ground herself in an unreal past.

In other areas too, change is, if not reluctant, slow. On the whole, references to lesbianism and homosexuality remain implicit and on the sidelines rather than central in British women's novels of the late forties and fifties (although the States seems to have been offered a wide range of popular paperback literature centring on homosexuality and lesbianism).[70] Barbara Pym's *A Glass of Blessings* (1958) does have a gay character, Bason, but his camp behaviour is stereotypical even if portrayed without overt prejudice; he contributes to the comic fabric of the novel.[71] However, there is one shining exception to this wariness, Mary Renault's *The Charioteer* (1953).[72] This novel deals centrally with a young man's gradual coming to terms with his, Laurie's, sexual orientation. We see him first protesting against the expulsion of his adored head of house, Lanyon, from their public school, for an (unnamed) homosexual offence. Later we meet Laurie in hospital, badly injured in the Dunkirk escape, where he gradually realizes he has fallen in love with a conscientious objector, the young Quaker, Andrew. Interwoven with Laurie's gradual acceptance of his sexual orientation are the prejudices of his heterosexual neighbour in the hospital ward, whose dysfunctional marriage undermines his defence of the superiority of 'normality'; and there is continual debate about the pacifism of the Quakers which, when confronted in person, fails to add up to cowardice. But homosexuality is the overriding issue, treated sensitively, with gay men debating their role in society and the attitudes society has to them. One character, Alec, puts his case eloquently:

> I don't admit that I'm a social menace ... I've never involved a normal person or a minor or anyone who wasn't in a position to exercise free choice. I'm not prepared to let myself be classified with dope-pedlars and prostitutes. Criminals are blackmailed. I'm not a criminal. I'm ready to go to some degree of trouble, if necessary, to make the point.
> (p. 233)

However, a gay friend, Ralph, responds by putting the case for what he himself terms 'normality', saying, 'even civilised people had better hang on to a few biological instincts ... They've learnt to leave us in peace unless we make public exhibitions of ourselves, but that's not enough, you start to expect a medal' (p. 233). Renault never allows her novel to adopt the tone of special pleading; she has a far more mature approach, simply showing, by her fine depiction of a range of characters, that her gays, like her heterosexuals, can be both admirable and despicable, as can any cross-section of humanity.

Disability, too is treated circumspectly at this time. The war wounded, as we have seen, remain visible in women's fiction, but other forms of disability tend to be either excluded or sidelined. However, one area of disability does gain increasing attention during the fifties, and this is the area of breakdown and madness, especially where these are clearly the result of social pressures.[72] Doris Lessing, for instance, shows in *The Grass Is Singing* (1950) how Mary breaks down under the strain of a marriage which is alien to her temperament, and the poverty of an isolated farm. Tragically, she cannot cope with the fact that the one person capable of giving her the comfort and reassurance she needs is black; she has been conditioned by her white-settler training to see such a possibility as literally beyond the pale. But women are not seen as the sole victims of social pressure; in Pamela Frankau's *The Offshore Light* (1952), a novel which can be usefully linked to Doris Lessing's *Briefing for a Descent into Hell* (1971), the diplomat Brooke Alder seems to divide his time between this world and the island of Leron, where he is known as the Guardian. It gradually becomes clear that he is undergoing some kind of breakdown in which he is trying to resolve the problems of this world on a flawed Utopian island created and sustained by his imagination. This novel shows a man bearing considerable responsibility in world affairs (a responsibility which society tends to see as a very 'masculine' province) and losing the support of his wife in the process. Just as novels like *The Fountain Overflows* and *The Flint Anchor* show the pressures imposed on a man to fulfil his patriarchal role within the family, so *The Offshore Light* shows the pressures of a career which pose too great a strain on a single individual, who cannot carry the burden of society's fear of a possible nuclear war.

Sometimes in the fifties there are brighter moments in dealing with those whom society either drives to madness or labels as mad. In Muriel Spark's comic novel *The Comforters* (1957), for instance, the novelist protagonist is labelled 'mad' by those who refuse to accept her wrestlings with the idea of author either as in control or as a channel through which creation is achieved; yet Caroline wins through into writing her own novel in her own way despite them all. But on the whole, women novelists use the theme of madness rather as Foucault will do in *Madness and Civilization* (1961), to expose the pressures that social expectation exerts on those who do not conform to received ideas on how men or women should behave. What is being explored in such novels is a concept which Iris Murdoch wrestles with in her early novels. In *Under the Net* (1954), for instance, her protagonist Jake ponders about his relationships:

When does one ever know a human being? Perhaps only after one has realised the impossibility of knowledge and renounced the desire for it and finally ceased to feel the need of it. But then what one achieves is no longer knowledge, it is simply a kind of co-existence; and this too is one of the guises of love.[74]

The idea that individual identity can be more important than a kind of submission to the partner, or indeed to society's expectation of submission to its tenets, is central to many of the novels of the fifties. Veronica Hull, for instance, analyses this notion of aloneness (not loneliness) in her novel *The Monkey Puzzle* (1958). Hull's protagonist, Catherine, sets out as a student of philosophy because 'to her, her existence was so tenuous that it needed the thoughts of others to confirm it' (p. 11). Later, lacking the external confirmation of her identity which she has needed, she breaks down, whereupon her family have her committed to a mental hospital. When she gets out, Catherine has to establish who she is for herself. She begins by refusing to live by the expectations of others; when told, for instance, that 'Having children isn't a *career*' (p. 96), she replies 'I don't mind having a job, but I don't want a career' (p. 97), a distinction which aligns her with dissenting children of suffragettes found in other novels of the decade. She links her struggles to establish her own identity, free from 'the thoughts of others' on the personal, private level, with a realization of the follies of society at large. Discovering the limitations of her own home life, she comes to the conclusion that

Considering that the commonplace and necessary facts of money, sex and death were taboo in many houses it was not surprising that such far-fetched horrors as war and madness overcame people almost without their putting up much resistance.

(p. 106)

At the same time, she refuses the advice of a disenchanted friend to 'be a cynic, sneer, be facetious' (p. 114). Eventually, shaken by her ordeals, she decides to concentrate on her own immediate concerns, eschewing the headier reaches of philosophy, which she terms 'the intellectuals' private cinema' (p. 205) for an empiricism she has experienced, not studied. She decides 'the world's madder than me', and goes her own way with a co-existing husband (to use Iris Murdoch's term for one of the guises of love) and a child, ignoring the pressures that once threatened to crush her. The redefining of her role is painfully achieved, and once again, although old notions of a submissive marriage are eschewed, the legacy of the suffragettes for one of its frailer daughters is shown as failing to offer all the solutions.

The politics of self-actualization and progressive social change: the sixties

During the sixties, the move towards redefining a personal identity and role, which Hull explores in *Monkey Puzzle*, intensifies, and the woman's point of view predominates in women's fiction; this is the decade when the pill will give women, potentially, far greater freedom, but will not by any means solve all their traditional problems. In *Talking to Women* (1965), Nell Dunn interviews a number of women writers who, she tells us in the introduction, believe 'that a woman's life should not solely be the struggle to make men happy but more than that a progress towards the development of one's own body and soul';[75] this extension of pre-war 'new' feminism is a major priority of women's fiction throughout this decade – women's sense of themselves is set beside battles over their legal status. In Dunn's book, we find Ann Quin repeating an old claim (one which Lessing's Martha recognized in *Martha Quest*, for instance) that:

> Men are always trying to assert themselves, a certain vanity, and women are not so conscious of trying to assert themselves, they're much more adaptable – they like playing a role that a man will throw upon them, they have many roles, there's a lot of the chameleon in women.
>
> (p. 137)

However, Edna O'Brien points to something which is less traditional: 'there's a fierce hollowness in relationships now. This creates a new morality. The morality of the lonely and the uncommitted' (p. 98). And O'Brien's own novels of the sixties are striking examples of this assertion. Her trilogy, *The Country Girls* (1960), *The Lonely Girl* (1962 – later retitled *Girl with Green Eyes*) and *Girls in Their Married Bliss* (1964), charts the lives of two girls brought up in the west of Ireland, and, breaking out of the claustrophobic repressions of their rural background, escaping first to Dublin and then to London.[76] Their tale is told with wit, lyricism and a painterly eye for descriptive detail, yet they never achieve happiness. Baba, the more resilient of the pair, rebels against the Dickensian strictures of their convent schooling, organizing their expulsion, but the freedom she craves ends in marriage to a husband who is often brutal, and whom she ultimately tolerates for the sake of her child, the result of an equally loveless affair. Kate is even more vulnerable. There are echoes of Jean Rhys's women of the thirties in her, as she is swept by her craving for romantic love from one disastrous relationship to another, losing her much loved child to her husband in the process. Where Baba suffers physical blows, what Kate encounters is largely mental abuse, and in the final volume of the trilogy she very nearly follows the route of so many women in novels of the fifties and sixties, teetering on the edge of madness. But finally she takes control of her own destiny in a devastatingly symbolic and final gesture of disillusionment with the promise of fulfilling relationships. She has herself sterilized, without any show of emotion (she who has always been a victim of her emotions); this is a bleak note to end on, as Kate, to Baba's dismay, signals her acceptance of what O'Brien will tell Dunn is 'the morality of the lonely and the uncommitted'.[77] The course O'Brien charts in these haunting novels has something in common with the course Doris Lessing's Martha takes in the Children of Violence novels – the move from a restrictive, rural background to the apparent greater freedom of the town, and the subsequent disillusionment with the men encountered there; Martha, like O'Brien's Kate, escapes a loveless marriage at the price of losing her child. But there the likeness ends. Where O'Brien concentrates exclusively on the women's relationships with each other and with the men who exploit them, Lessing shows her Martha as a child of her time, inextricably linked to the happenings of the world in which she lives. Yet both writers are deeply immersed in mapping what goes to establish a woman's identity.

The novel that has been taken as a flagship for this increasing concentration on woman's identity is Doris Lessing's *The Golden Notebook* (1962), which continues to be read as a classic feminist text. In part, Lessing engages in this work with what Irigaray defines as the crucial question of language.[78] However, Lessing's own preface, written ten years later, insists that her novel is not entirely about women's issues, but about the need not to compartmentalize, a priority which Lois McNay shares when she claims that the 'politics of self-actualization need not lapse inevitably into introversion but may contribute to wider forms of progressive social change'.[79] As I suggested earlier, this priority is precisely what we find in the culminating golden notebook of Lessing's novel, where Anna writes the first sentence of Saul's new novel and he offers the first sentence of hers, each of them, as it were, inscribing the other's body, but not with the urge for domination; Anna and Saul achieve a kind of coexistence which is rather different from the accepted ignorance of another's identity which Murdoch's Jake contemplates. For while Lessing has shown that Anna and Saul have, for a time, shared their identities, they nevertheless maintain each their own integrity, man and woman apart. Yet Anna supplies the masculine sentence for the beginning of Saul's novel, while he supplies the feminine sentence which will begin hers. Lessing suggests here something about the make-up of each individual which was not entirely in accord with the priorities of the incipient women's movement of the early sixties, and her novel was not interpreted in this way at the time.

Many novels of this decade look instead at the problems of marriage, conventional or otherwise. Elizabeth Taylor's *In a Summer Season* (1961), for instance, explores a marriage revolving entirely around passion, where the unknowable quality of another's identity is submerged beneath sexual enchantments for a time; this is not a question of the woman being dominated by the man, but of both being mesmerized by their mutual desire.[80] Taylor shows with her customary sensitivity the gradual jarring differences which threaten husband and wife; Kate is ten years older, and supports her husband, Dermot, financially (he cannot keep a job and drinks too much). Gradually, we find Dermot antagonized by those of Kate's memories and interests which she shares with old friends, fuelling his awareness of the vast difference between their temperaments. In a sense, the marriage is only saved by Dermot's death in a car crash, when Kate returns, conservatively, to her 'own kind', marrying her best friend's widower. Alongside this central relationship, Kate's children suffer their own rites of passage. Taylor explores the generation gap through each character's isolation within their own sexual longings, their contempt for the desires of others; yet while she gives us the poignancy of the inability to communicate, she also gives the comic absurdity of frank discussion between two older, unmarried women of the suffragette generation, Aunt Ethel and her friend, analysing, secure in their innocence, what they term 'the great mammary age' (p. 109). In the end, having met the young girl Araminta, old Sir Alfred sums up something of the legacy which the suffragettes have bequeathed to this new generation, and it is neatly ironic to have a man offer it, if somewhat condescendingly:

> Perhaps poor Ethel and her friends, he thought, with all their long-ago suffragette nonsense had achieved something after all – though it had not benefited themselves. Freedom to behave in her own style was what Araminta had from them. She made the most of it.

(p. 162)

Taylor here encapsulates something which inspired the new women's movements of the sixties: a sense that the promise of greater freedom for women which the suffragettes had worked for, while benefiting the Aramintas of society (although not perhaps in ways which those suffragettes might have approved of), had not as yet reached people like Kate. And this sense lies at the heart of a number of novels by women in the sixties.

In Penelope Mortimer's *The Pumpkin Eater* (1962), for instance, we find a wife who has been married three times and given birth to several children, simply because she can find no other role for herself.[81] In her latest marriage to Jake, symptomatically, 'Jake and life became confused in [her] mind' (p. 33), yet she is showing signs of a nervous breakdown, while Jake, exasperated, is drinking heavily; the woman's failure to find her own role is shown to inflict strain on both man and wife. She feels the solution would be to have another child, he objects, and when she does indeed become pregnant he cajoles her into an abortion. 'Really', she thinks, 'anyone would think that the emancipation of women had never happened' (p. 107), and, in a masochist moment, agrees not only to abortion but to sterilization, only to find that Jake is having an affair with her filmstar friend (herself married to a man who argues that 'women are made for bashing, and having kids' [p. 89]). For a time, she leaves Jake, returning in the end because of the children, but importantly, not in the same frame of mind. She is 'no longer frightened of [Jake]. I no longer needed him. I accepted him at last, because he was inevitable' (p. 158). The sadness of this novel is overwhelming; there is no sense that any woman of the narrator's acquaintance has experienced any form of emancipation, and, although we know this is not the whole picture of women's experience since the vote was won, it is dismaying to find so many works returning to this theme. Margaret Drabble explores it in *A Summer Bird-Cage* (1963), where Sarah watches her sister Louise marry a wealthy and mildly celebrated novelist, not for love but to avoid 'secretarial course-coffee bar degradation' (p. 8). Sarah is in essence a proto-feminist, thinking, 'The days are over, thank God, when a woman justifies her existence by marrying. At least that is true until she has children' (p. 74), but the novel concentrates on women entrapped in relationships which deny them any power over their own lives. Gill is one who has felt herself coerced by her husband into having an abortion and is haunted by it, despite her protestation that 'I know it isn't murder, I couldn't care less about abortions in fact' (p. 107). Finally, Louise does break out of her disastrous marriage and goes to live with her lover, but her decision does not appear to lead to any greater self-knowledge. And Drabble's next novel, *The Garrick Year* (1964), offers an even bleaker prospect.[82] It concentrates on the dreariness of domesticity, with the wife and mother in revolt at being 'packaged' for the husband's career. What Drabble shows, despite the wife's transient love affair, is a very conservative acceptance of marriage, even while the woman is shown straining at the bonds, and constantly stressing how unsatisfactory marriage is. This woman is shown as less than attractive as a personality; there is more than a little truth in the husband's assessment:

> we live in a hideous hybrid age, and I know you won't have that, will you? You swallow down your nasty sweet martini, you smoke your cigarettes, you watch the filthy television, you speak up in praise of posters and office blocks and speedboats and jazz, you spend a bleeding fortune on lacquer to keep your hair in ridiculous shapes, and then your stomach won't accept an ordinary useful inoffensive wardrobe. You can't just have what you want and throw out the rest, you know.
>
> (pp. 41–2)

Unnervingly, this novel seems to echo John Osborne's *Look Back in Anger*, with the husband playing Jimmy Porter, and the wife playing her female equivalent – an odd situation in a woman's novel.

Elizabeth Taylor, in *The Wedding Group* (1968), paints a much subtler picture of a young girl, Cressie, lured into an unsatisfactory marriage as the only route she can think of to rescue herself from the oppressive commune where she has grown up.[83] Here it is the mother-in-law, Midge, who tyrannizes over her youngest son and this new, inept wife; a friend observes that, while Cressy may have fought a hard battle to leave the commune, 'this one she'll never fight. She doesn't even know there's a war' (p. 178). Midge's stratagems to keep the young couple captive, especially after Cressy has a child, are legion, even to pretending a theft of diamond earrings which she has in fact hidden. Cressy's unhappiness grows, while her husband comforts himself by renewing his affair with a woman in town. In the end, although the couple may escape Midge's clutches, Taylor leaves the novel very open-ended. Cressy's baby is sickly, while she herself, utterly reliant on Midge in all practical matters as she has been, has no experience of looking after it; the marriage is already shaky. Cressy has no way of making a life on her own. Women's novels are haunted throughout the decade by such cases, even though the bulk of their women protagonists are middle class. The daughters and granddaughters of suffragettes are by no means all shown to be flourishing.

There are brighter moments: in *Memoirs of a Spacewoman* (1962), for instance, Naomi Mitchison constructs a future world in which women, no longer tied to marriage, choose the fathers for their children carefully, and retain friendships with former partners with no-one claiming to be dominant. Brigid Brophy's *The Finishing Touch* (1963) also strikes a lighter note, presenting a mischievous account of a French 'finishing' school which goes far beyond *Olivia* (1949) in its blatant eroticism, where the crushes of the girls feed the sexual appetite of Antonia, one of the joint headmistresses. But on the whole, those novels concentrating on gender and sexuality tend to show women consistently marginalized if they step too far out of their expected roles. Lynne Reid Banks, in *The L-shaped Room* (1960), shows her protagonist, Jane, quarrelling with her father because she is unmarried but pregnant, and going to live in a house where she has to learn that she is one with the marginalized; from seeing the prostitutes in the basement as 'strange animals from another part of the forest' (p. 7), she comes to accept them as her own kind, just as she also comes to accept the homosexuality of her black neighbour. Furthermore, in the course of her pregnancy, we are given a graphic account of the humiliation she undergoes when she visits a doctor who assumes she is asking for an abortion and does not even examine her; this humiliation drives her away from medical care, almost disastrously. Yet the novel ends consolingly: Jane is reconciled with her father and has her baby. However, we are left with the sense that Jane is fortunate in being middle class. Ultimately, she has a home to go to, unlike the prostitutes in the basement. Paddy Kitchen's novel, *Lying-in* (1965), also deals with pregnancy outside marriage, as we learn that the protagonist conceived William's child, and, grief-stricken after William's death, was married by John to protect her from the consequences of being a single mother. Significantly, she is, like so many women in novels of this time, consumed by guilt, since, as she says, 'I sometimes felt helpless at my inability either to discard old morals and conventions or to see any sense in them' (p. 34). We learn she has been pregnant before, by a man she did not love, and had great trouble getting an abortion (as in Banks's novel, we are given a graphic account of the humiliations she faced); when she succeeded, guilt again swamped her (women may have greater freedom in such novels, but they pay a high price for it), as she was again torn between seeing herself as immoral and wanting 'an extension of [her] untrammelled freedom' (p. 88) – conservatism and radicalism fight an evenly matched fight. And she is determined to have William's child. Like Banks's Jane, she is a middle-class mother, an architect; in the end, she is able to release John to his lover, Catherine, because she has a promising career. Again, the novel suggests that without the security of her background, her situation would be far more serious; as indeed we see in many of the situations in which women find themselves in Nell Dunn's *Up the Junction* (1963), a collection of short stories which is often hilarious, often devastatingly bleak in its exposure of a certain quality of life on the streets in the early sixties.[84] Yet this collection, too, is the product of a middle-class author, who has chosen to explore the life of the underprivileged; the mix of classes which Inez Holden showed in World War Two finds its echo in Dunn's work, but as a matter of choice.

As has already been mentioned, *The L-shaped Room* provides middle-class Jane with a gay black neighbour who becomes one of her closest friends, and homosexuals continue to crop up in novels of the sixties in subsidiary roles, on the whole without prejudice, although they are often presented in stereotypical camp guise. However, Maureen Duffy's novel *The Microcosm* (1966) gives a far bleaker picture of lesbian exist-ence in the sixties. What emerges is a dark, underworld life, where characters spend 'all the week wearing a false face', and feel like a lost tribe of aborigines buried deep in a social jungle,[85] harried by those who wish to 'civilize' them. As with the unmarried mother, guilt is a problem for Duffy's characters, simply because they do not fit in. They are 'the lonely ones. Afraid people will find out, outcasts; guilt too of course' (p. 35). The ghettoizing of Duffy's lesbians is a familiar situation for those whom the dominant culture will not accept, and Duffy also shows the pressures to conform on those who go, 'unloved and rejected, behind the bushes with the first boy who'll make them feel wanted, placed by their society' (p. 62). One of her characters tells how, submitting to the pressures, she allowed herself to get engaged, and she spares a thought for the boy in the case, also under pressure to conform, seeing them both as 'pressed into the mould by society before our bones had hardened into their individual shapes' (pp. 63–4). These women suffer from the slowness of society to accept them; one of them longs for the time 'when we can all be what individually we are and nobody gives a damn' (p. 236). The novel ends with a challenge which echoes Lessing's theme in *The Golden Notebook*, urging that we must not com-partmentalize:

> We're part of society, part of the world whether we or society like it or not, and we have to learn to live in the world and the world has to

live with us and make use of us, not as scapegoats, part of its collect-
ive unconscious it'd rather not come to terms with but as who we are,
just as in the long run it'll have to do with all the other bits and pieces
of humanity that go to make up the whole human picture. Society
isn't a simple organism with one nucleus and a fringe of little feet, it's
an infinitely complex living structure and if you try to suppress any
part of it by that much, and perhaps more, you diminish, you muti-
late the whole.

(p. 287)

This novel was written in 1966, but the plea is still relevant, as Sheila
Jeffreys suggests:

Lesbianism as a sexual practice is not a threat. If it were, then it would
not be the stock in trade of brothels and men's pornography. Lesbianism as an emotional universe which provides an alternative to
women from slotting into the heterosexual system, on the other
hand, is a threat. It is then anarchic and threatens the organising
principle of male supremacy.[86]

Yet at least Duffy's challenge to the dominant culture found a publisher,
although arguably, because her novel is written in a style that draws on
Joyce and Beckett, the style may have outweighed the content in the
book's reception.

However, small breakthroughs in writing about what would have
been unacceptable subject matter for fiction a few years earlier are
occurring. Penelope Mortimer, for instance, in her novel *My Friend
Says It's Bullet-Proof* (1967), writes about a woman who has lost a breast
to cancer.[87] This is a work which, although there is third-person narra-
tion, is written from within; the protagonist, Muriel, is not always
coherent either in actions or speech or when writing in her notebook,
and the anguish she feels at what she sees as a diminution of herself as a
woman is poignantly conveyed. Mortimer implies that society does not
encourage her to feel differently; she tells the man sitting beside her on a
plane that

she worked on a magazine which did not like to be thought of as a
woman's magazine because its policy was that women were people
like anyone else. At this he said, 'Ho, a feminist', and she knew it
would be useless to argue.

(p. 10)

This is a strange rejection of the term 'feminist', but Mortimer does not allow her Muriel to draw any comfort from solidarity with other women, or indeed to acknowledge that such a thing is possible. Furthermore, Muriel's introspection about her condition is deliberately presented as shocking, as when she writes in her notebook that 'the whole history of the Jewish race left me cold. Starving children, war, dismemberment, injustice – was that all?...This is the only thing that shocks me any more: my own deformity' (p. 11). Her desperate, angry identifying of herself by the 'horny, fluid-filled breast' which she can detach and carry, 'dangling from her hand', reduces her to feeling 'the obscene cheat of being a female impersonator' (p. 37). Gradually, a new lover, Robert, gives her the confidence to discard this artificial breast and to know herself as fully feminine; she experiences a Joycean epiphany when he says, 'I prefer you as you are' (p. 173). Yet Mortimer reveals blind spots, even as she liberates her protagonist; in passing, for instance, the narrative voice observes of whores that 'it was doubtful whether they suffered much from love' (p. 171). The intense concentration on Muriel's suffering as excluding the suffering of all others is maintained throughout; Mortimer does not pretend that suffering necessarily makes for heroism, and this is a major change from the traditional depiction of suffering heroines. The anguish and the anger, the sense of no compassion to spare beyond Muriel's own immediate situation is painfully and graphically conveyed; responsibility for the self takes undisputed precedence over responsibility for others.

Mortimer's novel is very much of her age, in Muriel's aggressively determined fight to regain her balance and re-establish her own identity. The sixties is the decade when Foucault's *Madness and Civilization* was published, and both he and such anti-psychiatrists as R. D. Laing in Britain (who was very influential on Lessing in the 1960s) attack and expose forms of society which Noam Chomsky, in *Deterring Democracy*, describes as offering 'free choice with a pistol to your head'.[88] Society may force into madness those who do not subscribe to its precepts, or may label them as mad – or they may seek to escape by a descent into madness, breakdown, and ultimate regeneration, as in Lessing's *The Golden Notebook* – which is not to deny the existence of mental illness as a devastating condition in its own right. It is as well to hear the voice of Jennifer Dawson, in her Afterword to *The Ha-Ha*, written for Virago in 1985, where she observes: 'In 1961...psychiatrists had not yet been pronounced the third arm of government'; and she goes on to remark drily,

I was lucky to have written *The Ha-Ha* before being influenced by the ideas of the mid-sixties. The high and prophetic status of insanity, neurosis and cold misery will continue to be questioned by those who have actually experienced it, nursed it, or seen people they love succumb. Insights. Reflections. But higher meaning? . . . A revolutionary revolt? A romantic option? A healing journey? Private enterprise psychiatry is the obvious activity for ipsonauts.[89]

This is a salutary warning against classing all mental illness in the same category as the kind of regenerative 'breakdown' that Lessing portrays in *The Golden Notebook*. Dawson's *The Ha-Ha* (1961) puts the case passionately for someone rejected by the dominant culture of her time. Early in the novel, links are made between social judgements on matters of political importance and attitudes to individuals. The protagonist hears an earnest supporter of the yearly 'Mission' to the university tell her mother,

> we are drifting near to a spiritual holocaust. Much as I admire these Aldermaston Marchers, and racial demonstrators, they surely tend to forget that in spite of all the material threats to our valuable Western contribution to civilization, a much graver one lies ahead in the form of a spiritual waste, a spiritual vacuum.
>
> (p. 12)

So much for the unity of body and spirit. The girl protagonist, almost inevitably according to her own estimation, finds refuge in a mental hospital, although she is dismayed when urged to get back to the 'real' world, 'as though there were two; one good and one to be avoided' (p. 22). Diagnosed schizophrenic, she is angry to find that this categorizes her as an outsider, when her only problem, as she sees it, is that she 'wanted the knack of existing. I did not know the rules' (p. 91), and she worries about the nature of 'reality', implying that 'reality' as defined by the dominant culture may not be entirely convincing. Gradually, she becomes institutionalized, until she sees herself as smothered to death, and runs away so as to find out for certain that she 'had not after all been extinguished, and that [her] existence had been saved' (p. 176). As with Hull's earlier novel (and Dawson and Hull knew each other), the madness of the world being a distinct possibility, its ability to label individuals as insane is called in question.[90]

Returning to Lessing's *The Golden Notebook*, we can perhaps see a way of reading her more optimistic version of breakdown. For, in a sense, what we are given is a breakdown of the novel form, offering a way for the novel to regenerate itself; the world of personal collapse in the middle of a gender crisis is merged with a world gone mad, and by structuring the novel so that we cannot lose ourselves among familiar linear developments of plot and developing characterization, by defamiliarizing the workings of the mind with verbal twists and images, we are being given new prospects of our contemporary world, where the individual knows so much more than he/she did before the overwhelming presence of the media, concerning the state of our world, yet also sees so much more clearly what an ineffectual position the private person holds when it comes to changing things. Sexuality and gender roles can become intimidating conundrums in such a world, but Lessing suggests one way through. Saul and Anna can share thoughts because Lessing's text gives them the words which convey sharing – just as we, the readers, can read those words on the page and make the connection between the sentence that Saul gives Anna and the sentence which begins Lessing's book – and can also share the conundrum that the sentence begins the novel which actually brings Saul and Anna into existence. Art in this novel is not naturalistic but patterns existence into ways by which we can see a happy ending for sexual and gender dilemmas in terms of a beginning. But the way forward is a perilous one, according both to this novel and *The Four-Gated City* (1969), and women are most at risk. The breakdown which novelists like Lessing, Dawson, Hull and Mortimer inflict on their female characters put women at odds with the normality defined by their dominant culture. These women are presented to us as marginalized, both by their sex and by their infringements of their perceived roles, just as surely as those suffering the alienation experienced by those of a race or class perceived as subordinate by the dominant culture.

5
Women in a Changing Society: Conclusion

When discussing the fiction I have been exploring in the previous chapters, it has seemed reasonable to suppose that many of these works reflect current ideas and trends within the writers' own society, and that their novels often act as mouthpieces for their contemporary female readership, both analysing and questioning issues within their own culture, and expressing this questioning eloquently and entertainingly. But is there supporting evidence for these suppositions? To show that there is, I am going to examine three nonfictional, feminist publications of the four decades I have been exploring, which will serve to confirm that the ways in which the novelists writing between 1928 and 1968 respond to their world do indeed reflect attitudes and expectations of that society, while at the same time the ways in which the vast majority of women were treated by their society (and in consequence were rated by themselves) were often less progressive than the suffragettes could have wished. These three middle-class assessments of women's position in society show how changing conditions affect the view of their priorities, their roles and their potential.

In 1929, in response to the granting of universal suffrage, the Hon. Mrs Dighton Pollock's *The Women of Today* was published. While the author acknowledges the limitations of her findings (interestingly, limitations she acknowledges in terms of race rather than class), she charts a clear way forward for newly emancipated women, urging that 'the ultimate use of freedom is to exercise the power of choice'.[1] Among other things, she discusses the way in which 'public opinion' has moved from the old morality of Puritan self-denial to a new outlook, based on the ideas of Freud and Jung, 'as to the dangers of repression' (p. 11); and she goes on to consider the pros and cons of monogamy – on the whole she favours it, but supports divorce rather than the continuation of a bad relationship. She lists various areas in which women still need to fight for improvement, ranging from greater efficiency in the running of the home to the right of women to continue in employment when they marry. She urges women to be seen to take their jobs seriously, and not to accept inferior status passively, and she also urges the profitable use of leisure, while not falling into the trap of merging this with the 'enforced idleness of unemployment' (p. 44). She urges the use of the newly gained vote, arguing against the familiar complaint made against political parties, that 'They're all alike, promise everything and do nothing' (p. 57), and listing areas that should be addressed, such as the cause of peace and the need for improvements in education. Finally she urges the young (for whom, she notes, the suffragettes are already history) to vote; frivolity, she says, is not enough. In sum, the tone of Mrs Pollock's book is positive; she sees that there is much to be done, both in society at large and with regard to issues specifically affecting women, but she sets out a programme which anticipates progress and greater involvement for women in the improvement of social and political conditions. And she is not alone. The Duchess of Atholl, for example, is equally positive in her book *Women and Politics* (1931), addressed to new women voters, although her tone is much less egalitarian; rather than concentrating on the tasks confronting women who want to improve their own opportunities and to exercise choice within their society, she sets out to instruct the woman voter on the duties of domesticity, the (conservative) politics of the day and the responsibilities of empire.[2] Yet, whatever their differences, both authors see universal franchise as the dawn of a new era for women, and, while obstacles are still acknowledged, this sense of the possibility of a positive role for women is, by and large, reflected in the women's fiction of the early thirties, although the growing fascist threat of a backlash against women's emancipation soon clouds this optimism as the thirties progress.

When we turn to the conclusions issuing from the Conference on the Feminine Point of View, which took place from 1947 to 1951, the impact of the War and its horrors is immediately obvious. The report on this conference sets out its motivation in dramatic terms: 'The discussion here summarized originated less in dissatisfaction with the position of women than in dissatisfaction verging on despair with the present state and future prospects of human society';[3] and it quotes the Director General of UNESCO as saying that 'mankind needs urgently the active intervention of women. If it is to survive, humanity must make use of all its inheritance' (p. 14). As a result, the report states that the conference abandoned the earlier priority of those 'dissatisfied with women's position' who emphasized the need for 'equality', 'meaning by that women's right to do, experience and express the same kind of things as men', and turned to another line of thought:

> we have focussed our attention on ways in which women seem to differ from men, and have considered mainly the good elements in their outlook, since it is by virtue of these that they should be able to contribute towards a better world.
>
> (p. 15)

This statement in itself suggests a change in thinking was felt to be necessary with the loss of confidence resulting from what Western civilization had shown itself capable of. Although there are frequent references in the report to Eleanor Rathbone, one of the champions of 'new' feminism before the War, concentrating as she does on issues (such as birth control and abortion) which directly affect women, 'those dissatisfied with women's position' can be seen as what Winifred Holtby called the Equalitarians, championed by Margaret Rhondda, who seem to be perceived as having gained the upper hand.[4] Already, the report seems to suggest, the priorities of those who were concerned for such women's needs as were different from those of men had been submerged in the course of World War Two beneath the demand for equality, and 'difference' needs to be restated (a point made in a number of the novels I have been looking at, where the daughters of suffragettes grow up feeling inadequate because they have not gone to university and pursued careers). Yet there are inconsistencies. The conference draws back from suggesting that women have a monopoly in what it defines as 'feminine' qualities (for example, intuitive sympathy, compassion, aversion to cruelty, selflessness, reverence for individual life). However, while it implies (rather than states) that views on men and masculinity are changing, the conference insists that women are the ones most likely to fulfil the need to inject 'feminine' qualities into the ruling ethos of the societies of their day, in the aftermath of World War Two. Despite the attempt to show masculinity and femininity as shifting their parameters, what the report goes on to demonstrate is that attitudes of men and women to each other and to themselves remain much the same as ever; when the delegates list the reasons for needing women's input into the pressing issues of the day, it seems that too little has changed since Mrs Pollock wrote her pamphlet, twenty years earlier. Women, they conclude, still lack confidence; men's standards (that is, the traditional views on 'masculine' standards) are still regarded as the norm (and the report refers to the BBC's refusal to allow Dorothy Sayers to speak about politics, a refusal which I shall return to).[5] The delegates deplore the use of sex appeal to gain power, as such manoeuvres rely on men's view of women as sex objects, and they deplore, above all, women's lack of economic power. They also deplore the lack of scope afforded to women when it comes to careers, and the dislike of intellect in a woman which is evinced by men – examples of women who have overcome such odds are, rather dismayingly, all drawn from the nineteenth century, suggesting that more recent examples are thin on the ground. Strikingly, they do not undervalue women in the home, as they see a prime need to educate women for all roles in life if they are to have an impact on society as a whole; they urge teachers, both men and women, to talk about marriage as a career, about marriage and a career, and about a career without marriage, and to provide good role models. This leads on to a consideration of whether women have their point of view represented in literature, or 'are women writers even today, when they write so much, influenced by a masculine pattern and masculine preferences'; they pick out Mary Webb and Virginia Woolf as two writers who have written from the woman's point of view this century, but claim that 'its newness has perhaps caused it to be only very partially understood' (p. 43). It is perhaps surprising that the report implies a real lack of a woman's point of view in twentieth-century fiction, given the number of writers who offer this in works I have been discussing. Already, it would seem, works rated as 'middlebrow' by the (largely masculine) academic establishment are being ignored, even (ironically) by the participants of this conference, who are for the most part highly educated; yet many of the novels they ignore were highly successful, judging by both sales and loans from public libraries, with a high percentage of women readers. But literary criticism is not by any means a high priority in this report. Again and again it returns to the need to make marriage less burdensome for women, and the need to grant them economic power if they are to fulfil the role which the Director General of UNESCO wishes them to play.[6] The blame for the present situation is placed squarely on men's attitude to women, and on women's deprecating attitude to themselves, while married women are urged, even when confined to a small circle, to recognize the value of their point of view in shaping the world. When reading this report, we need to remind ourselves that the conference has attempted to divide women's responsibility to human society as a whole from the improvement of women's lot *per se*. The crisis of confidence in Western civilization which resulted from World War Two clearly provides the motive power fuelling the debate.Yet while this crisis of confidence is clearly reflected in the fiction of the late forties and early fifties which I have been examining, many novelists do also explore the complexities of the lot of women within this disturbing context, as in Rose Macaulay's *The World My Wilderness* (1950) and Pamela Frankau's *A Wreath for the Enemy* (1954). In the end, what emerges from the fiction, as from the conference, is that the concerns of 'old' and 'new' feminisms cannot actually be separated; women can only make a successful contribution to society if their own needs are met, while the dominant culture must accept the necessity for a change in its attitude to women.

There is further concentration on women's view of themselves, and their uphill struggle to change traditional views of their role in a special issue of the journal *The Twentieth Century*, published a few years after the conference, in 1958.[7] This issue's subject is 'Women', but the male editor's introduction is very revealing. He acknowledges, like Mrs Pollock, that the issue is limited to experience in Western Europe and the United States, and he concedes readily that 'women, our companions and friends, have taken the place of ladies' (p. 99). But he notes that this special issue of his journal contains no article about political women, and the implication is that women are to blame for this, since he claims that 'only exceptionally have women chosen to avail themselves of the political possibilities open to them ... "Women's civic rights" seem uninteresting to the generation of Françoise Sagan and Brigitte Bardot' (p. 99); there is no mention of the obstacles put in women's ways to public office. Furthermore, while he has printed an article by Jacquetta Hawkes about CND (the Campaign for Nuclear Disarmament), he presents it as rather less than politically sophisticated, claiming condescendingly that 'Here women are on primeval territory. Even when they carry their men's clubs we may suppose that they hope somewhere in their dark bloodstreams that their men will not run into other men and so have occasion to use them' (p. 100). It would seem that while he can accept women as companions and friends, he takes up a traditional male stance of superiority when they do make political statements. However, he manages to ignore his own inconsistency in deploring the lack of women in politics by questioning whether Jacquetta Hawkes's concern about the bomb actually qualifies as 'a political statement' – a breathtaking example of tunnel vision. Yet he includes some articles by women which offer very clear grounds for why women have failed to take up what he claims as 'the political possibilities open to them'. Betty Miller, for instance, argues that, by and large, the young women of her day are indifferent to 'the heroic feats of the suffragette', not so much because of what Mrs Pollock called 'frivolity' (and which her editor might see as the concerns of Françoise Sagan and Brigitte Bardot), but because of continually frustrated attempts to use their skills to the full. Even when one of them does take a First from Oxford or Cambridge, says Miller, she cannot hope to reach the top of her profession, and often turns her back in disgust, opting for domesticity.[8] Miller finds that men do share more in the home, but she also reminds us that most young couples 'are necessarily conscious of the peril of bringing up a family under the steadily darkening shadow of Hiroshima', and have withdrawn into the nuclear family, 'a necessary reaction, perhaps, to the larger, and, as it must always seem to the individual, ungovernable menace of the world situation' (p. 129). Another contributor, Jenny Nasmyth, is precisely the kind of highly intelligent young woman whom Miller has in mind, and her article is candidly reactionary in argument; women, says Nasmyth, should not be educated in the same way as men. Even more alarmingly, she says she suspects that 'with few exceptions, able women are not as intellectually effective as able men',[9] and that work is an inadequate palliative for a woman as it is simply 'something that she does because she has not discovered how to be 100 per cent a woman in 1958' (p. 143), a point I shall return to. Her article is all the more telling as she is a young Oxford graduate of the kind Miller writes about; she has been in the Foreign Office, has failed to win advancement, and has now chosen marriage, with journalism as a secondary commitment. Her conservative view, if it is not intended to be read as heavily ironic, would seem to advocate a return to a near-Victorian view of women, but then, even Mary Warnock, the Oxford philosopher whom we might expect to be questioning why women do not have the chance to play a greater role in society, accepts the fact that many women return to the home after university, and sets out the importance of education specifically in terms of the married woman, blaming older dons for failing to value nonacademic qualities.[10] Marjorie Bremner, the sole American contributor, is less accepting and implicitly more critical. After offering a crudely essentialist view of the dominant American housewife and her husband, the New Man, she reiterates a point made at the earlier post-war conference: British women lack confidence, and this holds them back.[11] It is with some relief that we find Marghanita Laski taking a more combative line on behalf of British women, attacking advertizing companies for their tactics which she wittily presents in terms of religious revelations intent on moulding the women they target into 'a single chosen image'; she never suggests that women deserve such patronizing tactics.[12] But it is

Jacquetta Hawkes's contribution on 'Women against the Bomb' which actually shows women playing a role in society. Here is a woman who is not afraid to speak out on one of the most disturbing issues of the day (hers, it is worth repeating, is the one article which the editor accuses of lack of real understanding, querying whether opposition to the bomb does indeed count as 'political' and using the old tactic of diminishing the opposition by a ludicrous comparison, in this case that of the cave-woman trotting behind her man).[13] Yet the fact that Hawkes is alone in this number of *The Twentieth Century* to write about women who are taking action does tend to confirm the view borne out by a number of the novels I have been examining: that a large proportion of women in this country, taking women across all classes, had turned their back on matters of major political and social concern, in many cases because they were being denied a satisfying opportunity to make a difference, and were instead concentrating on the microcosmic politics of their private lives. Finally, in this same issue of *The Twentieth Century* which is devoted to women, we find Rayner Heppenstall linking homosexuality with 'the vampire mother', and Victor Musgrave largely stating that 'West Indians and Africans are expert ponces. Lazy by nature, lovers of women...' (p. 184). The sense that all those who are perceived as outside the sphere of the ruling ethos are still being constructed according to the specifications of mythical stereotypes is very strong.[14]

Yet Jacquetta Hawkes does name a wide range of women present at the CND meeting she describes, and certainly many of the writers whose work I have been exploring in this book can be read as consciousness raisers. The popularity of writers like Storm Jameson and Phyllis Bottome, to name only two, suggests that many women frequenting libraries during the thirties, forties and fifties were prepared to face the questions raised in their novels, and that the surface tension of the male-dominated society in which they lived was under pressure from beneath, preparing for the emergence of the women's movements in the sixties and seventies. But it is important to see the changing priorities throughout these decades if we are to understand some of the problems women faced when making decisions about the fiction they were writing. For instance, Mrs Dighton Pollock's clear view of women's way forward is clouded in the thirties and forties by the rise of Nazism, and the horrors of world war clearly influence the theme of the women's post-war conference, which states it has a greater concern for the state of the human race than for specifically women's issues, while in fact making a strong case for why both concerns are inextricably linked. The stark fact would seem to be that many issues specific to women's needs and their perceived roles have been crowded out by the events of the thirties and forties, and by the effect of these events on thinking in the fifties, and this fact is reflected in the 1958 number of *The Twentieth Century*, which reads as an advocacy of stasis for women, despite better educational prospects. Two issues recur in those thirty years: first, the implicit acceptance that the home will always play a major role in women's lives – there is no hint that this could ever be a man's domain, although in that 1958 number of *The Twentieth Century* there is one contributor, Betty Miller, who does acknowledge that men are taking a greater share in domestic matters. And secondly, time and again we read that women in Britain suffer from low self-esteem, and this holds them back in their social and political effectiveness.

These findings are inevitably reflected in the approach of women writers to their fiction. Storm Jameson is a case in point. In her out-standing autobiography, written during the sixties, *Journey from the North* (1969 and 1970), she repeatedly stresses her dissatisfaction with her own work throughout her writing career; the comments she makes on her own career strongly suggest that she suffers from that very lack of confidence which is so often noted in reports on women's progress throughout the decades.[15] Yet the work she did for refugees fleeing Europe during the thirties and forties was inestimable, and the novels she wrote sprang from her conviction that fiction could be a servant for social and political change: this conviction continues to permeate her work throughout the fifties and sixties. She, together with several others among the writers whom I have been discussing, represents the type of intellectual Edward Said describes as 'someone whose whole being is staked on a critical sense, a sense of being unwilling to accept easy formulas, or ready-made clichés'.[16] Jameson, whether in her role as PEN representative, espousing the cause of European refugees, or later, when she strives to improve her readers' understanding of the roots of war and social conflict, does indeed see her task as 'to universalize the crisis, to give greater human scope to what a particular race or nation suffered, to associate that experience with the suffering of others'; and she could be taken as an example of what Said argues, that, 'even if one is not an actual immigrant or expatriate, it is possible to think as one, to imagine and investigate in spite of barriers, and always to move away from the centralizing authorities towards the margins' (p. 33). It makes sense to see that Jameson's commitment to broad, humanitarian issues also underlies her prejudices; she is suspicious of those who set what she sees as too high a value on style – like her friend Queenie Leavis, she implies that social and political engagement is lacking in those who give stylistic experiment a high priority, as Virginia Woolf and Christine Brooke-Rose do. Yet is Jameson as far from these writers as she claims? She constantly writes on the importance of style serving subject matter, which is a concern she shares with both Woolf and Brooke-Rose. Where she does differ is in reaching out to a wider audience, giving them readier access to the social and political concerns she analyses – the perception of an audience, together with a capacity for responding swiftly to the shifting priorities of the responsibly minded of her day, would seem to be what separates her from those who experiment more obviously with style. We see, during the thirties, a shift in her work from women's issues to current affairs and international politics, a shift which is also found in the pages of *Time & Tide* during the thirties, where, as Deirdre Beddoe notes, 'women turned their energies to the struggle against unemployment at home and to the inter national fight against fascism and for peace'.[17] Like her character Philip in *Company Parade* (1934), Jameson sets out to be 'the conscience of un- thinking people';[18] she and her friend Queenie Leavis were very much of a mind in championing the moral responsibility of the novelist, and the need to cultivate that same responsibility in the reader, yet, as *Journey from the North* shows, Jameson never developed a strong sense of self- belief.

Jameson's talent for being 'the conscience of unthinking people' is very much in line with the aspirations for women's role expressed in Mrs Pollock's pamphlet, and echoed by the post-war conference. But when we take into account the sense of tasks still to be accomplished by women if they are to find their role in society, a theme which is there in Mrs Pollock's pamphlet, and still there thirty years later in the journal of 1958, the split in the ways women perceive their task when writing fiction becomes clearer, although many, in their different ways, explore issues similar to Jenny Nasmyth's when she observes that contemporary woman has not discovered how to be 100 per cent a woman. Increasingly throughout this period, there are those who address issues specific to women, from E. M. Delafield in the inter-war years to Margaret Drabble and Jennifer Dawson in the fifties and sixties; for these, the main requirement they make of style is accessibility, since they aim at a broad range of readers. Others, as we have seen, while not necessarily looking for a woman's style, search for a style which will reflect women's interiority, and we could count among them Dorothy Richardson, Virginia Woolf, Elizabeth Bowen and Stevie Smith. Such writers are those Storm Jameson confronts aggressively in her essay 'The Form of the Novel' (1949); she argues that in recent years, more serious novelists have been swayed, by the strength of the undersea current running against humanism, against the tradition, to give their greater effort to releasing in their work the little jet of their own personality...The change is also towards a detachment from the world, a withdrawal.[19]

More pertinently, Jameson goes on to argue in the same essay that

Life, at the level on which the great novelists must approach it, is so full of impurities. The pure novelist, intent on easing the bulges out of his form, is forced to exclude too much, and without being able to achieve the evocative precision and concentration of the poem. The writer becomes too important, the novel etiolated and narrow.

(p. 61)

Yet 'pure' novelists, as Jameson labels them (she is criticizing Bowen's *Death of the Heart* at the time) are not by any means all withdrawing from the world, even if they are shaping styles which can accommodate a woman's voice as they perceive it. Woolf, for instance, may not set the 'world' to the fore as Jameson does, but from *Jacob's Room* to *Between the Acts* it is insistently there by means of allusion, image, or aftermath, while in writing about *The Years*, Woolf famously says that she meant 'to give a picture of society as a whole, give characters from every side; turn them towards society, not private life', even though she adds, betraying the lack of confidence so often a feature of women writers of the period, 'Of course I completely failed'.[20] And Woolf, of course, is unfair to herself; as always she is her own harshest critic. *The Years* does make clear that private lives are inevitably moulded by the world in which they live; the Pargiters, by their prejudices and their aspirations, adopt the attitudes of their class in the early decades of the twentieth century and indeed show how such attitudes emanate as much from the family as from the world in which the family lives – the post-war conference on women is based on the same premise.

By citing different approaches to the novel, I have not tried to establish one point of view as superior to another, but to show why there was such diversity in the practice of so many of the women writers I have been exploring, and to argue that their reasons for writing as they do are very much grounded in the often conflicting priorities facing women during the 40 years under consideration: the concerns which, between the wars, were prioritized by 'old' (Equalitarian) and 'new' feminists develop and continue throughout the post-war years and inevitably affect decisions on how to write and about what. Jameson is unfair to such writers as Woolf and Bowen when she accuses them of being out of touch with their age; yet her criticism does highlight one of the problems any critic confronts when analysing the novel. The 'modernist' approach can be criticized as a matter of style and interiority, and so out of touch with wider issues; the 'realist' approach as old-fashioned and in the end confirming the values of the dominant culture, incapable of subversion. Champions of one or other camp will argue that such definitions are far too narrow, that either (depending on his/her allegiance) is supremely suited to reflecting 'modernity'. But it is all too easy to fall into the trap which Jameson does in her 1949 essay, seeing a great divide between the two camps, and insisting only one is capable of engaging fully with the challenges of the present, whereas, as I have attempted to show, engagement and innovation draw on the strengths of all forms of fiction, and even when apparently opting for traditional modes of expression, can subvert and question from within.

In a review written in 1940, Margery Allingham calls the period of the inter-war years 'the twenty-one years' armistice (as our great grand-children are almost certain to call it – knowledgeable little beasts)'.[21] She is already aware of how easy it is to judge a period with hindsight, as indeed we do when observing the confusions of the decades which I am contemplating. Certainly, it is very clear that fears about war and war itself account for the different priorities which women writers have throughout the thirties and forties. In 1941, for instance, Storm Jameson sees a semantic crisis facing the writer:

> Words no longer mean the same thing to men of equal intelligence in different nations – or two men of the same nation. The word for justice, the word for pity, the word for truth has a different meaning according as it is spoken by a Russian or a German or a Frenchman. Or by two Englishmen, one of whom is a party communist and the other an old-fashioned liberal.[22]

and she adds,

> too much has been quickly and brutally destroyed. Our sense of continuity with even the recent past has broken off like a torn nerve...we are always anxious. The new invention rushing on us may be an atomic bomb which will destroy so much that we can

> never begin again, even from scratch, or begin again only after a long
> blackout.
>
> (pp. 140–1)

By 1947, her worst fears appear to have been realized, as she observes the
huge ruin of Europe from the air: 'I saw that every stone was a question... Can we restore to man the human dignity he has lost?'[23] This is a
question reflecting the sense of existential crisis which finds expression
in the post-war women's conference, and Jameson appears to have
shelved the pre-war angst she saw in earlier essays of *The Writer's Situation*, for now she situates the main impetus for Sartre's thinking within
the French resistance during World War Two: 'The experience of the
Resistance gave a terrible point to the existentialist's belief that the
meaning of a man's life is in the exercise of his liberty: he is free just
so far as he is able to resist torture and death' (p. 23); and she goes on:

> Sartre... can demand of the individual to recognise his terrible
> responsibility for himself and his acts, his terrible and solitary free-
> dom... He cannot, within the human situation as he conceives it,
> erect brotherly respect as a universally valid human value.
>
> (p. 25)

She sees, at this date, just one question for the writer: 'Is he able to tell us
about the destiny of man, our destiny, in such a way that we have the
courage to live it, and gaily?' (p. 36). This is very much in line with the
perception of contemporary society and the role of women within it, as
envisaged at the post-war conference.

As the war drew to an end, Dorothy Sayers prepared the talk on 'Living
to Work' for the BBC *Postscript*, only to have it rejected because it
'appeared to have political tendencies, and... "our public do not want
to be admonished by a woman"';[24] this is the rejection quoted as
symptomatic of the times at the post-war conference. The piece which
Sayers submitted balances those who hate work as only interested in
money against those who love their work (she is drawing a very clear
line here between those with potentially satisfying jobs and those who
are employed as factory hands – like Mrs Pollock, she has a clear view of
very different middle- and working-class experiences). Sayers may often
be called conservative, but such a view is hard to justify in this talk,
where she argues that 'We have *all* become accustomed to rate the value
of work by a purely money standard',[25] the value placed on it by capi-
talism, and she insists:

I see no chance of getting rid of 'the system', or of the people who thrive on it, so long as in our hearts we accept the standards of that system, envy the very vices we condemn, build up with one hand what we pull down with the other, and treat with ridicule and contempt the people who acknowledge a less commercial – if you like, a more religious – conception of what work ought to be.

(p. 125)

Sayers may here appeal to 'religion' rather than to a secular ideology, but the use of religious vocabulary is common among women writers in the late forties and fifties when discussing value systems in the wake of the Holocaust and Hiroshima. It by no means always implies (in the works of Rebecca West, Sylvia Townsend Warner, Phyllis Bottome or Ethel Mannin, for instance) a whole-hearted subscription to institutionalized religion, any more than it did for the suffragettes or Marxists who had recourse to it. Phyllis Bottome is particularly interesting here. While she subscribes to Adler's ideas on the value of a Christian moral code, she does not link this with any church; in her novel *The Lifeline* (1946) she asserts that 'Christianity had been shrivelled into a dried mummy by the churches till its blood ran no more in its veins' (p. 259), and this is a frequent charge levelled against institutionalized religion in post-war novels by women. Most often, women writers use religious vocabulary to refer to such abstract concepts as justice and mercy which exist in the realm of human aspiration rather than invariable practice. Arguably, the ways in which they use this vocabulary reflects a quest for a mode of expression suitable for the kind of humanitarian contribution which the Director General of UNESCO envisaged women as making to the post-war world. The post-war conference on the 'Feminine Point of View' still sees the instilling of moral values as a crucial part of women's contribution to society, and Sayers is of her time in extending this concept into the workplace. Turning again to her essay, we find her, like Jameson, clear-eyed about the end of the war; victory, she says

will not leave us in a position where we can just relax all effort and enjoy ourselves in leisure and prosperity. We shall be living in a confused, exhausted and impoverished world, and there will be a great deal of work to do.[26]

Moral values may be seen by the post-war conference as the sphere where women have a major responsibility, but this hope takes as its given a stable family atmosphere. While most women writers of the forties conform to this view, there are voices which beg to differ. As we have seen, the woman damaged by domesticity or the dysfunctional family is there in Rosamond Lehmann's *The Ballad and the Source* (1944), in Betty Miller's *On the Side of the Angels* (1945) and in Elizabeth Taylor's *At Mrs Lippincote's* (1945), for instance, and in all three of these novels a woman's interiority is given a compelling voice. Susan Ertz, too, does not invariably offer the strongly centred family that appears in *Anger in the Sky* (1943); in *Two Names upon the Shore* (1947), the glamorous and able stepmother (Letty) dismisses her lacklustre stepdaughter, Mary, contemptuously when the girl shows signs of attaching herself to Letty's friend, Maud, saying, 'It's like having a valuable dog and going to endless trouble and expense over his training and so on, and then seeing him attach himself to strangers or the servants and show his teeth when you go near him'. As Maud says, 'What an unpleasant simile'.[27] Yet Ertz in the end offers a traditional solution: Mary does eventually escape into a marriage where she stands for moral values, caring for her husband's unbalanced mother, and eventually becoming reconciled to her father after he suffers a stroke. Letty, cruel though she is, is treated ambivalently. As an ambulance driver, she has done good work, but she is clearly condemned for abandoning her ailing husband – unfortunately, there is little attempt to analyse why she is as she is. However, we can make a link here with Rosamond Lehmann's far more subtly drawn Mrs Jardine in *The Ballad and the Source* (1944) – the woman who becomes dangerous to others is also shown as having been deprived of more positive outlets for her talents, largely because of old-fashioned ideas of a woman's role. Yet, in the end, where Ertz simply abandons Letty, having her lose Maud's approval, Lehmann's Mrs Jardine keeps the reader torn between distaste for her as a manipulater and compassion for her as a victim of society. There is no such ambivalence, however, in Barbara Comyns's *Sisters by a River* (1947).[28] Written early in the War to amuse her children, this work makes no attempt to show either family or mother as the purveyor of moral values; the mother is completely unmotherly, the children's cruelty to animals mirrors the father's cruelty to servants. While Comyns's tone is comic, often not unlike Stevie Smith's, she also shares Smith's capacity for showing us just how dark the underside of the comedy can be. It is, perhaps, significant that Comyns's *Sisters by a River* was not published during the War; of course, this may have been because of the severe paper shortage which affected all publishers, but it may also have been that her novel unnervingly asks questions which threaten to disrupt views on how women were supposed to think and act within a wartime family. Nor is there any sense in Comyns's novels that, if women ruled the world, they would do it 'cannily', while men and bairns would be free to 'dream and have their adventures', as Naomi Mitchison's Kirstie would have it in *The Bull Calves* (1947). Comyns, Lehmann and Ertz offer a domestic scene which mirrors the darkness perceived by writers like Jameson as engulfing European societies since World War One, and which gave rise to the near despair for human society which fuelled the post-war women's conference.

In the fifties, as we have seen, differences in the priorities of women writers continued, made more complex and diverse as the voices of women like Doris Lessing, Attia Hosain and Ruth Prawer Jhabvala articulated points of view formed far from Europe. While Sheila Rowbotham asserts that under the post-war Labour government of the late forties there was 'a broad faith that a better society was in the making [which] was widespread', this optimism was clearly not as widespread as she suggests, and the fifties did not retain it for long.[29] Throughout the decade, while the majority concentrated on their immediate tasks and their family lives in the context of an increasing media presence in the home, fear of the bomb was also increasing, together with a growing sense that the moral structuring of Western society was deeply flawed, imperialism an untenable concept and the odds still stacked against most women finding a role equal to a man's within society. Existential anxieties, increasing understanding of psychology, accelerating technological advances, were just some aspects of a rapidly changing world to bombard the writer. Inevitably, in this confusing world where the dominant culture still seemed largely hostile to women taking an equal part in its decisions and, as many of the contributors to the 1958 issue of *The Twentieth Century* assert, drove many women to turn their backs on public life, women novelists came to different decisions as to what they should prioritize. Rebecca West, for instance, observes in the same year:

> The experiences which the artist celebrates are not peculiar to him, they are common to all human beings; his only peculiarity lies in his power to analyse these experiences and synthesise the findings of his analysis. That being so, it is not surprising that the artist should deviate from his straight aesthetic course and occupy himself with the interests which preoccupy the society of which he is a member.[30]

Her point is strikingly called in question by Elizabeth Bowen's novel *A World of Love* (1955), since Bowen's 'straight aesthetic course' is not lost sight of, and her novel also shows Jameson's dismissal of a novelist setting a high value on style as less than fair.[31] In this novel Bowen sets up the apparently timeless continuity of the family kitchen in Southern Ireland:

> These [bowls, dishes, cups, etc.], with the disregarded dawdling and often stopping of the cheap scarlet clock wedged in somewhere between the bowls and dishes, spoke of the almost total irrelevance of Time, in the abstract, to this ceaseless kitchen.
>
> (p. 21)

Yet the apparent changeless continuity is soon shown to be complicated and potentially perilous, as we are told that

> Our sense of finality is less hard-and-fast: two wars have raised their query to it. Something has challenged the law of nature: it is hard, for instance, to see a young death in battle as in any way the fruition of a destiny, hard not to sense the continuation of the apparently cut-off life, hard not to ask, but *was* dissolution possible so abruptly, unmenacingly and soon?
>
> (p. 44)

Life in the old house revolves around the memory of a dead young man; the younger generation are, as a result, 'creatures of an impossible time, breathing wronged air' (p. 45), haunted by the past, yet desperately trying to claim the present and future for themselves. The novel plays with a timelessness which can become dictatorial – there is a need to acknowledge time past as not time present and to let the ghosts go; we are given a haunting evocation and interrogation of one of the central premises of modernism. The best, like Bowen, will not abandon entirely what West calls their 'particular grace', their aesthetic course, while never losing sight of the changing world around them.

Concerns which can be labelled spiritual or moral, depending on the reader's point of view, continue to haunt the fifties, just as the retreat to the personal does. Betty Miller's observation in *The Twentieth Century* that 'this retreat into a closed, intensely personal life is a necessary reaction, perhaps, to the larger, and, as it must always seem to the individual, ungovernable menace of the world situation',[32] could also offer an explanation for the ways in which West and other women writers, like Pamela Frankau, Muriel Spark and, in her distinctively ambivalent style, Iris Murdoch, explore the tenets of religion as some form of structuring in an uncertain world. However, while the novels of

Frankau and Spark confront the problems of their time through the lens of their Catholicism, Murdoch and West, each in their own ways, eschew the tenets of organized religion. They could be said to share the conviction of Ethel Mannin's protagonist in *Lover under Another Name* who has 'too deep a reverence for the religious spirit in man, as the creative spirit, the authentic Holy Spirit, to be able to tolerate its submergence in dogma and ritual';[33] for, as a character says in Iris Murdoch's *Under the Net* (1954), 'God is a task. God is detail. It all lies close to your hand' (p. 231). Or, as Murdoch says herself,

> the connection between art and moral life has languished because we are losing our sense of form and structure in the moral world...we need more concepts in which to picture the substance of our being; it is through an enriching and deepening of concepts that moral progress takes place.[34]

Again we can see that the language of religion or at least of Christian morality may be used without any allegiance to institutionalized religion, but as a means of expressing concerns about a scale of values which many writers of the period perceive as in danger of being lost. There is, among these writers, an insistent questioning of a state of affairs which Gillian Rose sums up in typically challenging style: 'Luther's faith delivers religion to the Prince and, in so doing, leaves the world exactly as it is, reinforcing its most divisive values'.[35] This is the situation which Muriel Spark explores in the novel *Robinson*, where the island's owner has his own 'private morality' that only works for one, and causes dangerous chaos when a plane crashes and he is faced with a group of survivors.[36] The world has changed radically from the one West ruefully recalls in 1953:

> When I was young I understood neither the difficulty of love nor the importance of law. I grew up in a world of rebellion and I was a rebel. I thought human beings were naturally good, and that their personal relations were bound to work out well, and that the law was a clumsy machine dealing harshly with people who would cease to offend as soon as we got rid of poverty. We were quite sure that human nature was good and would soon be perfect.[37]

By the fifties, such certainty about human nature has vanished; it is worth repeating what Iris Murdoch's protagonist Jake concludes in *Under the Net* (1954):

When does one ever know a human being? Perhaps only after one has realized the impossibility of knowledge and renounced the desire for it and finally ceased to feel even the need of it. But then what one achieves is no longer knowledge, it is simply a kind of co-existing; and this too is one of the guises of love.[38]

For a writer like Storm Jameson, with her strong commitment to the problems in society, whether in Britain or in Europe, the retreat from engagement in the face of the disintegration of certainties mirrored in the 1958 number of *The Twentieth Century* is distressing, although she does not underestimate the difficulties of commitment. As she says in *Parthian Words* (1970),

Our age is certainly a hell of an age to get to terms with...but a novelist, great or small, has no more imperative use for his intelligence. The deeper the tensions, conscious or unconscious, in his mind, the better his chance, if he has the insolence and reckless courage, of meeting head on the sharpest contradictions and anguish of his day. Whether he makes tragedy, comedy, or farce of them is his business.[39]

As I have tried to show, many novelists of the late fifties and the sixties do engage in the spirit that Jameson urges. For writers like Jameson herself, Margot Heinemann, Iris Murdoch, Doris Lessing or Christine Brooke-Rose, the sights are set on ethical dilemmas within society at large; their priorities reflect those of the post-war conference, setting human society ahead of issues specific to women. Yet many writers, from Veronica Hull and Maureen Duffy to Doris Lessing and Margaret Drabble, do centre on such women's issues; the gloomy tone of the *The Twentieth Century* number devoted to women finds corroboration in their novels, but such works also reveal increasing resistance to the situations in which their women protagonists find themselves. The protests giving rise to the women's movements of the late sixties and seventies are anticipated in such novels.

In writing about the four decades from 1928 to 1968, I have attempted to show that many women writers address political and social issues in their novels, sometimes echoing concerns being expressed within society at large, sometimes acting as 'the conscience of unthinking people'. Inevitably, I have only been able to scratch the surface of what was being written throughout the period, and have often been forced to omit, with regret, reference to works, both critical and fictional, because of constraints of space. But the issues I have addressed do give a glimpse of many writers' central concerns. The constant discussion throughout the period on how to write shows dramatically how priorities shift and change over the years as society's experiences change, and how different the solutions of different writers can be. Yet I have also ended my argument by showing that the position of women by the end of the fifties had in many ways failed to advance as far as the suffragettes might have hoped. Of course, advances had been made: educational opportunities were more widespread, health and living conditions had improved for a large proportion of the population. But as old certainties died, as social mobility increased, and greater social and political opportunities were ostensibly within women's grasp, many of the old prejudices affecting women were still in place, not only among men, but reflected in the view women had of themselves, as I have discussed in the context of Mrs Pollock's pamphlet, the report of the post-war conference and the number of *The Twentieth Century* on the subject of women, in 1958. In this context, it has become clear that women writers of fiction can indeed be seen as consciousness raisers, bringing social and political issues into novels, and paving the way for the women's movement of the late sixties and seventies. Works of the sixties like Lynn Reid Banks's *The L-Shaped Room* (1960), Jennifer Dawson's *The Ha-Ha* (1961) and Doris Lessing's *The Golden Notebook* (1962), gave voices to women which heralded the feminist upsurge at the end of the decade, and there are many other novels by women which, as I have shown, engage with issues affecting the whole of society, and showing women as full and able contributors to the intellectual, emotional and spiritual challenges of their times. It was no longer valid in 1968 to deplore the lack of literary mothers and grandmothers. The only pity is that so many of these earlier works are now out of print, so that we are in danger of losing sight of the continuities they so admirably demonstrate.

Notes

Introduction

1 Which is not to say that these dates are other than arbitrary. I should have liked to include a writer like Vernon Lee, for instance, who in 1908 is already debating the kind of issue which I shall be addressing in this book when she says: 'Reality is valuable to us only as the raw material for something very different; the artistic sense alters it into patterns, the logical faculty reduces it to ideas. Except for individual action, the individual case, which is the only reality, has no importance' ('Rosny and the Analytical French Novel', *Gospels of Anarchy and Other Contemporary Studies* [London: T. F. Unwin, 1908], p. 235). And of course there is Virginia Woolf in 'Mr Bennett and Mrs Brown', *A Woman's Essays: Selected Essays,* vol. 1, ed. Rachel Bowlby (Harmondsworth: Penguin, 1992), asking in 1923/4: 'But, I ask myself, what is reality? And who are the judges of reality?' (p. 75). See also E. Showalter, *A Literature of Their Own* (London: Virago, 1982), which gives an excellent insight into the forerunners of this period; although her dismissal of women's fiction as 'adrift' (p. 34) after Woolf's death is something I shall be questioning.

2 See, for instance, The Hon. Mrs Dighton Pollock, *The Women of Today,* Routledge Introductions to Modern Knowledge, no. 14 (London: George Routledge & Sons, 1929), for a discussion of what women needed to fight for after achieving the vote. She argues, among other things, for removal of the veto on Welfare Centres giving information on birth control, better nursery provision, family allowances paid directly to mothers, school dinners, improvement in the divorce laws, equal opportunities in the work place, and so on. Many of these issues are still unaddressed by the end of the fifties: see, for instance, the special issue on women, *The Twentieth Century,* vol. 164, no. 978, August 1958, 'Special Number on Women'. Both these publications will be addressed in my concluding chapter.

3 E. L. Doctorow, '"False" Documents', *Poets and Presidents: Selected Essays, 1972–1992* (London: Macmillan, 1994 [1993]), pp. 150–64 (159).

4 M. Nussbaum, *Love's Knowledge: Essays on Philosophy and Literature* (New York, Oxford: Oxford University Press, 1990), p. 390.

5 M. Foucault, *Power/Knowledge: Selected Interviews and Other Writings 1972–1977,* trans. C. Gordon, L. Marshall, J. Mepham, K. Soper (Hemel Hempstead: Harvester Press, 1980), p. 193. What Foucault claims here is, of course, not an unfamiliar idea for those versed in medieval and early modern attitudes to 'fact' and what we would call fictive reshapings to make a point.

6 S. Freud, *The Interpretation of Dreams,* trans. J. Strachey, ed. A. Richards (Harmondsworth: Penguin, 1976), pp. 223–4.

7 See E. Maslen, 'One Man's Tomorrow Is Another's Today: the Reader's World and Its Impact on *Nineteen Eighty-Four',* in *Storm Warnings: Science Fiction Confronts the Future,* eds G. E. Slusser, C. Greenland and E. S. Rabkin (Carbondale and Edwardsville: Southern Illinois Press, 1987), pp. 146–58. Also see Lev

Loseff, *On the Beneficence of Censorship: Aesopian Language in Modern Russian Literature*, trans. J. Bobko (Munich: Verlag Otto Sagner, 1984).

8 See D. Margolies, 'Introduction', *Writing the Revolution: Cultural Criticism from Left Review*, ed. D. Margolies (London: Pluto Press, 1998).

9 See S. Scaffardi, *Fire under the Carpet: Working for Civil Liberties in the 1930s* (London: Lawrence and Wishart, 1986).

10 N. Mitchison, *The Corn King and the Spring Queen* (London: Jonathan Cape, 1931), and *We Have Been Warned* (London: Constable, 1935).

11 Radclyffe Hall, *The Well of Loneliness* [1928] (London: Virago, Weidenfeld & Nicolson, 1998).

12 E. Buckley, *Destination Unknown* (London: Andrew Dakers, 1942).

13 E. Pargeter, *She Goes to War* (London: William Heinemann, 1942).

14 G. Beer, 'Representing Women: Representing the Past', in *The Feminist Reader: Essays in Gender and the Politics of Literary Criticism*, eds C. Belsey and J. Moore (London: Macmillan Education, 1989), pp. 63–80 (70).

15 A. Light, *Forever England: Femininity, Literature and Conservatism between the Wars* (London and New York: Routledge, 1991).

16 R. B. DuPlessis, *Writing beyond the Ending: Narrative Strategies of Twentieth-Century Women Writers* (Bloomington: Indiana University Press, 1985), p. 74.

17 I. Calvino, 'Right and Wrong Political Uses of Literature', *The Uses of Literature*, trans. P. Creagh (Orlando: Harcourt Brace Jovanovich, 1986), pp. 89–100 (99). See similar comments in D. Lessing's Preface to *The Golden Notebook* [1962] (London: Collins [Paladin], 1989).

18 K. Williams and S. Matthews, eds, *Rewriting the Thirties* (London and New York: Longman, 1997), p. 3.

19 M. Atwood, 'Amnesty International: an Address', *Second Words: Selected Critical Prose* (Toronto: House of Anansi Press, 1982), p. 394. I am grateful to Aamer Hussein for reminding me of this essay.

20 S. Ertz, *Woman Alive* (London: Hodder & Stoughton, 1935) and *Anger in the Sky* (London: Hodder & Stoughton, 1943).

21 B. Christian, 'The Uses of History: Francis Harper's *Iola Leroy, Shadows Uplifted*', *Black Feminist Criticism: Perspectives on Black Women Writers*, ed. B. Christian (New York: Pergamon Press, 1985), p. 168.

22 M. Atwood, *Second Words*, pp. 396–7.

23 V. N. Vološinov, 'Discourse in Life and Discourse in Art (concerning Sociological Poetics)', *Freudianism: a Marxist Critique* (New York: Academic Press, 1976), p. 97.

24 K. Ryan, 'Socialist Fiction and the Education of Desire: Mervyn Jones, Raymond Williams and John Berger', in *The Socialist Novel in Britain: Towards the Recovery of a Tradition*, ed. H. G. Klaus (Brighton: Harvester, 1982), pp. 166–85 (166–7).

25 S. Jameson, 'The Writer's Situation', *The Writer's Situation and Other Essays* (London: Macmillan, 1950), p. 1. See also Q. D. Leavis, *Fiction and the Reading Public* [1932] (London: Bellew Publishing, 1978), pp. 73–4, discussing the responsibility of the writer to his age.

26 See C. Harrison, *Modernism*, Movements in Modern Art Series (London: Tate Gallery Publishing, 1997), p. 6, for a parallel set of definition problems in modern art. See also C. Butler, *Early Modernism: Literature, Music, and Painting in Europe 1900–1914* (Oxford: Oxford University Press, 1994).

27 Sandra Kemp also reminds us that in a sense there is 'no such thing as modernism: that modernism is a retrospective description of common tendencies in a field of writing'. ' "But how describe a world seen without a self?" Feminism, Fiction and Modernism', *Critical Quarterly*, vol 32, no 1, 1990, pp. 99–118 (100).

28 M. Levenson, 'Introduction', in *The Cambridge Companion to Modernism*, ed. M. Levenson (Cambridge: Cambridge University Press, 1999), pp. 1–8 (3). See also D. Trotter, 'The Modernist Novel' in this volume (70–99) for an admirable discussion of the complexities involved.

29 E. D. Ermarth, 'Preface to 1998 Edition', *Realism and Consensus in the English Novel: Time, Space and Narrative* [1983] (Edinburgh: Edinburgh University Press, 1998), pp. xv–xvi.

30 S. Beckett, *Proust and Three Dialogues with Georges Duthuit* [*Proust* 1931] (London: John Calder Publishers, 1999), pp. 78–9.

31 C. Baldick, 'Estrangements', Review of *Metafiction* by Patricia Waugh, *Times Literary Supplement*, 15 March 1985, p. 295.

32 G. Gebauer and C. Wulf, *Mimesis: Culture–Art–Society*, trans. D. Reneau (Berkely, Los Angeles, London: University of California Press, 1995), p. 221.

33 I take this last phrase from Alexa Alfer's translation in an unpublished paper, where she points out an error in Reneau's version of 'es wird die mimetische Verfassung der Wirklichkeit selbst behauptet' (Gebauer and Wulf, *Mimesis* [Reibek: Rowohlt, 1992], p. 308). There is also, of course, Christine Brooke-Rose's very just observation that 'the very notion of mimesis is an illusion: unlike dramatic representation, narrative cannot imitate the story it is telling; it can only tell it, and give an illusions of mimesis, unless the object imitated is language (as in dialogue)' (*A Rhetoric of the Unreal: Studies in Narrative and Structure, Especially of the Fantastic* [Cambridge: Cambridge University Press, 1981], p. 320).

34 C. Craig, 'Going Down to Hell Is Easy', *Cencrastus*, 6, Autumn 1981, pp. 19–21 (19).

35 S. Rushdie, *Imaginary Homelands: Essays and Criticism, 1981–1991* (London: Granta, 1991), pp. 13–14.

36 This is as true for scientific theories as for works of art, as B. C. Van Fraassen and J. Sigman argue in 'Interpretations in Science and in the Arts', in *Realism and Representation*, ed. G. Levine (Wisconsin: University of Wisconsin Press, 1993), pp. 73–99.

37 B. Robbins, 'Modernism and Literary Realism: Response', in *Realism and Representation*, ed. Levine, pp. 225–31 (229).

38 J. Richards, 'Modernism and the People: the View from the Cinema Stalls', in *Rewriting the Thirties*, eds Williams and Matthews, pp. 182–201 (197).

39 E. H. Gombrich, *Art and Illusion: a Study in the Psychology of Pictorial Representation* (London: Phaidon, 1968), p. 148.

40 J. Malpas, *Realism*, Movements in Modern Art Series (London: Tate Gallery Publishing, 1997), p. 26.

41 T. Eagleton, 'Newsreel History', review of P. Conrad, *Modern Times, Modern Places*, *London Review of Books*, 12 November 1998, p. 8.

42 W. H. Auden, 'Psychology and Art Today' [1935], repr. in *The English Auden: Poems, Essays and Dramatic Writings 1927–1939*, ed. Edward Mendelson (London: Faber & Faber, 1977), pp. 332–42 (341).

43 J. Rose, *Why War: Psychoanalysis, Politics, and the Return to Melanie Klein* (Oxford: Blackwell, 1993), pp. 248–9. Rose goes on to point to how 'the opposition between the aesthetic and the historical is further displaced by the issue of memory' (p. 249).

44 B. Fowler, *The Alienated Reader: Women and Romantic Literature in the Twentieth Century* (Hemel Hempstead: Harvester Wheatsheaf, 1991).

45 D. Spender, ed., *Time and Tide Wait for No Man* (London: Pandora, 1984), p. 1. See also Maggie Humm, *Border Traffic: Strategies of Contemporary Women Writers* (Manchester and New York: Manchester University Press, 1991), for a feminist evaluation of a number of women writers of this period.

46 N. Beauman, *A Very Great Profession: the Woman's Novel 1914–1939* (London: Virago, 1983), p. 82.

47 J. Montefiore, *Men and Women Writers of the 1930s: the Dangerous Flood of History* (London and New York: Routledge, 1996).

1 Women's Ways of Writing

1 C. Brooke-Rose, *Stories, Theories, Things* (Cambridge: Cambridge University Press, 1991), p. 161.

2 R. West, *Black Lamb and Grey Falcon: a Journey through Yugoslavia* [1942], ed. T. Royle (Edinburgh: Canongate Classics, 1993), p. 55. See V. Goldsworthy, 'Black Lamb and Grey Falcon: Rebecca West's Journey through the Balkans', *Women: a Cultural Review*, vol. 8, no. i, Spring 1997, pp. 1–11, for an excellent analysis of this work.

3 S. Jameson, *Europe to Let: the Memoirs of an Obscure Man* (London: Macmillan, 1940), pp. 236–7.

4 See G. Orwell, 'Why I Write' [1946], *The Collected Essays, Journalism and Letters of George Orwell*, vol. 1, *An Age like This 1920–40*, eds S. Orwell and I. Angus (Harmondsworth: Penguin, 1970), pp. 23–30.

5 N. Mitchison, *The Corn King and the Spring Queen* (London: Jonathan Cape, 1931).

6 E. Mannin, *The Dark Forest* (London: Jarrolds, 1946).

7 S. Townsend Warner, *The Flint Anchor* (New York: The Viking Press, 1954).

8 M. Spark, *The Prime of Miss Jean Brodie* [1961] (Harmondsworth: Penguin, 1965).

9 See, for instance, D. Lessing, *The Grass Is Singing* [1950] (London: Collins [Paladin], 1989), and the first three volumes on the Children of Violence sequence: *Martha Quest* [1952], *A Proper Marriage* [1954] and *A Ripple from the Storm* [1958] (London: Collins [Paladin], 1990).

10 A. Gasiorek, *Post-War British Fiction: Realism and After* (London: Edward Arnold, 1995), p. 4; and see P. Lassner, *British Women Writers of World War II: Battlegrounds of Their Own* (London: Macmillan, 1998): 'While so many novels experiment formally with political aims, they do not invite new definitions of modernism; instead they invent new literary responses to modernism and to the era's socialist and proletarian fictions' (p. 5).

11 G. Hanscombe and V. Smyers, *Writing for Their Lives: the Modernist Women 1910–1940* (London: The Women's Press, 1987), p. 12.

12 C. M. Schenk, 'Exiled by Genre: Modernism, Canonicity, and the Politics of Exclusion', *Women's Writing in Exile*, eds M. L. Broe and A. Ingram (Chapel Hill and London: University of North Carolina Press, 1989), pp. 225–50 (231).

13 C. Brooke-Rose, *Stories, Theories, Things*, p. 172.

14 See R. Samuel, *Theatres of Memory* (London and New York: Verso, 1994).

15 N. Mitchison, *The Bull Calves* (London: Jonathan Cape, 1947), p. 411.

16 A. Gasiorek, *Post-War British Fiction*, pp. v–vi.

17 See M. Joannou, *'Ladies, Please Don't Smash These Windows': Women's Writing, Feminist Consciousness and Social Change 1918–1938* (Oxford and Providence: Berg, 1995): 'Traditional modes of writing are resilient' (p. 6); and 'To systematise a demarcation between traditional and experimental modes of writing is to perpetuate an artificial division more rigidly than many women of the 1920s and 1930s believed to be necessary. In practice, women writers often crossed the hypothesised demarcation line' (pp. 6–7).

18 S. Jameson, *Civil Journey* (Edinburgh: Constable, 1939).

19 Brecht's warning is quoted by Walter Benjamin in 'A Small History of Photography', *One Way Street and Other Writings*, trans. E. Jephcott and K. Shorter (London: Verso, 1979), p. 255.

20 V. Woolf, 'Modern Fiction', *The Crowded Dance of Modern Life: Selected Essays*, vol. 2, ed. R. Bowlby (Harmondsworth: Penguin, 1993), pp. 5–12 (7).

21 R. West, *Black Lamb and Grey Falcon*, p. 265.

22 S. Jameson, *In the Second Year* (London: Cassell, 1936); *The Fort* (London: Cassell, 1941); *Then We Shall Hear Singing: a Fantasy in C Major* (London: Cassell, 1942).

23 A. C. Francis, 'The Education of Desire: Utopian Fiction and Feminist Fantasy', in *The Victorian Fantasists: Essays on Culture, Society and Belief in the Mythopoeic Fiction of the Victorian Age*, ed. K. Filmer (London and Basingstoke: Macmillan, 1991), pp. 45–59 (49).

24 C. Brooke-Rose, *Stories, Theories, Things*, p. 210.

25 D. Cameron, ' "Words, Words, Words": the Power of Language', *The War of the Words: the Political Correctness Debate*, ed. S. Dunant (London: Virago, 1994), pp. 15–34 (17–18 and 26).

26 D. Cameron, 'Language: Are You Being Served?', *Critical Quarterly*, vol. 39, no. 2, Summer 1997, pp. 97–100 (99).

27 N. Mitchison, *The Bull Calves*, p. 408.

28 R. West, *Black Lamb and Grey Falcon*, pp. 1127–8.

29 P. Deane, 'Introduction', in *History in Our Hands: a Critical Anthology of Writings on Literature, Culture and Politics from the 1930s*, ed. P. Deane (London and New York, Leicester University Press, 1998), pp. 1–5 (9).

30 Q. D. Leavis, *Fiction and the Reading Public*, p. 20.

31 See A. Blunt, 'The Realism Quarrel' [April 1937], in *Writing the Revolution: Cultural Criticism from* Left Review, ed. David Margolies, pp. 76–9. Blunt argues that the working class is not ready for abstracts, but he suggests how the painter can use his knowledge of abstracts since geometric forms will suggest objects, and eventually 'the formal hint supplied by the subconscious can be utilised to convey some more rationalised and, therefore, more generally accessible idea' (p. 79). Margolies also includes Amabel Ellis's Readers' Competitions, giving advice on how to write (pp. 183–96 [183]). This is interesting to compare with Leavis's inclusion of advice given in the States

to writers for magazines; see E. Maslen, 'Naomi Mitchison's Historical Fiction', in *Women Writers of the 1930s: Gender, Politics and History*, ed. M. Joannou (Edinburgh: Edinburgh University Press, 1999), pp. 138–50 (140).

32 Q. D. Leavis, *Fiction and the Reading Public*, p. 51.

33 R. Fry, *Vision and Design* [1928] (London and New York: Oxford University Press, 1990), p. 15. Reading this comment, one can see why Ezra Pound was seduced by the politics of Mussolini's Italy.

34 Q. D. Leavis, *Fiction and the Reading Public*, p. 74.

35 M. Shaw, 'Feminism and Fiction between the Wars: Winifred Holtby and VirginiaWoolf', *Women's Writing: a Challenge to Theory*, ed. M. Monteith (Brighton: Harvester, 1986), pp. 171–91 (176).

36 See S. Kemp, '"But how describe a world without a self?"'.

37 M. Barrett, ed., *Virginia Woolf: Women and Writing* (London: The Women's Press, 1979), p. 189.

38 R. West, *The Strange Necessity: Essays and Reviews* (London: Jonathan Cape, 1928).

39 E. White, *Winifred Holtby: As I Knew Her* (London: Collins, 1938), pp. 133–4.

40 S. Jameson, 'Documents', *Fact*, no. 4, issue title 'Writing in Revolt', July 1937, pp. 9–18. Jameson did not of course invent documentary realism. See K. Williams: 'Post/Modern Documentary: Orwell, Agee and the New Reportage', in *Rewriting the Thirties*, eds Williams and Matthews, pp. 163–81. Williams observes that new reportage was 'a reaction against modernism's imploding preoccupation with self-analysis and experiment, but without merely regressing to nineteenth-century Naturalism's unproblematised mimesis. It eventually became an important position in the debate about the nature of the real, and the question of the most effective form of representing it'. The awareness 'that modernism's linguistic self-consciousness, together with new media technology, had transformed categories of realistic representation irrevocably, wasn't only aesthetic, but political' (p. 165).

41 S. Jameson, *Journey from the North*, vol. 1 [1969] (London: Virago 1984), p. 245. See also her earlier essay, 'The Form of the Novel', in *The Writer's Situation*, where she slates 'determined stylists' such as Romer Wilson, Djuna Barnes, Virginia Woolf and Gertrude Stein, because 'Writers, novelists, who devote themselves to the disintegration of language, may be innocent of the impulse that destroyed in a few days all the great libraries of Warsaw. But its roots stretch a long way, as far as it is from burning libraries to the concentration camps where men are burned' (pp. 55–6).

42 Storm Jameson, 'Documents' [1937], in *Modernism: an Anthology of Sources and Documents*, eds Vassiliki Kolocotvoni, Jane Goldman and Olga Taxidou (Edinburgh: Edinburgh University Press, 1998), pp. 556–60 (558).

43 See E. Gualteri, '*Three Guineas* and the Photograph: the Art of Propaganda', in *Women Writers of the 1930s: Gender Politics and History*, ed. Joannou, pp. 165–78. While some of the claims made by Gualteri may be challenged, her point about Woolf's different treatment of the two sets of photographs is useful.

44 V. Woolf, 'Craftsmanship', *The Crowded Dance of Modern Life*, pp. 137–43 (139–40).

45 Q. D. Leavis, *Fiction and the Reading Public*, p. 255.

46 V. Woolf, 'Craftsmanship', p. 143.

47   B. Miller (B. Bergson Spiro), *The Mere Living* (London: Victor Gollancz, 1933), p. 109.

48   See V. Cunningham, 'The Age of Anxiety and Influence; or, Tradition and the Thirties Talents', in *Rewriting the Thirties*, eds Williams and Matthews, pp. 5–22 (7).

49   T. Davies, 'Unfinished Business, Realism and Working-Class Writing', in *The British Working-Class Novel in the Twentieth Century*, ed. J. Hawthorn (London: Edward Arnold, 1984), pp. 125–39 (135).

50   A. Light, *Forever England*; G. Plain, *Women's Fiction of the Second World War: Gender, Power and Resistance* (Edinburgh: Edinburgh University Press, 1996).

51   A. C. Francis, 'The Education of Desire: Utopian Fiction and Feminist Fantasy', p. 47.

52   V. Cunningham, 'The Age of Anxiety and Influence; or, Tradition, and the Thirties Talents', p. 6.

53   G. Beer, 'Sylvia Townsend Warner: the Centrifugal Kick', in *Women Writers of the 1930s: Gender, Politics and History*, ed. Joannou, pp. 76–86 (82).

54   V. Woolf, *Orlando* [1928], *The Waves* [1931] and *The Years* [1937] (Harmondsworth: Penguin, 1993, 1992 and 1994), all originally published by The Hogarth Press in London. For valuable comment on *The Years*, see P. Marks, 'Illusion and Reality: the Spectre of Socialist Realism in Thirties Literature', *Rewriting the Thirties*, eds Williams and Matthews, pp. 23–36.

55   R. West, *Harriet Hume* [1929] (London: Virago, 1980); *The Thinking Reed* [1936] (London: Virago, 1984).

56   S. Ertz, *Woman Alive* (London: Hodder & Stoughton, 1935).

57   S. Jameson, *In the Second Year* (London: Cassell, 1936).

58   See E. Maslen, 'Naomi Mitchison's Historical Fiction', *Women Writers of the 1930s: Gender, Politics and History*, ed. Joannou, pp. 138–50. Also see J. Montefiore, *Men and Women Writers of the 1930s*, and J. Calder, *The Nine Lives of Naomi Mitchison* (London: Virago, 1997). See also Q. D. Leavis's comparison of her and Jameson in 'Lady Novelists and the Lower Orders', *Scrutiny*, vol. IV, no. 2, September 1935, pp. 112–32: 'where Naomi Mitchison displays snobbishness, complacency and intellectual pretentiousness, Storm Jameson's novel *Love in Winter* is a marked contrast to *We Have Been Warned*. Miss Jameson too has set out to give a cross-section of contemporary society, and the comparison...is entirely in her favour. She shows how much can be done by observing and composing with nothing more showy than stubborn honesty, humility and the sensitiveness that goes with solidity of character...the nearest thing to such a desirable kind of propaganda we have over here' (p. 117).

59   See, for example, S. Townsend Warner, *Summer Will Show* [1936] (London: Virago, 1987); K. Burdekin (writing as Murray Constantine), *Proud Man* [1934] (New York: The Feminist Press, 1993) and *Swastika Night* [1937] (London: Victor Gollancz, 1940; London: Lawrence & Wishart, 1985); E. Pargeter [now better known for her later pen-name, Ellis Peters], *Hortensius Friend of Nero* (London: Lovat Dickson, 1936); N. Mitchison, *The Corn King and the Spring Queen* (1931) and *The Blood of the Martyrs* (London: Constable, 1939).

60   E. Wilkinson, *Clash* [1928] (London: Virago, 1989).

61   W. Holtby, *South Riding: an English Landscape* [1936] (London: Virago, 1988).

62   A. Carter, *Nights at the Circus* [1984] (London: Pan [Picador], 1984).

63 R. West, *Harriet Hume*, p. 8.

64 N. Mitchison, *The Fourth Pig* (London: Constable, 1936); this is interesting to compare with Angela Carter's *The Bloody Chamber* [1967] (London: Virago, 1981).

65 C. Dane, *The Arrogant History of White Ben* (William Heinemann, 1939). See West's reference to a scarecrow mentioned above, *Black Lamb and Grey Falcon*, pp. 1127–8.

66 S. Smith, *Over the Frontier* [1938] (London: Virago, 1980).

67 M. Scott-James, 'News from Nowhere', *London Mercury*, 37 (February 1938), p. 456.

68 Quoted by F. Spalding, *Stevie Smith: a Critical Biography* (London: Faber, 1988), p. 134.

69 S. Smith, *Me Again*, eds J. Barbera and W. McBrien (London: Virago, 1981), p. 273.

70 S. Jameson, *Delicate Monster* (London: Ivor Nicholson and Watson, 1937), p. 38.

71 S. Jameson, *Europe to Let*, pp. 236–8.

72 *Time & Tide*, 8 June 1940, p. 620.

73 J. Radford, 'Late Modernism and the Politics of History', in *Women Writers of the 1930s*, ed. Joannou, pp. 33–45 (37); see also J. L. Johnson, 'The Remedial Flaw: Revisioning Cultural History in *Between the Acts*', in *Virginia Woolf and Bloomsbury*, ed. J. Marcus (London: Macmillan, 1987), pp. 253–78.

74 C. Wiley, 'Making History Unrepeatable in Virginia Woolf's *Between the Acts*', *Clio*, vol. 25, 1995, pp. 3–20 (20).

75 S. Ertz, *One Fight More* (London: Hodder & Stoughton, 1940); *The Bookseller*, 1 January 1942, also tells that Edith Pargeter's novel *Ordinary People* about a family living in a 'peaceful English setting . . . was written in cramped quarters during heavy blitzes' (p. 7).

76 S. Jameson, 'The Responsibilities of the Writer' (1941), *The Writer's Situation and Other Essays*, p. 165.

77 S. Jameson, 'The Responsibilities of the Writer', p. 177. Compare E. White, *Winifred Holtby*, pp. 133–4, quoted earlier.

78 S. Jameson, 'A Crisis of the Spirit' (written October–November 1941), *The Writer's Situation and Other Essays*, p. 139. Compare V. Woolf, 'Modern Fiction', *The Crowded Dance of Modern Life*, p. 7, quoted earlier.

79 D. Sayers, 'The Creative Mind' (Address given to the Humanities Club at Reading, February 1942), *Unpopular Opinions* (London: Victor Gollancz, 1946), p. 49.

80 See J. Labon, 'Tracing Storm Jameson', *Women: a Cultural Review*, vol. 8, no. 1, Spring 1997, pp. 33–47.

81 I. Holden, *Night Shift* (London: John Lane The Bodley Head, 1941).

82 See B. Fowler, *The Alienated Reader*, for a discussion of politically active women and escapist reading.

83 I. Holden, *There's No Story There* (London: John Lane The Bodley Head, 1944), p. 74. This novel also involves a murder mystery, but not as the driving force of the story.

84 S. Jameson, *Then We Shall Hear Singing*, p. 5.

85 E. Mannin, *The Dark Forest* (London: Jarrolds Ltd, 1946). As so often at this time, the date(s) of writing are given at the end of texts.

86 E. Pargeter, *She Goes to War* (London: William Heinemann, 1942).
87 *The Bookseller*, nos 1881–2, Thursday, 1 January 1942, p. 7: 'Leading Wren Pargeter...has helped in her fashion to sink the *Bismark*, for her watch was on duty while the German raider was being pursued though not when she sank. They left her damaged and burning, so to speak'. The *Bismark* was sunk in May 1941.
88 E. Pargeter, *Lame Crusade, Reluctant Odyssey* and *Warfare Accomplished*, The Eighth Champion of Christendom (London: William Heinemann, 1945, 1946 and 1947).
89 S. Smith, *The Holiday* [1949] (London: Virago, 1979), p. 53.
90 N. Mitchison, *The Bull Calves*, p. 515.
91 Bryher, *Beowulf* (New York: Pantheon Books, 1956), p. 22.
92 S. Jameson, 'The Novelist Today: 1949' (written May 1949), *The Writer's Situation and Other Essays*, p. 70.
93 E. Bowen, *The Heat of the Day* [1948] (Harmondsworth: Penguin, 1962).
94 E. Taylor, *Palladian* [1946] (London: Virago, 1985), p. viii.
95 D. Lessing, *The Grass Is Singing* [1950] (London: Collins [Paladin], 1989).
96 E. Taylor, *Angel* [1957] (London: Virago, 1984).
97 B. Comyns, *Sisters by a River* [1947] (London: Virago, 1985). The first sentence of her third novel, *Who Was Changed and Who Was Dead* [1954] (London: Virago, 1987), also announces its links with magic realism: 'The ducks swam through the drawing-room windows' (1).
98 Iris Murdoch also uses elements of magic realism within the existential realism of her early novels. See, for instance, *Under the Net* (London: Chatto & Windus, 1954), and *The Flight from the Enchanter* (London: Chatto & Windus, 1956).
99 S. Jameson, *The Green Man* (London: Macmillan, 1952).
100 S. Townsend Warner, *The Flint Anchor* (New York: The Viking Press, 1954).
101 See A. Hosain, *Phoenix Fled* [1953] (London: Virago, 1988); D. Lessing, *The Grass is Singing* (1950), and the Children of Violence Series.
102 M. Bradbury, 'Iris Murdoch's *Under the Net*', *Critical Quarterly*, no. 4, Spring 1962, pp. 47–54 (49).
103 I. Murdoch, 'Against Dryness: a Polemical Sketch', *Encounter*, no. 88, January 1961, pp. 16–20 (20); and see A. S. Byatt, *Degrees of Freedom: the Early Novels of Iris Murdoch* [1965] (London: Vintage, 1994), for excellent discussion of Murdoch's own early theory and practice.
104 C. Brooke-Rose, *The Languages of Love* (London: Secker & Warburg, 1957), p. 22.
105 C. Brooke-Rose, *The Sycamore Tree* (London: Secker & Warburg, 1958), p. 82. Her next novel, *The Dear Deceit* (London: Secker & Warburg, 1960), is less successful, experimenting with a reversal of chronological order of a man's life, with little of the earlier vitality of language. But the final 'realist' novel, *The Middlemen* (London: Secker & Warburg, 1961), has more of the explosive imagery of the first two.
106 See Brooke-Rose's comment on 'imagery' in *A Grammar for Metaphor* (London: Secker & Warburg, 1958), p. 288, as an example of her lucid attitude to language. She says we should be wary of using the term 'imagery' to include 'anything from metaphor to a literal fact or scene poetically described; and, as a corollary to this, the confusion between symbolism and metaphor. The

literal fact or scene may have symbolic meanings, more or less evident, more or less private; but this is achieved by the connotation that words and even syntax may have acquired in any civilisation or period, and not by means of the metaphoric relation of words to each other; the primary meaning of the symbolic word or sentence or poem is literal, indeed, the literal meaning is as much part of the effect and intention'. This lucidity is what makes her experimental writing so outstanding.

107   M. Borden, *The Hungry Leopard* (London: William Heinemann, 1956).

108   M. Spark, *The Comforters* [1957] (Harmondsworth: Penguin, 1963).

109   L. Reid Banks, *The L-shaped Room* (Harmondsworth: Penguin, 1962).

110   See, for instance, P. Mortimer, *The Pumpkin Eater* [1962] (Harmondsworth: Penguin, 1962); M. Drabble, *A Summer Bird-Cage* [1963] (Harmondsworth: Penguin, 1967); V. Hull, *The Monkey Puzzle* (London: Barrie, 1958); and J. Dawson, *The Ha-Ha* [1961] (London: Virago, 1985).

111   M. Gallie, *Strike for a Kingdom* (London: Victor Gollancz, 1959), and *The Small Mine* (London: Victor Gollancz, 1962). I am grateful to Prof. Stephen Knight for suggesting these witty and shrewd works to me. See his article '"The hesitations and uncertainties that were the truth": Three Welsh Industrial Novels by Women', in *British Industrial Fictions*, eds H. Gustav Klaus and Stephen Knight (Cardiff: University of Wales Press, 2000), pp. 1–8.

112   A. Hosain, *Sunlight on a Broken Column* [1961] (London: Penguin, 1992).

113   A. Carter, 'Introduction', C. Stead, *The Puzzleheaded Girl* [1968] (London: Virago, 1984), pp. vii–xv (x).

114   C. Stead, *Cotters' England* [1966] (London: Virago, 1980). In many ways, Stead's protagonist, Nellie, is also a working-class forerunner of Lessing's middle-class Alice in *The Good Terrorist* (London: Collins [Paladin], 1985).

115   N. Mitchison, *Memoirs of a Spacewoman* (London: Victor Gollancz, 1962).

116   B. Brophy, *The Finishing Touch* (London: Secker & Warburg, 1963), p. 7.

117   B. Brophy, *Hackenfeller's Ape* (London: Secker & Warburg, 1964).

118   M. Spark, *The Bachelors* [1960] (Harmondsworth: Penguin, 1963), p. 214.

119   D. Lessing, *The Golden Notebook* [1962] (London: Collins [Paladin] 1990).

120   M. Duffy, *The Microcosm* [1966] (London: Virago, 1989).

121   P. Waugh, *Postmodernism: a Reader* (London: Edward Arnold, 1997), pp. 7, 4.

122   H. Reyes, 'Delectable metarealism/ethical experiments: Re-reading Christine Brooke-Rose', unpublished Ph.D. thesis, University of London, 1998, p. 93.

123   C. Brooke-Rose, *The Christine Brooke-Rose Omnibus. Four Novels: Out, Such, Between, Thru* (Manchester: Carcanet Press, 1986). The novel *Between*, as Reyes points out, was begun in 1964, before *Such*, although published in 1968. The links with such French avant-garde writers as Alain Robbe-Grillet are well documented.

124   A. Quin, *Berg* (London: John Calder, 1964). Quin's experimentalism runs alongside that of such writers as B. S. Johnson.

125   A. Quin, *Three* (London: Calder & Boyars, 1966).

126   C. Brooke-Rose, *Stories, Theories, Things* (Cambridge: Cambridge University Press, 1991).

127   C. Brooke-Rose, *Stories, Theories, Things*, p. 231.

128   S. Jameson, 'The Writer in Contemporary Society', *American Scholar*, 35, Winter 1965–6, pp. 74–85 (76).

129 S. Jameson, *Parthian Words* (London: Collins Harvill, 1970), p. 137. In *Journey from the North*, vol. 1 [1969] (London: Virago, 1984), Jameson also says: 'I feel certain that any novelist who starts from the impulse to create a style... has begun to separate himself from his age. And that, carried too far, this separation must end in sterility and the breakdown of communication' (p. 300). Here she would seem to be attacking the kind of postmodern concerns that Carter attacks in her introduction to Stead's *Puzzleheaded Girl*, rather than the style Brooke-Rose develops, since Brooke-Rose's primary concern is to explore the effect of language on perception.

2   Wars and Rumours of Wars

1   S. Freud, 'Thoughts for the Times on War and Death' [1915], *Civilization, Society and Religion*, ed. A. Dickson, The Penguin Freud Library, vol. 12 (Harmondsworth: Penguin, 1991), p. 65.

2   S. Jameson, *The Clash* (London: William Heinemann, 1922), pp. 267–8. It is worth noting that by the end of the twenties there was a spate of novels about World War One – many writers had needed the ten-year interval to come to terms with that war and its implications.

3   Extract from Filippo Marinetti, 'The Founding and Manifesto of Futurism' [1909], *Marinetti: Selected Writings*, ed. R. W. Flint (London: Secker & Warburg, 1972), pp. 41–2.

4   W. Benjamin, 'The Work of Art in the Age of Mechanical Reproduction', in *Illuminations*, ed. Hannah Arendt, trans. H. Zohn (London: Fontana Press, 1992), pp. 219–44 (244).

5   M. Joannou, *'Ladies, Please Don't Smash These Windows'*, pp. 169–70.

6   Women's commitment to pacifism was, of course, by no means confined to Britain, gaining in strength in many countries throughout World War One and the inter-war years. See, for instance, Marie Louise Degen, *The History of the Woman's Peace Party*, The Johns Hopkins University Studies in Historical and Political Science, Series LVII, no. 3 (Baltimore: The Johns Hopkins University Press, 1939). Which is not to underestimate the number of women who were more than prepared to hand out white feathers in both world wars.

7   V. Woolf, *A Room of One's Own* and *Three Guineas*, ed. Morag Shiach, The World's Classics (Oxford: Oxford University Press, 1992). Also see V. Brittain's novel *Account Rendered* (London: Macmillan, 1945) for a sustained pacifist reaction to World War Two.

8   See *Time & Tide*, November 1939. I am grateful to Vesna Goldsworthy for giving me this reference.

9   M. Joannou, *'Ladies, Please Don't Smash These Windows'*, p. 170.

10 J. Bourke, *Dismembering the Male: Men's Bodies, Britain and the Great War* (London: Reaktion Books, 1996), p. 193.

11 The article quoted comes from 'Man Consciousness', *New Schoolmaster*, IV.20 (May 1923), p. 10.

12 M. Ulrich, ed., *Man, Proud Man: a Commentary by Mary Borden, E. M. Delafield, Susan Ertz, Storm Jameson, Helen Simpson, G. B. Stern, Sylvia Townsend Warner, Rebecca West* (London: Hamish Hamilton, 1932).

13 Ulrich, *Man, Proud Man*, p. 79. See also, for example, E. Cambridge, *Portrait of Angela: a Novel* (London: Jonathan Cape, 1939), where fighting is seen, ruefully, as a natural employment for a man; Woolf's anger fell on many sympathetic ears as the decade reached its end.

14 Ulrich, *Man, Proud Man*, p. 130.

15 S. Smith, *Over the Frontier* [1938] (London: Virago, 1980); A. Williams-Ellis, *Learn to Love First* (London: Victor Gollancz, 1939). This is not to align them with R. Baxter's misogynism in his works *Guilty Women* (London: Quality Press, 1941, reprinted six times before 1943) and *Women of the Gestapo* (London: Quality Press, 1943), where he claims, 'the male agents of the Gestapo are brutes, but the women agents are fiends who surpass the men in brutality and in their inhuman behaviour' (p. 16).

16 S. Jameson, *The Hidden River* (London: Macmillan, 1955); and R. Macaulay, *The World My Wilderness* [1950] (London: Virago, 1983).

17 J. Hartley, *Millions like Us: British Women's Fiction of the Second World War* (London: Virago, 1997), p. 6; see also G. Plain, *Women's Fiction of the Second World War: Gender, Power and Resistance* (Edinburgh: Edinburgh University Press, 1996).

18 S. Jameson, 'The Responsibilities of the Writer' (spoken at the opening meeting of the London Congress of the PEN, held on 11 September 1941), *The Writer's Situation and Other Essays*, p. 168.

19 S. Jameson, *The Black Laurel* (London: Macmillan, 1947).

20 V. Hull, *The Monkey Puzzle* (London: Barrie, 1958); J. Dawson, *The Ha-Ha* [1961] (London: Virago, 1985); P. Mortimer, *The Pumpkin Eater* [1962] (Harmondsworth: Penguin, 1964); P. Kitchen, *Lying-in* (London: Arnold Baker, 1965); and M. Duffy, *The Microcosm* [1966] (London:Virago, 1989).

21 Freud, *Civilisation, Society and Religion*, p. 72, and see *The Foucault Reader*, ed. P. Rabinow (Harmondsworth: Penguin, 1984).

22 A. Hosain, *Sunlight on a Broken Column* [1961] (London: Penguin, 1992).

23 N. Mitchison, *Memoirs of a Spacewoman* (London: Victor Gollancz, 1962); and D. Lessing, *The Four-Gated City* [1969] (London: Collins [Paladin], 1990).

24 Y. M. Klein, *Beyond the Home Front: Women's Autobiographical Writing of the Two World Wars* (London: Macmillan, 1997); C. M. Tylee, *The Great War and Women's Consciousness: Images of Militarism and Feminism in Women's Writings, 1914–1964* (Iowa City: University of Iowa Press, 1990); R. West, *The Return of the Soldier* (London: Nisbet, 1917).

25 M. Borden, *The Forbidden Zone* (London: William Heinemann,1929).

26 H. Zenna Smith, *Not So Quiet: Stepdaughters of War* [1930] (London: Virago, 1988), pp. 7–8. B. Hardy's introduction makes a strong case, defending Smith against earlier suspicions of plagiarism. See also, for comparison, R. Aldington, *Death of a Hero: a Novel* (London: Chatto & Windus, 1930).

27 N. Mitchison, *The Fourth Pig* (London: Constable, 1936), p. 5.

28 C. Dane, *The Arrogant History of White Ben* (London: William Heinemann, 1939). Dane's epigraphs are valuable pointers to the basis for her fable. I am grateful to Jenny Hartley for bringing this admirable novel to my attention.

29 The link at this date with the Nietzschean split between Apollo and Dionysus is clear. More recently Nazism tends to be seen as the product of a machine-like logic.

30 R. West, *Black Lamb and Grey Falcon*, p. 775.

31   S. Freud, 'Why War' 1932 [1933], *Civilization, Society and Religion*, p. 359; T. S. Eliot, 'The Hollow Men' [1925], *The Complete Poems and Plays of T. S. Eliot* (London & Boston: Faber & Faber, 1969), pp. 83–6 (83).

32   K. Burdekin, *The End of This Day's Business* (New York: The Feminist Press, 1989).

33   S. Ertz, *Woman Alive* (London: Hodder & Stoughton, 1935).

34   A. Williams-Ellis, *Learn to Love First*, p. 36.

35   S. Townsend Warner, *Summer Will Show* [1936] (London: Virago, 1987). More than one question is being raised here, although Warner leaves us to draw our own conclusions.

36   S. Smith, *Over the Frontier*, pp. 249–50.

37   S. Townsend Warner, 'The Drought Breaks' (1937), in *Spanish Front: Writers on the Civil War*, ed. V. Cunningham (Oxford: Oxford University Press, 1986), pp. 244–47 (247).

38   S. Townsend Warner, *After the Death of Don Juan* [1938] (London: Virago, 1988), pp. v–vi.

39   S. Freud, 'Why War?', *Civilization, Society and Religion*, p. 359.

40   P. Bottome, *The Mortal Storm* (London: Faber & Faber, 1937).

41   S. Jameson, *Europe to Let: the Memoirs of an Obscure Man* (London: Macmillan, 1940). Later, in *Journey from the North*, Jameson tells how this novel was based on actual conversations she had during her travels through east and central Europe in the thirties.

42   J. Labon, 'Tracing Storm Jameson', pp. 41–2.

43   S. Jameson, 'A Crisis of the Spirit' (1941), *The Writer's Situation*, p. 142.

44   S. Jameson, 'Creditors of France' (spoken at the closing meeting of the PEN congress, September 1941), *The Writer's Situation*, p. 180.

45   S. Jameson, *The Fort* (London: Cassell, 1941). The dates for the writing are given, as often at this time, at the end of the text. P. Lassner, in *British Women Writers of World War II: Battlegrounds of Their Own* (London: Macmillan, 1998), pp. 214–15, misreads the ending of this novel; all the characters in the final scene are in fact dead, as the presence of 'Jamie', a man killed in World War One, reveals.

46   S. Jameson, *Cousin Honoré* (London: Cassell, 1940).

47   S. Jameson, *Then We Shall Hear Singing: a Fantasy in C Major* (London: Cassell, 1942).

48   Recent commentators have suggested that none of the women are affected; but in fact only old Anna is untouched. Jameson is not making a radical feminist point here.

49   S. Jameson, *Cloudless May* (London: Macmillan, 1943).

50   Jameson, *Cloudless May*, p. 65.

51   See, for instance, p. 195.

52   S. Jameson, *The Other Side* (London: Macmillan, 1946). At the end of the text, the time of writing is given as 'August–December 1944'.

53   A number of women writers (Phyllis Bottome and Katharine Burdekin, for instance) saw fascism as the triumph of non-reason rather than the betrayal of rationalism, as Adorno would later claim.

54   E. Mannin, *The Dark Forest* (London: Jarrolds, 1946). The dates of the writing are given, as usual, at the end of the text.

55   J. Struther, *Mrs Miniver* [1939] (London: Virago, 1989) p. 62.

56 R. Ferguson, *A Footman for the Peacock* (London: Jonathan Cape, 1940). The adverse comment is Margery Allingham's, quoted in J. Hartley, *Millions like Us*, p. 5.

57 C. Dane, *He Brings Great News* (London: William Heinemann, 1944), p. 138.

58 R. Adam, *Murder in the Home Guard* (London: Chapman and Hall, 1942). She is cited by Q. D. Leavis in her review attacking *Three Guineas* as one of those who understood the social pressures of writing in a domestic situation.

59 P. Bottome, *London Pride* (London: Faber & Faber, 1941).

60 V. Sackville-West, *The Women's Land Army*, published under the auspices of the Ministry of Agriculture and Fisheries (London: Michael Joseph, 1944), p. 62. See B. Whitton, *Green Hands* (London: Faber & Faber, 1943), for a lively first-hand account of work on farms during the war.

61 P. Bottome, *Within the Cup* (London: Faber & Faber, 1943). This novel was published in the States as *Survival*.

62 See R. Baxter, *Hitler's Darkest Secret: What He Has in Store for Britain* (London: Quality Press, 1941), for a whole-hearted endorsement of the hawkish approach, with no distinction between military and civilian targets. He claims, amidst all too eager endorsement of various manifestations of xenophobia, that an informant has told him: 'Raids and more raids, bombs and more bombs, that is the answer to the Goebbels propaganda and the official dope issued out in Germany. Cities and towns must be remorselessly wiped out, thousands must be killed or injured' (p. 136).

63 S. Ertz, *Anger in the Sky* (London: Hodder & Stoughton, 1943).

64 B. Miller, *On the Side of the Angels* [delivered in 1944, although published in 1945] (London: Virago, 1985).

65 E. Pargeter, *She Goes to War*, p. 90.

66 R. Lehmann, 'When the Waters Came', in *The Penguin New Writing*, ed. J. Lehmann, Issue 3, February 1941, pp. 106–10.

67 R. Lehmann, 'Wonderful Holidays', in *The Penguin New Writing*, ed. J. Lehmann, Issue 22, 1944, pp. 18–24 (21).

68 P. Toynbee, 'The Decline and Future of the English Novel', in *The Penguin New Writing*, ed. J. Lehman, 1945, pp. 127–39 (138).

69 S. Jameson, 'The Responsibilities of the Writer', *The Writer's Situation*, p. 169.

70 P. Bottome, *The Lifeline* (London: Faber & Faber, 1946).

71 S. Jameson, *The Black Laurel*, p. 16.

72 In the released secret file, 'Russian Threat to Western Civilisation'. See *The Guardian*, Friday, 2 October 1998.

73 S. Jameson, *The Black Laurel*, p. 146.

74 E. Pargeter, *Lame Crusade*, The Eighth Champion of Christendom (London: William Heinemann, 1945), being the first book of the trilogy.

75 E. Pargeter, *Reluctant Odyssey* and *Warfare Accomplished*, being the second and third volumes of the trilogy The Eighth Champion of Christendom (London: William Heinemann, 1946 and 1947).

76 Jim's reaction exemplifies Theodor Adorno's assertion in his *Negative Dialectics* [1966], trans. E. B. Ashton (London: Routledge & Kegan Paul, 1973): 'After Auschwitz, our feelings...balk at squeezing any kind of sense, however bleached, out of the victim's fate...Our metaphysical faculty is paralysed because events have shattered the basis on which speculative metaphysical thought could be reconciled with experience' (pp. 361–2).

77   D. du Maurier, *The King's General* (London: Victor Gollancz, 1946).
78   N. Mitford, *The Pursuit of Love* (London: Hamish Hamilton, 1945).
79   Quoted by E. Rickword, 'Straws for the Wary: Antecedents to Fascism' [October 1934], in *Writing the Revolution: Cultural Criticism from Left Review*, ed. D. Margolies, pp. 105–13 (109–110).
80   B. Comyns, *The Skin Chairs* [1962] (London: Virago, 1986).
81   N. Mitford, *The Pursuit of Love*, p. 183.
82   R. West, *The Fountain Overflows* [1957] (London: Virago,1984), p. 11.
83   R. Macaulay, *The World My Wilderness* [1950], p. 149.
84   D. Lessing, *The Memoirs of a Survivor* [1973] (London: Pan [Picador], 1976).
85   L. Cooper, *Fenny* [1953] (London: Virago, 1987).
86   E. M. Butler, *Daylight in a Dream* (London: The Hogarth Press, 1951).
87   E. Mannin, *Lover under Another Name* (London: Jarrolds, 1953). See P. Lassner, *British Women Writers of World War II*, pp. 42–6, for a useful discussion of Mannin's work and attitudes.
88   P. Frankau, *The Offshore Light* (London: William Heinemann, 1952). This novel was too unlike her earlier novel for many of her readers, and the book had poor sales.
89   D. Lessing, *Briefing for a Descent into Hell* [1972] (London:Grafton, 1972).
90   See a much earlier example of concern with this theme: Rebecca West, *The Thinking Reed* [1936] (London: Virago, 1984), her 'writing back' to Henry James's *Portrait of a Lady*. West's novel plays throughout with the idea of violence, and her protagonist Isabelle has to resort to physical violence twice to assert her right to be heard as an individual.
91   B. Brophy, *Hackenfeller's Ape*, p. 40.
92   N. Mitchison, *Travel Light* [1952] (London: Virago, 1985).
93   N. Mitchison, *Memoirs of a Spacewoman*, pp. 26–7.

3   Marginalities of Race and Class

1   B. Gilroy, *Leaves in the Wind: Collected Writings*, ed. J. Anim-Addo (London: Mango Publishing, 1998), p. 58.
2   Z. Bauman, *Modernity and the Holocaust* (London: Polity Press, 1991), p. 92.
3   B. Gilroy, *Leaves in the Wind*, p. 58.
4   M. Ellman, 'The Imaginary Jew: T. S. Eliot and Ezra Pound', in *Between 'Race' and Culture: Representation of 'the Jew' in English and American Literature*, ed. B. Cheyette (Stanford: Stanford University Press, 1996), pp. 84–101 (101).
5   R. Samuel, 'Preface', in *Patriotism: the Making and Unmaking of British National Identity*, vol. 2, *Minorities and Outsiders*, ed. R. Samuel (London and New York: Routledge, 1989), pp. ix, xvi.
6   B. Cheyette, *Construction of 'the Jew' in English Literature and Society: Racial Representations, 1875–1945* (Cambridge: Cambridge University Press, 1993), p. 17.
7   P. Gilroy, *There Ain't No Black in the Union Jack* (London: Hutchison, 1987), p. 43.
8   G. Rose, *Judaism and Modernity: Philosophical Essays* (Oxford, UK, and Cambridge, UK: Blackwell, 1993), p. 35.
9   B. Cheyette, 'Introduction: Unanswered Questions', in *Between 'Race' and Culture*, ed. Cheyette, pp. 1–15 (14).

10 S. Renjen Bald, 'Images of South Asian Migrants in Literature: Different Perspectives', *New Community*, 17 (3), April 1991, pp. 413–31 (414).

11 Some atrocity stories during the First World War had indeed been found to be fabricated, but the evidence of the thirties was so strong that referring back to the earlier propagandist deceptions was a very thin excuse.

12 See R. H. S. Crossman, *The God That Failed: Six Studies in Communism by Koestler [et al.]* (London: Hamish Hamilton, 1950), p. 71; *The Brown Book of Hitler Terror: and the Burning of the Reichstag*, prepared by the World Committee for the Victims of German Fascism, intro. Lord Marley (London: Victor Gollancz, 1933); and for press censorship, see S. Scaffardi, *Fire under the Carpet*. I am grateful to Joanna Labon for reminding me of these works.

13 Stevie Smith, *Over the Frontier*, p. 158.

14 P. Lassner, ' '"The Milk of Our Mother's Kindness Has Ceased to Flow": Virginia Woolf, Stevie Smith, and the Representation of the Jew', in *Between 'Race' and Culture*, ed. Cheyette, pp. 129–44 (144).

15 P. Bottome, *The Mortal Storm*, p. 53.

16 Bottome is not alone in this; throughout the thirties and forties, this was common practice, even among Jewish writers, as for instance G. B. Stern and Betty Miller.

17 B. Cheyette, *Construction of 'the Jew' in English Literature and Society*, p. 268.

18 Communist Party of Great Britain, *Class against Class: General Election Programme of the Communist Party of Gt. Britain, 1929* (London: Dorrit Press, 1929), p. 12.

19 W. Holtby, 'Cavalcade' [1933], in *History in Our Hands*, ed. Deane, pp. 337–41 (340).

20 W. Holtby, *Mandoa, Mandoa!* [1933] (London: Virago, 1982).

21 B. Bush, 'Britain's Conscience of Africa', in *Gender and Imperialism*, ed. C. Midgley (Manchester and New York: Manchester University Press, 1998), pp. 200–23 (206).

22 J. Rhys, *Voyage in the Dark* [1934] (Harmondsworth: Penguin, 1969).

23 S. Nasta, 'Setting up Home in a City of Words: Sam Selvon's Novels', in *Other Britain, Other British: Contemporary Multicultural Fiction*, ed. A. R. Lee (London: Pluto Press, 1995), pp. 48–68 (50).

24 E. Savory, in 'The Jean Rhys Debate Forum: Jean Rhys, Race and Caribbean/ English Criticism', continuing the dialogue between Peter Hulme and Kamau Brathwaite (*Wasafiri* 20 [1990], 22[1992] and 23[1993]), *Wasafiri*, no. 28, Autumn 1998, pp. 33–8 (34).

25 E. Cambridge, *Portrait of Angela: a Novel* (London: Jonathan Cape, 1939), p. 59. See also T. Young, 'The Reception of Nancy Cunard's *Negro* Anthology', in *Women Writers of the 1930s*, ed. Joannou, pp. 113–122.

26 R. West, *The Strange Necessity: Essays and Reviews* (London: Jonathan Cape, 1928), p. 142.

27 R. West, *Harriet Hume*, p. 69.

28 R. West, *Black Lamb and Grey Falcon*, p. 843.

29 See J. Montefiore, *Men and Women of the 1930s*, for an admirable analysis of *Black Lamb and Grey Falcon*.

30 V. Woolf, *The Waves* [1931] (Harmondsworth: Penguin, 1992), and *The Years* [1937] (Harmonsworth: Penguin, 1994). See also D. Bradshaw's article,

'Hyam's Place: *The Years*, the Jews and the British Union of Fascists', in *Women Writers of the 1930s*, ed. Joannou, pp. 179–91.

31 L. Peach, 'No Longer a View: Virginia Woolf in the 1930s and the 1930s in Virginia Woolf', in *Women Writers of the 1930s*, ed. Joannou, pp. 192–204, (197).

32 V. Woolf, *A Room of One's Own*, and *Three Guineas*, p. 314.

33 N. Mitchison, *The Moral Basis of Politics* (London: Constable, 1938). This quotation taken from Deane, ed., *History in Our Hands*, p. 238.

34 M. D. Stocks, *Eleanor Rathbone: a Biography* (London: Victor Gollancz, 1949).

35 S. Townsend Warner, *Mr Fortune's Maggot* [1927] (London: Virago, 1978).

36 S. Townsend Warner, *Summer Will Show*, p. 43.

37 See F. Fanon, *Black Skin, White Masks*, trans. C. L. Markmann (London: Pluto Press, 1986).

38 R. McKibbin, *Classes and Cultures: England 1918–1951* (Oxford: Oxford University Press, 1998). He argues that the middle class greatly improved their position in the inter-war years at the expense of the working class.

39 S. Jameson, 'Documents', *Fact*, no. 4, pp. 10–11.

40 See P. Lassner, *British Women Writers of World War II*, for an interesting defence of *We Have Been Warned*, pp. 72–84.

41 Q. D. Leavis, 'Lady Novelists and the Lower Orders', p. 117.

42 A. Snaith, 'Virginia Woolf and Reading Communities: Respondents to *Three Guineas*', in *Virginia Woolf & Communities: Selected Papers from the Eighth Annual Conference on Virginia Woolf*, eds J. McVicker and L. Davis (New York: Pace University Press, 1999), pp. 219–26.

43 S. Jameson, *None Turn Back* [1936] (London: Virago, 1984); E. Wilkinson, *Clash* [1929] (London: Virago, 1989).

44 E. Wilkinson, *The Town That Was Murdered: The Life Story of Jarrow* (The Left Book Club, London: Gollancz, 1939).

45 E. Mannin, *Venetian Blinds* (London: Jarrolds, 1933). See also A. Croft, 'Ethel Mannin: The Red Rose of Love and the Red Flower of Liberty', in *Rediscovering Forgotten Radicals: British Women Writers 1889–1939*, eds A. Ingram and D. Patai (Chapel Hill and London: University of North Carolina Press, 1993), pp. 205–25.

46 R. West, *The Thinking Reed* [1936] (London: Virago, 1984).

47 D. Sayers, 'The Mysterious English' (Speech delivered in London, 1940), *Unpopular Opinions*, p. 67. While in many ways conservative, Sayers is full of surprises.

48 S. Jameson, 'The Stranger' (written June 1944), *The Writer's Situation*, p. 123.

49 E. Buckley, *Destination Unknown*, p. 8.

50 See R. Baxter, *Hitler's Darkest Secret: What He Has in Store for Britain*, p. 82. Baxter strongly supports internment, and warns against German nationals, whether Aryan or Jewish; they are 'enemy aliens, unprotected by diplomatic privileges, and as such were interned. They are still interned, and will remain in the camps in this country or in the Dominion of Canada, until victory is won'.

51 R. Adam, *Murder in the Home Guard*, p. 38.

52 M. Dickens, *One Pair of Feet* (London: Michael Joseph, 1942).

53 I. Holden, *There's No Story There*, p. 136.

54 B. Miller, *Farewell Leicester Square* (London: Robert Hale, 1941), p. 103.

55 S. Townsend Warner, *The Corner That Held Them* [1948] (London: Virago, 1988), p. 43. See G. Rose, 'Architecture after Auschwitz', *Judaism and Modernity*, on the dangerous attempt to ignore 'our implication as agents and as actors' with responsibility for the persecution of the Jews, etc. (p. 257).

56 S. Jameson, *Then We Shall Hear Singing*, p. 224.

57 D. Sayers, 'They Tried to Be Good', *Unpopular Opinions*, p. 100.

58 D. Sayers, 'The Gulf Stream and the Channel', *Unpopular Opinions*, p. 64.

59 E. M. Delafield, *No One Will Know* (London: Macmillan, 1941).

60 M. Gellhorn, *Liana* (London: Home and Van Thal, 1944).

61 A. Farjeon, 'The Rose', in *The Penguin New Writing*, ed. John Lehmann, issue 18 (July–September 1943), pp. 96–104.

62 E. Pargeter, *She Goes to War*, p. 128.

63 D. du Maurier, *Hungry Hill* [1943] (Harmondsworth: Penguin, 1967).

64 N. Mitchison, *The Bull Calves*, p. 45.

65 P. Bottome, *London Pride*, p. 12.

66 I. Holden, *Night Shift*, p. 20.

67 R. McKibbin, *Classes and Cultures*. See review of this work by Stefan Collini, *Times Literary Supplement*, 17 April 1998, pp. 3–4.

68 E. Pargeter, *She Goes to War*, p. 25.

69 S. Townsend Warner, *The Corner That Held Them*, p. 193.

70 P. Bottome, *The Lifeline*, p. 259.

71 V. Sackville-West, *The Women's Land Army*, p. 38.

72 M. Spark, *The Comforters*, p. 38.

73 S. Jameson, *The Green Man*, p. 297.

74 C. Brooke-Rose, *The Sycamore Tree*, p. 54.

75 A. M. Fielding, *Ashanti Blood* (London: William Heinemann, 1952), p. 5.

76 G. Rose's summing up (*The Broken Middle: Out of Our Ancient Society* [Oxford: Blackwell, 1992], p. 220) of Arendt's point in *The Origins of Totalitarianism* [1951] (New York: Harcourt Brace Jovanovitch, 1973), p. 150.

77 I. Murdoch, *The Flight from the Enchanter*, p. 45.

78 P. Bottome, *Under the Skin* (London: Faber & Faber, 1950).

79 See, for example, W. James, 'The Making of Black Identities', in *Patriotism*, vol. I, *History and Politics*, ed. Samuel, pp. 230–55: 'In the "mother country" no regard was paid to the complex hierarchy of shades; the pattern of racism which the Caribbean migrants experienced here did not correspond to the complexion hierarchy which they had left behind in the Caribbean. They were regarded monolithically as "coloureds", "West Indians", "blacks", "immigrants", and even "wogs", with no reference to differential shades' (p. 234).

80 S. Smith, *The Holiday*, p. 14.

81 A. Hosain, *Phoenix Fled* [1953] (London: Virago, 1988).

82 K. Markandaya, *Nectar in a Sieve* (New York: New American Library, 1954; London: Putnam, 1954).

83 R. Prawer Jhabvala, *Esmond in India* [1958] (Harmondsworth: Penguin, 1980).

84 H. Tiffin, 'Post-Colonialism, Post-Modernism and the Rehabilitation of Post-Colonial History', *The Journal of Commonwealth Literature*, vol. 23 (1988), pp. 169–81 (171).

85 D. Lessing, *The Grass Is Singing*, p. 18.

86 D. Lessing, *Martha Quest* [1952] and *A Proper Marriage* [1954] (London: Collins [Paladin], 1990).

87   D. Lessing, *Martha Quest*, p. 333.
88   G. Orwell, 'Marrakech' [1939], *The Collected Essays, Journalism and Letters of George Orwell*, vol. 1, *An Age like This 1920–40*, eds S. Orwell and I. Angus (Harmondsworth: Penguin, 1979), pp. 426–32 (431).
89   M. Spark, 'The Portobello Road' [*The Go-Away Bird*, 1958], *The Collected Stories* (Harmondsworth: Penguin, 1994), p. 7.
90   V. J. Mishra, 'Postcolonial Differend: Diasporic Narratives of Salman Rushdie', *Ariel*, 26: 3, 1995, pp. 1–9 (8). See Hanif Kureishi, 'London and Karachi', in *Patriotism*, ed. Samuel, vol. 2: 'it is the British, the white British, who have to learn that being British isn't what it was. Now it is a more complex thing, involving new elements' (pp. 285–7 [286]).
91   S. Nasta, 'Setting up Home in a City of Words: Sam Selvon's Novels', in *Other Britain, Other British: Contemporary Multicultural Fiction*, ed. A. R. Lee (London: Pluto Press, 1995), pp. 48–68 (49–50).
92   B. Gilroy, *Leaves in the Wind*, p. 213.
93   S. R. Bald, 'Images of South Asian Migrants in Literature', p. 416.
94   B. Pym, *Excellent Women* [1952] (London: Macmillan [Pan], 1995).
95   B. Pym, *Less than Angels* [1955] (London: Macmillan [Pan], 1993), p. 174.
96   C. Brooke-Rose, *The Languages of Love*, p. 112.
97   M. Spark, 'The Black Madonna', *The Collected Stories*, p. 47.
98   B. Comyns, *Who Was Changed and Who Was Dead* [1954] (London: Virago, 1987).
99   M. Gallie, *Strike for a Kingdom* (London: Victor Gollancz, 1959).
100 See S. Knight, '"The hesitations and uncertainties that were the truth"'.
101 M. Gallie, *Strike for a Kingdom*, p. 20.
102 P. Frankau, *A Wreath for the Enemy* [1954] (London: Virago, 1988).
103 S. Smith, *The Holiday*, pp. 104–5.
104 Review of E. M. Butler, *Daylight in a Dream*, *The Sunday Times*, 3 June 1951. See discussion of this novel in Chapter 2.
105 M. Spark, 'The Curtain Blown by the Breeze' [1961], *The Collected Stories*.
106 D. Lessing, 'The Black Madonna' [1964], *The Black Madonna* (London: HarperCollins [Paladin], 1992).
107 A. Hosain, *Sunlight on a Broken Column* [1961] (London: Penguin, 1992). Kamala Markandaya also continues to be published in Britain, the States and India.
108 R. Prawer Jhabvala, *Get Ready for Battle* [1962] (Harmondsworth: Penguin, 1981).
109 J. Rhys, *Wide Sargasso Sea* [1966] (Harmondsworth: Penguin, 1968).
110 B. Gilroy, *Leaves in the Wind*, p. 209.
111 D. Hinds, *Journey to an Illusion: the West Indian in Britain* (London: Heinemann, 1966), p. 11.
112 B. Pym, *No Fond Return of Love* [1961] (London: Macmillan [Pan], 1993), p. 260.
113 L. Reid Banks, *The L-shaped Room* [1960] (Harmondsworth: Penguin, 1962).
114 M. Duffy, *That's How It Was* [1962] (London: Virago, 1983).
115 M. Heinemann, *The Adventurers* (London: Lawrence and Wishart, 1960).
116 A. Sinfield, *Literature, Politics, and Culture in Postwar Britain* (Oxford: Basil Blackwell, 1989), p. 258.
117 S. Knight, '"The hesitations and uncertainties that were the truth"', p. 5.
118 M. Heinemann, *The Adventurers*, p. 312.

119 M. Gallie, *The Small Mine* (London: Victor Gollancz, 1962).
120 C. Stead, *Cotters' England* [1966] (London: Virago, 1980).
121 D. Lessing, *The Good Terrorist* [1985] (London: HarperCollins [Paladin], 1990).

4 Men, Women, Sex and Gender

1 S. Raitt and T. Tate, eds, *Women's Fiction and the Great War* (Oxford and New York: Clarendon Press, 1996), p. 1; and J. Montefiore, *Men and Women Writers of the 1930s*, pp. 1–2.
2 L. Irigaray, *Je, tu, nous: Toward a Culture of Difference*, trans. A. Martin (London and New York: Routledge, 1993), p. 20. See also G. Rose, *The Broken Middle*, p. 185, on 'woman' as 'the Lear of modernity'.
3 C. Hall, *White, Male and Middle Class: Explorations in Feminism and History* (Cambridge: Polity Press, 1992), p. 13. See also J. W. Scott, 'Rewriting History', in *Behind the Lines: Gender and the Two World Wars*, eds M. Randolph Higonnet, J. Jensen, S. Michel, M. Collins Weitz (New Haven and London: Yale University Press, 1987), pp. 10–17 (13).
4 M. van der Wijngaard, *Reinventing the Sexes: the Biomedical Construction of Femininity and Masculinity* (Bloomington: Indiana Press, 1997), offers a challenging reading of the history of biomedical research.
5 E. Badinter, *XY: On Masculine Identity*, trans. L. Davis (New York: Columbia University Press, 1995), p. 26.
6 K. Clatterbaugh, *Contemporary Perspectives on Masculinity: Men, Women and Politics in Modern Society* (Boulder: Westview Press, 1990), pp. 159–60.
7 E. Badinter, *XY*, p. 103.
8 L. Irigaray, *Je, tu, nous*, p. 19.
9 C. M. Tylee, *The Great War and Women's Consciousness*, p. 187.
10 M. Randolph Higonnet et al., 'Introduction', in *Behind the Lines*, pp. 1–9 (4).
11 G. Rose, *Love's Work* [1995] (London: Vintage, 1997), p. 131. See also E. Wilson, *The Sphinx in the City: Urban Life, the Control of Disorder, and Women* (London: Virago, 1991).
12 W. Holtby, *Women* (London: John Lane The Bodley Head, 1934), p. 192.
13 M. Shaw, 'Feminism and Fiction between the Wars: Winifred Holtby and Virginia Woolf', in *Women's Writing: a Challenge to Theory*, ed. M. Monteith (Brighton: Harvester, 1986), pp. 171–91.
14 J. Bourke, *Dismembering the Male*, p. 11.
15 W. Holtby, *Women*, p. 2.
16 W. Holtby, *Virginia Woolf* (London: Wishart, 1932), p. 178.
17 R. West, *The Return of the Soldier* [1918], and G. B. Stern, *A Deputy Was King* [1926] (London: Virago, 1988). See also Dorothy Sayers's detective novels for one of the most famous sufferers from neurasthenia in the inter-war years, Lord Peter Wimsey.
18 M. Borden, *The Forbidden Zone*, p. 60.
19 See B. Melman, *Women and the Popular Imagination in the Twenties: Flappers and Nymphs* (Basingstoke: Macmillan, 1988), p. 18, for the perception of the threat posed by the surplus of women, both morally and in the work place. See also Jane Dowson's admirable introduction to *Women's Poetry of the 1930s: a Critical Anthology* (London and New York: Routledge, 1996).

20 W. Holtby, *Virginia Woolf*, pp. 27–9. Not, of course, that such concerns only emerged after the Great War. Holtby's arguments have much in common with those of Vernon Lee, for instance. See Lee's 'The Economic Parasitism of Women', *Gospels of Anarchy and Other Contemporary Studies* (London and Lepsic: T. Fisher Unwin, 1908).
21 See M. D. Stocks, *Eleanor Rathbone*.
22 M. Borden, *The Technique of Marriage* (London: William Heinemann, 1933), p. 127; see also Clemence Dane, *The Woman's Side* (London: Herbert Jenkins, 1926), for a liberal analysis of women's responsibilities in society, but conservatism over women 'inspiring' male genius (p. 138).
23 E. Wilkinson, *Clash*, p. 190.
24 R. Bowlby, 'Walking, Women and Writing: Virginia Woolf as *flaneuse*', *Still Crazy after All These Years: Women, Writing and Psychoanalysis* (London and New York: Routledge, 1992), pp. 4–5; see also S. Rowbotham, *A Century of Women: the History of Women in Britain and the United States* (Harmondsworth: Penguin, 1997), p. 10, where she speaks of the hidden costs for an independent woman in politics in the twenties, and also see Anthea Trodd, *Women's Writing in English: Britain 1900–1945* (London and New York: Longman, 1998).
25 R. West, *The Harsh Voice* [1935] (London: Virago, 1982).
26 R. West, *The Thinking Reed*, p. 134.
27 J. Rhys, *After Leaving Mr Mackenzie* [1930] (Harmondsworth: Penguin, 1971), p. 11.
28 J. Rhys, *Voyage in the Dark* [1934] (Harmondsworth: Penguin, 1969); *Good Morning, Midnight* [1939] (Harmondsworth: Penguin, 1967), p. 75.
29 H. Simpson, *Saraband for Dead Lovers* (London and Toronto: William Heinemann, 1935).
30 K. Burdekin, *The End of This Day's Business* (New York: The Feminist Press at the City University of New York, 1989).
31 M. Ulrich, ed., *Man, Proud Man: a Commentary by Mary Borden, E. M. Delafield, Susan Ertz, Storm Jameson, Helen Simpson, G. B. Stern, Sylvia Townsend Warner, Rebecca West* (London: Hamish Hamilton, 1932). See E. Maslen, 'Man, Proud Man? Women's Views of Men between the Wars', in *Women Voice Men: Gender in European Culture*, ed. M. Slater (Exeter: Intellect, 1997), pp. 53–60; and K. Williams, 'Back from the Future: Katharine Burdekin and Science Fiction in the 1930s', in *Women Writers of the 1930s*, ed. Joannou, pp. 151–64.
32 G. B. Stern, 'Man – without Prejudice (Rough Notes)', in *Man, Proud Man*, ed. Ulrich, p. 179.
33 E. Badinter, *XY*, pp. 25–6.
34 R. Graves, *Goodbye to All That* [1929] (Harmondsworth: Penguin, 1960), p. 238.
35 R. Aldington, *Death of a Hero: a Novel* (London: Chatto & Windus, 1929), p. 258.
36 J. Bourke, *Dismembering the Male*, p. 59.
37 H. Simpson, *Boomerang* (London: Heinemann, 1932), pp. 234 and 290.
38 V. Cross, *Martha Brown M.P., a Girl of Tomorrow* (London: T. Werner Laurie, 1935). See also N. Bowman Albinski, *Women's Utopias in British and American Fiction* (London and New York: Routledge, 1988), for contextualization within women's utopian fiction.

39 S. Milgram Knapp, 'Revolutionary Androgyny in the Fiction of "Victoria Cross"', in *Seeing Double: Revisioning Edwardian and Modernist Literature*, ed. C. M. Kaplan and A. B. Simpson (Basingstoke: Macmillan, 1996), pp. 3–20 (19).

40 C. Hall, *White, Male and Middle Class*, p. 12.

41 S. Townsend Warner, *Lolly Willowes* [1926] (London: Virago, 1993).

42 L. Cooper, *The New House* [1936] (Harmondsworth: Penguin, 1946).

43 R. Hall, 'Miss Ogilvy Finds Herself' (1934), in *Women, Men, and the Great War: an Anthology of Stories*, ed. T. Tate (Manchester and New York: Manchester University Press, 1995), pp. 127–35 (129).

44 W. Holtby, *Women*, p. 8.

45 E. Mannin, *Men Are Unwise* (London: Jarrolds 1934).

46 P. Bottome, *The Mortal Storm*, p. 188.

47 E. Taylor, *At Mrs Lippincote's* [1945] (London: Virago, 1988), p. 5.

48 B. Whitton, *Green Hands* (London: Faber & Faber, 1943).

49 V. Sackville-West, *The Women's Land Army*, p. 22.

50 A. Lant, 'Prologue', in *Nationalising Femininity: Culture, Sexuality and British Cinema in the Second World War*, ed. C. Gledhill Swanson (Manchester: Manchester University Press, 1996), pp. 1–24 (22).

51 E. Pargeter, *She Goes To War*, p. 108.

52 D. Sayers, *Unpopular Opinions*, p. 7.

53 S. Jameson, *Then We Shall Hear Singing*, p. 229.

54 K. O'Brien, *The Land of Spices* (London: William Heinemann, 1941).

55 K. O'Brien, *The Last of Summer* (London: William Heinemann, 1943).

56 R. Lehmann, *The Ballad and the Source* (London: Collins and the Book Society, 1944). See also D. Trilling, 'Fiction in Review', *The Nation*, 14 April 1945, vol. 160, p. 423, for a shrewd assessment of this novel.

57 R. Adam, *Murder in the Home Guard*, p. 106.

58 D. Sayers, 'Are Women Human?' (Address given to the Women's Society, 1938), *Unpopular Opinions*.

59 R. Adam, *Murder in the Home Guard*, p. 132.

60 P. Bentley, *The Rise of Henry Morcar* (London: Victor Gollancz, 1946).

61 R. Ferguson, *A Stroll before Sunset* (London: Jonathan Cape, 1946).

62 Olivia [Dorothy Strachey], *Olivia* [1949] (London: Virago, 1987).

63 G. Plain, *Women's Fiction of the Second World War: Gender, Power and Resistance* (Edinburgh: Edinburgh University Press, 1996).

64 S. Rowbotham, *A Century of Women*, p. 292.

65 E. Taylor, *A Game of Hide and Seek* [1951] (London: Virago, 1986), p. 3. See also D. Lessing, *Retreat to Innocence* (London: Michael Joseph, 1956), for a daughter who is utterly (and, in the event, disastrously) apolitical, in rebellion against her left-wing mother.

66 D. Philips and I. Haywood, *Brave New Causes: Women in Postwar Fictions* (London and Washington: Leicester University Press, 1998).

67 See D. Philips and I. Haywood, *Brave New Causes*, pp. 58–71 and, on Mills and Boon, pp. 80–8.

68 R. West, *The Fountain Overflows*, p. 274.

69 C. Brooke-Rose, *The Languages of Love*, p. 132.

70 See, for instance, the situation as described in *Outwrite: Lesbianism and Popular Culture*, ed. G. Griffin (London and Boulder, Colorado: Pluto Press, 1993).

71   B. Pym, *A Glass of Blessings* [1958] (London: Macmillan [Pan], 1989).
72   M. Renault, *The Charioteer* (London, New York, Toronto: Longmans, Green and Co., 1953).
73   It had, of course, surfaced before in women's fiction. A famous nineteenth-century example is Charlotte Perkins Gilman's *The Yellow Wallpaper* [1892], ed. D. M. Bauer (Basingstoke: Macmillan, 1998), and Jean Rhys's novels of the thirties frequently show women in a state of mental breakdown, as in *After Leaving Mr Mackenzie* (1930) and *Good Morning, Midnight* (1939). See also the hugely successful novel of the forties, set in America: Mary Jane Ward's *The Snake Pit* (London: Cassell, 1947), where the protagonist suffers the latest 'cure' – the inhumanity of mental hospital wards: 'Shock treatments. Why bother with insulin, metrazol or electiricity? Long ago they lowered insane persons into snake pits; they thought that an experience that might drive a sane person out of his wits might send an insane person back into sanity. By design or by accident, she couldn't know, a more modern "they" had given V. Cunningham a far more drastic shock treatment than Dr Kik had been able to manage with his clamps and wedges and assistants. They had thrown her into a snake pit and she had been shocked into knowing that she would get well' (p. 209).
74   I. Murdoch, *Under the Net*, p. 239.
75   N. Dunn, *Talking to Women* (Bristol: MacGibbon & Kee, 1965), p. 9.
76   E. O'Brien, *The Country Girls* [1960] (Harmondsworth: Penguin, 1963); *The Lonely Girl* [1962] (retitled *Girl with Green Eyes*, Harmondsworth: Penguin, 1964); *Girls in Their Married Bliss* [1964] (Harmondsworth: Penguin, 1967).
77   N. Dunn, *Talking to Women*, p. 98.
78   See, in relation to this, G. Greene, *Changing the Story: Feminist Fiction and the Tradition* (Bloomington, Ind.: Indiana University Press, 1991), p. 117.
79   L. McNay, *Foucault and Feminism* (Oxford: Polity Press, 1992), p. 197.
80   E. Taylor, *In a Summer Season* [1961] (London: Virago, 1983).
81   P. Mortimer, *The Pumpkin Eater* [1962] (Harmondsworth: Penguin, 1964).
82   M. Drabble, *The Garrick Year* [1964] (Harmondsworth: Penguin, 1966).
83   E. Taylor, *The Wedding Group* [1968] (London: Virago, 1985).
84   N. Dunn, *Up the Junction* (London: MacGibbon & Kee, 1963).
85   M. Duffy, *The Microcosm*, p. 21.
86   S. Jeffreys, *Anti-climax: a Feminist Perspective on the Sexual Revolution* (London: Women's Press, 1990), p. 24.
87   P. Mortimer, *My Friend Says It's Bullet-Proof* [1967] (London: Virago, 1989).
88   N. Chomsky, *Deterring Democracy* (London: Vintage, 1992), p. 347. See also, for instance, R. D. Laing, *The Politics of Experience, and The Bird of Paradise* (Harmondsworth: Penguin, 1967).
89   J. Dawson, *The Ha-Ha*, pp. 180–1. See also, for this whole issue of madness, Jacqueline Rose, 'On the "Universality" of Madness: Bessie Head's *A Question of Power*', *States of Fantasy* (Oxford: Clarendon Press, 1996), pp. 99–116.
90   See also Hannah Green (Joanne Greenberg), *I Never Promised You a Rose Garden* (New York: Holt, Reinhart and Winston, 1964; London: Gollancz, 1964), which poignantly captures the life in hospital of a young girl diagnosed as schizophrenic, together with the reactions of her doctors and family. The ways in which she negotiates with an alternative world within her own consciousness bear comparison with Pamela Frankau's earlier *The Offshore Light* (1952) and Doris Lessing's later *Briefing for a Descent into Hell* [1971].

5 Women in a Changing Society: Conclusion

1 The Hon. Mrs. Dighton Pollock, *The Women of Today*, p. 2.
2 The Duchess of Atholl, MP, *Women and Politics* (London: Philip Allan, 1931). The Duchess is a fine example of conservatism and radicalism in the individual; later she would go to Spain, and prove by no means unsympathetic to the Republican cause.
3 *The Report of a Conference on the Feminine Point of View*, drafted by Olwen W. Campbell (London: Williams & Norgate, 1952), p. 13.
4 See Marion Shaw, 'Feminism and Fiction between the Wars'.
5 See D. Sayers, *Unpopular Opinions*, p. 7.
6 See Betty Friedan, *The Feminist Mystique* [1963] (Harmondsworth: [Pelican] Penguin, 1965), p. 24, writing on the fifties and stressing the huge range of tasks facing the modern housewife, and observing that when 'a woman tries to put the problem into words, she often describes the daily life she leads. What is there in this recital of comfortable domestic detail that could possibly cause such a feeling of desperation?' Rose Macaulay addresses the same problem in 'Some Problems of a Woman's Life' (1923), in *Things My Mother Should Have Told Me: the Best of Good Housekeeping 1922–1940*, eds B. Braithwaite and N. Walsh, *Good Housekeeping* Nostalgia Series (London: Ebury Press, 1991), pp. 12–16 (14), urging 'Do not keep house. Let the house, or flat, go unkept. Let it go to the devil', for otherwise there is no time for 'reading, walking, sitting in the woods, playing games, making love, merely existing without effort'. And E. M. Delafield's *The Diary of a Provincial Lady* [1930–40] (London: Virago, 1984) is just one of a host of other works on the same theme.
7 *The Twentieth Century*, August 1958, vol. 164, no. 978: 'Special Number on Women'.
8 B. Miller, 'Amazons and Afterwards', *The Twentieth Century*, pp. 126–35.
9 J. Nasmyth, 'The Wages of Freedom', *The Twentieth Century*, pp. 136–43 (138).
10 M. Warnock, 'Nymphs or Buestockings?', *The Twentieth Century*, pp. 145–50.
11 M. Bremner, 'Good Wives?', *The Twentieth Century*, pp. 159–69.
12 M. Laski, 'The Image on the Penny', *The Twentieth Century*, pp. 151–8 (151).
13 J. Hawkes, 'Women against the Bomb', *The Twentieth Century*, pp. 185–8.
14 R. Heppenstall, 'Jocasta', and V. Musgrave, 'Women outside the Law', *The Twentieth Century*, pp. 170–7 and 178–84.
15 S. Jameson, *Journey from the North*, vols 1 and 2 [1969 and 1970] (London: Virago, 1984).
16 E. Said, *Representations of the Intellectual: the 1993 Reith Lectures* (London: Vintage, 1994), p. 17. Said appears to be borrowing Gramsci's concept of 'the organic intellectual' here, as Morag Shiach reminds me.
17 D. Beddoe, *Back to Home and Duty: Women between the Wars, 1918–1939* (London: Pandora, 1989), p. 140.
18 S. Jameson, *Company Parade* (London: Cassell, 1934), p. 111.
19 S. Jameson, 'The Form of the Novel', *The Writer's Situation*, p. 58. See also Q. D. Leavis's last paper, 'The Englishness of the English Novel', *English Studies*, vol. 62, nos 1–6, 1981, pp. 126–32; she names George Eliot, D. H. Lawrence and Solzhenitsyn when claiming that the novelist is a 'necessary critic of society' (p. 128), and cites Iris Murdoch as one of those writers who

has 'an original mind and so inevitably [is] an innovator – not one who plays irresponsible technical games or puts together a fiction to illustrate an arbitrary literary theory' (p. 129). She deplores the concentration on women's problems in the novels of the seventies and eighties.

20 V. Woolf, Letter to Stephen Spender, 7 April 1937, *The Letters of Virginia Woolf*, eds N. Nicolson and J. Trautmann (6 vols; London: Hogarth Press, 1975–80), vi, pp. 115–16.

21 M. Allingham, review of Storm Jameson's *Europe to Let*, *Time & Tide*, 14 December 1940, p. 1235.

22 S. Jameson, 'A Crisis of the Spirit' (October–November 1941), *The Writer's Situation*, p. 137.

23 S. Jameson, 'The Writer's Situation' (1947), *The Writer's Situation*, p. 20.

24 D. Sayers, *Unpopular Opinions*, p. 7.

25 D. Sayers, 'Living to Work', *Unpopular Opinions*, p. 124.

26 D. Sayers, 'Living to Work', *Unpopular Oppinions*, pp. 126–7.

27 S. Ertz, *Two Names upon the Shore* (London: Hodder & Stoughton, 1947); in the USA published as *Mary Hallam* (New York: Harper and Brothers, 1947), p. 14.

28 B. Comyns, *Sisters by a River* [1947] (London: Virago, 1985).

29 S. Rowbotham, *A Century of Women*, p. 243.

30 R. West, *The Court and the Castle: a Study of the Interactions of Political and Religious Ideas in Imaginative Literature* (London: Macmillan, 1958), p. 241.

31 E. Bowen, *A World of Love* [1955] (Harmondsworth: Penguin, 1983).

32 B. Miller, 'Amazons and Afterwards', *The Twentieth Century*, p. 131.

33 E. Mannin, *Lover under Another Name*, p. 69. See also her *The Lady and the Mystic* (London: Hutchinson, 1967).

34 I. Murdoch, 'Against Dryness', *Encounter*, no. 88, January 1961, p. 17.

35 G. Rose, *The Broken Middle*, p. 161.

36 M. Spark, *Robinson* [1958] (London: Macmillan, 1958), p. 163; see also Rose Macaulay, *The Towers of Trebizond* (London: Collins and The Book Society, 1956), for a perhaps surprising (given the fact that she was a High Anglican herself), if highly comic, critical view of a woman seeing her mission as the spreading of Anglicanism among Moslems.

37 R. West, 'This I Believe', in *This I Believe: the Personal Philosophies of One Hundred Thoughtful Men and Women in All Walks of Life*, ed. Edward Morgan (London: Hamish Hamilton, 1953), pp. 98–108 (100).

38 I. Murdoch, *Under the Net*, p. 239.

39 S. Jameson, *Parthian Words*, p. 143.

Primary Sources

Adam, Ruth, *Murder in the Home Guard* (London: Chapman and Hall, 1942).

Aldington, Richard, *Death of a Hero: a Novel* (London: Chatto & Windus, 1929).

Allingham, Margery, review of Storm Jameson's *Europe to Let*, *Time & Tide*, 14 December 1940, p. 1235.

Atholl, The Duchess of, MP, *Women and Politics* (London: Philip Allan, 1931).

Banks, Lynne Reid, *The L-shaped Room* (Harmondsworth: Penguin, 1962).

Bentley, Phyllis, *The Rise of Henry Morcar* (London: Victor Gollancz, 1946).

Borden, Mary, *The Forbidden Zone* (London: William Heinemann,1929).

—— *The Technique of Marriage* (London: William Heinemann, 1933).

—— *The Hungry Leopard* (London: William Heinemann, 1956).

Bottome, Phyllis, *The Mortal Storm* (London: Faber & Faber, 1937).

—— *London Pride* (London: Faber & Faber, 1941).

—— *Within the Cup* (London: Faber & Faber, 1943).

—— *The Lifeline* (London: Faber & Faber, 1946).

—— *Under the Skin* (London: Faber & Faber, 1950).

Bowen, Elizabeth, *The Heat of the Day* [1948] (Harmondsworth: Penguin, 1962).

—— *A World of Love* [1955] (Harmondsworth: Penguin, 1983).

Brittain, Vera, *Account Rendered* (London: Macmillan, 1945).

Brooke-Rose, Christine, *The Languages of Love* (London: Secker & Warburg, 1957).

—— *The Sycamore Tree* (London: Secker & Warburg, 1958).

—— *The Dear Deceit* London: Secker & Warburg, 1960).

—— *The Middlemen* (London: Secker & Warburg, 1961).

—— *The Christine Brooke-Rose Omnibus. Four Novels: Out, Such, Between, Thru* (Manchester: Carcanet Press, 1986).

Brophy, Brigid, *The Finishing Touch* (London: Secker & Warburg, 1963).

—— *Hackenfeller's Ape* (London: Secker & Warburg, 1964).

Bryher, *Beowulf* (New York: Pantheon Books, 1956).

Buckley, Eunice, *Destination Unknown* (London: Andrew Dakers, 1942).

Burdekin, Katharine [Murray Constantine], *Proud Man* [1934] (New York: The Feminist Press, 1993).

—— *Swastika Night* [1937] (London: Victor Gollancz, 1940; London: Lawrence & Wishart, 1985).

—— *The End of This Day's Business* (New York: The Feminist Press, 1989).

Butler, E. M., *Daylight in a Dream* (London: The Hogarth Press, 1951).

Cambridge, Elizabeth, *Portrait of Angela: a Novel* (London: Jonathan Cape, 1939).

Campbell, Olwen W., ed., *The Report of a Conference on the Feminine Point of View* (London: Williams & Norgate, 1952).

Carter, Angela, *The Bloody Chamber* [1967] (London: Virago, 1981).

—— *Nights at the Circus* [1984] (London: Pan (Picador), 1984).

Comyns, Barbara, *Sisters by a River* [1947] (London: Virago, 1985).

—— *Who Was Changed and Who Was Dead* [1954] (London: Virago, 1987).

—— *The Skin Chairs* [1962] (London: Virago, 1986).

Cooper, Lettice, *The New House* [1936] (Harmondsworth: Penguin, 1946).

—— *Fenny* [1953] (London: Virago, 1987).

Cross, Victoria, *Martha Brown M. P., a Girl of Tomorrow* (London: T. Werner Laurie, 1935).

Dane, Clemence, *The Woman's Side* (London: Herbert Jenkins, 1926).

—— *The Arrogant History of White Ben* (William Heinemann, 1939).

—— *He Brings Great News* (London: William Heinemann, 1944).

Dawson, Jennifer, *The Ha-Ha* [1961] (London: Virago, 1985).

Delafield, E. M., *The Diary of a Provincial Lady* [1930–40] (London: Virago, 1984).

—— *No One Will Know* (London: Macmillan, 1941).

Dickens, Monica, *One Pair of Feet* (London: Michael Joseph, 1942).

Drabble, Margaret, *A Summer Bird-Cage* [1963] (Harmondsworth: Penguin, 1967).

—— *The Garrick Year* [1964] (Harmondsworth: Penguin, 1966).

du Maurier, Daphne, *Hungry Hill* [1943] (Harmondsworth: Penguin, 1967).

—— *The King's General* (London: Victor Gollancz, 1946).

Duffy, Maureen, *That's How It Was* [1962] (London: Virago, 1983).

—— *The Microcosm* [1966] (London: Virago, 1989).

Dunn, Nell, *Up the Junction* (London: MacGibbon & Kee, 1963).

—— *Talking to Women* (London: MacGibbon & Kee, 1965).

Ertz, Susan, *Woman Alive* (London: Hodder & Stoughton, 1935).

—— *One Fight More* (London: Hodder & Stoughton, 1940).

—— *Anger in the Sky* (London: Hodder & Stoughton, 1943).

—— *Two Names upon the Shore* (London: Hodder & Stoughton, 1947); published as *Mary Hallam* (New York: Harper and Brothers, 1947).

Farjeon, Annabel, 'The Rose', in *The Penguin New Writing*, ed. John Lehmann, issue 18 (July–September 1943), pp. 96–104.

Ferguson, Rachel, *A Footman for the Peacock* (London: Jonathan Cape, 1940).

—— *A Stroll before Sunset* (London: Jonathan Cape, 1946).

Fielding, Ann Mary, *Ashanti Blood* (London: William Heinemann, 1952).

Frankau, Pamela, *The Offshore Light* (London: William Heinemann, 1952).

—— *A Wreath for the Enemy* [1954] (London: Virago, 1988).

Gallie, Menna, *Strike for a Kingdom* (London: Victor Gollancz, 1959).

—— *The Small Mine* (London: Victor Gollancz, 1962).

Gellhorn, Martha, *Liana* (London: Home and Van Thal, 1944).

Gilman, Charlotte Perkins, *The Yellow Wallpaper* [1892], ed. D. M. Bauer (Basingstoke: Macmillan, 1998).

Graves, Robert, *Goodbye to All That* [1929] (Harmondsworth: Penguin, 1960).

Green, Hannah [Joanne Greenberg], *I Never Promised You a Rose Garden* (New York: Holt, Reinhart and Winston, 1964; London: Gollancz, 1964).

Hall, Radclyffe, *The Well of Loneliness* [1928] (London: Virago, Weidenfeld & Nicolson, 1998).

—— 'Miss Ogilvy Finds Herself' [1934] in *Women, Men, and the Great War: an Anthology of Stories*, ed. T. Tate (Manchester and New York: Manchester University Press, 1995), pp. 127–35.

Heinemann, Margot, *The Adventurers* (London: Lawrence and Wishart, 1960).

Holden, Inez, *Night Shift* (London: John Lane The Bodley Head, 1941).

—— *There's No Story There* (London: John Lane The Bodley Head, 1944).

Holtby, Winifred, *Virginia Woolf* (London: Wishart, 1932).

—— *Mandoa, Mandoa!* [1933] (London: Virago, 1982).

—— *Women* (London: John Lane The Bodley Head, 1934).

—— *South Riding: an English Landscape* [1936] (London: Virago, 1988).
Hosain, Attia, *Phoenix Fled* [1953] (London: Virago, 1988).
—— *Sunlight on a Broken Column* [1961] (London: Penguin, 1992).
Hull, Veronica, *The Monkey Puzzle* (London: Barrie, 1958).
Jameson, Storm, *The Clash* (London: William Heinemann, 1922).
—— *Company Parade* (London: Cassell, 1934).
—— *In the Second Year* (London:Cassell, 1936).
—— *None Turn Back* [1936] (London: Virago, 1984).
—— *Delicate Monster* (London: Ivor Nicholson and Watson, 1937).
—— 'Documents', *Fact* no. 4, issue title 'Writing in Revolt', July 1937, pp. 9–18.
—— *Civil Journey* (Edinburgh: Constable, 1939).
—— *Cousin Honoré* (London: Cassell, 1940).
—— *Europe to Let: the Memoirs of an Obscure Man* (London: Macmillan, 1940).
—— *The Fort* (London: Cassell, 1941).
—— *Then We Shall Hear Singing: a Fantasy in C Major* (London: Cassell, 1942).
—— *Cloudless May* (London: Macmillan, 1943).
—— *The Other Side* (London: Macmillan, 1946).
—— *The Black Laurel* (London: Macmillan, 1947).
—— *The Writer's Situation and Other Essays* (London: Macmillan, 1950).
—— *The Green Man* (London: Macmillan, 1952).
—— *The Hidden River* (London: Macmillan, 1955).
—— 'The Writer in Contemporary Society', *American Scholar*, 35 (Winter 1965–6), pp. 126–32.
—— *Journey from the North*, vols 1 and 2 [1969 and 1970] (London: Virago, 1984).
—— *Parthian Words* (London: Collins Harvill, 1970).
Jhabvala, Ruth Prawer, *Esmond in India* [1958] (Harmondsworth: Penguin, 1980).
—— *Get Ready for Battle* [1962] (Harmondsworth: Penguin, 1981).
Kitchen, Paddy, *Lying-in* (London: Arnold Baker, 1965).
Leavis, Q. D., *Fiction and the Reading Public* [1932] (London: Bellew Publishing, 1978).
—— 'Lady Novelists and the Lower Orders', *Scrutiny*, vol. iv, no. 2, September 1935, pp. 112–32.
—— 'The Englishness of the English Novel', *English Studies*, vol. 62, nos 1–6, 1981, pp. 126–32.
Lehmann, Rosamond, 'When the Waters Came', in *The Penguin New Writing*, ed. J. Lehmann, issue 3, February 1941, pp. 106–10.
—— *The Ballad and the Source* (London: Collins and The Book Society, 1944).
—— 'Wonderful Holidays', in *The Penguin New Writing*, ed. J. Lehmann, issue 22, 1944, pp. 18–24.
Lessing, Doris, *The Grass Is Singing* [1950] (London: Collins (Paladin), 1989).
—— *Martha Quest* [1952] (London: Collins (Paladin), 1990).
—— *A Proper Marriage* [1954] (London: Collins (Paladin), 1990).
—— *Retreat to Innocence* (London: Michael Joseph, 1956).
—— *A Ripple from the Storm* [1958] (London: Collins (Paladin), 1990).
—— *The Golden Notebook* [1962] (London: Collins (Paladin), 1989).
—— *The Four-Gated City* [1969] (London: Collins [Paladin], 1990).
—— *Briefing for a Descent into Hell* [1971] (London: Grafton, 1972).
—— *The Memoirs of a Survivor* [1973] (London: Pan [Picador], 1976).
—— *The Good Terrorist* [1985] (London: HarperCollins [Paladin], 1990).

Lessing, Doris, *The Black Madonna* (London: HarperCollins [Paladin], 1992).

Macaulay, Rose, *The World My Wilderness* [1950] (London: Virago, 1983).

—— *The Towers of Trebizond* (London: Collins and The Book Society, 1956).

Mannin, Ethel, *Venetian Blinds* (London: Jarrolds, 1933).

—— *Men Are Unwise* (London: Jarrolds 1934).

—— *The Dark Forest* (London: Jarrolds, 1946).

—— *Lover under Another Name* (London: Jarrolds, 1953).

—— *The Lady and the Mystic* (London: Hutchinson, 1967).

Markandaya, Kamala, *Nectar in a Sieve* (New York: New American Library, 1954; London: Putnam, 1954).

Miller, Betty (B. Bergson Spiro), *The Mere Living* (London: Victor Gollancz, 1933).

—— *On the Side of the Angels* [1945] (London: Virago, 1985).

—— *Farewell Leicester Square* (London: Robert Hale, 1941).

Mitchison, Naomi, *The Corn King and the Spring Queen* (London: Jonathan Cape, 1931).

—— *We Have Been Warned* (London: Constable, 1935).

—— *The Fourth Pig* (London: Constable, 1936).

—— *The Blood of the Martyrs* (London: Constable, 1939).

—— *The Bull Calves* (London: Jonathan Cape, 1947).

—— *Travel Light* [1952] (London: Virago, 1985).

—— *Memoirs of a Spacewoman* (London: Victor Gollancz, 1962).

Mitford, Nancy, *The Pursuit of Love* (London: Hamish Hamilton, 1945).

Morgan, Edward, ed., *This I Believe: the Personal Philosophies of One Hundred Thoughtful Men and Women in All Walks of Life* (London: Hamish Hamilton, 1953).

Mortimer, Penelope, *The Pumpkin Eater* [1962] (Harmondsworth: Penguin, 1964).

—— *My Friend Says It's Bullet-Proof* [1967] (London: Virago, 1989).

Murdoch, Iris, *Under the Net* (London: Chatto & Windus, 1954).

—— *The Flight from the Enchanter* (London: Chatto & Windus, 1956).

—— 'Against Dryness: a Polemical Sketch', *Encounter*, no. 88, January 1961, pp. 16–20.

O'Brien, Edna, E., *The Country Girls* [1960] (Harmondsworth: Penguin, 1963).

—— *The Lonely Girl* [1962] (retitled *Girl with Green Eyes*, Harmondsworth: Penguin, 1964).

—— *Girls in Their Married Bliss* [1964] (Harmondsworth: Penguin, 1967).

O'Brien, Kate, *The Land of Spices* (London: William Heinemann, 1941).

—— *The Last of Summer* (London: William Heinemann, 1943).

Olivia [Dorothy Strachey], *Olivia* [1949] (London: Virago, 1987).

Pargeter, Edith, *Hortensius Friend of Nero* (London: Lovat Dickson, 1936).

—— *She Goes to War* (London: William Heinemann, 1942).

—— *Lame Crusade*, The Eighth Champion of Christendom *(London: William Heinemann, 1945)*.

—— *Reluctant Odyssey*, The Eighth Champion of Christendom (London: William Heinemann, 1946).

—— *Warfare Accomplished*, The Eighth Champion of Christendom (London: William Heinemann, 1947).

Pollock, The Hon. Mrs Dighton, *The Women of Today*, Routledge Introductions to modern Knowledge, no. 14 (London: George Routledge & Sons, 1929).

Pym, Barbara, *Excellent Women* [1952] (London: Macmillan (Pan), 1995).

—— *Less than Angels* [1955] (London: Macmillan [Pan], 1993).

—— *A Glass of Blessings* [1958] (London: Macmillan [Pan], 1989).

—— *No Fond Return of Love* [1961] (London: Macmillan [Pan], 1993).

Quin, Ann, *Berg* (London: John Calder, 1964).

—— *Three* (London: Calder & Boyars, 1966).

Renault, Mary, *The Charioteer* (London, New York, Toronto: Longmans, Green and Co., 1953).

Rhys, Jean, *After Leaving Mr Mackenzie* [1930] (Harmondsworth: Penguin, 1971).

—— *Voyage in the Dark* [1934] (Harmondsworth: Penguin, 1969).

—— *Good Morning, Midnight* [1939] (Harmondsworth: Penguin, 1967).

—— *Wide Sargasso Sea* [1966] (Harmondsworth: Penguin, 1968).

Sackville-West, Victoria, *The Women's Land Army*, published under the auspices of the Ministry of Agriculture and Fisheries (London: Michael Joseph, 1944).

Sayers, Dorothy, *Unpopular Opinions* (London: Victor Gollancz, 1946).

Simpson, Helen, *Boomerang* (London: Heinemann, 1932).

—— *Saraband for Dead Lovers* (London and Toronto: William Heinemann, 1935).

Smith, Helen Zenna, *Not so Quiet: Stepdaughters of War* [1930] (London: Virago, 1988).

Smith, Stevie, *Over the Frontier* [1938] (London: Virago, 1980).

—— *The Holiday* [1949] (London: Virago, 1979).

—— *Me Again*, eds J. Barbera and W. McBrien (London: Virago, 1981).

Spark, Muriel, *The Comforters* [1957] (Harmondsworth: Penguin, 1963).

—— *Robinson* (London: Macmillan, 1958).

—— *The Bachelors* [1960] (Harmondsworth: Penguin, 1963).

—— *The Prime of Miss Jean Brodie* [1961] (Harmondsworth: Penguin, 1965).

—— *The Collected Stories* (Harmondsworth: Penguin, 1994).

Stead, Christina, *Cotters' England* [1966] (London: Virago, 1980).

—— *The Puzzleheaded Girl* [1968] (London: Virago, 1984).

Stern, G. B., *A Deputy Was King* [1926] (London: Virago, 1988).

Struther, Jan, *Mrs Miniver* [1939] (London: Virago, 1989).

Taylor, Elizabeth, *At Mrs Lippincote's* [1945] (London: Virago, 1988).

—— *Palladian* [1946] (London: Virago, 1985).

—— *A Game of Hide and Seek* [1951] (London: Virago, 1986).

—— *Angel* [1957] (London: Virago, 1984).

—— *In a Summer Season* [1961] (London: Virago, 1983).

—— *The Wedding Group* [1968] (London: Virago, 1985).

The Twentieth Century, vol. 164, no. 978 August 1958: 'Special Number on Women'.

Ulrich, Mabel, ed., *Man, Proud Man: a Commentary by Mary Borden, E. M. Delafield, Susan Ertz, Storm Jameson, Helen Simpson, G. B. Stern, Sylvia Townsend Warner, Rebecca West* (London: Hamish Hamilton, 1932).

Ward, Mary Jane, *The Snake Pit* (London: Cassell, 1947).

Warner, Sylvia Townsend, *Lolly Willowes* [1926] (London: Virago, 1993).

—— *Mr Fortune's Maggot* [1927] (London: Virago, 1978).

—— *Summer Will Show* [1936] (London: Virago, 1987).

—— 'The Drought Breaks' (1937), in *Spanish Front: Writers on the Civil War* , ed. Valentine Cunningham (Oxford: Oxford University Press, 1986), pp. 244–7.

—— *After the Death of Don Juan* [1938] (London: Virago, 1988).

—— *The Corner That Held Them* [1948] (London: Virago, 1988).

Warner, Sylvia Townsend, *The Flint Anchor* (New York: The Viking Press, 1954).

West, Rebecca, *The Return of the Soldier* (London: Nisbet, 1917).

—— *The Strange Necessity: Essays and Reviews* (London: Jonathan Cape, 1928).

—— *Harriet Hume* [1929] (London: Virago, 1980).

—— *The Harsh Voice* [1935] (London: Virago, 1982).

—— *The Thinking Reed* [1936] (London: Virago, 1984).

—— *Black Lamb and Grey Falcon: a Journey through Yugoslavia* [1942], ed. T. Royle (Edinburgh: Canongate Classics, 1993).

—— *The Fountain Overflows* [1957] (London: Virago, 1984).

—— *The Court and the Castle: a Study of the Interactions of Political and Religious Ideas in Imaginative Literature* (London: Macmillan, 1958).

White, Evelyn, *Winifred Holtby: As I Knew Her* (London: Collins, 1938).

Whitton, Barbara, *Green Hands* (London: Faber & Faber, 1943).

Wilkinson, Ellen, *Clash* [1928] (London: Virago, 1989).

—— *The Town That Was Murdered: the Life Story of Jarrow* (The Left Book Club, London: Gollancz, 1939).

Williams-Ellis, Amabel, *Learn to Love First* (London: Victor Gollancz, 1939).

Woolf, Virginia, *Orlando* [1928] (Harmondsworth: Penguin, 1993).

—— *The Waves* [1931] (Harmondsworth: Penguin, 1992).

—— *The Years* [1937] (Harmondsworth: Penguin, 1994).

—— *The Letters of Virginia Woolf*, eds N. Nicolson and J. Trautmann (6 vols; London: Hogarth Press, 1975–80).

—— *A Room of One's Own* and *Three Guineas*, ed. Morag Shiach (The World's Classics, Oxford: Oxford University Press, 1992).

—— 'Mr Bennett and Mrs Brown', *A Woman's Essays: Selected Essays*, vol. 1, ed. Rachel Bowlby (Harmondsworth: Penguin, 1992).

—— *The Crowded Dance of Modern Life: Selected Essays*, vol. 2, ed. Rachel Bowlby (Harmondsworth: Penguin, 1993).

Select Bibliography

Adorno, Theodor, *Negative Dialectics* [1966], trans. E. B. Ashton (London: Routledge & Kegan Paul, 1973).

Albinski, Nan Bowman, *Women's Utopias in British and American Fiction* (London and New York: Routledge, 1988).

Atwood, Margaret, *Second Words: Selected Critical Prose* (Toronto: House of Anansi Press, 1982).

Badinter, Elizabeth, *XY: On Masculine Identity*, trans. L. Davis (New York: Columbia University Press, 1995).

Bald, Suresh Renjen, 'Images of South Asian Migrants in Literature: Different Perspectives', *New Community*, 17 (3), April 1991, pp. 413–31.

Barrett, Michèle, ed.,*Virginia Woolf: Women and Writing* (London: The Women's Press, 1979).

Bauman, Zygmunt, *Modernity and the Holocaust* (London: Polity Press, 1991).

Baxter, Richard, *Guilty Women* (London: Quality Press, 1941).

—— *Hitler's Darkest Secret: What He Has in Store for Britain* (London: Quality Press, 1941).

—— *Women of the Gestapo* (London: Quality Press, 1943).

Beauman, Nicola, *A Very Great Profession: the Woman's Novel 1914–1939* (London: Virago, 1983).

Beckett, Samuel, *Proust and Three Dialogues with Georges Duthuit* [*Proust* 1931] (London: John Calder Publishers, 1999).

Beddoe, Deirdre, *Back to Home and Duty: Women between the Wars, 1918–1939* (London: Pandora, 1989).

Beer, Gillian, 'Representing Women: Representing the Past', *The Feminist Reader: Essays in Gender and the Politics of Literary Criticism*, eds Catherine Belsey and Jane Moore (London: Macmillan Education, 1989), pp. 63–80.

Benjamin, Walter, *One Way Street and Other Writings*, trans. Edmund Jephcott and Kingsley Shorter (London: Verso, 1979).

—— *Illuminations*, ed. Hannah Arendt, trans. H. Zohn (London: Fontana Press, 1992).

Bourke, Joanna, *Dismembering the Male: Men's Bodies, Britain and the Great War* (London: Reaktion Books, 1996).

Bradbury, Malcolm, 'Iris Murdoch's *Under the Net*', *Critical Quarterly*, no. 4, Spring 1962, pp. 47–54.

Braithwaite, B. and Walsh, N., eds, *Things My Mother Should Have Told Me: the Best of Good Housekeeping 1922–1940* (*Good Housekeeping* Nostalgia Series; London: Ebury Press, 1991).

Brooke-Rose, Christine, *A Grammar for Metaphor* (London: Secker & Warburg, 1958)

—— *A Rhetoric of the Unreal: Studies in Narrative and Structure, Especially of the Fantastic* (Cambridge: Cambridge University Press, 1981).

—— *Stories, Theories, Things* (Cambridge: Cambridge University Press, 1991).

Butler, Christopher, *Early Modernism: Literature, Music, and Painting in Europe 1900–1914* (Oxford: Oxford University Press, 1994).

Byatt, A. S., *Degrees of Freedom: the Early Novels of Iris Murdoch* [1965] (London: Vintage, 1994).

Calder, Jenni, *The Nine Lives of Naomi Mitchison* (London: Virago, 1997).

Calvino, Italo, 'Right and Wrong Political Uses of Literature', *The Uses of Literature*, trans. Patrick Creagh (Orlando: Harcourt Brace Jovanovich, 1986), pp. 89–100.

Cameron, Deborah, ' "Words, Words, Words": the Power of Language', *The War of the Words: the Political Correctness Debate*, ed. S. Dunant (London: Virago, 1994), pp. 15–34.

—— 'Language: Are You Being Served?', *Critical Quarterly*, vol. 39, no. 2, Summer 1997, pp. 97–100.

Cheyette, Bryan, *Construction of 'the Jew' in English Literature and Society: Racial Representations, 1875–1945* (Cambridge: Cambridge University Press, 1993).

—— ed., *Between 'Race' and Culture: Representation of 'the Jew' in English and American Literature* (Stanford: Stanford University Press, 1996).

Chomsky, Noam, *Deterring Democracy* (London: Vintage, 1992).

Christian, Barbara, ed., *Black Feminist Criticism: Perspectives on Black Women Writers* (New York: Pergamon Press, 1985).

Clatterbaugh, Kenneth, *Contemporary Perspectives on Masculinity: Men, Women and Politics in Modern Society* (Boulder: Westview Press, 1990).

Communist Party of Great Britain, *Class against Class: General Election Programme of the Communist Party of Gt. Britain, 1929* (London: Dorrit Press, 1929).

Craig, Cairns, 'Going Down to Hell is Easy', *Cencrastus*, 6, Autumn 1981, pp. 19–21.

Davies, Tony, 'Unfinished Business, Realism and Working-Class Writing', *The British Working-Class Novel in the Twentieth Century* , ed. Jeremy Hawthorn (London: Edward Arnold, 1984), pp. 125–39.

Deane, Patrick, ed, *History in Our Hands: a Critical Anthology of Writings on Literature, Culture and Politics from the 1930s* (London and New York: Leicester University Press, 1998).

Degen, Marie Louise, *The History of the Woman's Peace Party*, The Johns Hopkins University Studies in Historical and Political Science, Series LVII, no. 3 (Baltimore: The Johns Hopkins University Press, 1939).

Doctorow, E. L., *Poets and Presidents: Selected Essays, 1972–1992* (London: Macmillan, 1994 [1993]).

Dowson, Jane, ed., *Women's Poetry of the 1930s: a Critical Anthology* (London and New York: Routledge, 1996).

DuPlessis, Rachel, *Writing beyond the Ending: Narrative Strategies of Twentieth-Century Women Writers* (Bloomington: Indiana University Press, 1985).

Eagleton, Terry, 'Newsreel History', review of Peter Conrad, *Modern Times, Modern Places*, *London Review of Books*, 12 November 1998, p. 8.

Ermarth, Elizabeth Deeds, *Realism and Consensus in the English Novel: Time, Space and Narrative* [1983] (Edinburgh: Edinburgh University Press, 1998).

Fanon, Franz, *Black Skin, White Masks*, trans. Charles Lam Markmann (London: Pluto Press, 1986).

Foucault, Michel, *Power/Knowledge: Selected Interviews and other Writings 1972–1977*, trans. Colin Gordon, Leo Marshall, John Mepham, Kate Soper (Hemel Hempstead: Harvester Press, 1980).

Fowler, Bridget, *The Alienated Reader: Women and Romantic Literature in the Twentieth Century* (Hemel Hempstead: Harvester Wheatsheaf, 1991).

Francis, Anne Cranny, 'The Education of Desire: Utopian Fiction and Feminist Fantasy', in *The Victorian Fantasists: Essays on Culture, Society and Belief in the Mythopoeic Fiction of the Victorian Age*, ed. Kath Filmer (London and Basingstoke: Macmillan, 1991), pp. 45–59.

Freud, Sigmund, *The Interpretation of Dreams*, trans. James Strachey, ed. Angela Richards (Harmondsworth: Penguin, 1976).

—— *Civilization, Society and Religion*, ed. A. Dickson, The Penguin Freud Library, vol. 12 (Harmondsworth: Penguin, 1991).

Fry, Roger, *Vision and Design* [1928] (London and New York: Oxford University Press, 1990).

Gasiorek, Andrzej, *Post-War British Fiction: Realism and After* (London: Edward Arnold, 1995).

Gebauer, Gunter and Wulf, Christoff, *Mimesis: Culture–Art–Society*, trans. D. Reneau (Berkely, Los Angeles, London: University of California Press, 1995).

Gilroy, Beryl, *Leaves in the Wind: Collected Writings*, ed. Joan Anim-Addo (London: Mango Publishing, 1998).

Gilroy, Paul, *There Ain't No Black in the Union Jack* (London: Hutchison, 1987).

Goldsworthy, Vesna, 'Black Lamb and Grey Falcon: Rebecca West's Journey through the Balkans', *Women: a Cultural Review*, vol. 8, no. i, Spring 1997, pp. 1–11.

Gombrich, E. H., *Art and Illusion: a Study in the Psychology of Pictorial Representation* (London: Phaidon, 1968).

Greene, Gayle, *Changing the Story: Feminist Fiction and the Tradition* (Bloomington, Ind.: Indiana University Press, 1991).

Griffin, Gabrièle, ed., *Outwrite: Lesbianism and Popular Culture* (London and Boulder, Colorado: Pluto Press, 1993).

Grigson, Geoffrey, ed., *The Arts Today* (London: John Lane The Bodley Head, 1935).

Hall, Catherine, *White, Male and Middle Class: Explorations in Feminism and History* (Cambridge: Polity Press, 1992).

Hanscombe, Gillian and Smyers, Virginia, *Writing for Their Lives: The Modernist Women 1910–1940* (London: The Women's Press, 1987).

Harrison, Charles, *Modernism*, Movements in Modern Art Series (London: Tate Gallery Publishing, 1997).

Hartley, Jenny, *Millions like Us: British Women's Fiction of the Second World War* (London: Virago, 1997).

Higonnet, Margaret Randolph, Jensen, Jane, Michel, Sonya and Weitz, Margaret Collins, eds, *Behind the Lines: Gender and the Two World Wars* (New Haven and London: Yale University Press, 1987).

Hinds, Donald, *Journey to an Illusion: the West Indian in Britain* (London: Heinemann, 1966).

Humm, Maggie, *Border Traffic: Strategies of Contemporary Women Writers* (Manchester and New York: Manchester University Press, 1991).

Ingram, Angela, and Patai, Daphne, eds, *Rediscovering Forgotten Radicals: British Women Writers 1889–1939* (Chapel Hill and London: University of North Carolina Press, 1993).

Irigaray, Luce, *Je, tu, nous: Toward a Culture of Difference*, trans. A. Martin (London and New York: Routledge, 1993).

Jeffreys, Sheila, *Anti-climax: a Feminist Perspective on the Sexual Revolution* (London: Women's Press, 1990).

Joannou, Maroula, *'Ladies, Please Don't Smash These Windows': Women's Writing, Feminist Consciousness and Social Change 1918–1938* (Oxford and Providence: Berg, 1995).

——— ed., *Women Writers of the 1930s: Gender, Politics and History* (Edinburgh: Edinburgh University Press, 1999).

Kemp, Sandra, ' "But how describe a world without a self?" Feminism, fiction and modernism', *Critical Quarterly*, vol. 32, no. 1, 1990, pp. 99–118.

Klaus, Gustav H., ed., *The Socialist Novel in Britain: Towards the Recovery of a Tradition* (Brighton: Harvester, 1982).

Klein, Yvonne M., *Beyond the Home Front: Women's Autobiographical Writing of the Two World Wars* (London: Macmillan, 1997).

Knapp, Shoshana Milgram, 'Revolutionary Androgyny in the Fiction of "Victoria Cross" ', in *Seeing Double: Revisioning Edwardian and Modernist Literature*, eds. Carola M. Kaplan and Anne B. Simpson (Basingstoke: Macmillan, 1996), pp. 3–20.

Knight, Stephen, ' "The hesitations and uncertainties that were the truth": Three Welsh Industrial Novels by Women', in *British Industrial Fictions* , eds H. Gustav Klaus and Stephen Knight (Cardiff: University of Wales Press, 2000).

Labon, Joanna, 'Tracing Storm Jameson', *Women: a Cultural Review*, vol. 8, no. 1, Spring 1997, pp. 33–47.

Laing, R. D., *The Politics of Experience, and The Bird of Paradise* (Harmondsworth: Penguin, 1967).

Lant, Antonia, 'Prologue', in *Nationalising Femininity: Culture, Sexuality and British Cinema in the Second World War*, ed. Christine Gledhill Swanson (Manchester: Manchester University Press, 1996).

Lassner, Phyllis, *British Women Writers of World War II: Battlegrounds of Their Own* (London: Macmillan, 1998).

Lee, A. Robert, ed., *Other Britain, Other British: Contemporary Multicultural Fiction* (London: Pluto Press, 1995).

Lee, Vernon, *Gospels of Anarchy and Other Contemporary Studies* (London: T. F. Unwin, 1908).

Levenson, Michael, ed., *The Cambridge Companion to Modernism* (Cambridge: Cambridge University Press, 1999).

Levine, George, ed., *Realism and Representation* (Wisconsin: University of Wisconsin Press, 1993).

Light, Alison, *Forever England: Femininity, Literature and Conservatism between the Wars* (London and New York: Routledge, 1991).

Loseff, Lev, *On the Beneficence of Censorship: Aesopian Language in Modern Russian Literature*, trans. Jane Bobko (Munich: Verlag Otto Sagner, 1984).

McKibbin, Ross, *Classes and Cultures: England 1918–1951* (Oxford: Oxford University Press, 1998).

McNay, Lois, *Foucault and Feminism* (Oxford: Polity Press, 1992).

Malpas, James, *Realism*, Movements in Modern Art Series (London: Tate Gallery Publishing, 1997).

Marcus, Jane, ed., *Virginia Woolf and Bloomsbury* (London: Macmillan, 1987).

Margolies, David, ed., *Writing the Revolution: Cultural Criticism from Left Review* (London: Pluto Press, 1998).

Marinetti, Filippo, *Marinetti: Selected Writings*, ed. R. W. Flint (London: Secker & Warburg, 1972).

Maslen, Elizabeth, 'One Man's Tomorrow Is Another's Today: the Reader's World and Its Impact on *Nineteen Eighty-Four*', in *Storm Warnings: Science Fiction Confronts the Future*, eds George E. Slusser, Colin Greenland and Eric S. Rabkin (Carbondale and Edwardsville: Southern Illinois Press, 1987), pp. 146–58.

—— 'Man, Proud Man? Women's Views of Men between the Wars', *Women Voice Men: Gender in European Culture*, ed. Maya Slater (Exeter: Intellect, 1997), pp. 53–60.

Melman, Billie, *Women and the Popular Imagination in the Twenties: Flappers and Nymphs* (Basingstoke: Macmillan, 1988).

Midgley, Clare, ed., *Gender and Imperialism* (Manchester and New York: Manchester University Press, 1998).

Mishra, V. J., 'Postcolonial Differend: Diasporic Narratives of Salman Rushdie', *Ariel*, 26: 3, 1995.

Montefiore, Janet, *Men and Women Writers of the 1930s: the Dangerous Flood of History* (London and New York: Routledge, 1996).

Nasta, Susheila, 'Setting Up Home in a City of Words: Sam Selvon's Novels', in *Other Britain, Other British: Contemporary Multicultural Fiction*, ed. A. Robert Lee (London: Pluto Press, 1995), pp. 48–68.

Nussbaum, Martha, *Love's Knowledge: Essays on Philosophy and Literature* (New York, Oxford: Oxford University Press, 1990).

Orwell, George, 'Why I Write' [1946], *The Collected Essays, Journalism and Letters of George Orwell*, vol. 1, *An Age like This 1920–40*, eds Sonia Orwell and Ian Angus (Harmondsworth: Penguin, 1970), pp. 23–30.

Philips, Deborah and Haywood, Ian, *Brave New Causes: Women in Postwar Fictions* (London and Washington: Leicester University Press, 1998).

Plain, Gill, *Women's Fiction of the Second World War: Gender, Power and Resistance* (Edinburgh: Edinburgh University Press, 1996).

Raitt, Suzanne and Tate, Trudi, *Women's Fiction and the Great War* (Oxford and New York: Clarendon Press, 1996).

Rose, Gillian, *The Broken Middle: Out of Our Ancient Society* (Oxford: Blackwell, 1992).

—— *Judaism and Modernity: Philosophical Essays* (Oxford, UK, and Cambridge, UK: Blackwell, 1993).

—— *Love's Work* [1995] (London: Vintage, 1997).

Rose, Jacqueline, *Why War: Psychoanalysis, Politics, and the Return to Melanie Klein* (Oxford: Blackwell, 1993).

—— *States of Fantasy* (Oxford: Clarendon Press, 1996).

Rowbotham, Sheila, *A Century of Women: the History of Women in Britain and the United States* (Harmondsworth: Penguin, 1997).

Rushdie, Salman, *Imaginary Homelands: Essays and Criticism, 1981–1991* (London: Granta, 1991).

Said, Edward, *Representations of the Intellectual: the 1993 Reith Lectures* (London: Vintage, 1994).

Samuel, Raphael, ed., *Patriotism: the Making and Unmaking of British National Identity*, vol. 1, History and Politics; vol. 2, Minorities and Outsiders (London and New York: Routledge, 1989).

Samuel, Raphael, *Theatres of Memory* (London and New York: Verso, 1994).

Scaffardi, Sylvia, *Fire under the Carpet: Working for Civil Liberties in the 1930s* (London: Lawrence and Wishart, 1986).

Schenk, Celeste M., 'Exiled by Genre: Modernism, Canonicity, and the Politics of Exclusion', in *Women's Writing in Exile*, eds Mary Lynn Broe and Angela Ingram (Chapel Hill and London: University of North Carolina Press, 1989), pp. 225–50.

Shaw, Marion, 'Feminism and Fiction between the Wars: Winifred Holtby and *VirginiaWoolf*', in *Women's Writing: a Challenge to Theory* , ed. Moira Monteith (Brighton: Harvester, 1986), pp. 171–91.

Showalter, Elaine, *A Literature of Their Own* (London: Virago, 1982).

Sinfield, Alan, *Literature, Politics, and Culture in Postwar Britain* (Oxford: Basil Blackwell, 1989)

Snaith, Anna, 'Virginia Woolf and Reading Communities: Respondents to *Three Guineas*', in *Virginia Woolf & Communities: Selected Papers from the Eighth Annual Conference on Virginia Woolf* , eds Jeanette McVicker and Laura Davis (New York: Pace University Press, 1999), pp. 219–26.

Spalding, Frances, *Stevie Smith: a Critical Biography* (London: Faber, 1988).

Spender, Dale, ed., *Time and Tide Wait for No Man* (London: Pandora, 1984).

Stocks, Mary D., *Eleanor Rathbone: a Biography* (London: Victor Gollancz, 1949).

Tiffin, Helen, 'Post-Colonialism, Post-Modernism and the Rehabilitation of Post-colonial History', *The Journal of Commonwealth Literature*, vol. 23 (1988), pp. 169–81.

Trodd, Anthea, *Women's Writing in English: Britain 1900–1945* (London and New York: Longman, 1998).

Tylee, Claire M., *The Great War and Women's Consciousness: Images of Militarism and Feminism in Women's Writings, 1914–1964* (Iowa City: University of Iowa Press, 1990).

van der Wijngaard, Marianne, *Reinventing the Sexes: the Biomedical Construction of Femininity and Masculinity* (Bloomington: Indiana University Press, 1997).

Volšinov, V. N., *Freudianism: a Marxist Critique* (New York: Academic Press, 1976).

Waugh, Patricia, *Postmodernism: a Reader* (London: Edward Arnold, 1997).

Wiley, Catherine, 'Making History Unrepeatable in Virginia Woolf's *Between the Acts*', *Clio*, vol. 25, 1995, pp. 3–20.

Williams, Keith and Matthews, Steven, eds, *Rewriting the Thirties* (London and New York: Longman, 1997).

Wilson, Elizabeth, *The Sphinx in the City: Urban Life, the Control of Disorder, and Women* (London: Virago, 1991).

Index

abortion and pregnancy, 157–8, 164, 177, 179

Adam, Ruth, *Murder in the Home Guard*, 80–1, 115, 120, 163–4, 217

Adler, Alfred, 73, 75, 82, 85, 197
  see also Freud, Sigmund

Adorno, Theodor, *Negative Dialectics*, 217

Albinski, N. Bowman, 224

Aldington, Richard, *Death of a Hero*, 154, 215

Alfer, Alexa, 206

Allingham, Margery, 195, 217, 228

anti-Semitism, 17, 73, 74, 76, 78, 80, 86, 101–2, 106, 114–16, 123, 127, 133, 143
  see also empire; fascism; imperialism; Nazism; racism

Arendt, Hannah, 124, 221

art, 21, 22, 23, 28, 31, 34, 36
  see also experimental style; modernism; modernity; realism; reality

Atholl, The Duchess of, 186, 227
  Women and Politics, 186

Atwood, Margaret, 6, 7, 205

Auden, W. H., 14, 206

Badinter, Elizabeth, 145–6, 154–5, 223

Bailey, Paul, 48

Bald, Suresh Renjen, 101, 129–30, 131, 219

Baldick, Chris, 10, 206

Banks, Lynne Reid, 52
  The L-Shaped Room, 52, 139–40, 179, 180, 203, 213, 222

Bardot, Brigitte, 189, 190

Barrett, Michèle, 30, 209

Bauman, Zygmunt, 99, 218

Baxter, Richard, 71
  Guilty Women, 71, 77, 215
  Hitler's Darkest Secret, 217, 220

  Women of the Gestapo, 215

Beauman, Nicola, 18, 207

Beckett, Samuel, 10, 26, 56, 58, 181, 206
  Waiting for Godot, 26

Beddoe, Deirdre, 193, 227

Beer, Gillian, 5, 37, 205, 210

Benjamin, Walter, 63, 84, 208, 214

Bennett, Arnold, 31, 34
  The Old Wives' Tale, 35

Bentley, Phyllis, *The Rise of Henry Morcar*, 164

Blunt, Anthony, 208

The Bookseller, 45, 212

Borden, Mary, 51
  The Forbidden Zone, 67, 149, 215
  The Hungry Leopard, 51, 169, 213
  The Technique of Marriage, 149, 224

Bottome, Phyllis, 1, 65, 73, 76, 191, 197, 216
  The Lifeline, 85, 122, 197, 217
  London Pride, 81, 102, 119–20, 143, 217
  The Mortal Storm, 73, 102, 158, 216, 219
  Under the Skin, 125, 221
  Within the Cup, 82, 164, 217

Bourke, Joanna, 64, 154, 214, 223

Bowen, Elizabeth, 42, 193, 195
  Death of the Heart, 194
  The Heat of the Day, 48, 87, 90, 162, 164, 212
  A World of Love, 199–200

Bowlby, Rachel, 149–50, 204, 224

Bradbury, Malcolm, 212

Bradshaw, D., 219

breakdown, 151, 172, 182–4
  see also madness

Brecht, Bertolt, 23, 24, 61, 208

Bremner, Marjorie, 190

Brittain, Vera, 63, 92
  Account Rendered, 85, 214

Brontë, Charlotte, 38

241